The
Nameless Man

THE
NAMELESS MAN

L.M. BROWNING
and Marianne Browning

HOMEBOUND
Imprint of HIRAETH PRESS

Visit our website: www.homebound.hiraethpress.com
Visit the author at: www.lmbrowning.com

FIRST EDITION
ISBN 13: 978-0-9835852-4-4 (pbk)

BOOK DESIGN
Front Cover Image: The Temple Mount
Front Image Attribution: © Boris Katsman (Shuttershock.com)
Back Cover Image: Gehenna (Hinnom) Valley Near Jerusalem
Back Image Attribution: © Slavapolo (Shuttershock.com)
Book Design: Leslie M. Browning and Marianne Browning
Typeface: Adobe Garamond Pro

HOMEBOUND
Imprint of HIRAETH PRESS

DEDICATION

K now this,
   you who are distant
yet close to my heart,
if your search for
understanding has brought you
to open this book and read
these words sympathetically,
then along your path you have
found a companion in me.

Table of
Contents

THE JOURNEY

It begins innocently.
Taking us to places we cannot foresee—
    those places that bring us
    to a speechless awe
    as well as those that bring us
    to devastating tears.

The journey was begun
by the reaching heart
    calling into the unseen.

We live forever changed by the day
when we were taken by the hand
and led into all that we did not know.

CHAPTER I

The Man

HE NEVER INTENDED TO GO BACK. No, not all his memories of this place were painful. Overwhelming joy and deep contentment were had while they resided here. Yet, when looked back on, the happiness he had known in this country was overshadowed by the dominant sorrow; for he could not think of the joy felt, without recalling how that time of innocence was violently brought to an end.

For a long time the man struggled over whether or not to return but the time finally came when he found himself moving toward the very place he had fled years ago, in that past life. *There was no going forward without going back—* he knew this. This resounding fact defined the last decades of his family's life; as such some part of him should have known that this day would inevitably come when he would need to return.

He came back in a desire to roam the countryside of his former home, hoping to experience a renewed connection to the man he had been before the scars maimed him. For a week, he and the younger of his two sons, Yoseph, had traveled the landscape. They walked from the northern port where their boat had made berth, down along the coastline and into the countryside he once knew so well.

In the past when he came home after a journey, the bleating lambs and swaying tops of the fig trees always called him home. Yet the trees had long since been beheaded and their fibrous bodies yielded to decay in the arid dirt. Over the long years since his family made their home in this region, the landscape had been drastically altered; leaving the disfigured face of the motherland barely recognizable, even to the man's native eyes.

⸙

He had wanted to make this pilgrimage alone. He knew that, if ever he were to brave a return, the stipulation would be that he do so on his own. He simply wasn't willing to risk the safety of the family by allowing them to return with him to this volatile place. Yet despite his wishes, Yoseph refused to be left behind. The young man had cared for his father for decades—acting as his companion on the long journey—and he had no intention of allowing his father to take this pivotal trip alone.

Yoseph had been raised on a foreign land of green shores, far removed from the parched hills rolling underfoot. Stranger to his birthland, the young man took in the landscape for the first time; while his father looked for remnants of old landmarks still recognizable after the ages of upheaval. Walking upon the land of his family's past, Yoseph was at last able to tie the stories he had heard all his life with a place, like putting a face to the name of someone you had heard spoken of since you were a babe.

Yoseph had been born the third child of four. He had the pronounced look of his father. By appearance one would say he was in his mid-twenties, though he held himself as though he were much older. A healthy young man of average build, he was slightly shorter than his father. He dressed in plain clothes—brown pants and a loosely fitting midnight blue shirt, accompanied by a neutral tan shawl wrapped about his shoulders and neck. It had been given to him by his father who insisted that its protection would be needed in the lands to which they were headed. Yoseph's hair was mid-brown in color and was slightly overgrown; it bushed out around his ears and was strewn thickly along the slope of his brow. He had not shaved since their arrival, leaving a faint beard shadowing the tanned cheeks of his thin face.

Over the course of their walk south Yoseph carried two bags—one rucksack on his back and one handcrafted canvas bag slung at his side. Each sagged heavily with supplies, though did not seem to burden the young man's strong back.

Walking side by side, the father held himself different than the son. While it was apparent in their faces that both had seen a hard life, the man was clearly more apprehensive than the boy. The man's trauma manifested in subtle ways, the most obvious being that of his shawl in contrast to his son's. While Yoseph walked with his shawl wrapped around his neck, drawn up slightly—just barely covering the crown of his head, the man had his shawl drawn up completely over his head, creating a deep hood of anonymity into which he could withdraw, preventing any passersby from being able to discern his appearance.

In the logical part of his mind, the man knew that any who could potentially recognize him had long since moved on in their journey yet he still felt the need to conceal himself. As though something in him feared that, even those he had never met before, could still potentially put a name to the face. From the moment their ship made port he had felt vulnerable. It felt as if no time had elapsed since the night of his exodus and, no matter the precautions taken, he would easily be recognized and persecuted.

Wanting nothing more than to blend into the backdrop, the man wore an indistinct set of clothes—dark gray pants, a white shirt and a neutral tan colored shawl, the same color as the one he wrapped around his son as they disembarked the boat. Lightweight brown leather shoes, which had been creased with age and wear, covered the well-worn soles of his feet.

He had gentle features, a strong jaw and intense brown eyes that had the ability to look past skin and into the character of another. In his late forties, the man's dark brown hair and short unkempt beard now held flecks of gray. The man's hair was far longer than that of his son's—reaching the base of his neck, falling just a few inches above his shoulders.

Slung across his chest rested the strap of the solitary canvas bag he carried. The bag was weighted by its bulky contents but the man could manage it without too much trouble. He was fit, so much so that one would think he did not physically need the aid of the wooden staff he walked with; nonetheless, there was internal wear bearing down his heart, causing him to lean on the staff more than he should have needed to.

~

At an easy pace, it had been a five day journey from the Bay of Haifa, where the ship had made port, to his former homelands in the south. They had taken their time, walking through their past life at a casual pace. But sadly, no matter the efforts taken to ease into this return, the man felt increasingly tense with each passing mile. Staying more than one night when stopping in the villages along their path was out of the question. As irrational as it may have seemed to an outsider, the man simply could not shake the feeling of being chased—hounds at his heels driving him onward.

It was only when he reached the old homelands that he consented to linger. He had returned with the intention of treading the paths of his youth in search of some remnant of his lost fervor to help reconnect him with who he had once been, before the pain over took him and the fatigue robbed him of his reason.

The man circled the site of the old homestead, desperately trying to recall what the land had looked like in the past, in a desire to paint a mental picture for his son. The man had envisioned a rush of renewed memories bursting into his mind when once again he set foot on the old lands. Yet this restoration of the faded and frayed memories had not taken place. Like an Alzheimer patient he shuffled along the dusty plot trying to recall where the old house had once stood and where the gardens had once bloomed.

It had been a calm day, there had been a few other pilgrims wandering in the distance—travelers who had come compelled by their religion longing for an epiphany that would pull together a cohesive answer concerning the greater truths. And then there was the man who had come compelled by a personal need to reconcile the difficult truths of his life that had formed after he had sought insight into the greater matters. But then it happened—something was stirring. Straining for clarity, his contemplation was disturbed when a shift came to the general atmosphere. The serene countryside suddenly woke with activity. The farmers came out of their houses, the villages in the distance woke from a sleepy day and the very air itself seemed to hum with the whisper of frightening news.

A crowd composed of pilgrims, farmers and townspeople had gathered. The man and his son walked towards them to learn what was happening. Panic broke out—word of bombings and fighting to the north. The war that raged years ago when their family worked these land, raged still. The opposing sides now went by different names but it was the same hatred—the same struggle to see who would stand on the pedestal, dominant over all others.

The accounts of killings and raids had reached the southern villages, as did the fear that the fighting would sweep down. Men and women were choosing to pack their vital belongings and make for the city rather than stay and face the ravaging militants that would surely descend.

The pilgrims who had come from stable lands were distraught when hearing the news—proximity to war was something the western world was often spared; while in contrast the natives who lived daily with such threats took the news in stride, they had become accustom to the predictable insanity of living in a region of unrest.

For the man the news came like the jab of a knife, reopening a wound that had festered within him for some years. Upon hearing the news, a flash of a memory vividly ripped through his mind—he could see himself hatefully cast down onto the rocky ground, the skin of his nearly bare body scraped away by the abrasive gravel and grit. Drowning in the past, a hysteria of helplessness threatened to overtake him. His bearded face contracted; he recoiled, shutting his eyes tight, trying not to look at the scenes playing out within his mind.

He had returned to his homeland to awaken the memories of what had been *before* the attack, not to once more relive the wounds suffered during. And yet as he stood faced with the prospect of returning to that place he feared the most—that place where the violent memories had been made—he felt certain that this pilgrimage of intended re-connection would do nothing more than tear wider his already bleeding wounds.

꙰

He had entered his adult life with a belief in a natural justice, wherein those who are loving are protected from those who are spiteful. Experiencing the direct opposite of this during his chaotic life, the man was left pondering why the wicked are routinely permitted to come and, in the course of a single night, undo years of growth and work. The good-hearted build and the ill-hearted destroy—history had proven thus; nonetheless, be it common, it was still wrong. *Love is the greater force yet also the eternal victim.* He thought to himself. Such paradoxes ran his strained mind in circles.

It was this cycle of senseless loss that caused the questions of *how* and *why* to fester within him; putting him at odds with the idealistic man he once was and the educated, albeit more pessimistic man, he had come to be. He had endured the soldiers with swords who came with the authority of the state and the mentality of the mob, lashing out at any and all. ...The broken in doors, fleeing in fear, found through betrayal; then left helpless in the custody of the immoral.

He was born with a desire to ease the internal ails of those around him yet the compassion he extended had been repaid with betrayal. He endured becoming the object of the mob's derision and the resource from where the greedy extracted their spoils. Jaded and hurt, he had since withdrawn from society and had no desire to reenter, what he viewed, to be the center of the madness.

No, he thought to himself. —*No.* He turned away from the speculating crowd, pulling his son gently by the arm as he made to leave.

"Wait!" a balding gray-haired man bellowed at the back of him. The stranger had a thick, well-kempt beard so long the eye could follow it down like a trail to his rounded belly. Deep lines creased his face; he was obviously a native to the local lands, aged by the searing sun.

Turning to face the stranger, the man observed a contradiction. The old man's hands were thickly calloused—the trait of a workmen, which starkly contradicted the middle-income clothes of a businessman the old man donned. These small signs hinting at the sense of shame the old man carried concerning his station in life and his wish to distance himself from that low-class affiliation whenever he could.

"You mustn't go off on your own," the old gray-haired man argued. "You do not know how things are in this country. You must come with us to the city."

"I-will-not-go-into-that-city," the man replied without room for negotiation. "And you are mistaken to think I do not know how these lands are," he added in a dismissal. His voice was uncharacteristically sharp.

"You must come with us. It is for your own safety," a farmer within the crowd firmly insisted.

"That city has never been safe," the man rebutted. "It was not safe when my family lived here and we all know that it is not safe now," the man finished. His answers were seemingly spoken from a place of reason but were actually rooted in his fear and not any logical conclusion.

An even-toned voice sounded amongst the bullies, "If you lived here before then you know these lands are not safe. We should all go to the city until the threat is passed, then resume our journeys." This voice of calm reason belonged to a man of average build and height in his mid-thirties; he stood with a woman who seemed to be his wife. The couple looked faintly familiar to the man.

Both the husband and wife had a trustworthy, loyalty about them—a gentleness that seeped through in the compassionate quality of their voice. The two were obviously of humble means. This was apparent by the clothes the husband wore. His pants shown mending stitches here and there around the knees and cuffs; while the long mid-blue cotton shirt he wore had a simple hand-made quality to it. Finally, covering his head there was a white linen shawl, which had the wide-weave trait of homespun cloth. The man's shortly cut light brown hair could be seen high on his forehead where the shawl ended. He had a close cut beard growing across his round face which, despite the panic, was smiling at both the man and his son.

Seemingly good natured, the stranger did have a distinct look of wear about his face, as if aged by prolonged physical and emotional labors. He and his wife shared this look of fatigue; nonetheless, the years of hardship did not seem to leave either of them embittered; rather, they had a manner that spoke of a longing for mercy in what had been a difficult existence.

"I will not force you sir," the husband continued. "But you seem reasonable enough. You must realize that two lone men are vulnerable in these lands. We shall find safety together in the city. ...*Please*," he added moments later in a desperate whisper.

Taking a strained breath, the man visibly shook with emotion. His eyes filled; the tears sat trembling on the edge of his lower eyelids as he wrestled with the inexpressible agony overtaking him. The stranger's words had reached past his fear, appealing to his reason but it still took every ounce of courage for the man to consider returning to that city. He knew deep down—underneath his terror—he should listen to the stranger's words yet despite the good argument the stranger had made, the man did not feel empowered. Be it the prudent thing to do, nausea rose in his churning stomach at the thought of passing through those gates again.

"Please, you must come with us," the woman said, echoing her husband's words. She wanted to shake the man from the dark place his fears were taking him.

Lost in his thoughts, the man finally placed where he had seen the couple. Every time the man and his son had come into a village while on the course of their journey south, they had come upon this same couple, as if the two pairs were walking parallel paths. The woman had a genuineness about her. Her long wavy hair fell to her waist; most of it was pulled back—enveloped safely within the cloth cone her cotton veil made as it draped. She was wrapped in a long brown skirt, had plain shoes and a rose colored blouse, which had been delicately embellished with embroidered patterns of scrolling leaves all about the neck and sleeve ends. Her oval face was full and a warm gaze shone through, despite the signs of wear.

Neither the man nor Yoseph had ever spoken with the couple. The man rarely spoke to anyone outside his immediate family. When approached by those he did not know his response usually consisted of a half-polite, half-melancholy nod before he continued on his way. Nevertheless, despite the lack of a formal introduction, due to the frequency of their run-ins on the road south, the man did feel that he and the couple already had some sort of undeclared acquaintance. Enough so that it was not strange for the couple to speak to him as if they already knew him.

"I cannot go back," the man confessed in a strangulated whisper only his son could hear. He felt pressured on all sides—bullied by the approaching forces, by the impatient crowd and by his own fears.

"Just leave the fool be!" the older gray-hair man bellowed in exasperation. "If we are going to leave we must do so now." At his order, most of the crowd began to disperse, heading off to make preparations for the retreat into the city. Apparently the word of this man carried weight with the locals.

Leaving his wife's side for a moment, the husband walked up to the man and his son—close enough so that only they two could hear, "I do not know what happened to create such a fear of the city in you...I can only imagine. But let me say this: If you don't go, both you and your son will fall into the hands of the fighters. You must believe me when I say: this is not something you want."

Looking up from his own terror the man met his son's eyes and in that instant the situation shifted. The man's fear could make him risk his own life but not even the strongest fear could compel him to risk his son's safety.

The city was unsafe—it always had been and most-likely would always be. But falling into the hands of moralless men blinded by fanaticism was far more dangerous. A struggle raged within the man, every organ within him trembled; vomit swelled from his stomach and rose up his throat, bringing the taste of bile to his mouth.

Gripping his staff as if it were the hand of his mother and he were but a frightened child, every fiber of his being pleaded with the unseen forces not to make him endure a return to that place. Yet in the taut silence no answers came, no reprieve was given and he bitterly stepped forward on an unsteady footing, setting out on the path that would return him to that same place his life had once ended.

"What is your name?" the husband asked; extending an introduction that went unreciprocated by the preoccupied man.

Trying to make up for his father's understandable lack of manners, the young man spoke up, "My name is Yoseph."

The husband met Yoseph's hand. "Good to meet you, albeit under regrettable circumstances. I am Samuel. This is my wife Maria," he said, drawing his wife over with a loving touch to stand closer to him. "And your name sir?" Samuel patiently asked the man again.

"What?" the man replied distraughtly in a half whisper. His face was red and sweaty as he struggled to fight back the terror within him. Tears glazed the sides of his face.

"Your name…?" Samuel repeated calmly.

He was at a loss. "I'd rather not say," the man replied in a tormented voice; not speaking meanly but rather, sadly—protectively.

CHAPTER II

The City

THE MARCH TO THE CITY BEGAN. The dry dirt on the rural road clouded underfoot as the caravan of weary souls shuffled onward. The low growing brush grew sparsely along the roadside. In the distance the balding green hills were parched, yearning for rains that seldom came.

Now and again, a clump of thin, pointed cypress trees or the outline of a huddled village rose on the horizon. Yoseph took in these sights as he walked; however, the man was blind to it all. He stared transfixed at the looming figure of the ancient city growing larger in the distance. It was as if the city had fed off his fear. *How it has swelled with time,* he thought to himself. The urban sprawl stretched the width of his gaze. It was more forbidding than he recalled.

The man walked closely by his son; his sole source of comfort lie within the boy and he lacked the strength to venture too far from him. It could have been his imagination but the man felt that everyone in the caravan was watching him. Feeling their questioning eyes on him only served to heighten his alienation.

Yoseph took his father's arm in an effort to steady him, both within and without. It had always been disconcerting for the young man to see his father—one of the strongest hearts in their family—in such a terribly vulnerable state.

Yoseph knew his father to be a resilient man; nonetheless, having grown up in the aftermath of the attack that had crippled their family, he knew thoroughly his father's wounds. The young man had not been alive to see his father in the time before the evil had come upon them. Stories of the relatively peaceful time of insights and hope known before the attack had filled Yoseph's childhood yet the reality of the trauma suffered had defined the boy's life since his birth.

Over the years the two had traveled together. They were father and son but they were also brothers and friends; while on their journey the bond had evolved and at times even reversed—Yoseph becoming the father, and the father becoming the child in need of care. It was not a failure on the man's part to need his son in such a way; rather, it was simply their reality after how brutally deep the wounds went and how long the hard path had drawn out.

"It will be alright," Yoseph whispered comfortingly to his father. "No one will know us. It will be different this time. We will be safe," he offered, wanting to reassure his father. Yet he could sense that, despite his good intentions, none of his assurances had managed to penetrate the dense fear wrapped around his father's heart.

❧

Usually a level-headed person, the man simply could not control his emotions when it came to the events that had taken place in that city. He could not pull himself out of his reeling; he could not shake himself from the nightmare evil had conjured all those years ago. While marching towards the city he felt disembodied from reality; for what was happening, could not actually be happening.

Withdrawn into his mind, the man thought silently to himself as the miles passed, *So many precious moments from the past—moments I never thought I would forget—have become distant in my mind. Why couldn't the traumas be among those memories forgotten? Why was the joy able to be so easily overshadowed? The happiness once known had been full—resplendent, yet it is only faintly recalled, as though some suppressive presence pushes it down in me where I can no longer reach it.*

Watching the man try to compose himself, Samuel moved closer. "Do you have a wife?" he inquired kindly; trying to distract the man from his worries.

"Yes," the man replied. He was preoccupied yet still felt the need to answer.

"Is she in danger?" Samuel asked. "Is that why you are hesitant to go to the city? …Because your family is at risk in another part of the country?"

Upon hearing this question the man looked mournful. *…Is she safe?* This question was one that both father and son asked themselves daily—a question for which they had no solid answer.

"She is not safe at home, as I would wish her to be," he replied. "But her safety is not the cause of my present worries." The man could have left his response there but to Samuel's surprise, he went on, "We have not seen each other in a very long time. She is always on my mind," the man added quickly. "But for once, I am glad she is not by my side; I would not want her to come back with me," he finished darkly.

As he withdrew back into himself, Samuel felt the short conversation come to its end. It did not seem as though the man's thoughts were dwelling upon the city but rather some other heartache of which Samuel and Maria had no knowledge.

As he squinted, the glint of a tear shone in the sunlight running along his rough cheek. A silent agony revealed itself. While thinking of the distance between them always was a source of pain for him, thinking of her did seem to calm him in that moment. She drew his focus away from his terror, even if only for a short time.

❦

This mysterious man had a certain aura about him triggering many to speculate about his identity. The fact that he had refused to give his name led some to whisper that he had to be a criminal. Yet it was clear to Samuel and Maria that this man, while a mystery, was not sinister.

He seldom spoke, and while this might have appeared a trait of coldness to some in the caravan, Samuel and Maria knew it to be a result of some wound the man borne upon his heart, which had broken his trust. No one yet knew the source of these wounds; nonetheless, to a certain group within the caravan, other things about the man were becoming clearer and stronger with each passing mile.

It could be sensed by anyone not willfully blind that this man had lived a different life, and had much insight to impart. His gaze was striking. His eyes revealed the depth of his pain; there was a deepening world-weariness behind his tired, pleading stare. Yet those same eyes spoke of a reservoir of hard-earned knowledge. He had a certain look about him— an uncommon gait—he moved through the world alienated by part of it and yet, at the same time, communing with part of it. This strange aura, which drew so many eyes to stare, seemed otherworldly.

❧

Over the course of the afternoon many people had taken to the roads, joining the march of the displaced. The highways were flooded yet, this country being a convergence of the ancient and the modern, the open lands were filled as well, by those traveling on foot and camelback. What had started off as a small caravan had slowly gathered into a herd as news of the fighting reached other villages and inhabitants thought it prudent to flee to the city.

The caravans traveled up the slopes of maroon soil, gravitating toward the promise of sanctuary. Pulled from his sorrow by a flicker of color, the man noticed the same golden wildflowers that had grown on these hills during the springs of his past, bloomed still. The generations of seeds had resiliently managed to continue on uninterrupted, growing across a land besieged so many times throughout history. Engrossed in this one pleasant thought, the man was taken aback when he looked up from his reflections to see that they had at last come to the mouth of the city.

The first feeling to strike him was terror. He thought the city had looked large miles away but it was even more intimidating up close. It looked like a swollen leech stretched across the countryside. Thick clouds gathered overhead casting a patchy darkness on the buildings. The man felt an ill omen mounting. With each step he took he felt as though he was approaching a beast found in some innermost circle of Hell.

As they moved close to the outer walls the noise began to rise. The scattered crowd bottle-necked as they herded onto the short bridge leading up to the gate. The man faintly heard Samuel and Yoseph speaking in the background. "It is nearly sunset. It will be busier than normal," Samuel warned.

Yoseph's face creased with concern. "Why?" he asked, having to shout above the racket.

"Concern after the attacks and Shabbat," Samuel shouted back.

With a heavy breath, the man passed under the tall, stone arch of the gate, a shadow crossed his path and he emerged from the darkened passage out into a busy marketplace.

The claustrophobic scene came as a slap in the face. He was dazed. There were merchants crying on all sides trying to entice the arriving pilgrims, arguments erupted over prices and melodramatic haggling began. Within the mob conversations played out in a half-dozen different languages, loud techno music rumbled from a club that had just opened its doors to the evening crowd and the call to evening prayer erupted from a P.A. system. It all melted together into a disorienting din. All the man could see were blurred faces. The constant stream of bombarding noise came at him from all sides. Unsettled and unbalanced the man flashed between images of the past and the present. Modern buildings fell away, the ancient stone roads shifted back into dirt and the merchants transfigured into a mob of onlookers—their bargain cries audibly morphing into that of insults and condemnation.

The dense crowd of shoppers and pilgrims moving through the market broke the entering caravan into pieces. In the upheaval the man was separated from his son and shunted along the length of the main street. Lost in a wave of panic, the man couldn't breathe. Soaked with sweat, panting heavily, he pushed his way through the pressing crowd, trying to make his way to an isolated corner where he could try to spot his son. Yet upon extracting himself from the suffocating mass, the man crumpled—collapsing back first against the stone wall of a building, sliding to the ground as his legs buckled. Balled up, knees against his chest, the man clutched himself tightly, trembling in terror of the chaotic surround.

Yoseph's eyes had followed his father's jilted progress through the congested crowd. The young man fought his way through the oblivious shoppers and overeager merchants to reach his father; while at the same time, from the corner of his eye, watching the position of their caravan moving through the market. He did not want the two of them left alone in the forbidding city.

Yoseph heard the wail of a classical guitar, the metallic shifting of a tambourine and the rapid pulse of a calf-skin drum, which beat in sync with his heart, echo from a street band playing nearby. There was a scramble for supplies as the sun fell to the horizon. Then, quite suddenly, a lone man dressed in black waded into the crowd. The people parted to make way for him. Blowing hard on the shofar, the man trumpeted the start of Shabbat. In that moment, all Jewish shop owners observing the tradition closed to begin their day of rest. Much of their caravan dispersed, each small group striking out with their own destination—heading towards the homes of family or acquaintances but thankfully some still remained in the market to buy supplies.

As the mob thinned Yoseph was at last able to push his way through to reach his father. He knelt down beside him and tried to speak to him—to reach him in the depths of his terror and raise him above the surrounding din. "Father. ...father! We must find a place to stay. You have to come with me. ...father!" he repeated. He shook him slightly but the man made no response. Yoseph's mind raced as he tried to think of what to do next. Such attacks had happened before. Yet it had never been this serious—never this gripping.

The man was there but at the same time, not. His body was in the market but his mind had been pulled backward, into past events. He was elsewhere, in a place where he could not hear his son. In a time before his son had even been born, when here—in this city—he was attacked and betrayed by those he called his friends.

Long ago the broken bones had healed and the cuts had been stitched shut yet today the poor man could feel all the old wounds ache; it was as though, triggered by the vivid memory, the bruises had re-bloomed. He winced as Yoseph laid a hand on him. Tears began to swell behind his closed eyelids. The stream of racket around him battered his

21

heightened senses. He needed quiet. He needed calm. The fierce velocity of his hammering heart against his ribs shook his entire body. The courage was gone from him—it had been taken from him years ago in this very place.

His eyes were closed shut yet that did not black out the scenes replaying inside his mind. He once again felt the strike of bats and sting of the whips; he coughed as the stench of blood, urine and infection he smelt in that rancid holding cell choked him once more. The silent hysteria coiled tightly inside his chest—strangulating him. It was inexpressible—the maddening terror that comes when you realize that you no longer have the power to safeguard the sanctity of your body; for you are the prisoner of the immoral ones who have a thirst for the suffering of others and no sense of shame to stay their hand.

Submerged deep within the nightmare he was helplessly reliving, the man could not hear his son; he could not feel the pain of his own fingernails digging into his arms and head as he gripped and clawed at himself. He was utterly incapacitated—trapped in an attack he had survived but never fully escaped. Crying and shaking, he cowered before the fully awoken memory of all that had happened upon this ground.

Placing his hands firmly on his father's shoulders, Yoseph leaned in close, resting his forehead upon his father's, trying to calm him.

"Father!" he said strongly, trying to shake him from his reeling. "We must get off the street and find a place to hold up."

An unexpected tap on his shoulder caused the young man to jump violently.

"I am sorry," Samuel said quickly. He was genuinely apologetic.

Yoseph turned back to his father once he saw that there was no threat.

Samuel continued on, "We are moving on from the market. Most of the hotels are full but we were told of a vacant building a short ways from here. We have been permitted to take refuge there."

Knowing he had to get his father off the streets and into a more controlled setting, Yoseph gathered himself and stood up. He pulled his father's shawl up high, in an effort to shelter him in some small way from the damaging surround. Then, taking his father under the arms, he pulled his limp body upright and rested him against the wall.

The man legs had been so weakened by fear, he was unable to stand upon them. He felt useless. He was unable to open his eyes, unable to bring himself into the present— unable to make the violent memories cease looping.

Knowing that they had to push forward, Yoseph pulled one of his father's arms over his shoulder, then wrapped his arm around his father's back, taking all the weight upon himself.

"Where is the building?" he asked Samuel with single-minded focus; ignoring the weight of his father's body bearing down on his shoulder.

"This way," Samuel answered, moving quickly to the other side of the ailing man, in an effort to aid Yoseph in carrying the weight of his father's wounds.

⁂

Down the busy road and up a narrow corridor of concrete stairs, they came to what would be their inn until the threat passed. This sanctuary they all were to stay in was nothing more than a bombed out building. There were no furnishings; the room was utterly bare. Curls of peeling paint clung to the walls; while plaster dust, shards of glass and debris coated the floors.

Yoseph had settled his father against a wall on the far side of the room, away from the others in the caravan who shuffled in. There were no room divides; rather it looked as though it had once served as an office space. It was completely open; several dead power outlets and phone jacks dotted the pallid gray baseboard.

Yoseph counted eighteen people from the caravan who chose to stay in the large room: the gray-hair man, whose name he gathered to be Ari after listening to introductions being made between those who had gathered from across the room; Ari's wife and their three adult sons; a farmer, his wife and their young daughter; a group of students on pilgrimage; Samuel and Maria and of course himself and his father.

As each group of travelers came up the stairwell and entered the room, they claimed a space for themselves and began to settle in. Yoseph had cleared a space for his father, took out a thin bedroll from among their belongings and eased him down to rest. Yoseph was thankful that the room was quiet and away from the bombarding streets. As he leaned back against the wall, gripping his father's hand tightly, Yoseph pleaded that his father's terror would ease and the coming night would pass gently.

☙

Despite Yoseph's hopes for a peaceful night, it had been a period of silent, fevered fear. It had taken several hours for the man to calm down enough to fall into a sleep.

Waking mid-morning, the man found himself being tended to by Maria; his son was nowhere in sight. Startled, he sat up quickly.

"He is fine," Maria said reassuringly. "Yoseph and Samuel went back to the market to gather supplies. He did not think that you would wake up until he was back. He did not want to leave you alone but he said you needed supplies and it seemed a safe time to go. Several others went out in the early morning and said the streets seemed quiet."

Upon hearing this, the man relaxed slightly but he still felt uneasy. He understood his son's reasoning but was still upset with his decision; he had not wanted them to separate while in the city.

"You do not look well," Maria said, in a concerned voice. "Here, I made tea," she said consolingly. "I always bring some with me on journeys and the farmer let me use his propane stove."

The man wrapped his trembling hands around the mug and brought it close to his face. The cinnamon and anise steam broke across his face. His appetite was non-existent but there was something comforting about holding the warm mug. The heat seeped through the heavy ceramic and went deep into the joints of his aching hands.

She gave him a supportive smile and a kind nod trying to hearten him. He took a sip. She continued, "Your son will return soon with food. I do not have much to offer until my Samuel gets back but you are welcome to what we do have." She removed various small packages from the basket at her side.

He swallowed the hot amber liquid. "Thank you, no," he answered gratefully. "I am not hungry."

"You will need to eat," she said in a firm yet caring voice.

"No," the man said, motioning that she sit back down. "Really, I am fine," he added. He did not want to be rude but he was nauseated by the fear churning within him, to the point that food was simply repulsive.

"So," she said awkwardly. She stared down at her hands, at a loss as to what to say. She did not know what she could offer to alleviate the obviously tormented man. She knew that the man was private and most-likely did not want to talk; however she felt the need to break the tension of the situation.

"What do you do? What is your trade?" she asked, beginning with the routine question in an obvious effort to make conversation.

In an effort not to hurt her feelings the man pushed himself to speak. "I have done many things in my time," he offered; willing to share this personal detail with one who had been so understanding and helpful. Adding a bit sadly, "I was a woodworker as a younger man and hope to be again some-day. But it has been a long time since I was able to simply tend to the needs of my family's home. I was a teacher for a short time," he added in a factual voice.

"And what are you now?" Maria asked.

"A traveler of sorts, I suppose," he replied unenthusiastically.

Across the room a few of the bright-eyed students from the caravan listened to the conversation. Upon hearing that the man had been a teacher they felt compelled to chime in.

"What subject did you teach?" one of the students asked with interest.

Less willing to speak with others in the room, the man's tone altered slightly. He was noticeably more guarded and hesitant. "No one subject," he replied. "I was not a formal teacher in a classroom. I suppose," he said slowly, "if I had to place myself in a category, which mind you I do not often do, *spirituality* would be the answer."

The student's interest peaked.

The man ignored this invite into conversation. He could hear footsteps echoing up the stairwell that led down to ground level. A moment later Yoseph came through the doorway with a full bag of supplies in hand, Samuel following directly behind him. Disturbingly it was in that same moment—as Yoseph and Samuel crossed the threshold—that a blast sounded, rocking the ground the building stood upon.

Everyone fell to the floor. The man tried to keep his eyes fixed on Yoseph during the chaos but a fine plaster dust descended from overhead and blinded him.

When the bomb sounded all conversation stopped, as did the heart of every person in the room. The man's heart had paused mid-beat, right in the center of his throat—lodged there like a lump of fear he could not swallow.

With aftershocks still reverberated along the foundation and up through the hearts of those in the room, the older man—Ari and his three sons jumped to their feet, running to a broken window where they saw smoke billowing from one of the old Quarters.

CHAPTER III

The Request

SEVERAL HOURS HAD PASSED SINCE THE BUILDING and the nerves of all those within it, were shook by the attack. Word had come of the suicide bombing at a café only a mile away. Four people had been injured and twenty killed. When the man was told this news he sat to himself for a time. No, he had not been at the café. He had not known the victims. But he could feel the loss. He always could. From the very beginning of his life, the pain of a stranger had been his own.

Sickeningly, the announcement of bombings was commonplace in this age. As jaded and alienated as he felt, he could not help but ache for humanity. Only hours before, the morning crowd was sitting at the tables set outside the café, sipping their tea and coffee. A child sat across from her parents, swinging her small feet in the air between the wide legs of her chair, elbows propped up on the rim of the table as she nibbled the edges of a golden, honeyed pastry. A business man sat oblivious to his surroundings as he punched-off a text message on his phone. A beaming young woman walked up to the counter to place an order for a dessert to accompany the dinner she was making for her boyfriend; while a waitress picked up a paper cut out of a white box, folded it together and began placing the sweets neatly inside. All of them went about their morning unaware that in some dark apartment not too far away a lone man was blindly stretching out his trembling fingers towards destruction.

In that moment when the blast sounded, in the thin space before their last breath, each and every life about to end had their final thought—their last rush of feeling, which sadly was one of terror and confusion. The parents surrendered themselves to the awful truth that they could not protect their daughter. The child looked up—eyes wide—to see the ghostly figures of her adult-self approaching her, only to brush past her. The business man stared blankly at the mundane message he was responding to on his phone, to view in the letters the full horror of a life wasted; having given years of loyalty to a company that did not see the worth of his life, until a point came when he could not see it either. The youthful woman placing the dessert order, flashed to the wedding that would never come and to the faces of the children that would never be born.

The potential of these hearts was cut short all because it was deemed virtuous to bring their life to a violent end in the name of a *loving* God. The blast wave would stretch out far beyond the radius of the shrapnel as one by one the loved ones of those lost learned of the attack and descended into chaos. Decades of torment rippled out from any bomb detonated, from any bullet fired or from any weapon wielded. This morning a new group of mourners joined the procession of those wandering this world asking *how* and *why*.

❧

For hours after the attack Ari and his sons debated the possible parties responsible. The conversation was so loud it was offensive. The argument dominated the atmosphere of the room, driving out what little peace could be found.

"...I am telling you it was them. They were responsible for the last café bombing. It is their method, they...."

Entering this conversation towards the end, Samuel spoke up out of exasperation, "It does not matter what the name of the faction is," he said, cutting across Ari's eldest son. "None of this is done in the name of God; it is done in the name of *power*—to gain it, to keep it, to exert it."

The nameless man looked up. For hours now he had been unsuccessfully attempting to block out the pointless debate. Samuel's words had acted like a fresh wind of reason dispersing the thick cloud of ignorance and for the first time since the debate began the man was interested in what was being said. His eyes fixed intently on Samuel.

"I am tired of these violent acts being carried out in the name of what is sacred. If these groups are going to kill they should at least have the courage to come out and make plain their true motives. Those leaders who spur their lessers on with assurances of *divine will* are not following God. They are following their own ambitions. Behind their devout cries is a desire to dominate, and behind that is the tormenting insecurity they cannot seem to come to terms with, whispering to them that they are powerless, pathetic men," Samuel finished in a frustrated tone. It was obvious that this speech had built up in him a line at a time over the hours that the asinine speculation had persisted until he finally had to speak.

Surprisingly no one argued with Samuel. The nameless man had felt sure that a rebuttal would come from Ari, who seemed to fancy himself well-versed in politics. Perhaps it was something in the firm tone of Samuel's voice that let the others know that there was no room for debate. Or perhaps the silence was simply due to the fact that the debate had already been carrying on for hours and none of them had it in them to start a new argument. Either way, the talk was brought to an end when Ari's wife called to him, telling him that their afternoon meal was ready.

❦

After everyone had eaten and the arguments had stopped the momentum of the day seemed to slack. Most everyone sat drowsily resting with a full belly. Across the room the students talked amongst themselves trying to distract their minds from the disconcerting situation. The man and his son sat in the corner of the bare room, off to themselves; Samuel and Maria situated a few feet down from them.

The man and his son were in the middle of a private conversation when, curious about the mysterious stranger, one of the students came over to speak to him.

"Sir," the bright-eyed student started shakily, "my friends and I were hoping you might speak with us. You said you are a teacher of spirituality…? We are all students of religion and, well, we were thinking it might be pleasant to have a conversation to pass the time. We came here on pilgrimage, traveling to our new school in the south. It seems a waste to sit here in the presence of a teacher and not have a conversation."

The young boys, none of whom were older than twenty-five, all came over assuming that a conversation was already beginning. Overhearing the young student's words, a few of the others in the room, looked up out of simple curiosity—all of them wanting to learn more of the nameless man's story.

Samuel and Maria could not help but turn to listen as well. They did not want to pry into the man's life; rather, they were following a rising feeling that told them this man had the answers. A conclusion they could not logically explain but that was undeniably strong.

The man felt the pressure of the moment. He found he was being brought unto a pivotal moment in his journey and he honestly did not know what choice to make.

&

The first time they had asked the man answered, *no*. He was going through far too much within himself and did not feel up to interacting with anyone beyond his son or perhaps Samuel and Maria, who thus far seemed a warm presence.

Determined to have their way, the students had persisted into the late afternoon; bringing the man to the point where he had little choice but to address this request.

"You have asked me to share what I have learned over my spiritual life," he said, feeling slightly beleaguered.

"Please," the eager student affirmed.

"You do not know what you ask," the man said morosely; speaking from a place of painful awareness.

"I don't understand," the student said at a loss. Clearly he thought his request was rather normal and not worthy of this fuss.

"I know you don't," the man said, in a meaningful way. Adding, "What is your name young man?"

"Asa," the student offered in a soft voice.

Asa was obviously the youngest among the other students. He had full cheeks, which were nearly always pushed back with a broad smile. There were no strains upon his bright gaze. He had short full hair, dark brown in color. His skin had been tanned by the hot sun. It was clear that the boy had been raised in this area, which made it all the more remarkable to the man that the boy still retained such an innocent, optimistic air about him.

"Asa—*the healer*," the man said in a reflective voice.

"Excuse me sir?" Asa asked respectfully.

"That is the etymology of your name—the healer."

"Yes sir, I know. My father chose my name deliberately for its meaning. He hoped my birth would heal my family's grief after having lost another son before me."

"How did he die?" Ari's eldest son interjected insensitively.

This man was harsh, brutish and militant in appearance. His hair was shaved very short, calling to mind the style of a soldier. Unconcerned with the emotional sensitivities of those around him, he had a pitiable mental dullness about him.

Taken aback by the brute's abrupt entry into the conversation, Asa fumbled for words.

The nameless man spoke up, "And what is your name sir?" he inquired. There was a mild sharpness to his voice. He wanted to bring the brash man to a pause, so as to reflect on the manners he lacked, as well as provide Asa a moment of support during which he could regroup.

"Aden," the brute answered. Still oblivious to any offence he might have given, he pushed on, asking again in an equally insensitive manner, "So, how did your brother die?"

"In a bombing," Asa offered meekly. Clearly the young man felt dominated by Aden's demands.

After his unfeeling question was answered, Aden seemed to have nothing more to offer to the conversation and faded into the background. The group lapsed back into silence and the nameless man continued, turning to address Asa once more. Picking up where he and the young man left off before the interruption.

"Having lived with those bearing wounds, you may be able to understand what it means when I say that I too have wounds—wounds that I received after speaking unwanted truth.

"I was begged to speak, just as you beg me now, only to be spited when I did; in this you may see why I am hesitant to speak now."

"All we sought was a conversation," another student offered as Asa pondered the man's words silently.

"*All* you sought was a conversation," the man echoed; not stressing the words to be harsh with the young man but rather, as a means of bringing forward a point. "What is your name young man?" the man asked kindly.

"Gideon," the student replied.

Looking to be about the same age as Asa, Gideon gave off a different feel than his fellow. Gideon seemed jaded by the events of his life thus far; he did not have the bright-hearted fervor of Asa. He had lost the motivation to delve too deeply and the deeper significance of small actions seemed to escape the young man.

The nameless man looked the boy over; his dark hair was thin and grown out, following the slope of his forehead it hung down, partly concealing his blue eyes. He had a pallid complexion, a thin face and a pointed chin. It was clear in how he held himself that, though he was young, he wanted to be treated as a man.

"You speak as if a conversation were a harmless thing. Yet few things are more impacting than words, be they spoken or written. Few things are more perilous than offering unwanted truth unto a group of people. We never risk more than when we share our beliefs with another.

"You would say that you seek the truth and admire those who would speak bluntly, yet I have heard such things before and felt the sting of a whip upon my back when I heeded my heart and spoke without restraint."

"We simply wish to talk—to learn," Gideon reasoned in a serious tone; still sounding like a child in spite of himself. "We came here to this city to explore our faith. So, speak to us—preach as you say you once did and let us all just speak for a time. What else is there for us to do here?"

The man drew in a long heavy breath. "You would enter into a conversation, discussing such serious matters simply as a way of *passing time*. I take such conversations with the utmost seriousness and do not enter into them as a diversion," the man said defensively. "Speaking idly without first knowing the character and intentions of those I am conversing with has cost me a great deal already. I will not speak arbitrarily again. I will not enter into a recreational debate. What I have learned on my path is saved for my family and for those who, like us, have sought the answers out of a deeply-felt need to know the truth."

Samuel and Maria seemed drawn to this statement. A profound yearning showed on their faces.

"We are students of religion; we have devoted our lives to the study of the sacred texts. We are serious in our pursuit for truth," Gideon said; in an all too unaware manner.

"Of what faith are you?" Aden said, rudely interjecting once again. He had begun to question the character of his company. By his manner he seemed to be addressing the whole group, as if wanting everyone to sound off before the discussion went any further.

"Wait," the nameless man interceded before any answers were given. "No," he said firmly. "No labels—no naming our religion. As soon as each person here declares his or her religion boundaries will be drawn between us and preconceived notions concerning followers of each faith shall be attached to their holders.

"If we are to speak, I suggest that we must all remain nameless in this respect."

"Why?" Aden asked again in an aggressive voice. "You are talking about having a debate about God. How can we have this if we don't know what faith everyone is?" he finished dully.

"I think it is necessary that we withhold our religion so as to remain free of judgment and be known for who we are, not what we are painted to be by public perception.

"I personally don't desire to know your religion," he added in a matter-of-fact tone, "only if you have faith."

"What's the difference?" Aden asked in an exasperated tone. "Semantics," he spat out condescendingly.

"It is not semantics," the man insisted. "Faith is the willful act of believing in that which, as of now, cannot fully be comprehended. *Faith* has to do with the individual; whereas *religion* concerns a *movement*. Religion is inherently political—complex; whereas faith is inherently personal.

"Today—in this circle, we shall speak of our personal beliefs. Every person seeking knowledge of the sacred knows the established paths of religion open to them but what we don't know are each other's personal conclusions—those truths we each have come to on our own.

"Following a religion will bring you to the values at the center of that religion—values that can bring us closer to our better selves or further away. Yet if we wish to find the divine each of us must make our own path to it—following not the blazed path of doctrine but choosing instead to venture through the wilderness of the unknown led by our heart, guided by the signs we perceived while in that heady altered state that is belief."

"I just don't understand how we can discuss God, without speaking of religion," Aden argued. "They are one in the same."

"Each religion is composed of the ideas of mankind concerning the divine; while God—the divine—exists separate, independent from what we might think it to be. In the end, my point is this: Do you wish to study what has been written or do you wish to know truth? For I have found that the two seldom align.

"You ask me to speak and in this, you ask me to share my personal truth," the man said, returning to the original request. "But I would now ask you how far you are willing to go to follow that truth?"

With a pained look on his face the man realized that, in spite of himself, the conversation he sought to avoid had already begun. Upon his face there was a look that spoke of the inner-struggle occurring. He wanted to go on—he wanted to attempt to explain his point but at the same time the wounded part of him now screamed at him to hold his tongue.

It was his nature to share and engage. He had tried to train himself not to do so; for every time he had tried to speak— tried to share, he had been met with deafness, denial and dire consequence. Yet, for all his self-restraint, for years on end he had inwardly sought the opportunity to do it all over again, regardless of how dearly his first attempt had cost him. On the surface it might have seemed illogical for him to wrestle so fiercely over a seemingly harmless conversation with a group of young students; however, there is no such thing as a harmless conversation. And this inner-conflict occurred in him because in this moment, for him, there was a greater choice being made—in entering this conversation he was reentering a world where he was misunderstood and hunted, and he did not know if he was ready to do so.

His nature battled against his past trauma. His hopes that the truth could be set straight battled against all the futile past encounters had. At times he found these inner-battles a madness of duality—his nature struggling against the unchanging reality of the place he was in and the choices of the people. Would he ever stop going around in circles? Would there ever come a day when he would no longer feel the need to give the truth to those who, in the end, would not want it and would hate him for his attempts to awaken them to a reality they went to great lengths to deny?

Would it be different this time? he asked himself. He felt naïve for even considering the possibility.

Yoseph looked at his father, seeing all too plainly that he was considering entering into the conversation. The boy would not hold back his father, but at the same time he could not hide his rising fear at the prospect of entering into this type of debate given their current vulnerability. Yoseph was the one other who knew the greater significance of events that escaped the others around them. The young man sat beside his father, waiting and watching just as all the others were, wondering if he would speak or if he would let the moment pass.

The internal struggled played out silently. He had always spoken out of a desire to connect. He had told himself otherwise—he had told himself that he had spoken out of a desire to *inform*, but this was not true. Underneath it all, he had always spoke out of a desire to *connect*—to find bonds with strangers, which all rooted back to the idealistic dream he was still trying to realize, wherein the family of humanity would reunite.

Regardless of his past reasons for speaking the man knew that if he were to speak again—if he were to risk it, he would have to do it for the shear sake of the truth alone. To hear the truth spoken and to have it known, no matter if it were accepted or rejected. …No matter if he was welcomed or again condemned.

One part of him told him he was a fool for even considering speaking again, especially given where he was. *Here of all places…here is where it would happen.* Thinking this, the man could not help but laugh within himself at the irony of the fates. *You led me here knowing I would do this,* he spoke silently within himself, to the one that can hear the unspoken things.

Resigning himself to his inalterable nature…. Confronting the fact that, while he had escaped this city all those years ago, he had still been trapped here since that day, the man began.

"The long nights of torment and hysteria in the garden come not before the marked day but *after*," he said, bringing an eerie hush to the group. "We give ourselves over in our heightened piety—pledging that we will do what is right, completely ignorant of what shall be asked of us.

"In this world of unspoken rules and unchallenged lies the truth has a cost for those who bear it unto the masses. The illusions in this world are guarded by a spiteful element—by those who have become evil. Every word of truth breaks down a part of a great illusion the movement of evil has woven, bringing down the wrath of those who depend on its continued existence," the man finished. The words settled over those present.

The silence stretched. "Is that why you are hesitant to speak?" an older student asked. The man had heard the other students call this young man by the name of Judah. "You believe the words you speak here, with us, will bring down the wrath of this evil of which you speak?"

Judah was by far the eldest among the students, most likely in his mid-late twenties. The boy was lean and thin-faced. He had sandy blonde hair, light eyes and newly sun-kissed skin, which hinted that he had traveled to this land from a country to the north. Despite not being a native, the young man did not seem intimidated by his surroundings; he was confident, mature and had the fatherly presence within the group.

The nameless man wordlessly affirmed Judah's conclusions.

Asa spoke up, "But this evil you speak of is surely not present here. You need not fear speaking the truth to us. All of us here welcome the end of illusions."

"Your words are spoken in the tongue of youth," the man said, half reminiscing, half pitying. "Of some things your youth makes you wiser than any of us and still, of other matters, you know only the children's tales and not the reality.

"What am I ignorant of?" Asa said, unoffended. He was inexplicably drawn to hear this nameless man's insights.

"When I say the word 'evil' unto you, most likely fairy tale images of beastly demons enter your mind; however, evil possesses neither a forked tongue nor cloven hooves. True evil is harmless in appearance; the horror lies in its actions and its inner-features.

"You say that all those who are gathered here desire the end of illusions, yet to what degree? If the truth I revealed unto you brought to an end the only world you ever knew, would you still urge me to speak? Would you embrace me still if I was the one to wake you from the ease of your ignorance and bring you into a harder life? Or would you reject me and condemn me in a desperate effort to silence the words I spoke, that you might return to your former ease of unknowing?

"Would you respect the sanctity of the words passed down to me in confidence from those who came before, which I choose to share with you? Or, hearing the profoundness of this truth, would you go unto your fellow man and preach the words as your own—craving the reverence given to the false prophets?"

"I do not understand," Asa said, feeling daunted by the mounting complexity of a seemingly simple request.

"I am not insulting you dear boy," the man was quick to reassure. "I am asking all here, who would say they seek the truth, to be aware of why they desire to find it. Not all seek the truth with purity of intention; some seek not to know but to find that which can be packaged and sold unto the desperate."

Simplifying his point, the man went on, "Ask yourself this question: Do you seek to know God? Or do you seek to *be* God? If the answer your heart whispers is the latter—if you would possess, dominate and be revered, you are part of the negative element of which I speak and I would have this conversation end now; for I would rather give no more wisdom to be exploited.

"If we would speak, I would have the conversation be taken seriously. We seldom admit to ourselves, let alone others, when we have settled. The choice to become evil is a subtle one at times; it occurs when we no longer find the need for the distinction between truth and lie but only between easy and hard. Waking to the truth is a hard road many would rather not take. If you sense within yourself that some part of you would rather remain ignorant—if your desire for truth will last this day alone, then you should leave this circle and return to the life you have resigned yourself to lead.

"So now," the man said calmly, "if after I have begun to reveal the nature of the path you have declared the desire to travel, if any of you are still eager to continue, we shall. But if you should feel a sense of idealism is driving you to stay and listen," the man's eyes fell on Asa's bright-eyed, eager face, "… if you feel unafraid and undaunted by what my words will begin for you, you have listened but have not heard a word I have said.

"Many of you walk the path your parents started you on when they passed down their traditions to you. If I asked each of you whether or not you wish to know the deeper meaning in all that is taking place around you, many of you would say beyond a doubt that your answer is yes. Yet sadly, while many would declare this, it is not always genuinely meant. You see," he said frankly, "all of us have the chance to learn the truth, whether it be the truth of the divine, of the world around us or of our self, and we simply decide that we do not want to know.

"As unconscionable as it is, many prefer ignorance to awareness and I have learned to respect this choice. I no longer try to change the minds of those who would rather be left in their denial. Yet, if having heard me—if having understood me, if having some appreciation for the cost of bearing the truth—there are those among you who would have me speak, stay and we shall have a conversation."

No one made to leave the group. Whether out of a genuine desire to listen, a curiosity as to what the man could possibly know that could be worth his fear to share it or simply not wanting to appear to be one who is content in their ignorance, everyone stayed. All the students remained seated;

Samuel and Maria looked utterly absorbed. Off to the side, decidedly apart from the group, Ari and his three sons waited, outwardly appearing uninterested but inwardly hushed.

Seeing this, the man knew it was time to begin. The greater significance was inescapable—he could not bear to look it full in the face but neither could he turn away. He found himself doing what he swore to himself a hundred times over, he would never again do.

"As cold as it may sound to you, I chose long ago not to try to teach again. In another life, I spoke once in a desire to ease those around me, only to lose everything when those who once listened forsook me for an easier path. So this time, if I shall speak, I must do so for myself alone, as a way to reaffirm who I am after conceding myself bit by bit over the course of the silent years."

Samuel and Maria looked puzzlingly at him, wondering as to the context behind his words. Seeing their wordless inquiry, he continued on, directing his words to them, "Years ago, I chose to never again share my innermost thoughts with anyone outside my family. At the time, I did not think my silence would change what I knew to be true within myself; I thought I would still be myself, I would simply force myself to hold back what I might have otherwise shared. Yet I have found that throughout each meeting and encounter that I forced myself to hide who I am and held back the words I felt compelled to speak, I became lost to myself and the knowledge I once knew so thoroughly became all the harder to recall.

"Afraid of the evil who initially wounded me and who eternally hunts, I hid the truth that attracts it—like a wounded animal trying to cover their tracks. Only, in my terror, I hid the truth too deep and now even I cannot fully recall all I once knew.

"And so," he said in a steady exhale, "after many nights spent battling—trying to come to terms with the fact that I would again be faced with this situation, I choose to speak, not to awaken the truth in you but to reawaken it within me."

Chapter IV

The Truth

"TELL US WHAT IT IS YOU BELIEVE. Tell us your story," pronounced asa, in his unfailingly eager voice.

Looking at the young student with a mixture of admiration and despair, the man waded into the deep conversation they all had sought so fervently. "Tell my story," he began hesitantly. "This is a tale few could arrange in a graceful way. I find it is easier to tell the story of all mankind, than attempt to encompass the vast inner-life of just one person. I sense that, beyond my story, what you actually seek to discuss is the *greater story* we are all a part of, of which I have indeed been given small parts; however, as I said, I have only *parts*. I have never known how to go about assembling the book that would tell the story from beginning to end."

The man settled in, turned a page in his memory and began to delve. Without even trying he drew the attention of those in the room with the skill of the most gifted storyteller. "At times, it is hard to see where the true beginning of a story is. I do not know where the beginning of this greater story took place and I do not presume to know how it all shall end. So I fear that, as I undertake the telling, you will have to take what bits of truths I give you and arrange them yourselves." He paused. The room was silent. Every eye was set upon him—a fact that left him decidedly ill at ease.

Those in the room were captivated by the man; something about him, which they were hardly aware of, drew their gaze. He felt familiar to them and yet was a complete unknown. None of them knew why it was so important to hear this man speak; the need was simply there—unable to be denied. The violence that had driven them all into the city faded to the background; as if they had not been brought here by danger at all but rather, led here by fate's hand to hear this man speak.

For those few who listened begrudgingly the Fates who had plopped them at the man's feet were acting as a parent guiding them to learn an unwanted but much-needed lesson. As though putting them into proximity of this man was a means of, if only once, making them listen to that which they did not want to hear.

He began.

"You ask me to tell you what I believe. Tell me," he asked in return, "have you ever tried to recall the face of a loved one long passed? …The face of your husband or wife perhaps?" His steady voice wavered.

"She was the one I shared all things with...my wife," he clarified unnecessarily. "Ours is a union more intimate than any to come before. Yet now her face only reveals itself to me when I bring forward the memory of a specific moment we shared. If I try to recall an image from the general space of my mind her face remains indiscernible within the vagueness.

"My beliefs—the truths I was given long ago—have become like her face—lost until a specific memory is brought to mind. And so, you cannot make this general a request of me: 'Tell me what you believe?' Instead you must ask me of specific matters and in the end gather what pieces I am able to bring forth from my memory and make a mosaic that shows the greater whole."

The man's question was posed to the group and the first minds to start pondering the topics of discussion were those of the students. For Maria and Samuel personal questions regarding their individual difficulties came to mind yet for the students of Theology and Rhetoric the greater questions asked by every generation of humanity were what ought to be discussed.

Gideon was the first to break the silent thought. From beneath his dark hair he gazed at the man. "You say you know of evil—that you have 'encountered it'...been 'hunted by it' and 'seen its forms.' You say that all we know of evil comes from fictitious stories. So tell us then of the *true* evil."

With a heavy breath the man replied, "You ask me to remember the worst first." Adding in a tone of irony, "The truth about evil is the one thing I need not try and recall." His tone darkened for a moment, as the irony turned bitter in his mouth. He recomposed himself. "Some would think that you have chosen the wrong place to begin this talk but ironically enough, evil is the right place to begin."

"Why?" Gideon asked musingly.

"Because the world we know and all that we have been taught as truth was affected by the emergence of evil and, if we are to take in the truth, we must first rid ourselves of the lies we live with as a result of evil's influence.

"I wish I could say that awakening to the truth begins with the gentle sight of love's depths revealed, but it doesn't. At least, it didn't for me," he added. "Instead I find, we must first awaken to the deceptive, negative presences surrounding us. In the end, I suppose, given the nature of this world it is necessary to see the illusions before we can understand the workings of our reality. But still," he added regretfully, "to know the truth about evil you must also be told the story of love and vice versa; for, while the two are opposites, they are forever linked in that they share the same roots in humanity. To tell you the truth about the devil I must share with you the story of God. And to speak with you of God I must first disillusion you of who and what you may believe God to be. More importantly than my telling you is your willingness to hear me—to hear ideas that contradict that which you were taught."

"To reach original truth we must shed all myth—we must do without the drama and theatrics that normally surround both the evil and the divine, so as to let the simple story stand alone."

The man paused, it seemed he was flipping through a book in his mind, looking for the right page to begin at; while those listening sat wondering as to what direction he would go—what religious view did he hold and what familiar doctrine would he recite. Unbeknownst to them, he was preparing to give them a story they had never before heard, drawing from a faith that had all but died out.

Finding his mental page, the man spoke, "The struggle with evil began, not with a falling out between a *God* and his *fallen servant* but between a *father* suffering a falling out with his *son*. The wise one—the elder of us all—is not a deity. The God figurehead is a myth," he said baldly, "a persona evolved over the course of history. A myth built up around two things, which must be respectively separated and then redefined in your mind. The term 'God' is an idea—a myth that encompasses a man and an immortal force, binding them into one all-powerful, supernatural being. When in fact the man and the force, while connected, are separate.

"There is the all-powerful force that brings deeper meaning to our life—fulfillment of potential, transcendence of daily life and a progression of knowledge that brings about a heightened awareness. This force is also the life-bringing force, having been the catalyst that encouraged life to come forth upon this once barren Earth—the force of *love*."

The man was cut off by a few dark laughs. Obviously some disagreed with what they believed to be a sentimental explanation of the divine power. Not altogether unexpectedly, the laughs came from Ari's corner.

Having encountered such reactions countless times before, the man knew their objection without having to ask. "I know why you laugh. You hear the word *love* and think: what is this emotion love when compared to the terrifying power of *God*," he replied in an understanding tone. "Some of you find humor in my declaration. You undoubtedly think me to be sentimental in my beliefs. And I do not begrudge you your skepticism; for I know the reason you think this of me is because of what you have been taught God to be and what you have come to perceive love to be.

"For most, God equates unparalleled power that is to be feared—a deity who is to be revered and cowered before." He paused. His voice rose and he continued in a questioning tone, "I always regarded fear of the divine as an oxymoron. We need not fear that which is sacred. We need only fear those who are willing to destroy it—those who have become evil.

"Only those who are insecure or narcissistic require reverence. I hold the deepest respect for that which I regard as divine; however, I hold no fear of it." He turned, staring at Ari and the others who had laughed. "You regard your God—your divinity—as that which is terrifyingly powerful. I too regard my—greater force—as an unparalleled power, only it invokes compassion and connection. Not fear," he stressed.

"Many of you have been taught that love is purely an emotion—that love is infatuation, that it is lust or even frailty. You may even subconsciously equate love with the feminine and in turn the feminine with weakness. Yet the divine one I have come to know is genderless. It has the strengths of both man and woman—of the father and the mother. Love is both the seed and the womb for all things that grow.

"We are taught preconceived notions about the divine and, accepting them without question, the true identity and character of the greater force is seldom found.

"You think love to equate weakness because love has been demeaned—redefined by those who do not believe in the virtue of *being loving*." The tone of his voice rose as his point built, "What if I were to tell you that all you have been taught of this world—of yourself, of love and of the divine, has been taught to you by *evil*—by those who do not believe in the virtues of love?"

The group sat quietly. They did not sense the precipice they were on. They thought his last comment was simply the posing of a "what if" meant to insight further discussion, not a revelation meant to awaken them from a lifetime of misconception.

Failing to grasp what he meant, the conversation was redirected—rolled back slightly. "You said that our idea of God is wrong, how so?" Maria asked timidly. She did not want to pass over the point at hand but she needed clarification.

Knowing that the deeper layers of meaning in his words were yet to be appreciated, the man understood the need to take things slowly. He knew that solidified falsehoods are broken down one radical thought at a time.

He turned and addressed Maria, "Many of the world religions portray the divine as something separate from humanity, something to be known from *a distance*. The divine is portrayed as a God—a supernatural being, all-controlling, at times even cold or indifferent to the sufferings of his creation. The divine has been put in the shape of a man. This human portrayal of the divine happened millennia ago and the evolution continues still. Some think this distortion happened—that man put his own face upon the divine—in his longing to be all-powerful. I believe it was a combination of a deliberate skewing of facts and the degradation of truth that occurs over the generations.

"You see," the man said, wanting to clarify, "in the beginning there was the human man who learned the most about the greater force and then there was the force itself. These two separate things were merged into one being throughout the course of history—becoming one all-powerful being known as God. Yet the wise man and the greater force, while connected, are not one singular supernatural deity.

"The persona—the figurehead of God—is a collection of fictions; while the story of the human man who was entangled in the myth of God was lost. Tales of God were woven and the history of both the greater force and the man—his life, his wife, his family and his insights were lost."

"What text do you site for these ideas?" Gideon inquired, requiring corroboration before he would give the view credence.

"No third-hand text sources," the man confessed to the boy's dismay. "I have learned the truth after making a journey to reach it and after listening to those who lived it. I understand these sources may not seem adequate," he added, in response to the young man's furrowed brow. "It would seem now that, if occurrences are not recorded in the annals of history, they did not happen. Yet I would reason, recorded history is new; while mankind is old. The most pivotal acts have gone unrecorded."

Veering off his point a bit, the man paused, re-centered himself and waded forward; returning once more to the question that began this conversation. "If you truly want to know of evil I must tell you many shocking revelations." His tone was foreboding, "The first concerns the place that would be evil's plane—the world commonly known as *Hell*."

The man hesitated. He locked eyes with his son; in that moment many unspoken things were said. Yoseph knew it was going to take a great deal of daring for his father to speak the words rising in his mind.

He chose to continue, "Can a person live in a world their entire lives and not be aware of the nature of the place into which they were born? —*Yes.* Just as we can think we know an individual yet still remain unaware of their true character, until at last a revealing moment comes to show us the side of them we never saw before." Making a solid point, the man continued to build, "You see, each person has an inner-balance that when tipped, can change the nature of who and what they are; likewise this world that mankind has created upon the Earth has a balance. It was tipped when the desire to possess surged throughout mankind and those who abandoned the ways of love suddenly outnumbered those who held to it, causing the nature of the world we are endeavoring to build to be corrupted and the balance of life to be plunged into chaos."

Yoseph watched intently as his father struggled to share so much of himself. It was clear to the boy that his father was fighting for the courage to speak these personal insights aloud. There was a latent fear in the timber of the man's voice— tremors reverberating from the inner-battle occurring.

"There are two disturbing revelations that change our life completely—awakening us to truth yet also into a time of difficultly. They are as follows: Evil is not found in a single demon. Evil is not sequestered to a cavernous Underworld. Evil surrounds us; for evil is human or rather, those who were once human. Outwardly one who chooses evil looks the same as one who chooses love; for all human beings utilize the same vessel—the same body to house our Being. It is *inside* the body, that the drastic difference between those who choose to become evil and those who choose to remain faithful to their humanity, can be seen.

"The difference between one who has chosen an evil way of life and one who has chosen a loving way of life, lies in what they have come to crave and the intentions that they hold towards others. One who has become evil is one who has become inhuman—they no longer embody the virtues of humanity. And sadly, they degrade the reputation of humanity as a whole through what they choose to do.

"Contrary to how it is portrayed, evil is not demonic or supernatural. Those who are evil are neither devils with horns nor snakes that crawl on their belly. In behavior, mind-set and cravings, evil is certainly savage—a human transmuted into a dark creature, whose negative presence drains any fullness around it. Nonetheless, those who are now evil began as human and they are met every day upon the streets of this world; for you see, contrary to the mythos of many religions, evil does not reside in an Underworld; evil is a movement that dominates the world in which we dwell at this very *moment*."

Dazed by the information, the group's reactions came slowly as though they each were rising out of a deep sleep and attempting to reorient. "This cannot be true," Asa said feebly. The optimistic child had trouble believing his own argument. "There *are* devils in this world that lie at the root of all chaos. Tempting man away from the goodness he has in him."

The man fully understood the boy's reluctance to accept such a hard truth; nonetheless, it was truth. "Those who have become evil are portrayed very dramatically, as demons that emerge from a layer of the unseen to tempt us and strike bargains to be signed in blood for our soul." His voice had a flourish of overacting—his way of highlighting the hilarity of the overdramatized exaggerations of both evil and the divine. "In truth," he continued seriously, "evil's influence is much more subtle; its disguises much more cunning.

"We pass evil as we walk down the road, we sit at its table, heed its opinions and bring it into our homes; we are employed by it, we socialize with it and even help it strive. Some of us even find the evil, when we gaze at our own reflection."

"Evil is human?" Samuel echoed slowly; still stuck at the beginning of the conversation and seeking affirmation.

"Yes," the man said, affirming his first revelation. "Evil's origin has its roots in humanity. And just as evil is different than we are led to believe, so too is evil's part of the world: Hell."

As the group was still trying to grasp the first revelation, the man proceeded into the second. Not trying to rush them but rather, allow them to see the greater picture.

"How can Hell be different than we believe?" Aden asked, disgusted with what he had heard so far and clearly not receptive to what was coming next.

Despite Aden's aggressive tone, the man answered the question. "Hell is not the punishment of the wicked, it is the world the wicked created—the world they rule and thrive in. Dwelling in Hell is not the punishment of the immoral; it is the unjust punishment of the innocent.

"The second revelation," he emphasized, "that redefines our very existence is that this world mankind has created upon the Earth is *Hell.*"

Ari and Aden sounded a grunt of incredulity. Whispers rose among the students.

Not surprised by this skeptical response, the man proceeded undeterred. He wanted to tie his insights together into a cohesive truth. Rebutting the disbelief with a thoughtful tone, he proceeded, "While I cannot hear what you whisper to each other. I know what you must think of my declarations. Furthermore, I know that some of you have already begun to go deaf to my words and might even wish to walk away.

"At the same time however, I know that some of you who are open to listening have begun asking questions—the same questions I once asked as to how this can be true. *How is this possible? How can this Earth, which is still dotted with green, be the inferno of legend?* The answer to these questions is simple: Because this World is not what it appears to be; it is not what it once was…it is not what it *should be*," he stated firmly.

"To hold the Earth in its current state as the full glory of what it should be, would be to hold an emaciated prisoner of war as the embodiment of human health and beauty—the embodiment of what a thriving human being should be.

"The Earth, as it has been left, is not what it appears to be. Peel back the bark of the Great Tree to see that underneath the facade it is dying. Festering and rotting—hollowed out by the insects of this world—the maggots, worms—all manner of invertebrate creatures who greedily fill their mouths, gorging themselves on the flesh of the Great Tree to satisfy their bottomless lusting. Until finally she stands as but a shell, on the verge of collapse.

"Just as the body reflects the health of the soul. The Earth reflects the nature of the world we have raised upon her. This Earth, while still dotted with green, is the location upon which Hell has been raised. The Earth itself is not Hell. There is the natural world that was here before us and then there is the infrastructure of a world that we—humankind—have erected upon her. It is that man-made world that is Hell. A world dominated by a movement of loveless people—by evil. And just as the starved prisoner of war still shows a shadow of the healthy human they once were, before they were abused, starved, enslaved and put at the mercy of twisted men, so too the Earth shows signs of what she once was before she was taken by those who became evil and from her lands the old ways, wherein the culture of love flourished, were wiped clean."

The moment was suspended in silence. Some pondered what he said, others denied it adamantly.

The first voice to speak was that of a questioning one.

"I do not understand how this world can be Hell," Asa said, desperately trying to grasp the new idea; realizing that the conversation of spirituality, which he had so deeply wanted, was not going to go in the direction he had anticipated.

The man addressed the confused boy kindly, "You are having difficulty understanding my words because they are going against all the information that is already instilled in your mind. If the truth is to take its rightful place, one must allow for the lies that are held to be truth, to be replaced. For some of us who are set in our ways, this is a painful, maddening process of redefinition, wherein the only world we have ever known comes to an end and we frighteningly find ourselves in an entirely new reality.

"I know how hard grasping entirely new concepts can be—the mind recoils at such new ideas that throw our known reality into chaos. We all think we know the world we live in and it is mentally jarring when we find out that we do not. We must make the transition from the lies we have been taught to the truth we find while living, slowly. One thought at a time you were taught the history of this world, the information given to you were lies; nonetheless, one thought at a time your perspective can be righted. To awaken to the truth, we must first awaken to the extent of the lie. This process is shocking to the point of devastating. But regardless of the upheaval, having the truth is worth the ruin we must endure.

"You say you cannot understand how this world can be Hell, part of your inability to understand is due to the fact that you do not know the true nature of Hell, only the mythology of a place. Neither those who are evil nor Hell are what they are portrayed to be. The truth of the place has been distorted by fantastical fiction involving fire and brimstone. The most prominent differences between the Hell you have read of and evil's true place are as follows."

"Firstly," the man said, "Hell is not a torturous inferno to which all evil is sent upon dying. —This is myth. In truth, Hell is the world that those who have chosen to become evil have built upon this natural Earth during their lifetimes. It is an *Underworld*, not in that it lies at the molten mantel of the Earth but in the fact that those who created Hell and who chose to dwell in it have sunken beneath what it is to be human and allowed their radiant soul to descend into darkness."

"This world man built is and always has been a world of evil?" Asa asked, utterly confused.

"No," the man said, correcting him. "Evil's world was built overtop another world—a world built by those who believed in love.

"Both love and evil are *philosophies*—perspectives on the world and self that one chooses to adopt. Evil and love are cultural choices that we make depending upon what we desire to pursue. Our philosophy determines the biology of our soul. The beliefs we choose define our identity—loving we are love, inhuman we are evil. Those who are evil do not come forth as such from their mother's womb—everything that holds life is composed of sacred materials; rather, evil is something we make ourselves into by choice.

"Very simply put, evil is a *movement*—it was begun by one man and was joined by others who agreed with his philosophy. The balance of the Earth tipped when those embracing and condoning of evil's ways became the majority and the old world of wholesomeness, love and community was overturned to make way for the new dominant philosophy to be set into place."

The man shifted tones, "There are texts well-known for their foretelling of how the end of the world will come—the breaking of the seven seals, the Armageddon, and so forth. But you see, humanity holds the seven seals—seven degrees to which we can descend before we bring about our own end. Each time we pervert the innocent. Each time we defile what is natural and pure. Each time we try to manipulate what should be left alone. Each time the twisting of humanity takes another full turn, a symbolic seal is broken and the inevitable outcome of irrevocable loss those who have chosen evil have set themselves upon, draws nearer. We wait for the messenger to come forth and break the seals, yet the seals are bound to the integrity of mankind and the end we await has already come to pass. Dig at the foundations of this modern age and there you will find the crumbling fragments of the already-broken seals.

"Look out the window," he said boldly. "Behold the wake of the end." He raised a hand towards the gapping window overlooking the city. "The great harlot has seduced mankind and brought us to our end. Consumed by our lust for her we all sell ourselves, our morals…our very mother the Earth, just to have a taste of her—this whore that is wealth and power."

Realizing that he had diverged from his original point the man slowly redirected the conversation. "The second difference between the Hell of myth and the reality of evil's world is that Hell—evil's world—was not created by the divine as a place of punishment. Hell is a world created, ruled and maintained by those who have joined the movement of evil—by those who are gripped with greed and lust, to the extent that they have become numb to the sufferings of those around them and indifferent to the distinctions of right and wrong.

"You see, Hell is not the punishment for evil; it is the place in which those who have chosen evil's way of life *flourish*. Founded upon a rejection of love's virtue, those who began evil chartered their world upon a renouncement of the natural and ancient ways, shaping their world through condoning greed and encouraging perversion.

"Evil's histories are lies that have slowly become accepted as truths. Hell's strongest walls and the central pillars are made by monumental denials, which those who live here will not allow to be torn down. Hell's foundation was laid through intimate betrayals and consensual wrongdoing.

"Hell is the pain of the loving being, not the wrongdoer. It is not the nightmarish fate awaiting those who are twisted but rather one that is endured by those who are innocent. Hell is not justice for the guilty, it is the injustice for those who have done no wrong—the fate dreaded by the loving heart but preferred by the perverse.

"Hell is an extreme. We, humanity, make choices that effect our individual lives yet what we refuse to take into account is that, even our smallest choices become part of the *greater choice* that defines the nature of the world we are helping to build.

"The nature of the world is defined by the dominant species that dwells upon it. For now that species is humanity and within humanity the current majority are those siding with the movement of evil. The world reflects the choices of the majority and in this age those choices are of detrimental ways—evil ways. This is how Hell came to be. Hell's populous are those who have left loving ways behind for other self-gratifying ambitions; for they no longer believe in the virtues of a loving life of integrity and compassion. They do not believe that a life of loving pursuits is enough to fulfill them. So they abandon those ways of home, family and community in favor of their individual ambitions of influence, reverence, possession and detrimental pleasures."

When at last he stopped, the man saw uncomprehending faces looking back at him; many of those present weren't able to transition to this new perspective after living for so long with another. He could have stopped here—deeming that he had said enough, nonetheless, he chose to continue, unable to stop in the middle.

"Hell is a culture created by those who have a twisted vision of what it is they want and what it is that gives them joy. Hell is a world perpetuated by those who are driven by their ambitions to possess and dominate rather than love.

"When we think of Hell and evil, we think of *otherworldly* creatures; while the reality of the situation goes overlooked. Those who have become evil are not obscure demons, their features are very real. They are those who hoard rather than give; who would rather rule than unite; who see themselves but no others. And Hell—the world where evil's culture is central—is real as well. It is a world built by a people who were not able to pursue their dark lustings within a world based upon love's ways and so tore down that world, making way for one where perversion and greed are acceptable."

"So," one of the students said, speaking up rather forcefully. "You claim some perfect civilization once existed. One wherein all people were *loving* towards one another; if that were true, there would be some remnants of its history. Mankind has always been brutal, greedy and depraved." Clear tones of resentment and disbelief resounded in the student's voice. This was the first time this particular student had entered into the conversation. He was young, though had a much more logical air about him than the other young students. The boy had short brown hair, striking hazel eyes and a sharply focused gaze. He went by the name of Elijah.

"Hell does hold remnants of the old way of life, wherein love's culture was prevalent," the man replied in an even-toned voice. "Truths are scattered throughout the lies, like ruins of a world that once existed, protruding through the lifeless desert sands of our current reality. But as happens so often, truth has become myth; historians piece together what fragments they find and come to false conclusions. Their perspectives colored by the stories they have been raised with.

"We view our world and all that we know through the lens of the stories we listened to as we grew. Be the stories true or false, they give context to all that we learn and in this, the stories we regard as true define our reality...even when they be overdramatized myths and lies."

The students watched the man intently; they seemed half open to him, half wary of him.

"You each view the world through the stories you have made central in your life—most of these stories having been gathered from the particular religion to which you belong. Yet if I was to give you another story—if you were told an alternate history of humanity and the forces at work in this world, you would then see the world anew. You then might see that there is indeed proof of another world that once thrived, erected by those who believed in love, wherein all people were indeed gentle toward one another."

Ira, Ari's second son, took issue with these words. "You speak as if one can simply choose a story to live by from among the many that are written. There is only one truth—there is *only one story* that tells the real history and reveals the actual truth of God. We cannot simply *choose* which story we like best. We must find the truth and live by it." Unlike his elder brother, Ira was not as thuggish or dull-witted; rather, he was that most dangerous mix of intelligence and blind fanaticism.

"You are correct," the man admitted, choosing his words carefully. "There is only one true history of humanity—one course of events that actually happened. The paradox with all accounts of history is that each person saw the events differently. Tyrants see themselves as liberators and paint their victims as the troubled party. Those who are spited see their inflictors as demons and vilify them in stories to the point that they are no longer human but horned beasts. Exaggerations, bold-faced lies, cover-ups, hidden agendas—history is distorted a hundred different ways, until it seems to be all but impossible to reach the original truth of events.

"However, in the end, the true story of what actually occurred does remain intact behind the lies and denials. And despite all attempts made to bury the fact so that the fiction could be asserted, we can discover what really happened. We each can find the truth, if we so desire to," he emphasized. "We each can connect with a heart who was *actually present* during the period we wish to know of—who *lived* the history we seek to learn; for, though our ancestors be gone, they are far from dead."

Gideon looked stone-faced; he clearly was not happy with the man's reply. The man felt the need to make one further point. "I tell you the truth I have found because you urged me to. But I will not force my truth upon you in any way. I will never declare that, unless you believe what I believe you shall suffer some damnation. Any person or group who deals in such threats reveals their ignorance of actual truth.

"If you desire to hear no more tell me to be silent and we can wait here for the threat to pass and then go our separate ways. It is enough for me that I know what I know and that I live with the truth. The validation of my belief does not come through outside approval rather through what my heart knows and what the experiences of my life have taught me.

"The pieces of the *greater story* I have were given to me by those who I have come to trust and respect. I was told a story that contradicted *everything* I had been taught by the religion under which I was raised, and I did not accept this new story *blindly*—I was given the freewill to question it—to test it, and so I did. I lived my life and experienced affirmations that confirmed the new truth I was told. I did not *need* for the things I learned to be real. I did not take this story as truth out of some longing to bring meaning to my life. This truth was taken without desperation and it was proven by firsthand experiences, not second or third-hand reasoning."

Chapter V

The Descent

THE MAN STOOD UP TO STRETCH. He thought it best to pull back from the conversation for a time. "It is near night fall. I am going to eat and sit quietly for a time."

The crowd broke up wordlessly. The students seem a bit lost after the talk. They did not know what to think. The conversation was not going in the direction they anticipated. When they approached the man to talk, what they subconsciously expected was the same rehashing of well-known texts—a debate on the old topics, not an encounter with such radical ideas. The new perspective strained their pre-set minds like a silent migraine. Everyone in the group was speechless for their own reasons: The students were confused, Ari and his sons were frustrated and Samuel and Maria were captivated.

The man moved away from the others in the room for a brief respite, joining his son in the far-off corner they had claimed. Yoseph was unpacking the supplies he had purchased at the market.

"I did not know what to get," Yoseph said as he rummaged through a canvas shopping bag. "I have some preserved fish, some hard cheese, a bag of assorted dried fruit and nuts, a cake of dried dates, ten or so flat breads, a jar of olives, some fresh fruit: pears and apples."

"Just some bread," the man replied.

Yoseph looked up from the bag towards his father with a disapproving look. "How about some cheese to go with it?"

"I am not very hungry. I just need some time with my own thoughts."

"Have it with some milk then. I only got a small jar. … it will be spoiled by the end of the day," Yoseph justified. He did not bother waiting for his father's reply; he unscrewed the air-tight metal lid with a *snap* and set the glass pint jar in from of him.

The man said nothing. He knew his son's intentions were well-meant.

"Here." Yoseph took out a few of the flat breads and the wedge of hard cheese wrapped in wax paper. He sliced down a few hunks with a dull knife from their traveling kit. Then intentionally moved the paper so that it was between them— sliding it ever so slightly towards his father's side.

As the two began eating questions rose in Yoseph's mind; the foremost one being *why* his father had chosen to enter into such a debate. However, knowing that his father had already been asked too many questions that afternoon, Yoseph did not speak. He simply ate and let his father's taxed mind rest in the quiet.

Going into their bags, each group brought out their food. Like the man and Yoseph, most everyone ate preserved foods bought in the market that could keep without refrigeration and be prepared without the conveniences of a pan and stove.

The students were seated on the floor in a circle. As they ate, Asa, Gideon, Judah, Elijah and the other two students, who had thus far chosen to remain silent in the conversations, sat together discussing the topics that had been introduced. All the students wore the same layered linen robes, as most who followed the more conservative religions in the area did. The robe stretched across the breadth of their lap as they sat cross-legged on the dusty concrete floor; for most, wax-paper bags of preserved fruits and portions of bread sat atop this taut table of stretched cloth.

Ari and his sons remained cloistered—not feeling afraid of the others in the room per se but rather, above them. Yoseph eyed the men from across the room. Chewing slowly, his fixed eyes spoke of hidden fears. He stood beside his father whenever he chose to speak and he always would. Yet Yoseph could not deny the backlash that came in the wake of his father's words. He found himself worried that an incident would occur while they were in the city.

Like Ari, each of his sons were dressed in more modern clothing—a mixture of traditional clothing and the look of the business men of the west. All four of them wore trousers with starched dress shirts that had been slightly dirtied over the elapsing days of confinement. Their mother, Ari's wife,

wore strictly traditional clothing in comparison to her husband and three sons. This woman was withdrawn—not shy
but *quiet*—her face had been hardened and showed an age
that was certainly beyond her years. She had the look of a
resigned woman—one who was strong enough in character
to change her obviously difficult circumstances though, for
unspoken reasons, had chosen not to. Never given an introduction, the man would not have even known her name if he
had not overheard Ari say it while pointing at some food out
of arm's reach during their meal. "*Nira,*" he said impatiently,
shaking a finger at a wrapper holding strips of dried lamb.

Elsewhere in the room, the farmer and his wife, along
with their young daughter, sat to themselves in a far off corner completely uninterested in the conversations taking place.
They had set themselves up a cozy little living space, laying
down a blanket as a carpet and makeshift beds. The little girl
could not have been more than eight years of age. She was
well behaved, sitting quietly and contentedly near her parents.
Reading the wife's gestures towards her husband, the man
concluded that the two had a happy marriage but that both
were wearied by the hard life they had known in this country.

Sitting there, chewing the bite of cheese he had just taken,
the nameless man could not help but stare at the small family,
which so strongly reminded him of his own family. At one
point in time, it would have been his family off to themselves,
content in their own company. He looked at the small family
longingly. They felt no need to get involved with the things
occurring in this city—they were completely, focused on each
other and the survival of their family in this precarious country.

The man was pulled out of his quiet contemplation by the offer of a sticky date made by his son.

To Yoseph's surprise, his father took one.

Pulling a sticky date off the cake of a few dozen, he placed it in his mouth and was taken back to that past life. The morsel tasted the same as it once did. Ages later the trees were still yielding fruit with that same taste. He bit down; his teeth broke through the remainder of the date's thin skin. He savored the sweetness of the chewy, molasses body, grainy on his tongue. Finished, he took another. Yoseph smiled.

Not far from the man and his son sat Samuel and Maria, quietly eating their own meal. The break in conversation had lasted over an hour, when at last Maria posed a question. She gently swept her long hair aside—pulling it out of the way as she finished gathering the remnants of wrappers and papers. Settling herself, she had the distinct look of someone wanting to speak but who was afraid to do so. She and Samuel had sat quietly throughout the whole break, thinking of what had been said, until at last, Maria felt the need to confirm something.

"I have long felt this world to be empty—devoid of meaning—as if something that once flourished had died, leaving all of us starved. Does this feeling I have had, come from what has happened? What I mean to say is, do I feel this way because this world is built by those without a belief in love?"

"Yes," the man replied, a hint of sorrow to his voice. He felt as though he were informing her that she was suffering from a terrible disease.

He had not planned on speaking any further but he did not feel as though he could leave her question unanswered. Finished with his own meal he turned to her and spoke, not as a teacher but as a friend bringing bad news. "The emptiness you feel is due to the way of life you are confined to. The way of life that could have brought us each meaning was abandoned and now we are all born into this barren place," he stressed in a frustrated tone. "Life as it has been made to be in this age is inherently empty.

"This world leaves the soul malnourished. One who believes in love seeks the meaning that comes from connection, union, simplicity, home, family, learning, growth and so on, because it feeds our soul and fills our life. Whereas one who has emptied themselves of love, no longer seeks the meaningfulness of loving pursuits—they no longer see the virtues or fulfillment in such acts. Instead they have come to seek self-gratification alone, forsaking bonds with other humans, choosing instead a narcissistic relationship with themselves.

"We call those who have given up their belief in love— those who have been consumed by greed, perversion and the desire to dominate, 'evil.' This is the name given to them by history. What the word means to me is suffering—incomprehensible, senseless suffering. One who has chosen evil and one who has chosen love are polar opposites, unable to coexist."

The man paused as Asa, who had been listening to the side-conversation from across the room, came over to give his opinion. "You say that, these loveless people are the evil in this world? While this world is Hell. And the people of this age feel a sense of emptiness about their lives because this place mankind has constructed, is inherently empty?" He spoke, as though he were trying to take in the words as they passed from his lips.

"Correct," the man said with a soft sigh. He realized the larger conversation had once again resumed as the other students walked towards him. "The nature of any place is determined by the world-view of the people who populate it. Hell is a rotting shell that has nothing to fill it; for most of the people within its walls are disingenuous, driven by attaining what is empty. Thus all interaction becomes meaningless theatrics, which do not feed a loving heart's need for interaction and exchange."

"In the end, anything conceived without love is dead—it bears no soul. The hands can build a structure but it is the heart that brings forth the meaning to fill it. Like a loveless mother giving birth to a soulless child, those without love have built a hollow world and arranged a fruitless, cancerous way of living, which is unsustainable in the long-term.

"Behind the façade of the present world's apparent virtues is a rotting cavity. We all sense the emptiness of the world we live in," he said, motioning to Maria. He was clearly vexed by humanity's current circumstances. "People are suffering from illnesses that are not only caused from the toxicity of the modern world but also because they are starved of meaning and are dying from the existential famine that has been expanding for centuries.

"The way of life that mankind has set into place," the man said with conviction, "gives nothing to those who adopt it; for it is not properly centered on loving, virtuous pursuits. Humanity took up the modern hammer and built with the sole intention of self-profit and domination, and in doing so built a world detrimental to all life—a torture, a plague...a place of enslavement, despair and injustice—a Hell."

"Was it ever any different?" Maria asked longingly. Wanting to hear of a place where meaning was abundant.

"Yes," the man affirmed. "Throughout the course of humanity's history there have been other cultures—other 'worlds,' we built upon this Earth. Worlds built by villages of families with a compassion for each other, whose purpose is helping the community flourish. Some call this old world that was built by loving hands 'the old kingdom' or 'the old culture'—it is the world of love and honorable pursuits. I simply call it, 'the old world.'

"Tell us of it," Maria said.

The man obliged, "It was an age of abundance, wherein greed had not yet emerged and the natural world—the Earth—had yet to be defaced for the sake of its resources. It was a wholesome time, when the way of life had within the villages, brought a fullness to the heart.

"Layer upon layer of meaning and possibility, the old world—the old culture of love—had the means to feed the heart. Now the old ways are confined to a small isle hidden away but once they were held by all who drew breath.

"An island?" Maria echoed with wonder.

"Yes. It is a place beyond this backwardness. The shore on the other side of this Hell." His voice softened, "It is a sanctuary of abundance, where the very air we take in sooths and keeps all parts of us sharp—awake and aware. An ageless land where the ways past are the ways still kept.

"The beauty of the place goes beyond words. The thick mossy blanket of the valley's grasses creep up the sides of the steep black tors, which stand like megaliths framing the threshold of a wall-less, roofless temple. Tufts of tall grass spot the smoothly rolling lands; while banks of low growing bushes and brambles skirt the bases of the sloping hills. Taking in a breath, you inhale salty air, fragrant with heather and hearth smoke. The swollen blue lochs are afire with the white sunlight blazing across their surface. Looking out across the horizon, you see a nesting of thatch roofs settled cozily at the base of a far off mount; curls of smoke rise from chimneys; the stark whitewash walls of each cottage clearly visible…painted the color of freshly risen heavy cream. Wading into the waist high golden fields, the beams of a gentle sun streak through the cracks in the silver clouds dominating the cerulean sky above, embossing the rolling vista below. A warm happiness is carried in the wind. Walking these lands you are surrounded by a loving presence. No weights are carried across those hills—the miles do not drain us; rather, with each step taken, we are refilled. There the wellspring of enthusiasm overflows, washing away fears, drowning doubts and putting out the wildfires of hopelessness. Those lands are alive—each part of the scene before you breathes; the patches of each different color course with a dazzling, fluid vibrancy.

"But more than the land it is the ways of the people that make this place sacred. No greed. No perversion. No hatred. A community that is a family—giving, compassionate, wholesome, honest…feeling…." The man's voice tapered off, he stared into the vision of the landscape.

"It sounds idyllic," Maria said.

"It sounds like a fantasy," Ari entered darkly. Apparently he had been listening from across the room. He sat leaning against the wall, casually picking at his back teeth with his pinky finger. His fat belly full from his meal.

"I have been to both worlds—lived in both cultures. The world built by the loving may sound so perfect that it could not possibly be real, but I assure you that it is."

"I don't need to construct such fantasies. I am strong enough to deal with the flaws of the world I live in," Ari retorted.

"This world," the man replied, "is the delusion. Gazing upon the surface of love's depths is like living on an ever-expanding landscape—there is no edge to the world of love; length, breadth and depth—there are no boundaries. Yet the world evil has made is a mere illusion of a thriving world. If you plunge your hands into this backward world seeking to draw forth meaning for your life, you will find it is like punching through a thin sheet of paper that has been painted with a mural of a happy life—a facsimile of contentment. And when at last you withdraw your empty hand you will find the hole you made has begun to rip the façade, creating a tear that soon spreads across the face of the world before you. Until at last the mural—the illusion—tears away completely and you stand there gazing into a frightening oblivion."

The man underlined his final point on the matter, "Hell—this culture you take part in—is a madness of meaningless things, of senseless suffering and irrational choices. It is a madness of twisted ideals—a condoned warping of humanity itself. Hell is the womb of perversion and violence; kept immortal through accepted wrongs and through lies that are preferred to truth.

"The foundational doctrines of this dark world were made by taking weak lies and repeating them over and over again, until they became strong in the minds of all and thus real in those minds. The thin, fragile material with which this world is built can easily be torn down by those desiring truth. Yet as with any society built upon lies, the unwritten law while in this world is that we do not question that which we are told is true; for questions weaken the structure of lies. Questions hurled at lies wear down the illusion and make the lies more obvious—making the empty, corrupt nature of the world mankind has built, obvious—when all that its architects and inhabitants want, is to deny this fact.

"Beware those who fear questions; for they feel the inward need to protect that which they know to be false."

⁊

"How did this happen?" Maria asked, beside herself. "How did it all come to this? How did so much of humanity become so...*inhuman?*" She had listened to the man and, after having lived her life within the same backward world he spoke of, she could accept his words yet not understand how they had come to be true.

"Firstly, let me say that 'inhuman' is exactly the right word to describe what the majority of humanity has become. 'Evil' is a word that seems to link to something 'otherworldly' in our minds. 'Inhuman' is more precise.

"As for your question of *how* this all came about.... I can share the answers that I have found but even after you have listened to me the questions of *why* some people make the choices they do, will remain."

Maria nodded her head. Her eyes urged him to continue.

"I have learned that those who are evil cannot be understood through explanation, rather we must see them unmasked to understand what they have become. We must *see people* for what they are; for many have made incomprehensible choices that have turned them into something *inhuman*—something that is unimaginable to the innocent mind. Anything that is inconceivable can only be understood through firsthand experience," he emphasized darkly. As he spoke he began absentmindedly rubbing his hands. Battling an unconscious stress.

He tremulously continued, "I know that there are the questions of *how* and *why* echoing in your mind when you look at what people have become; for these same questions once plagued my mind—questions that I needed to have answered. Yet now, after having passed through Hell and seen with my own eyes, I have since learned that the descent of humanity happened *gradually*. With each generation pushing the limits of immorality a little further.

"The majority of those who have allowed themselves to become evil—inhuman—have done so slowly. We, as a society, have moved from love's culture to the culture of evil *slowly*. In many instances, becoming evil is the result of a course of choices made without regard for the greater significance of even our smallest actions.

"You see," he said, "evil is never called 'evil.' Within the psyche of man 'evil' is something that must be resisted—never taken part in, never embraced or even condoned for a moment. This moral imperative to resist evil is ingrained within mankind. Yet, if a thing is not labeled 'evil'—we take no issue with participating in it.

"So, with all this being true, how then did mankind become evil? —By not calling what we were becoming 'evil.' By calling descent, progress. By calling the breaking of families, *liberation of responsibility.* By calling the greedy, *the ambitious.* By abandoning the sacred union that can exist between two souls and calling it *a sexual revolution.* By calling the concubine *the modern woman.* And by calling the unfaithful man without honor simply *what a man is.*

"When a person becomes evil they rarely state: 'I am choosing to become evil.' Instead, they become evil by gradually twisting their original self and emptying themselves of love—by gradually bringing themselves away from the good, loving person who they were born as and becoming something *inhuman*—dark, indifferent and twisted in nature. All the while justifying what they are becoming, never calling it 'evil,' simply calling it 'change' or even 'progress.'

"Mankind's descent is slow, spanning generations. As such the knowledge of how far we have fallen cannot be fully perceived. If we were to compare what we, humanity, have become in contrast with what we are meant to be, we would see clearly how far we have descended. But because pure hearts are rare and dark hearts are 'the norm' we see nothing wrong with what we have become.

"There are some who would deem to look into the glass that reflects the true state of their soul and, finding themselves ill-altered, would do what they can to recover their original self. Yet in general, the majority of humanity chooses to look away—to cover that *Great Mirror of the Internal*—in an effort to remain blind to what it is they have become.

Hell is inhabited by an evil
who thinks they are loving.

By beasts
who think they are human.

By savages
who think they are civilized.

By faithless men
who think they are pious.

By attackers
who think they are victims.

By devils
who think they are gods.

By the ignorant
who think they are educated.

By the guilty
who think they are judges.

By human beings
unwilling to recognize
what they have become.
…unwilling to abandon a way of life
    that leaves them empty.
…unwilling to dismantle a world
    that is detrimental to all living things,
    including themselves.

CHAPTER VI

The Accusation

"Y OU SAY THAT THE MAJORITY OF PEOPLE CHOOSE evil, but there are many people out in the world doing good," asa reasoned optimistically. "I cannot see how the bad people of this world outnumber the good."

"Then you are blind," Aden spat. "I may not agree with this man but even I can see there are few righteous men left."

Stepping over a comment that he felt could lead to a vain debate, the man continued, "*Yes,* there are good people in this world," he assured Asa. "But, sadly a great many people—the majority—are indifferent. There are those people who actively engage in exploitive, hurtful endeavors, who are the evil in this world. But then there are those people who allow these actions to take place—the consenting mob who makes the culture of evil acceptable; who, through their indifference, have made themselves a part of the movement. Becoming

81

evil is not always a matter of stating a preference for dark appetites; many people align themselves with the movement by watching wrongful deeds be carried out in front of them but choose to say nothing and in doing so, make themselves complicit in the act. The movement of evil is allowed to flourish as it does, not because of the vast numbers of the willfully evil but due to the fact that the majority of people are indifferent to right and wrong, truth and lie."

"So you would say then, that most people become evil without ever knowing it?" Asa said rather feebly; his naïveté showing itself once more.

"There is a difference between not *knowing* what we have become and not *admitting* what we have become. If we allow ourselves to be fully self-aware, we all know on some level what we are—be it good or evil.

"As I have said, there are those who are evil, not because of what they do but because of what they *don't do*. Indifference is a choice. And then there are those who are *willfully* evil— those who do not speak the word of what they have become but who, deep within themselves, are aware of the choice they have made. Those who are willfully evil hurt others deliberately, bent on carrying out their own selfish ambitions.

"You say there are good people in this world," the man said, echoing the young student's declaration once more. "Yes," he affirmed, wanting to throw the boy some small assurance as he sank into his disillusionment, "there are good, wholly loving people in this world. In fact, while evil is the majority at present, a great number of the people you encounter will not appear to be evil. The willfully evil—the ones so purely and obviously inhuman—are a minority within evil as a whole;

they only number thousands among the millions. It will be the indifferent that you encounter most often. Those who see the evil—who know the wrongful nature of this world mankind has built and yet do nothing.

"These indifferent ones can appear to be, in many senses, good people. They will do kindness unto you. They can love to some degree. They even hold some faded sense of morality. However, the good man who ignores the acts of evil, allows evil to carry out that act. In his silence, he becomes culpable for the acts that evil carries out," the man continued, his voice gradually becoming short-tempered. "It is this mob of indifferent people who frustrate me the most. I can see clearly the aims of the willful ones; even if I cannot understand the reasoning behind their choices. But those who are indifferent—they are the ones I simply cannot comprehend. They are the ones who infuriate me. Be they good people, in the end, they are as heartless as the most vile evil; for they do not care to stop the wrongful acts. Willfully deaf, blind and mute, they allow evil to exist—allow the movement to progress.

"The power to tip the balance—make love the central and evil the exile—lies within the indifferent mob. If this group were to rise up and declare evil's culture no longer acceptable, change would come swiftly," the man concluded decisively.

"I have never encountered this evil you speak of. Those I know are good people, in every sense," Elijah said, feeling as though he lived in a different world than that of the man

"Perhaps those who you have around you are among those who believe in love. Yet within your lifetime, I dare say, you have encountered evil dear boy," the man said in a gentle voice; delicately breaking a hard truth to this youthful heart.

"You simply did not know it." The man sighed. He hated being the one to bring these hard facts. "Hell is inhabited by an elusive yet ever-present evil who will never declare to you in words what they are. They carry out their acts under cover of veils and masks—pretense and deceptions. Making it so you rarely see what they are capable of or what it is they truly want from you—be it your downfall, your gifts or your life itself.

"The evil that has come about is abundant yet in the beginning it is indiscernible to our eyes; for outwardly we look the same as them. In the beginning, the presence of evil is hard to discern; for those who are evil are adept at hiding their true face. The evil cannot be confronted until un-masked—defrocked—revealed for what it has become *within* and brought thrashing into the light.

"The nature of the savage of which I speak is to control—to feign caring, to exploit and finally spite or castaway in disregard. As inconceivable as it is, those who are willfully evil shall come close to you, speak to you in loving tones as, behind your back, they steal all that is precious to you. Then when they are finished with you or feel they are losing their power over you they shall incapacitate you in some way bodily, emotionally, mentally or financially; for thus is the nature of the beast. Those who have become evil are leeches upon your life and your heart—draining emotion, momentum, self-esteem, clarity, freedom...everything," he said in a soft voice. "And if somehow you survive these unforeseen attacks, break away and go in search of your inflictor—if you go once again before those who hurt you, being evil they shall deny their attack to the end, no matter the memories you possess of that moment of betrayal. Cowardly the evil that wrongs us, seldom allows us to confront our true tormentor; it leers in the shadows as we uncover its true nature; in the end denying that such a smirk ever crossed its lips. When we try to hold them responsible for the numerous wrongs done, they will twist the situation around until they are not evil but the misunderstood victim, while we are their inflictor; for thus," he ended morosely, "is the nature of the evil."

"Blasphemy!" Ari said in a quick, harsh whisper.

There it was—the familiar verdict had been flung again. Having heard it many times before, the man had expected it; nonetheless the sharp word, with its perilous stigma, still struck deep.

"I have heard enough," Ari continued, rising to speak. The lamp light in the dark night illuminated his aged face and long silver bread. He had a forbidding look upon his face. "Who are you to speak as an authority on such matters?" he scolded in a deadly tone. "Evil is caused by the devil. Wiser men than you have learned this and passed down this knowledge so that mankind may be aware of the presence of the Dark one. You are a young man who ought not question the wisdom of the old prophets. I have seldom seen such displays of vanity as I have here today; your ego is swollen sir and I am disgusted.

"You speak of these matters as if you were there to witness them; as though you out of all others have been told a truth that none of us know. Vanity and lies," he concluded hurtfully.

Ari remained standing, as if daring the man to enter into debate. Collecting himself, the man took a moment. His heart was pounding hard in his chest from a mixture of anxiety and frustration. But regardless of his inner-disarray the man spoke with an even-temper, "Sir, I have indeed seen evil with my own eyes. I have learned truths concerning our history and the current state of this world through decades of firsthand experience and contemplation. I have the truth—of this I am certain. However, I am not the only one who knows these truths. There are many of us, we have simply come to terms with the current stance humanity has taken to maintain their detrimental ways and turned our attention toward the preservation of what innocence remains. We choose to no longer pass on what we have been told, for fear of our safety as well as our soul-fatigue, having spoken several times during our respective ages, only to meet the same condemnation.

"I cannot address all that you would accuse me of but I can say this—an unwillingness to listen reveals much about the state of a person's belief. Unwillingness to listen shows a fear concerning what might be said.

"If you do not wish to listen you do not have to do so," the man concluded succinctly. "But I would ask that you take your leave without hatred toward myself or ridicule towards what personal beliefs I shared with you and not mock what I deem to share from my heart."

Pulling out of the inevitable circular debate that would ensue if he addressed the matter any further, the man tried to refocus on the topic at hand and press on. Ari looked sharply at the man, obviously not finished voicing his disapproval but choosing, for whatever reason, to sit down and hold his tongue for the moment.

Flustered, the man noticed the faces of the students still looking at him expectantly, willing him to continue even though they too had come to doubt his views. After an awkward moment, the man found the place he had left off. "There are some things, that I am no longer certain of but to my sorrow, evil is the one thing I understand very well," the man began slowly, gradually finding his lost train of thought. "I speak of evil's mindset, culture and workings not in generalities or in theory but with intimate detail; for I understand the descent of man well. Of course, it did not begin this way...I did not always know evil as well as I do now.

"On my journey I have learned of evil the only way one can—through experience and years of reflection and mediation that must follow the scarring exposure. I have borne witness to the evil and slowly come to understand the psychology of those who make inhuman choices. I have been able to discern the mindset of the insane creature through interaction. I have been able to understand what one who chooses evil seeks and lusts after, in observing what they hold of value and what they discard.

"I have seen the values of those in this place as I watched all that is priceless be sold, and the precious be extorted and ravaged without shame. I have seen all that is sacred exploited and the innocent led into a perversion that is said to be their liberation. It has been a journey of scarring images, repulsive acts and horrifying, heart wrenching shocks. Yet coming to the end of my journey I can say, at the very least, that I have learned the truth of the situation."

"What does it say to us when you declare that you know evil so well? That you know evil 'the best,' having 'intimately' learned of it?" Ari asked, inferring that the man might have a dark history of his own from which he drew his insights.

Insinuations not lost on him, the man chose to address the question and not the insult, "I am not evil but have endured Hell. Like the generations of loving hearts that have come before, I have longed for what is meaningful in a world of shallowness. I am in need of what is real—what is genuine, among people who refuse to be. I want only closeness—the intimacy of open souls—yet am among a people who see no virtue in offering up the deepest parts of themselves to one another.

"I believe in love, while traversing this world built on a choice to not believe in love. Over the course of my life, I have felt alone among the vast mob of those with whom I cannot identify yet I am not the first to be outcast for a belief in compassionate, honest ways. For generations, the culture of evil has been chosen by the majority yet there have been those rare hearts who have refused its ways, who have sought to transcend themselves back to a purer way of living and being.

"There are still those who strive to remain loving in this apathetic world. This is the movement I join myself to. In these people I place all my hopes. It is for these people that I continue on and it is from these people that I draw hope for a better future; for I believe that it is possible for all the loving hearts who remain to be brought together and carried beyond this backward world, to that place which evil has not been allowed to spread to—that Other Shore that was set apart as a sanctuary, where we might have a chance to live the old ways." Calming, the man turned to address Ari directly, "You would accuse me of *wanting* to know evil, as if suggesting I am somehow fascinated by it. Yet I came to know evil as part of the process of healing from the wounds I suffered as a result of attacks carried out upon me. I have seen the shocking acts of evil but what I desire is to see the striking acts of love, and in this, return to my original intention, which was to know better the workings of the divine.

"I know the many recesses of Hell—the lowest points of this backward world; now I live to know the beautiful heights of a loving world. I want to cross the threshold from the barren to the abundant; moving out of this cold numbness and into that which is vibrantly alive with feeling. I wish to find the ends of this Hell that I might rest whole and at peace in the healing place that is home."

"How poetic," Ari said patronizingly. "What is so Hellish about these current circumstances. Hell itself will be much harsher than this and rightfully so; for, despite what you say, it is a punishment earned by the most wicked."

"This world is harsh enough for those who are innocent," the man rebutted bluntly. "You would think Hell to be a place of bodily torture, fire and such.... Bodily torture, while horrendous is quick compared to the drawn out inflictions put upon the mind and heart. And I can say this having suffered all forms," the man added, giving no further context.

The man paused. He looked down and shook his head slightly. He stared at the floor as he murmured, "Backward. It is all backward."

"This Earth is overtaken by those who have chosen to become beasts, so many of us are now born into Hell. Deep within ourselves we sense something is wrong with this world—we sense there is something that we know, yet do not know—unspoken truths of which we are never able to be certain; for while we sense the wrongness, we turn to those around us, only to see them accepting, without hesitation, what we would question and so we think that we must be mistaken.

"The majority of us remember nothing that came before the emergence of evil and in this age few are ever taught of the old world that came before. We are born into a world of evil's creation and are taught that this culture is the one rightful way of living; remaining unaware of its backward nature. Until the instinctual knowledge every human possesses of right and wrong rises in us strongly enough to compel us to disregard the widely-accepted wrongs and follow our heart above all else." The man raised his head, looking into the face of each of those around him—his penetrative gaze passing beyond their eyes into what lie within. "Some of you have asked how I have come to know what I do. I learned by asking questions, some of which were unpopular.

"The truth is always there to be had, all we must do is *want it*. The wisdom of the old ways have been lost yet there are those who have preserved that knowledge and we are connected with these keepers of our true history. I found the truth," he said plainly, "after *asking* for it.

"I, like you—like all people, had been born into Hell; however I, unlike the majority, did not want any part of it. And so I sought a way to make the world better and reach out to mankind offering my love and every insight, wanting it to somehow aid in alleviating the suffering in this world. Later, after the violent betrayals carried out by those I tried to aid, I began to sense that no one could shut down the great machine evil has built except evil, and so, I subconsciously began looking for a way to leave this world behind.

"Scarred by my encounters with an inhuman movement that I could not see or confront, I asked for a way to break from all that has been endured here, so that I could have the chance for a life elsewhere—in a place beyond this emptiness. And in making this request I had asked to be awoken to all that I did not know. At the time I had not known what I was asking for. I did not know what I needed. I did not know where I was or what had happened to me. But I asked the questions. And when I woke to the world around me it was unbelievable.

"Having endured many a personal trauma at the hands of evil, yet not understanding what evil was, I had reached *the limit of what could be borne* and it was there on the edge I called for the truth, not knowing the greater endeavor I was beginning.

"When I was younger, I asked for the truth concerning the *divine element* when, in a moment of fervor, I wanted to connect with the immense force I felt in the beyond. Later, as a wounded man, I asked for the truth again, only this time it was the truth concerning the *hurtful elements.*"

He paused for a moment. His context was thin but his meaning was deep. All those in the room listened, even those who would have rather not.

"It was during a time in my life, when I was plagued by the holes in my understanding after having met many elusive evils, that I called for the truth about the inhuman. In a moment when I felt run around by the mind games and lost in the tangle of lies spoken to me, I demanded truth. I made a declaration within myself, not fully appreciating the power of my request, even though in my youth I had seen firsthand the power that the desire to know holds. At the time, I did not

91

know for sure that anything would come of my pronouncement," the man vulnerably confessed. Adding in as a candid
side note, "How often do we plead for answers, only to be left
still waiting in need?

"In my youth, when I was fearless and full, I asked to know
the divine. Then, later, when I was empty and traumatized,
I demanded to understand the evil. Not because I wanted to
know of the evil rather than the divine but because I was simply,
unable to go any further without the truth of the situation.
Specifically, I demanded to know the truth hidden from my
eyes by those who betrayed me. After this impassioned
moment of declaration passed, exhausted by my turmoil, I
laid down as with the end of any other day. Not knowing
that one life had just come to an end as another leg of the
great journey I have been on since coming into existence, was
beginning—an arduous leg, through a desert of harsh truths.
So you see," he said in a tired voice, "I started off seeking the
divine. It was while attempting to heal from evil's attacks that
the need to understand the other side came about."

The man paused, took a deep breath, held the air in
his lungs and then exhaled slowly, as if he were trying to
draw in some substance from the wind that might fortify
his exhausted self. "The day is spent," he said, allowing his
tiredness to show, "and I have already said too much. We all
need time to think and rest."

"Will we speak more tomorrow?" Asa asked, clearly
echoing the desires of some of the others in the group, as
Maria, Samuel and the other students turned their faces
expectantly towards him.

"I would be willing to continue talking with any who
might wish to."

The crowd rose, many said nothing—their minds reeled with the revelations they had been given. The man knew that perhaps those who said nothing might have actually heard what he had shared. Yet as Ari and his sons began to talk amongst themselves; the words that were said were indiscernible but the disapproving tone unmistakable.

"I want to make one thing perfectly clear," the man said, loud enough for all to hear, disrupting the whispered condemnations of Ari and his boys.

"Understand this," he said in a clear voice, "for it is more important than anything else we spoke of today. I did not say all this—all that I have said of evil—to *demonize* humanity but rather to *humanize* evil. Evil is not some otherworldly creation; humanity is its source and thus its end. The underlining truth is evil is something we create, carry out, perpetuate. Without our consent it would not exist," the man finished, in a decisive tone. Bringing the days talks to a close.

CHAPTER VII

The First Night

WITH EVERYONE RETIRED TO THEIR RESPECTIVE areas the room was quiet. A square hole in the plaster wall framed where a window had once been situated. The man approached. He unraveled his shawl from around his neck and wiped his face with the tails. The cool evening breeze relieved his clammy nausea. He was smoothed by the dark. Some feared the unknown when staring into the dark but he found solace in the night; the world was at rest and there was less pressure under the moonlight than the daylight.

It was a starless night. The sky was the color of inky blue velvet. White and red electric lights dotted the dark cityscape. Black clumps of trees silhouetted against the moonlight filled in the gaps between the stout buildings.

The man stood there for a time looking out past the lights of the surroundings to the horizon. Bursts of light flared into existence in the murky night, then extinguished themselves. Several seconds later the faintest rumble reached him—a sound wave carrying the thunder of the mortar shell strikes. Each shell strike was like a fence post rising, keeping him confined in the city.

Consumed in his thoughts the man walked absentmindedly back over to he and his son's small corner.

"Are you alright?" Yoseph whispered as his father sat down. With the curiosity of the group satisfied for the day, the two of them were at last able to talk alone.

"I'm fine," the man said. He feigned a reassuring voice, albeit unconvincingly.

Yoseph did not ask his father why he had chosen to speak, he knew him too well. He knew that, in his father's mind, sometimes it simply *had* to be done—it was the inexorable end that his father could not help but come to. Since he was a boy Yoseph had watched his father struggle when asked to speak; for when a person made that declaration of "wanting truth," his father found it hard to deny them the knowledge he had been given. But at the same time, it was hard to sit down and spill forth to strangers, knowing all too well that the majority—if not all of them, were going to reject what they heard and condemn him for uttering it.

"We'll be alright," Yoseph said; as much for his own benefit as his father's.

"Yes, we will be alright," the man replied; taking the assurance then giving it back.

"I am sure this is all happening for a reason. I don't think we would have been led here, unless it was for a reason," Yoseph said, a bit weakly. His sentiment was more a hope than a certainty.

It was still too early for the man to wholeheartedly agree. "Yes, I am sure something will come of it," he replied; aspiring to hope.

"Is it anything like it was?" Yoseph asked curiously.

"By sight, no, it is nothing like it was. By feel however, it is the same. In the past, to me, it always felt like a fortress or a prison and it still does," the man's voice dragged a bit. He was exhausted.

"How long do you think we will be here?" Yoseph asked, feeling it best to change topics.

The man knew what he hoped for—he hoped they would be leaving within a few days but he knew better than that. He knew that, given the instability of the area, the fight could last weeks, even months. He could not even consider that long a stay and yet, could not stop thinking about it.

"Hopefully we will not be here long," he finally offered, deciding it was better to be hopeful than realistic.

"Samuel and Maria seem as though they are good people," Yoseph remarked, trying to focus on a good.

"Yes, so far they seem good-hearted, very caring," he admitted, cautiously.

"He seems like he could be trouble," Yoseph said, staring over toward the area where Ari lay sleeping with his wife and three sons.

"Hmmm," the man offered, partly frustrated and partly exhausted.

"If you plan on speaking tomorrow he is going to keep on provoking you," Yoseph said, telling his father what he already knew; at the same time, subtly inquiring as to whether or not he was actually going to continue these *conversations*.

Sensing the questions Yoseph wanted to ask him, the man decided to say nothing—not because he didn't want to speak with his son but because he did not have an answer. At the moment, he hardly knew who he was or what he was doing, and if he tried to talk about the situation in his fragile mental state he would surely unravel.

There were other questions Yoseph wanted to ask that, for his father's sake, he dare not speak aloud. Too young to recall the first time their family had been in the city—all those years ago during the first attack, Yoseph wanted to ask if they were near the place the family had once stayed. He wanted to know how the city had changed with time. Yet even with dozens of questions filling his mind Yoseph's sensitivities towards his father's wounds told him to hold his tongue. He knew there were certain things that could be spoken about and certain subjects and events that could not be broached, lest they trigger a reliving of those traumatic moments.

"Do you need anything?" Yoseph asked, letting his questions die silently within him.

"No. I don't think I can eat anything but you should," he said in a fatherly way. Adding quickly in a worried tone, "And I meant what I said, I do not want you going to the market without me."

There was a flash of memory—the man remembered the panic he felt while wading through the crowd at the market and then another image thrust forward to the front of his mind—that of being driven by the vicious mob encircling him, down an ancient version of the same streets he had walked just yesterday evening.

Yoseph looked regretful.

"I understand why you went without me," the man said slowly; visibly disturbed by what he was silently reliving. "I just don't want us splitting up; it is simply not safe."

They were always stronger together; everyone in their family was like this. It was not safe for them to be apart anywhere within this world hostile towards love but especially here, in this city.

"It's late. You should try to sleep," Yoseph said lovingly; trying to ease his father down onto one of the makeshift beds.

He had set up his father's bed flush against the wall and then laid out his own bedroll in front of him—in an effort to give his father some feeling of privacy, however slight.

Yoseph had learned how to accommodate his father's wounds. After years of living with those traumatized in his family and then traveling with his father on the journey, Yoseph knew what accommodations a specific wound required and was considerate enough to see to those little details that could help his father live more easily day-to-day.

After a short debate, the man consented to lie down. Was he tired? —No. But he saw the fatigue in his son's shadowed eyes and knew Yoseph would not sleep until he did. The man knew that his son would stay up with him all night if he asked him to—he had many times before but he did not want that. Despite the events of the day, there was nothing the man was eager to talk about. He simply needed rest—they both did.

The morning, afternoon and evening had been so full, the single day had felt like three. And at the days end, he told himself that rest would make the chaos quiet and the feeling of unraveling lessen. In the past, rest had always helped reorder and stabilize his fraying mind yet as he readied myself to lie down he had a sinking feeling that, even if he did manage to get some sleep, it would not help…not here.

Watching his son lie down, he too eased down onto his thin bedroll, resting his taut, exhausted body. He lay there staring at the back of his son's head and felt an overwhelming fear come over him that something would happen to them while they were stuck in this perilous city.

For a long time he stared unblinkingly at his son, pleading to whoever could feel him from across the distance to keep them safe and bring them home again. His eyes slowly closed as he tried to drift to sleep yet he could not help but think back on the surreal day.

He thought he had fully realized what he had chosen to do when he opened his mouth. He had felt the weight of the moment while it was upon him yet not until now, when he was left alone, did the reality of the situation penetrate him. The self-doubt and self-loathing spread.

What am I doing? he thought to himself.

What-am-I-doing? he repeated silently in his mind. With each repetition he became harsher with himself.

He could not breathe. He hugged his bag tightly. His walking stick lie next to him. His knuckles had turned white as he dug his fingers into the wood.

Flinching at the thought of where he was, nauseated by the danger entailed in what he had consented to do, he found this night he was casting stones at himself—wondering if he would ever learn to keep his mouth shut.

I used to rise at dawn. I was that full—that expectant. During that brief window after adolescence but before waking to the bleak state of the world—that was the time I formed my belief. A belief I would mourn for and chase after for the remainder of my adult life.

Reaching throughout the long nights, I was replenished each day not by rest but by passion. Night would surrender to day and I would dress, venturing out into the twilight expanse to walk between worlds. It was there I met you—there I listened as you spoke the first truths I would learn. Those days I spent connected to you filled me with an enthusiasm for the truth—a bursting that I brought home with me, which led me to share all you had told me.

Safe among my family yet I was not safe with all. They came to me as brothers. How was I to know they were my betrayers? They asked me to speak. How was I to know they were gathering all that I gave to sell unto the desperate? How was I to know how the truth was regarded here? How was I to know of the backlash entailed? Should you not have warned me? Should you not have placed in me a prudence—a wariness, instead of an enthusiasm? You saved me and in the same act condemned me. I do not regret the way of things but I cannot help but think there could have been another way.

How you must dread awakening we who ask the questions, knowing what we will face when you give us our answers. Are you ever tempted to let us sleep—to leave us in our ignorance if it means we find some bliss, however hollow? I should think you are, because I know that, even the most devout of followers, question the virtue of the right path when the passing days become hard enough.

In the end I suppose the lifetime of difficulty that is entailed with breaking from those who are evil is better than the empty eternity spent wandering the labyrinth of their lies. You wait ever-vigil for us to ask the question. You remain there, throughout our lives, hand extended with the truth of it all—always offering it, never forcing it. Yet with the truth should you not also give a warning? Should you not tell us that, though it be our choice to listen, it is not the choice made by the many? Regardless, in the end, even if you did warn, I would still speak. I cannot seem to help but do so, even when I know the dangers. In this am I strong or am I foolish?

Despite what the cost had been for speaking the truth the first time, he still felt the urge to speak again and over time he had come to hate himself for the very urge that defined him. He did not know why he still felt this urge. He did not believe that humanity would change. He did not expect the truth to be embraced. He knew full-well how futile it all was. For lifetimes on end he had been going around in the unending cycle of opening his mouth, speaking the truth and being rejected and spited for it.

He knew the gain to be nought and the cost to be *everything* and yet he still felt a stirring from time to time to gather all he had learned and share it. It was when this feeling rose that the self-loathing did as well. He hated himself for continuing to go around in this circle and risking his family's safety every time he did so.

If it were he alone—if only he had to pay the cost for his actions, if only he had to face the wrath of the mob—he would follow his feelings and speak to whatever end. But he was not alone, he had followed the feelings compelling him to speak—he acted on his nature and when the backlash came it was his family who felt it.

Oh yes, he had borne the attack all those years ago, when his truths brought down the wrath of those who depended on lies for their livelihood. He had the scars to prove how extensive evil's denial is and how deep their greed goes.

What they had done to him had traumatized him but it was what they had done to his loved ones—the emotional costs, the loss of their home, their security and freedom, that pained him the most. He felt as though he had become a plague upon all those who loved him. He had brought down the evil upon them. They all had fled, leaving behind their precious life but the evil had followed them—hunting for him. Because of *his name*, the family lived in fear; if his name was uttered—if he was recognized—they would have to leave everything behind and once again start over with nothing.

Before the attack, life had been peaceful. Long days spent in the ease of each other's company and the contentment of a simple life of tending lands and home. That was the lifetime before they were forced to live in terror; it was the life before the torment...before the evil knew who they were.

He had opened his mouth and they had been forced to leave behind their home—their sanctuary—fleeing the countryside in the dark of night in disguise. They had been forced into poverty by the greed of the evil he had foolishly attracted. All because he was too blind to see the true nature of those he gathered around him...all because he had opened his mouth.

Logically he knew it was not his speaking that brought the time of difficulty; he knew that the source of the heartache lay solely with the people who chose evil and did not want to hear, and those who wanted to use his gathered insights to become gods among men. He knew all this to be true in his mind but not in his heart. And so in his heart he had come to hate the very things that made him who he is.

Deep down he knew that his family did not blame him for all that had been lost. But on some level, he knew that, like himself, they could not understand how he could consider speaking again after all that had happened.

It was not that he was naïve; it was not that he was idealistic; it was not that he was self-righteous; it was not that he craved attention; it was just who he was—as though, after realizing the truth the next step was to share it.

He had been going around in the same tormenting cycle for longer than he could remember. He lay there, silently writhing in the torment and the self-condemnation. He knew it was an innocent thing—to share what was in his heart. But here—in this backward place, it was not that simple.

Last time he was in this city it had been all others who judged him—it had been the evil that condemned him but this time, ironically, he was condemning himself. He wanted to go back in time a few weeks to stop himself from coming back to this country. He wanted to go back a few hours and stop himself from consenting to speak. But he could not. All he could do was force himself to be silent come morning and not chance his and Yoseph's safety any further than he already had.

There—it was done, he thought to himself. This resolution was the only thing that calmed him. It was the only thing that allowed him to ease into sleep, however disturbed.

Though, he knew full-well that come morning, the resolve he felt so clearly this night, would fade and he would consent to speak again. It had happened before…it had happened so many times. And so he lay there, trapped in the vicious cycle of torment, feeling the self-loathing swell once more.

It was maddening.

CHAPTER VIII

The Origin

HE HAD HOPED IT WAS A DREAM. During those first moments as he woke, while his mind was still suspended in that hazy place of unconsciousness in-between dreams and reality, he thought he felt grass beneath him instead of the cold concrete. He exhaled in relief. For the first time in days his body relaxed. He melted into his bed, ready for a few more hours of sleep after the restless tossing he had endured all night. But then in the background he heard it: the general stirrings of those in the room. His mind rose out of that blissful place and moved back into cold reality. He opened his eyes and his heart sank. The stark room was in front of him and the noise of the city streets below was rising up through the gaping windows.

With a heavy sigh he shut his eyes again.

"Did you sleep?" Yoseph asked; noticing that his father had moved.

"Not well," he replied. His eyes were still shut.

"Neither did I."

"Any news?" the man asked; fishing for a reason to hope it would be a better day.

Still lying on his bedroll, he opened his eyes and stared at his son. Yoseph looked disappointed.

"Militants have moved in from the north and west. More bombings took place over the night. I don't know all of it; I just heard bits and pieces. I don't think it is going to be safe for us to leave today. With all the instability, everyone is advised to stay in the city…indoors when possible."

"Perhaps tomorrow," the man said fatigued; desperately trying to be optimistic.

"Want breakfast?" Yoseph reached for his food bag.

"No. I just want to sit for a little while," the man replied.

This was normal; the man hardly ever ate a large breakfast. He sat up as Yoseph pulled out an orange and set to peeling it.

The man pulled himself over to the wall and sat against it. He picked up his shawl from his bedroll—it had been his pillow during the night and he wrapped his shawl around him like a scarf; he did not need it for protection from the sun while indoors but something about the softness of the fabric against his skin was comforting to him. The cloth had been woven by his daughter and it felt soothing to have something from home near him. He tilted his head back, closed his eyes and tried to find something calm within himself to grab hold of.

As the man knew it would, the decision he had come to before falling to sleep had faded with the rising of the sun. He sat there, sipping some water as his son ate the wedges of his orange, naively hoping that no one would approach him for a few hours. Only to be disappointed as, upon seeing that he was awake, the small group of students started gathering.

"We have all had time to think about what was said yesterday. Many of us have questions," Asa said, in a slightly pleading tone. The boy did not want the conversations to stop.

Nearby Samuel and Maria saw what was happening.

Hardly able to breathe under the weight of his dread, the man forced down the voice of self-condemnation. He knew he had no choice but to act on his nature.

The students looked as though they wanted to dominate the topics of conversation; however, the one to pose the first question to the group was Samuel, who had been rather quiet the day before. Sitting with Maria beside him, his hand in her's, he began, "I have seen enough in my time to be open to the notion that this world man is creating is backward. What I do not understand is how all this came about. I know we spoke of how a human being descends but I still don't understand how this all began if, as you say, a loving culture reigned. How did this all come to pass? I was told the story of the fallen Angel—his breaking with God and his corruption of man. Yet you tell us that this is a myth. So my question is: what is the truth?"

He felt daunted by the immensity of the request. The answer rushed to his mind as a dozen different points that needed to be addressed. Thankfully, after a moment of inner-settling, his overwhelmed mind focused to one singular point—one story that held in it the history of us all.

"I told you yesterday that, to tell you the story of the Devil I would have to tell you the story of God. And that the story of evil is not a story of a falling out between a servant and his master but between *a father and a son*," he emphasized. "In the beginning there wasn't God and man, rather there was the *original family* from who all mankind descends.

"This family was—is composed of an immortal man, an immortal woman and the children who sprung forth from their union. This original family dwelt in an age before evil had come into existence. It is hard for us to conceive of what the old world must have been; I never saw it in its glory but I have met those who were there in the beginning and I have listened to their accounts just as you sit listening to mine. The old world came to an end when the original family was divided in two. This division came by way of a choice made by the eldest son—a man around whom the myth of the devil has been spun. He divided the family, by becoming the first evil in a loving circle."

"How did he become evil?" Asa asked. "Did something tempt him?"

"—No," the man said quickly and firmly. "Nothing *tempts* us to become evil. Evil did not approach the man; as I said, evil is not an entity but a *movement*. This man conceived of the philosophy that would become the movement of evil. Without any cause to twist himself with these new dark appetites, the man gathered together the ideals that would become evil; like a virgin birth from a woman's womb—evil was conceived in this man's heart purely by his own will. As his perspective of the world shifted he did not reject it—he did not fight the distortion—he embraced it and in doing so he brought forth we know as 'evil.'

"It was this first son who became the father of evil. He stopped believing in love—stopped believing in the virtues of love as a way of life and as he abandoned his old life for his other darker ideals he created evil—he became evil."

"No one simply becomes evil," Judah asserted skeptically, "something or someone tempts them. I have seen a good child grow to be a bad man but there was always a *cause*. Evil could not simply rise in a person without cause—without some wrong done to them; unless that is, you think humans to be evil by nature?"

"Becoming evil is a matter of *choice*, not cause. It is true that, in the beginning, we all are victims of evil—nearly all have been coerced, influenced and wronged by evil at some point within our lives. However, being wronged by evil is neither the justification nor cause for becoming the evil."

"Some do commit horrible acts because they have no choice," Judah said, in a defensive manner.

"There is always a choice," the man replied without room for argument. "We can start out as the victim but at some point, no matter what has happened to us or what pressures may be upon us, we alone are responsible for our actions." The man paused; his tone of voice shifted as he shared an example. "A son can be taught his father's prejudices—he can be raised to hate people of a certain creed or nationality and when he is young the boy will carry out hateful acts based on the skewed perspective he has been given. During his childhood the boy is a victim of his father's evil; however, at some point that boy becomes a man and he faces a moment when he chooses to either adopt his father's prejudices or reject such thinking. Either way, after this moment the boy is no longer a victim; he alone is responsible for his choices." The example ended and the man reiterated his point, "We all find ourselves a victim at some point but this is no justification for becoming an inflictor. Fear, desperation, abuse, hardship, poverty—circumstance has been made out to be the cause of evil but it is not." As he spoke the man looked troubled. "Too busy to be conscious. Too poor to be moral. Too lonely to be chaste. Too afraid to be honest. Too dependent to be equal. Too desperate to be particular. Too realistic to have hope. Too religious to have faith. Too tired to be kind. ...we explain our grievances away and take no responsibility for what we do or what we become. Yet the long train of inflictor and victim began with the simple choice one person made to hurt another, even though they themselves were never a victim."

"You say that it was good, loving hearts who brought forth evil?" Samuel asked. He was understandably confused.

"Yes, in the beginning becoming evil was purely a senseless act and to some degree it remains so to this day. The movement of evil began with one man but there were others who embraced his new distorted perspective. Without previous wrong done to them and without any other person's influence driving them to do so, these once loving hearts twisted themselves. They became inflictors without anyone having ever inflicted upon them. No provocation, no justification, no explanation but rather, just the sheer will to betray their better, loving self—this is how evil was created.

"Those who first became evil—who created it and embody it—defined the process of how one becomes evil. The transformation from loving heart to evil has no root in anything previously done to you; becoming evil stems directly from choice—it is not a consequence we must live with after enduring the poor choices of others. Becoming evil does not stem from what our past has been but rather, what we desire for our future.

"Those who choose evil hurt us, influence us and deceive us. Consequently it would seem that all they do would weigh heavily upon our individual development—that, what their hand deprives us of or inflicts upon us, would tend to sway what we become later in life. Nonetheless, in the end, it is not their acts but *our choice*. It is a matter of whether we desire to hold to our original selves or pursue that which degrades us.

"Either we want to be free of the evil ones who harm us or we want to take-up their own sword and impale them in kind. Either we want to be rid of the game or we want to master it. Either we seek the same power as those who have attempted to dominate us and so enter the great pursuit or we reach out to love, regarding it as the one and only power we wish to know.

"In this world where evil is so dominant, choosing not to be evil can be a matter of breaking a cycle—choosing not to follow in the footsteps of our parents, peers, mentors and leaders who, whether through their indifference or willful desires, have become a part of evil's movement.

"Some will say that those children who are beaten will grow up to become those who beat. Likewise that those who were kept powerless become those who seek power over others. Proposing that who we are is solely a matter of this cause and effect, suggests choice does not shape our path at all but rather circumstance sets us on one path that we must inexorably travel unto a fate beyond our capability to change. Despite the popularity of this opinion, I have seen otherwise."

"What *have* you seen?" Ari challenged.

The man was quiet. In place of the certainty he had only moments ago there was now a timidness emanating from a deep-seated fear. He was hesitant to share the specific events of his past, even if they could give credence to his argument.

"Suffice it to say, I have seen good people—people who were made to want for nothing and who were given love in abundance—choose to make themselves a part of evil. While, on the other hand, I have seen the abused, the repressed and the battered—those who have every reason to hate—turn away from the evil person they might become; choosing instead to remain sources of love. I have seen both the conception of evil and the immortality of love."

"To think that our development is *not* based upon our environment is foolish," Elijah argued. "Of course our surroundings will shape what we become."

"Shape, yes. *Define*, no," the man replied. "I will not deny that, without influences—be they loving or hurtful—the course of our life would progress differently, as would our individual evolution of self. However, the ultimate choices we make that decide our way of life rest with us alone. Many parts of us can be influenced; nevertheless, we each have a *core* that is impervious to manipulation and it is within this place that we make our defining life choices.

"Evil can strike at you, it can scourge and torture you, take and deprive, and *still*, after having absorbed nothing but this ruthlessness, your heart can have no desire to attack. One who is covered with scars—who bleeds from every surface of their body and within every depth of their soul—can still be incapable of raising a hand against another. One who has been betrayed—lied to for the whole of their life—can still be incapable of lying to another. The character of those surrounding us and what they have done—this may dominate many things: our memory, our thoughts…it may traumatize us and haunt us year upon year, but one thing that it *does not* do is dictate our choices, and those who say it does are simply refusing to take responsibility for their own desires. Believing that the origin of evil lies with the actions of a tempting devil has only served to misplace blame."

Ari and two of his sons, Aden and Ira, all made incredulous grunts. They were still not convinced. The man pushed forward, turning his attention to the others sitting around him. He did not see the virtue in justifying himself to those who would never validate what he was saying.

"When making your pivotal choices, what has been done to you by others is irrelevant; for in these moments there is only you and what you want for your life. Do you want a life based on love? Or are there dark ambitions attractive to you? Will you embrace the twistedness that is out there? —Do you see it as twistedness at all?"

"Can one become evil without knowing it? Take the wrong path without being aware of it?" Samuel asked.

"At one point in my life, I thought that yes—many people walk down the wrong path unaware of what they have chosen. It was this assumption that made me preach so long ago; I thought that, if only the truth of the situation was known, those who are going down the path of suffering would turn around. I thought it was simply a matter of helping to trigger an awakening. What I did not realize is that many people who are a part of evil's movement are asleep because they choose to be. What I mistook as sleep was actually a state of deep denial. The truth is, deep down we can each sense the nature of our choice—anytime we twist ourselves by wrong action we can feel the pull of our poor choice on the fiber of our morality.

"If you have already decided what you want but are unsure of the virtue of the way you have chosen, look down your future path and ask yourself if you will have to leave behind all morals and all bonds of love while in pursuit of your vision. If you answer yes, then the path you have chosen is that of becoming someone less than a human should be— evil. In the end, becoming evil is not about what has been done to you, it is about what you *want* to do. The nature of what we come to crave defines what we in turn become.

"In your moment of choice your past is cut away and the surrounding people are pushed back, so as to play no part in the choice you must make. In this moment there is only you and what you want for your life. And it is what *you* choose— what *you* desire—that shall define who and what you are. After this moment of choice, no matter what you choose, you shall never again be a victim of evil; for either you choose to become the evil of your own accord, thus joining their circle becoming an inflictor. Or you have chosen to live as one who believes in love; thus choosing to part from the evil and dwell in a reality beyond them.

"In the end, when we stand before the internal mirror and must look at who we are, the evil that spites us is not in the reflection with us. The circumstance of our life may show as the wear upon our face and body but still there is only us—there is only what we have done in the face of all that was done to us. There is only what we desire. There is only what we believe in.

"Any wrongs committed against us, no matter how traumatizing, never justify any act of wrong we carry out," he stated without exception. "When we are faced with making a choice we can feel it in our heart—what the right thing and wrong thing to be done is; those who are evil can distort our perception but we can get to the right decision, if we *desire* to.

"Victims are even more knowledgeable when it concerns what is right and wrong, and therefore more capable of making a clear choice. Those of us who have endured mistreatment may have never had an example of goodness to look to. We may have never experienced a loving touch or known decency or consideration; however, in our heart we are painfully aware of how we should have been treated; thus the uncaring of others hurts us so deeply.

"Within ourselves—contained in that most human part of us, we know how we should treat one another; we know right from wrong and hollow from meaningful; we know human from inhuman and wholesomeness from vulgarity. We can feel when we are being twisted into something we are not and likewise when, either through indifference or with deliberate action, we are twisting ourselves—transmuting ourselves into evil.

"Those of us who have been struck may never have experienced the touch of love but we know how the sting of uncaring feels. As such we can make a choice whether or not to inflict that pain upon another. We can choose to pass on the infliction or let it end with us; choosing instead to reach out and give the love that we ourselves should have been given.

"Evil can hurt us, mislead us and coerce us. It can at times impair our judgment and lead us into places that we would not have otherwise gone. Yet in the end, when we come to that moment when the two paths are before us there stands only us.

"Evil came about through choice and is perpetuated through choice. We can choose to let suffering end with us or we can choose to let it spill over to the next generation and the other innocents around us. What evil did to us and who we are—in the end these are two separate things. We carry the marks that show the wrong choices of others but that does not mean we bear no responsibility for the choices we make.

"One cannot be caused to become evil; evil has always been and will always be, a choice. We are never fully lost until we cast ourselves away. The innocence within us cannot die by evil's hand, only by our own." After the lengthy recitation, he finished; certain in what he had said.

"Do you say then, that evil is something that lies dormant in mankind to be awoken?" Asa asked. Adding, "I do not believe that humanity is inherently evil. The source of evil must be demonic."

Suddenly, before Asa could receive an answer, Aden interjected with a violent declaration directed at the nameless man. "Look out the window man!" Aden shouted. He pointed out the window toward the horizon, where smoke rose in the aftermath of the daily bombing. "There is more going on here than can be explained by mankind's actions alone. There is a battle occurring between what is righteous and what is evil, and men are merely pawns in it!"

"Wait," Uri reasoned. Heads turned, this was the first time the man had spoken. He was the youngest of Ari's sons. Surprisingly he was in opposition to his brother. "Now, there are many things that this man has said that I cannot agree with but mankind being evil is the one thing I have no trouble accepting."

The nameless man gave a small nod of appreciation to Uri for his act of defense. "I appreciate your words but I do want to make one thing clear. I have seen much of the world and, while I believe mankind to be the source of evil, I do not believe mankind to be *inherently* evil. It may seem like a small distinction but it is, in fact, a drastic one." The man explained, "To say that we are inherently evil—to say that evil is part of our nature. This may seem reasonable given the crimes humanity has committed, but in the end we are creatures descended from an embodiment of love."

"If you can honestly believe that evil is not a part of human nature you have not seen as much of the world as you would claim," Aden jabbed sharply.

For the first time since meeting him, the people in the room saw anger in the face of the gentle-mannered man. When he spoke again, outrage could be clearly heard in his dry, blunt, tone of voice, "I have seen more than you will ever know. You all have the right to disagree with my beliefs, and I respect that right enough not to force my views upon you; respect me now—respect what I have been through in my life, even though the details remain unknown to you, and do not demean what I have endured." The nameless man shook as he spoke. His voice quivered. Silence fell over the room. No one spoke.

CHAPTER IX

The Family Divided

IN THE SILENCE THE MAN ROSE AND WALKED ACROSS the barren room. All eyes were upon him. He turned his back on the people to face the sight of the city he feared through the gapping frame of a broken window.

It was apparent by his demeanor that he had little desire to continue speaking. Some in the room did not seem to mind this; for they had already heard more than they desired. Yet despite those who were content in the quiet, others in the room wanted the conversation to go on; for they had heard the beginning of the answers they had long-sought and were eager to know the missing pieces yet to be discussed.

Skipping over the argument and returning to the original subject, Samuel knew he may not have understood what he was hearing but he wanted to hear it all. "Why is it that you think evil is not part of human nature?" he asked.

With his back to the room and his eyes set on the hills in the distance, the nameless man said nothing. He felt the gaze of those in the room focused upon his back, some waiting for his answer, others silently pleading within themselves that he not speak.

"Please continue," Samuel said politely. "I have a belief in people, which is slowly being lost. I want to know why it is you think that evil is not our nature, when it seems so predominant in us."

Samuel's soothing tone of voice eased the man, his trembling sternum began to calm. He took a deep jerky breath then exhaled steadily out into the evening air. The day was almost spent.

Eyes still facing the city skyline the man resumed his story. "I once asked the same questions that you do Samuel. For a long time my belief in people was lost; I found myself convinced of mankind's beastly nature. However, one night, when pondering our nature I was led to a truth I could not ignore. Instead of looking at what mankind is today as a means of defining the baseline for human nature, I pondered what was in the heart of the first human being. My thinking being that, what was in his or her heart must show what we are at our root."

"What conclusion did you come to?" Samuel asked.

The man retraced the line of reasoning that he had followed that night, now so long ago.

"With evil being so predominant and the decent, loving hearts being so few I came to a point when I felt the need to ask the question: Are human beings evil by nature? My conclusion had always been that love was the baseline of humanity and evil was the digression. But that night, I found myself asking, what if evil is the baseline nature and love is the transcendence? —Is it that so few have risen above what human nature is or is it that so many have fallen from it?

"To accept that the ideals embodied in evil's philosophy reflect the nature of humanity we would have to concede that evil is the natural way—that evil was there in us from the beginning.

"Such an argument is logical, especially as we look out into the world," the man's voice descended. "The bloodied masses claw at one another; starved children lay incapacitated in some forgotten place; greed driving the spear of war ever-forward—through the innocent man's heart without concern for cost, only gain. Oh yes," the man stressed with emotion, "if all the blood spilt could be gathered up and all the tears wept pooled together we all would drown in an ocean of salty maroon waters high enough to deluge the world." Realizing he had sunken into the horror of the evil, his voice rose as his focus returned. "Evil is certainly abundant—even dominant, but to say evil is humanity's nature—such a concession is impossible for me to make because I cannot, even for a moment, think evil is natural. To me evil is everything that is unnatural—evil is the imbalance, the backwardness, the twisting of what is pure.

"Evil is common now," the man commented in an ironic, offhanded manner. "Many of its ways have been adopted, even become acceptable and preferred but this does not show the natural way of humanity. These facts simply show humanity's sharp decline.

"To concede that the nature of humanity is evil would be to take *choice* out of the equation. It would be to say evil is what man is, instead of what he has *become*, and this is not something I believe to be true. We would be stating that purity is not something we are born with, it is something we attain. And while this reasoning may at times seem true, I believe that we all are born pure. Purity is simply something that is stripped from us or something that we freely forsake, and so becomes something to be reclaimed.

"The true nature of humanity has been drowned out by the swell of evil. Nevertheless, a human being is not born a beast—he becomes one. Love is not the higher path; it is the place we all start. Renewing ourselves to our loving nature—to our belief in the virtues of love—we reaffirm our *original self* and preserve what the surrounding evil tries to twist in us.

"Where love is absent, the savage man dwells. When filled by love for another, love compels our every act—we are caring, genuine, honorable and never harmful. When filled with love we embody *humanity* and when filled with a desire to dominate, we embody *evil*," the man concluded. "The two are quite separate."

"There are so many corrupt people but I cannot believe that there would be so many who would choose to become evil without any kind of outward influence deceiving them into wrongdoing. If evil is not demonic then it must be part of human nature," Asa debated respectfully.

Back still to the room, eyes fixed on the horizon, the man stared out at the low rising moon. "Evil is the majority. There is no denying its prominence. But despite its commonplace and the ease with which I see people bring it forth from within themselves, I cannot believe man is born with the foulness within them.

"Looking out at the mob I ask myself what mankind was born to be, knowing I will not find my answer by looking into the hearts of those I pass on the street; for so many of them are twisted beyond recognition—barely human, hardly feeling, verging on death—decayed from what they originally were.

"Instead, to find my answer I find that I must look back. I must reach into the past and try to envision the first being to emerge into existence. I must connect with the soul of them that endures still, and ask myself if I believe this first being to be a loving heart or an unfeeling beast?

"Behold the first being," the man said out in a clear, reflective tone. "Was their heart a twisted one or did it beam? Did they raise a hand to the next human to come forth or go unto them wanting closeness? Did they find in them one to rule or the answer to that aching plea for companionship? Were the first two adversaries or kin?

"The first heart reflects the nature of us all and when I reach out to this ancient one I do not feel malice but gentleness; I feel not torment but peace...not hate but caring. Evil is familiar to me, easily recognizable in both sight and feel. Yet reaching out to this first heart—the father and mother of us all—I do not feel the root of evil; I feel the embodiment of love. In that first soul I feel the intensity of all loving emotion at last taking the form of flesh—I feel the soul of Love, and in this I know what we all were born to be.

"The hearts we descended from are pure," he said, turning around to face the room. "Evil is the betrayal of what it is to be human, not the fulfillment of our nature. Love will always connect us into our original self. Through love we remain faithful to who we were in the beginning as well as to those we wish to honor as we live," he concluded; sitting down beside his son.

"You spoke of how this all began with an 'original family' and the fall of a son. Can you tell us any more of the original family and how this struggle with evil came about?" Samuel asked open-mindedly. Despite all that had been spoken of, he was ready to hear more.

The man gazed towards Samuel and Maria in the lamplight; he was willing to go on with the conversation. The couple noticed shadowed circles around the man's intense eyes; he was tired—worn, not by this day, but by the many that had come before. "For a great number of years I did not know the story. I did not know anything other than the depth of the pain I felt at the hands of evil and the torment of my own unanswered questions when it came to the reasons and methods of the evil I had encountered. That said, I wanted the whole truth, just as you do now. However, the answers I needed were not something I could find in the recorded history of man; for that part of humanity's history has been lost.

"There are fragments of truth scattered throughout the myths of mankind hidden like ruins among the shifting sands of time; they are indistinguishable from fiction unless you already know some small part of the truth you seek.

"After living without answers for the majority of my life, my family was finally given some insight when we met those who knew the lost story we sought. They did not tell us all that they know nevertheless, I do have the basic timeline of the events," the man proceeded. "The name of the son has become synonymous with evil, but once it was just a name and he was a good man. In time, this eldest son began to change as his desires shifted from the pure to the perverse. You ask: 'How does one become evil?' The answer is: The transformation from loving being to evil being occurs when we lose our original self—the pure, wholesome heart we were born as.

"We can indeed lose ourselves. I realize that this sounds like such an existential statement but it is a very real condition, and it does happen with disconcerting ease."

"How does it happen?" Asa asked. "How can we lose who we are? We are always ourselves," the boy added in a confused tone.

"We can lose ourselves in betraying ourselves," the man replied. "What is our identity? Is it contained in our mind or in our soul? No, it is neither. Our identity lies in our beliefs and desires. We become evil when we abandon our belief in love by choosing to take up another belief—a belief in possession, domination, greed and lust. Purity of action equates purity of self. The more corrupt the action the more damaged the self. The son's desires changed, his perspective changed and subsequently his identity was lost, and he became evil. He betrayed his original self and became what he is today. He was raised in the old world, which was based upon a belief in love, family and community. However, in time, he chose to create a new philosophy by which to live.

"Instead of a community of equals he wanted a Lord and subjects. This is a common concept to us at present but at that time, it was inconceivable. Before he changed all were loving. Humanity sought to unite with each other and to free each other. The emergence of evil came about when the son desired to possess others instead of free others—to dominate, rather than support. His desires twisted and thus he twisted. At first evil began as this dark lusting, but then the breadth of evil widened to encompass other foul appetites never conceived of before—the desire to harm, to inflict pain, to spite...to kill.

"Tolerating his son's vulgarity for many years, the father waited in hope for the return of the good-hearted boy he once knew, but there came a day when the father and mother could no longer condone their son's choices. And so, the father did the only thing he could—he gave his son an ultimatum: The son could renew his pure self and return to love's ways or leave the family's lands to start another life elsewhere.

"Outraged by this pronouncement, the son painted his father a tyrant—judgmental and self-righteous—one to be feared and not loved. As evil always does, the son turned the situation around until it was backward—the son portrayed his father as the one who wanted to dominate and himself as a victim that wanted only to be free.

"It had not been easy for the father and mother to turn their son from the house. Such an act had never been heard of before this time. They had let him stay within the community for as long as they could—too long some would say—out of a hope that their loving boy would once again resurface from within the moods and delusions of this monster who had come into their midst. But the time came, when the son's actions were hurting others in the village stealing the innocence of those in the surround—pressing the father into action.

"The father turned the son from the lands, forced him to leave the village if he would not change. Upon hearing the ultimatum the son defied his father and raged against him. Before leaving the Homelands the son went unto his brothers and sisters—gathering the surrounding community and preached his new found philosophy unto the open-hearted masses. He condemned his father and—made himself appear the victim. He put off his new desires and ambitions as a natural evolution of civilization.

"Rebelling against the beliefs of love, the son was unwilling to change; he continued to bring vulgarity unto the wholesome society and so the son was exiled from the Homelands and set out into the undeveloped lands that surrounded.

"Doing this—breaking with their own son—broke the hearts of the father and mother. The family had taken a tremendous hit and the age of the old world of loving ways began its slow decline. The family was divided and with that act a wound that would linger for lifetimes was made. The hearts in the family were broken, no one knew what had happened to bring about these events. The age of mourning and torment had begun.

"The son left the Homelands, choosing his new found ambitions over his family. He took with him those people who had identified with his sermons, having come to crave what he did, and with them he founded his own world. The ages passed, and the world and the culture he founded have become this," he said, raising his arms slightly. "The world he created is the one you live in."

"Impossible!" Aden replied. "You're making it up as you go along."

"No," rebutted the man. "It was the son who 'made it up as he went along.' With his newfound ambitions and blinding pride driving him, the son laid the foundation for another world—imposed new beliefs within his society and with it a new reality. Many years passed and evil progressed their world while love tried to rebuild theirs yet evil and love did not part ways quietly. Evil became a terror to those in the Homelands; for while the immoral had been forced to leave they returned unto the Homelands, first to preach their lies and then later to harm those who refused to condone the new ways.

"Violence erupted in the old Homelands. Innocent, loving people were taken, beaten, robbed, raped—atrocities that had never before been carried out. Evil had evolved from a lustful craving to a spiteful hatred. The son reentered the lands to preach and then to demand.

"The father told his children and the extended family of the community not to listen. He gave them all the choice to stay or leave; for, contrary to what he was made out to be by his son, the father was not trying to control his family—he was not trying to be that of a Lord—he was simply a man who did not want to lose what was most precious.

"The father's attempts to hold together the family were carried out in vain. The son gained more followers and eventually succeeded in tearing apart the family of humanity. In doing so he also tore the Earth in two wherein there was a society of love and one of evil."

When the man finished most everyone was anticipating a moment of silent reflection, but instead Ira—Ari's second born— who apparently had been steadily building in frustration, verbally leapt upon the nameless man to denounce his story.

"I don't even know where to begin. You simply made it up—you altered the scriptures as if they were fiction that could be rewritten. I will not listen to this any longer," he declared in outrage. His tone seemed rather dramatic—overacted; as though he were trying to act offended when, on some level, was indifferent.

"I was told this story by those who witnessed the events."

Ira had no reply to this; his face remained fixed in a look of mocking disbelief.

"You have spoken to those who were present at these events that you say, 'took place millenniums ago.' How is such a thing possible?" Ira asked, in an obvious attempt to make the man appear insane or a lair.

"Yes," Judah echoed in agreement. He had been waiting to return to this subject for some time. "It makes no sense," he added, not wanting to appear part of Ira's attack but rather, simply wanting an answer to the question posed.

"As I have said," the man replied calmly, "the world was different before the movement of evil came about. As impossible as it is to believe, in the old culture there was no aging. You know dying is known as a *natural process* but long ago, in a forgotten time, there was no aging—no dying. One grew to maturity, time passed but there was no wear. One was filled but never drained."

A general question rose from many mouths at once, "How?"

"Love," the man replied simply. "Love has the ability to sustain us indefinitely—to maintain the body of one who is filled with love. Time does not apply to those filled with love. Love does not weaken or wear, only deepen. And in this, love is immortal. Love brings life and sustains life."

"Even if, I believed you, which I don't," Aden replied aggressively. He set aside the absurd notion without a second thought. "What are the names of those within this original family? What is this defiant son's name?"

"You already know his name—nearly everyone knows his name. The story of this man is embedded in humanity's storytelling. He has been given a different name by each culture to relate his story. Many myths have sprung up around the simple truth, grown thick over time—obscuring the original facts. I will not deny that the story is an epic one; however, the reality is much less surreal than it has been made out to be.

"I hesitate in speaking his name here because, when I give you the name, your mind will travel to the myth, leaving the truth overshadowed by all the lies that you know of him. That said, I will tell you this—the first son has become the being known as the devil; while the father became known as God. Ironically, most all that we know in this world concerning the divine element has been taught to us from evil's perspective. The original story still exists in some form within the literature of mankind. Some of the stories are there in the histories of different faiths yet the truth has been dramatized and lost its emotional resonance.

"The father of the original family was made into God; the mother was forgotten—swept aside with evil's disregard for women. The son who brought forth the movement became the devil. The other sons and daughters had myths formed around them as well, portrayed as Otherworldly beings, angels, servants and so on.

"Likewise, the old world has had myths formed around it; going by a dozen names, each peoples having their own term for the world based upon the old culture—love's Reality: Paradise, Heaven, Elysium, Aaru, Arcadia, Tir Na NÓg, Eden, Shambhala, Utopia...and so on. Likewise the world evil founded has gone by a dozen different names depending upon the culture and language of the writer: Hell, the Underworld, Hades, Jahannam, Avīci, the Inferno and so forth. Yet there was a disconnect in that, we perceive both evil and love's worlds to exist on other planes rather than upon this Earth." The man's voice tapered off as he rested in the wake of the truths he just shared.

Maria picked up the thread of thought, "This old world that was there in the time before evil, is it entirely gone?" She asked mournfully; wanting to continue the conversation even though the day had long-since passed into night.

Obliging the good woman, the man continued, "When the family divided the Earth was divided as well. When those who became evil were turned from the house they went out into the area of the Earth yet to be developed and founded their own world.

"It was not the father's intention when he turned his son from the house, that another way of life be established. When making the ultimatum he was doing what was necessary to protect the family's innocence, hoping in time that, those who had twisted themselves would awaken to their actions, experience a change of heart and return home.

"No one could have foreseen what evil would grow to become or that it would last this long. After those who became evil were asked to leave there was a short time when the two peoples lived apart, without much incident. Those in the Homelands agonized over the inexplicable change in the character of their loved ones—deeply mourning the loss of their family members. While those in evil's movement were occupied on establishing the basic infrastructure of the new world they were creating. Yet, as I said, fighting eventually broke out when evil started reentering the Homelands and began striking at those who would not join them. Over time, as the numbers of evil swelled, their world did as well.

"In the old world we lived in harmony with each other, the Earth and all living creatures. Evil however, does not live in balance; they believe that their ambitions supersede any and all laws of nature. In their mind the ends justified the means—they stripped the Earth of all resources: cutting down forests without replanting, slaughtering herds and flocks without regard for their continued existence. Never before had such waste been seen; as evil rose the balance was lost and pain was born unto the world. Suffering sprung from evil's existence: illnesses, plagues, wars, lies…these things had never been suffered before yet once evil came into being so did these inflictions.

"In time the situation came to the point where evil's burgeoning world threatened the Homelands and something had to be done to protect the innocent. Those who still believed in love needed a sanctuary, wherein the ways of love could be preserved and those who did not want to partake in evil would have a place to live as they wish. And so there was a divide made between the Homelands and evil's lands."

"What do you mean?" Maria asked.

"A part of the Earth was hidden away—out beyond the reach of evil. We call this place the Other Shore but it has gone by many names depending upon the culture."

"Nonsense," Ira said restlessly. "If such a world once flourished upon the Earth there would be a record."

"No there wouldn't," the man insisted. "Not a complete history anyway—not if evil were holding the pen.

"Born into Hell I was taught evil's version of history. But upon arriving on the Other Shore I found *truth*."

"You have been to this place?" Aden said with a slight laugh.

"For a time," the man replied vaguely. Offering nothing more, even when pushed.

"While there it was explained to us that, in the time before evil existed, all living beings—humanity itself—was a family. And the chosen way of life was based upon a belief that love was all-fulfilling. All people believed in union, in family and in community. For ages on end, this world of love flourished.

"During this time the Earth was without suffering, without pain and without poverty, without illness, hate, greed, lust and perversion. Until, the change took place and the son brought forth a new ill perspective—evil. First it was just him—just one—a single individual who seemed to lose his belief in love and crave other things—other ideas of power, other ambitions."

"What prompted the change?" Samuel inquired.

"To this day his choice is regarded as inexplicable. There was no reason—no provocation, no trauma, no unfulfilled need, that caused him to become what he *did*—he simply did. He tired of the loving way, and churned within himself new ambitions. He no longer saw the virtue in being a part of a community. He wanted to possess, to control—to rule. It was—is, his belief that only these endeavors, not love, are fulfilling." The man refocused. "Gradually as more people converted to evil the loving hearts were out-numbered. The Homelands were seized by the evil, those who believed in love were persecuted and the history of the old world was erased. Evil overturned everything so to be free to reshape the world in its own, warped image.

"The movement of evil swept the world—they stripped the natural Earth bare and built their own world, at the heart of which, lay the self-centered way of life they prefer. Afterward they wiped out all evidence of the great crime committed; presenting the emerging generations with a new reality. A world of 'new possibility,' of 'invention,' of 'progress'—*civilized*, when it is anything but. A reality where it is taught that deceit, greed, hate and lust are unalterable traits within humanity, when they are actually the signs of humanities descent. A reality where crime, poverty, war, sickness, death and despair are an inevitable part of life, when, in actuality, they are the byproducts of evil's culture alone."

"So this Other Shore—the last of the Homelands, were taken?" Maria asked sadly.

"No, the Other Shore is the last foothold of the old world. It was preserved generations ago, when evil began to spread. Protected by Love, placed out of the reach of evil, it acts as a refuge for the survivors.

"I have told you that Hell's true location is on Earth. The next revelation is that Heaven's is as well. Every culture has a myth based upon this sanctuary. These myths are the fragments of truth that managed to survive the upheaval and evil's rewriting of history. Some of the descriptions are simply myth—just as with Hell. Heaven is not celestial light and heralding angels. It is a world built by those with a deep belief in love, whose inhabitants have come to understand the power of love and many of the unseen workings of the world. It is a world where love and the old culture have managed to survive."

CHAPTER X

The Second Night

MEALS HAD BEEN PREPARED, prayers had been made and the evening had blended into night. Everyone was sleeping after the long day. The room hummed with the sound of deep breathing. Samuel and Maria however, sat awake whispering to one another, as did the man and his son.

Feeling grateful to have the couple's voice among the group, the man decided it was time to strike up a conversation of his own. He moved quietly over to them.

"Good evening," he whispered warmly. A faint smile moved across his bearded cheeks.

Taken aback by the man's approach, the couple took a moment to respond. "Good evening," Samuel replied awkwardly.

The man smiled. "Do you mind that I came over?" he asked politely. "I understand if you wish to be alone after such a long day."

"No," Maria replied quickly. "We don't mind. In fact, we were just talking about everything we discussed today. After learning all that we have, it seems things will never be the same." Maria stopped herself. "But I am sure you don't wish to speak more about the day. You have already talked enough."

"It's fine," the man said, giving her leave to speak.

"It's me," Samuel said. "I appreciate everything you have told us these last days. We are excited to have met you. You are the answer to many prayers. But, there is another side to it all, isn't there? As we learn these truths, we are also learning that everything we have believed in thus far has been a lie. It is...."

"Unbelievable," the man replied, putting Samuel's struggles into words.

"Yes," he agreed sorrowfully. The conversations of the day had pulled his mind over some invisible line of awareness, from which there was no going back. "How do you even know what is true? There are so many hidden agendas; how does one even go about learning genuine truth? How did you do it?" he asked, wanting to be pointed towards the right sources.

"I was given it. It was passed onto me, just as I pass it onto you now."

"From those you mentioned on the Other Shore?" Samuel asked.

"My family and I were given a great deal of information during our brief stay on the Other Shore but we had begun learning before that. I began asking questions as a young man. The problem was, those who had the answers I needed were not nearby. I did the normal things one does when seeking insight; I read books and spoke to 'religious men.' But they did not have the answers I needed. I did not know what exactly I was looking for but I knew the answers I received from those I spoke with and gleaned from books just did not feel complete.

"Of course I know now that the vast majority of books would not be helpful, given the fact that their texts are skewed. Many of the teachers around us limit our mind instead of expand it. The people who knew the answers I needed were out there, I simply had to find them. As it happened they found me, in a rather unexpected way.

"You see, at times, those who have the truth we are in need of, are not physically nearby, so the lessons must take place from afar. We are able to learn from those who are at a distance by way of *the connection* we each have. It was through this process of distance learning that I was taught much of what I know." The man paused. He could tell that they were not following what he meant by "connection." He decided to go further back.

"When I was a younger man, back when my family made our home in this country, I use to go out before the sunrise and walk among the hills near our home. One morning in particular, I rose and went walking in the stillness. The questions I sought answers to were resounding in me. And it was as I roamed through the silence, reaching out to what I thought at that time in my life was God, that I felt a thought come into my mind, only it was not my thought. Information came into my mind fully-formed—striking insights that I had never considered before, let alone figured out so clearly.

"You see, those who had the truth I needed did indeed exist, they were simply at a distance and so the truth had to be sent to me from afar. At times I have received the insights of our ancestors, while at other times I have connected with Love itself—the ancient consciousness. What came to me in the beginning were simple thoughts—an alternate viewpoint—a perspective that was different from the philosophies imparted to me by all others. During those first years, I filtered the truth received through the perceptions already embedded in me by teachings I had received; this resulted in a semi-distorted truth. However, in time, the preconceived notions of the divine, the world and myself were removed and a clean and whole truth was able to be had.

"That morning I heard it—the calling in the calm. These first thoughts began a progression of learning, which lasts to this day. This is what I mean when I say that we are all connected. I do not simply mean in a 'web of life' sense—one's actions effecting the next—but rather, we are physically connected to one another. Those thoughts that were given to me traveled from the heart who sent them, across the distance and into my mind. This connection flows from soul to soul—running through the fabric of the unseen. Every living thing is part of this network. I am connected to you," he said to Samuel. "And you to me. Through the connection all things can be shared: love, insight, healing, memory.... If you were ever far from me and I wanted to learn a truth you knew, I could use the connection to reach out the question I need an answer to, to see if you had some answer to give back. Truth can be shared without words," the man said simply. "It can be shared through the connection, spoken in an inaudible language, which is heard, not with the ears but with the receptors of the soul.

"I know that, right now, after all that we have spoken of these last days, you are confused. All you can see is the lies you were told and the harm done by evil. But there is more taking place within you and around you, and when you clear the initial shock you will be able to perceive it. You will be able to see the greater reality taking place beyond the surface of these conversations."

"What do you mean?" Samuel asked, wanting to see another side to the matter so that his focus would turn from the negative.

"Things are never what they are on the surface alone," the man replied. "There are many layers to what is occurring; in time, you will be able to appreciate each of them.

"There are three planes to our reality: what is taking place *within us*, what is taking place in *the unseen* and what is taking place in the *physical*. We must be ever-mindful to take into account what is happening simultaneously on these planes, if we are to be aware of the deeper meaning in what is occurring—in what we are a part of.

"Through emotional awareness, we know what is taking place *within us*. And by means of our connection and our inner-senses we become aware of what is taking place in the *unseen*."

"Inner-senses?" Samuel asked. Maria likewise looking confused by the term.

"We all have inner-senses that enable us to be aware of what is happening in the unseen. Utilizing our inner-senses and our connection we have the means to: find genuine truth, gain an awareness of our full reality and finally judge the legitimacy of the information we are given by others."

"I still don't understand," Samuel answered, wishing he did.

"It is my fault," the man said. "The day has been a long one and I am not being clear. You see, there are the senses of the physical body," he began slowly. "The outer-senses of smell, sight, sound, touch, taste but there are also the senses of our *Being*. These senses are mainly grouped in with our 'instincts,' due to the fact that the senses of the Being are based upon feeling."

"The Being?" Samuel inquired. "You mean the soul?"

"Yes, I suppose soul would work as well. You see, your Being—your soul—is contained in your body though, is apart from your body. Your Being is *you*—the individual that is you. Your Being is the identity that was created before you came into this body. Some call it 'the soul.' I hesitate to use this word because it seems to me that the soul is regarded as a piece of the whole that is you, whereas your Being is you, in your entirety. Your body is merely a vessel for your Being. If your body dies, your Being does not. Your body is something you reside in now yet can transition from if need be. Your body is, in a way, the interface through which your Being interacts with the physical world. Whereas your Being is your identity in the world that lie behind this physical one.

"Your body obeys your Being. You probably know this phenomenon as 'mind over matter' or 'the mind-body problem.' The body reflects the state of the Being; for example, a Being emptied of love equals a body that sickens whereas a Being filled with love equals a body sustained immortally from within." The man paused, issuing a quiet laugh. "I gave examples of two extremes but of course, there are other 'middle ground' examples. I know I am venturing into something that seems unbelievable," he said, wanting them to know he related to their disbelief and confusion. "Setting aside these ideas for now, it is enough that you understand that you are more than your body. And your reach extends beyond the end of your fingers. Through your Being you are connected—connected to others as well as the most ancient consciousness. Just as your body can reach out a hand and touch another, so your Being can extend from the heart and you can touch another, even if they be at a much greater distance than arm's length.

"The inner-senses of which I spoke have many uses. Our most helpful ability, given the extent of lies in this world, is the testing of truth. You see, our inner-senses help us in finding truth because we are able to evaluate what we are learning by passing it through our heart to see what reaction arises. The bodily senses upon which we rely the most to define our reality—sight and sound—can be easily deceived. Our ears can be told lies and our eyes be fooled by illusions. However the senses of our Being are different. Through the inner-senses we can see clearly what is being hidden from us by one who is trying to mislead us. Through our inner-senses we can feel the truth of the matter, which can at times be hard to determine when dealing with those who are duplicitous.

"As I am sure you know, people come unto us and declare they are our friends, when in their heart they wish to harm us. At times people say they want nothing from us, when in their heart they want to possess us. If we simply listen to their *words* with our ears without using our inner-senses to confirm what they are declaring, we will be deceived. Through using our inner-senses we can get to the genuine reality of what is taking place in front of us. Extending your heart to feel what is in the heart of those in front of you, can act as an affirmation of what they have declared. Does the feeling of what is in their heart match their words or differ?

"These senses can give you the truth you have been denied, that is, if you are able to trust what your heart is telling you above all else. Above what the books may say and what the teachers may tell you and what the people around you may declare. You see," he said, expanding on a new aspect. "Because these senses are telling us something that we cannot always confirm with our eyes or ears, the senses of the Being cannot be fully utilized by one who does not possess some level of self-trust—some degree of confidence in what their heart is telling them.

"When using the senses of the Being, as compared to the senses of the body. There isn't always a 'visible' confirmation of what is being sensed within. For example, when you detect an aroma using the body's sense of smell, there is a confirmation—most always you can find what it is you are smelling. However, when you are sensing something within your heart via the inner-senses, there isn't always visible confirmation—we can sense something occurring in the unseen but have no visible affirmation to substantiate what we are sensing; instead, it is simply a matter of trusting what our inner-senses—our instincts...our heart— is telling us.

"To utilize the senses of the Being we must have confidence in the ability of our heart to sense what goes unseen. We must also have emotional clarity; for many things can come to taint what our inner-senses are telling us such as fear, despair and other outer-influences. The senses of the Being are mainly based upon *feeling*; therefore we must try to maintain the purity of our feelings, by remaining ever-conscious of our anger, fears and so on. Many in this age, do not give credence to their inner-senses because they cannot trust anything that cannot be confirmed by eye or instrument. Yet, while the senses of the Being are different from those of the body, they are no less reliable or exact.

"In many instances the senses of the body are more easily deceived than the inner-senses because they detect only the visible surface of something, which is the part of any person or situation that can be easily disguised and thus misjudged. Whereas the inner-senses detect what lies within a situation— what is emanating from within another, which is much harder to hide.

"The inner-senses are the part of us that can detect what goes unseen or what lies beyond the surface of something or someone. Through our inner-senses we cannot only detect the true intentions of others but we can also become sensitive enough to feel things—events—taking place on a greater scale within the world or within our life. The inner-senses are based on feeling and utilizing them is based mainly on trust, clarity, awareness, sensitivity and belief. Through the outer-senses we have the surface. Through the inner-senses we have the deeper meaning and through the connection we have a full appreciation for the scope of what is occurring." The man took a breath. "I know you feel lost—dazed. Right now, you both are in an in-between—you are leaving behind one world— one way of life, and preparing to enter a new. Transitions are always difficult; some more than others," he said, with a bit of irony. Trying to lighten what had been a heavy day. "But remember, you are leaving behind something false and in doing so, freeing yourself to find something real. By listening with such an open-mind you have shown your courage."

The man finished, leaving Samuel at ease. There was still the reality of the life-long misconceptions, nonetheless after the talk the couple felt there was also an entirely new world of untold possibility waiting to be explored. They had been opened to a new way of thinking—one that excited them.

As excited as they were to continue talking, the couple knew it was late—well past midnight, and they didn't think their mind could process much more. It had already been a day of tremendous revelation and they could feel the strain of the significant newly-learned truths pushing the limits of their perceptions. So, while their heart longed to continue, their mind cried out for rest.

"We should let you rest," Maria said kindly, seeing that the man was likewise strained by the amount of information he had conveyed throughout the day.

"I hope we did not push you," Samuel added; realizing that, in their eagerness to learn, they had deprived the man of his night's rest.

"I enjoyed talking with you both," he assured them. "Mind you, I think we probably discussed more than we should have; I think we have exhausted ourselves."

"We can talk more tomorrow," Samuel reasoned, looking as though he could not hold his eyes open another moment no matter how much he desired to.

"Yes," they all agreed.

Samuel and Maria lay down and the man moved back to his area, where his son was laying still awake in his bed, having listened to the conversation.

"Are you alright?" Yoseph asked in the darkness.

"Yes. I am fine. Are you alright?"

"Yes," Yoseph replied, tired.

The man lay down upon his thin bedroll—Yoseph fell asleep instantly; while the man laid awake for a time with his thoughts.

᠌

Yoseph would have stayed up if his father had asked him to, but he did not. It had been an entire day of talking—so much so that the conversation blurred into a confusing jumble, and the man just needed quiet.

At times, when he was talking, he felt a feeling of unconsciousness, as though a question asked by the crowd awoke some dormant knowledge in him that he never knew was there; as though his mouth spoke, disconnected from his mind.

Throughout his life there had always been knowledge he possessed that he had never learned of or was taught. It was almost as though he was drawing from embedded knowledge and the unconscious memory of all loving beings.

Perhaps, he thought to himself.

The fear of what had been shared was not as consuming this night as it had been the night before. He was able to bury the fearful reality of where he was and what he was doing deep within his mind, temporarily giving him the ability to handle the situation. Nevertheless, at the same time, he was fully conscious—acutely aware—and he did not know how he felt about the choice he had made to speak.

His thoughts moved beyond the room he was in, beyond the city walls, to pass over his family—wherever they might be in their journeys. *How will this end?* he thought to himself.

He asked those in the unseen this question, just as those around him had been asking questions of him. Only the answers he received were not as clear as the ones he gave. Or rather, his trust in them was not as strong as it once had been.

He had no reason to doubt in the ability of love to guide him; the family had made it this far and not due to mere happenstance. *No,* he thought to himself. *Trust was not the issue—I do not lack trust in what we are doing, rather I lack enthusiasm.*

He was tired, the momentum of his convictions was gone, it had been faint before the journey and now, after years of tasks and separation from those he loved, it was all but dead.

He knew those who guided him to be wise enough to see the family through all the obstacles that lie ahead and untangle them from all that lie behind them. But he could not help thinking that the stamina of their hearts had been overestimated.

We will never give up on each other—we can't. You used that fact when planning this, didn't you, he thought to himself, speaking to those who could hear his thoughts.

You knew we could endure it all if it meant we were doing it for each other. Did you put our reunion as the destination, knowing that it would help us accomplish the journey? he asked.

No answer came, but at the same time, he felt a confirmation.

Evil overshadows all, he thought to himself, slightly angry with himself. He was frustrated that he had once again allowed himself to lose focus of love and dwell once more on all that the heartless had done to them.

145

We left the Other Shore…. We agreed to make this journey in order to learn the truth about what evil had done to us…all so that we might heal. We did not come here for evil itself. We did this for each other, out of love and concern, he reminded himself. *We came back here to finish it because we could not live, broken as we were.*

Let it be done, he declared within himself, sending the declaration through his heart and out into the unseen; pushing back against all fatigue and depression that weighed him down.

Let us do what need be done and face what need be faced, so this may come to an end and each of us may be free to resume our rightful life.

The broken man within him felt resilient; the helpless man felt empowered; the terrified man felt courage; the exhausted man felt a surge of determination and the battered man stood up, willing to fight.

CHAPTER XI

The Other Side

THE DAY HAD BEGUN EARLY FOR THE MAN. He rose just before dawn, intending to have a few moments to himself. Sitting beside the gaping window, reflecting on all that had come to pass over the night, he did not hear Ari's approach.

"Early to rise?" Ari inquired. His voice was soft and smooth. He ran his hand down the length of his long beard.

The man turned from the window. He said nothing at first. Giving time for Ari to make his intentions clear. The two stared at each other for a few moments as though summing each other up. While they had not spoken a great deal during the conversations themselves, an uneasy relationship had silently developed between the two.

"I can sense that you do not wish company," Ari said. The man did not contradict this assumption. Ari continued,

"I came over to give you a piece of advice. You are in a city of three traditions. It is lethal enough to hold one of these faiths as your own in an environment of such rivalries. It sets you at odds with the other two. But to openly contradict all three is suicidal. So, while I appreciate your unique views," he said condescendingly, "I council caution." The man still remained silent, waiting for the end of the pretense.

Ari went on, "I can tell by how you hold yourself with the others during these conversations that you believe what you are saying but you do not understand the politics of religion here. In this city, everything is taken to heart. If you speak against my God, it is as though you speak against my father. I can let these recreational *talks* proceed only so far." The man still said nothing. Ari persisted.

"The boys are only students, they do not yet understand the serious responsibilities entailed within the religious life they have chosen. They are amused by you, they indulge you, but their masters would not. I have survived in this city for many years. I have learned how to balance the politics of religion. Listen to me," he urged, feigning care. "Let the remainder of our time here pass quietly," he finished in a seemingly friendly way, though with a subtext permeated with threat.

"Politics," the man replied, "in this instance, is the truth verses the opposing popular opinion and the personal ambitions of the greedy. Taking in mind the 'politics' is taking in mind the will of the mob and the ambitions of those rising in power. I know the popular opinion but I do not alter the truths I know to suit it. When I speak, I do so knowing I am giving a message that few desire to hear. When last I came to this city I learned the harsh reality of the politics of religion here. I would not change my words to suit the mob then and I will not do it now. I will speak with the group for as long as they desire me to do so. I am not forcing any truth upon them. I know that will not ease your worries. You will still view me as a threat."

"I do not see you as a threat. I speak out of concern for you," Ari replied in a silk tone of smooth, boldfaced lies.

"Of course," the man said, hearing all that went unspoken quite clearly. "Be assured, I understand your message. And I have no doubt that you have understood mine."

Ari turned and began to walk away.

"Something to consider," the man spoke up in a genuine brotherly tone. "We all are presented with moments wherein we can change. All we must do is allow ourselves to take in those truths we have long fought away."

Ari turned on his heel and walked away. As he did the students began to stir at the noise. The man gave a tired sigh.

*

The morning passed. The others rose and ventured out into the city to gather fresh news and supplies from the streets. The farmer had reluctantly parted from his wife and daughter to gather food in the market. Upon his return, he had brought with him an assortment of newspapers, which brought slightly more reliable reports than the rumors Aden and Ira gathered from the back alleys. Headlines of mortar attacks and suicide bombings that had occurred in the Bank—just north of the city—were splattered across the front page. More attacks were expected in the city as well. Everyone was on edge.

With no hope of leaving that day, once again, after the morning meal had been eaten the crowd gathered around the man, as though the building they were staying in wasn't a makeshift shelter at all but rather a school and when the sun rose the bell rang, calling everyone to the first lecture.

The students moved close, as did Samuel and Maria; while Ari and his sons chose to keep to themselves this morning, apparently having heard enough. Ari casting wordless glances at the man from time to time.

It was the students that began the conversation of the day, asking the man to continue telling them about the struggle between evil and love. Upon hearing the request the man felt wearied, he wasn't keen on returning to the topic of evil considering the realization he came to last night when he lay to himself. He wanted to shift the focus to love. Thankfully, before the man could even begin, Maria spoke up— pleading for a different tone, apparently just as wearied by the focus on evil.

"We have been talking so much about evil. Tell us something of love," Maria asked.

"For pity sake. Must we do this again today?" Ira complained as he walked across the room to his father. He halted staring at the group. All eyes in the room turned to him.

"Leave him be," declared Maria, coming to the man's defense. She rose and stood face-to-face with Ira.

"Learn to control your wife," Ira said to Samuel in a dangerous tone. Samuel made to rise. The nameless man beat him to it. "Enough," he said firmly. "Enough," he repeated again, in a calming voice. "I feel no need to speak," he finished, defusing the situation.

"Well we have a need to listen," Maria spoke up.

"You all gather around him like he is a bloody prophet," Ira quipped, waving a dismissive hand in the direction of the nameless man. "All he spouts is sacrilege. He just wants attention."

"That is the most foolish thing I have ever heard," Maria replied. She stood at least a foot shorter than Ira. Dwarfed by his wide stature, she was still unafraid. "All-he-wants, is to be left alone. Not attention. He speaks because we ask him to."

"Don't argue with a woman," Aden said in an exhausted voice. "Thoughtless thing," he jabbed.

Maria's eyes were still fixed on Ira, she ignored Aden. Samuel however, could not. He stepped forward standing behind his wife in a show of support.

"Oh look, there he is, right behind his wife. How suiting," Aden remarked jokingly as he sat reclined against the wall watching the events. The atmosphere in the room was taut. Everyone had been confined for days and the differences of opinion were becoming clearer with each passing moment.

One argument shot down, Ira dredged up a new grievance. "You boys," he said, pointing at the students, "you do not even defend your faith when he rips it down. You should be ashamed. You say you are students of the scripture yet listen to a man who does not even follow it. When you find your faith, you defend it against those who attack it—that is how the truth remains intact. But instead you let him insult it. It is not his place to question God's truth."

"Don't question it. Don't test it," Maria repeated. "That is how lies remain intact, not truth. Truth is truth, it endures no matter what we may do to it; for it does not require our belief to make it what it is. Lies however, they crumble when questioned; they are undone when not followed. Blind faith isn't faith at all; it is laziness. And fanaticism isn't devotion; it is hatred wrapped in the guise of righteousness. What does it hurt to let him speak?" she reasoned. "You listen, you open your mind to a new perspective and if you don't agree with what he says, you go on your way, no harm done. Why must you run him down? What nerve do his words strike in you that make you hate him so?

"I have sat here listening to your comments for two days and from where I stand your faith has not made you compassionate. The words you live by have not opened your mind but closed it. Those who use religion to find God, at some point, veer off the beaten path because they must find their own way to the truth. But you and so many others use religion as a means of drawing battle lines. You don't even know what it is to have faith," she finished. Her heart pound in her chest—resounding in her soul.

"Ahhh," Ira grunted in a dismissive manner. "I will not stay to listen to this. Foolish woman!" he spat. "There are better things to be done than sit like brainless-sheep listening to this nonsense. Aden," Ira called. Aden rose, jeering at Maria as he made his way towards the door to join his brother. The two left.

Even with the two men gone, the room was still tense. Afterward, Ari neither approved nor disapproved of his sons' behavior. He said nothing. He simply sat there, watching the nameless man quietly, the way a cat watches a bird.

Everyone was still, even the daughter of the farmer and his wife had stopped playing to watch the events. Uri, the youngest brother had remained quiet beside his mother the entire time. The students were speechless, unsure as to whether or not Ira had been justified in his accusation. Yoseph had risen. He stood like a guard at his father's side—steadfast. The man laid a hand on his son and then walked quietly to the window; he was obviously alienated. His face was fixed in a pained expression. Keeping a respective distance, Maria approached him and spoke in a pleading voice, "Please...don't let them stop you. After all these days of hearing about evil, tell us of the other side," she asked.

Everyone waited. Ira's words still echoed in the room. Others, besides the man, had been shaken within themselves. All except Maria, Samuel and Yoseph, who were sure of themselves before and after.

A long time passed. The man stood silently to himself, his back to the room. All he could hear were Ira's words: "All he wants is attention." ...*attention?* he thought to himself, struggling in-between a need to shout and a need to cry. The morning light was bright upon his face. His eyes were glazed with tears of torment. He gripped the edge of the windowsill until his knuckles were white. He finally released his grip when Maria's pleas rose in his mind, louder than Ira's insults. He would not let the day be taken by one man's anger.

Straining against the tight bands of muscle strangling his chest, he took a ragged breath. He walked back over to his normal seat near Yoseph. He rubbed his face his fingers pushing hard on his temples before passing down his cheeks along his beard. Then, wiping his sweaty palms on the knees of his trousers he cleared his throat. "To learn of love," he began slowly, trying to move past the outburst, "one must possess an open mind—a truly *open mind*," he emphasized seriously. The irony was not lost on him, given the argument had only moments ago. "For love," he pressed on, "has no limits and so, if we are to understand love's workings, we must learn to think and to perceive our world without limits." With the first thought expressed, the momentum gradually began to return. "Open-mindedness is simple in theory but harder in practice. Throughout our adolescence we are bombarded with false information—we are taught of a reality that does not apply to the force of love or to those who are filled with it. We are taught what is possible and impossible; we have limits instilled within our minds and we begin to see the world and ourselves within those narrow limits. And in doing so, we become blinded to the vastness of our world; held back from achieving the full potential that lay within us.

"There are many different sides of love," he said. The heaviness that had been weighing on him after the argument lightened. "There is love the force, there is the being of love—the most ancient soul—and then there is the love that bonds us together. Over the ages, following the fall of the Homelands, the legacy of love has been in the hands of those writing history: evil. Lacking a belief in it, evil has belittled love. As it is now, in this age, love is known as an emotion; emotion equating a chain of chemical reactions in our brain—far removed from an occurrence taking place in our soul," he said with noticeable disgust.

"What love is, truly…. What the force of love is and what genuine love is between hearts, is much different than what it has been made out to be. In this age love is primarily linked to sex and infatuation; for that is what evil has decided to degradingly equate it to. Yet love is not lust—love is not so shallow. Love is a bond between hearts. It is an embrace that goes deeper than flesh. It is a bond that *physically exists* running between hearts; able to be felt, even if it is not able to be seen," the man struggled with words. His mind was going in every direction at once. Following the way of evil was linear—explaining its pathology was done step-by-step, but love on the other hand was circular—limitless; existing in countless forms and bringing untold abilities.

Having found the direction he wished to go in, he began again, "Love is a force and a being but for humanity it is also a practice—a choice—a way of living.

"Love is the life-bringing force, not just metaphorically but physically. Without love this body decays yet when filled with love, this body is healthy and immortal. Devoid of love this body weakens and our heartbeat grows faint yet overflowing with love we are sustained indefinitely and hold a power that we can hardly fathom. Do not mistake the food you eat and the water you drink as what nourishes you; it is love that feeds the fibers of your body and soul. Without love we are starved and our soul becomes distended with emptiness. Hungry for love, we gorge ourselves with food into obesity yet never feel fulfilled.

Love unites us—
    love fills us,
    compels us,
    inspires us,
    empowers us,
    completes us,
    awakens us,
    enlightens us.

"When love flows through us, life beams from us. It is the one thing we can give infinitely and yet never be emptied of; for love only ever grows."

The man stopped again. He was overwhelmed. "There is so much to say about love...so much to share with you. We have all sought an all-powerful omnipresence. Well love is ever-present. It is what the fabric of the unseen is woven with. Love is the true identity of the divine.

"There is still so much to learn. I know a great deal of love yet I also know I have hardly even begun to learn all that there is. Each one of us has to explore this force on our own and in doing so, bring another side of its ability forward for all to learn of."

"How do we explore it?" Asa asked. "By practicing compassion?" There was curiosity in his voice but, at the same time, something had changed in the boy. The brightness was gone from him.

"Yes. Showing love is the best way to let it flow through you. It is one way we explore its depth," the man affirmed. Adding, "Of course, there is more than one way. Just as some would believe religion to be mankind's interface with God, I find family to be my interface with love...with the divine. Through exploring my bonds, not only with my immediate family but with the Earth and all living creatures, I come to understand love. I find that I meet an embodiment of love, in those who are loving."

"What do you mean?" Gideon followed up in a flat voice.

"When there is a person who reveals the hidden meaning in your life—they are an embodiment of love and through interacting with them, you may interact with the divine they are allowing to flow through them.

"Exploring our bonds is one way to explore the aspects of the divine. Another way is through *the connection.*"

This comment brought querying looks from the students.

"We each have a connection to what came before us. We are each connected to our ancestors who, though they have left this world, live on elsewhere. And finally we are each connected to the consciousness of love—the being of love. We have the means to explore love from *within*—through reaching out into the unseen from our heart, directly unto the consciousness of love. Where we can then listen to the truth firsthand."

"This is how you learned your truth?" Gideon asked.

"A great deal of it. Yes," the man offered. "We—each of us—have a connection to the divine."

"You hear a voice?" Gideon asked in a judgmental tone.

"It is not a voice in your mind. The words are not *heard,* they are *felt.* It is as though you have a thought but are aware that it is not *your* thought. When you think, you do not hear your thought audibly echo in your mind it simply comes. Such is the way with the connection, only what is coming is not from you.

"We all have the means to connect to each other and the unseen. The connection is there within each of us; it simply goes unutilized. This world, as it is now, makes connecting difficult."

"What do you mean?" Maria inquired. Her voice added warmth in what was becoming a cold-toned discussion.

"The way of life had here does not encourage us to develop our connection to the unseen. The pace of our lives in this age is not conducive to maintaining a higher consciousness. Humanity suffers from the two extremes of exhaustion and boredom. We fear life lacks any deeper meaning and so we fill it up with shallow busy-work so to distract us from the fraying holes within us. We fear the silence, as we equate it with emptiness. Yet it is only within the quiet that we can hear the whispers coming from within. It is only when living at a moderate pace that we can maintain the proper level of consciousness and ordered priorities, so to be aware of the things of deeper significance occurring around and within us."

"How did you do it? How did you develop your connection while in this world?" Maria asked.

"I did while within the walls of our sanctuary," he answered.

"The Other Shore?" Maria asked.

"No. The sanctuary my family built—our *home*, and of course, the protective, nurturing circle of our love for each other," he explained. "If we are to develop our connection to the unseen, which at this moment lies within each and every heart, we must push back the emptiness within ourselves and remove ourselves from the hollow way of life so prevalent in this world. We must give priority to a search for meaning. The daily shallowness we are forced to put up with here just to earn what we need have shelter and food can be consuming—drowning out all other higher pursuits. We work like slaves and are so depleted by our effort to survive that we never live. We must maintain focus on what is truly important. This world is centered on ambition—possession. All this is unimportant. And so we must push it all back and make a place for reflection and growth—a sanctuary that we may enter, to explore ourselves and all that we are connected to.

"There are such places left on this Earth—untouched wild places where the hushed, un-intruding surround allows rumination to be had. Yet we can also create such places, wherein our connection to love—to the divine—is clear and we are able to explore what is out there and in here," he said, pointing to his chest. "Our home—the small space upon this Earth that we work for can be a sacred space wherein we can explore and believe without hindrance. Any home can be a womb.

"These types of sanctuaries must be created...they must be sought. We can choose a space, even if it be a small room, push back all that is detrimental to our well-being—all negative people, all the bombarding media—and establish in that space a place where we can commune with love.

"Our home is our refuge. As are those people who are loving. Among those who genuinely love us we are safe, nurtured and given the freedom and support to explore ourselves. From within our sanctuaries we can see more of the vast landscape of love's potential."

"You have a very *unique* view of love," Gideon said patronizingly. He glared at the man from beneath his grown out black hair.

"My thoughts bring me to the same conclusion. I do not believe I will come to know God by knowing my family," Judah added.

"Agreed. The divine cannot be known through the ordinary," Elijah said, leaving no room for a change of mind.

The man did not reply right away. Within himself he had pulled back from the conversation. A shift had occurred. The man felt the projected resentment, fear and judgment. The once open-minds of the students were closing. He did not feel as though he was exchanging thoughts with the students but rather defending himself from their attacks.

"I do not know of your relationship with your family," he said in reply to Elijah and Judah's comments. "I am going to venture to say your relationship with your family is not a true one and therefore you have not yet experienced the sacred nature of each bond. In feeling our love deepen we understand the divine workings of this world more intimately.

"In my instance, I came to know the divine through better knowing my wife, my children, my brothers, sisters and parents. In feeling the depth of their love for me, I know love to be limitless. In seeing what they are capable of when acting on their love for me, I know love to be powerful. In joining to their hearts, I join to what is sacred and know better the deeper meaning in living."

"Why would someone demean love? If love is indeed all the things you say it is, why would the truth be hidden? It sounds paranoid," Gideon reasoned.

Trying to disregard the insult and answer the question the man replied, "When the old ways were left behind and new ways were founded—a new reality not based upon a belief in love. When an old civilization is wiped out, the conqueror's will impose their way of life on the survivors, and so it was when evil took the Homelands. New explanations were needed for the workings of all things—ones that were not based upon the old beliefs. Science provided the new explanations needed and the redefinition and reeducation of humanity began.

"Yet, while they swept away the old world, love survives. While evil's mark has been left upon the Earth and upon us all, love makes the only lasting difference. Though we are now driven by gratification, humanity was once driven by love and community. It is how we began. It is the reason I go on. Love is my deeper meaning in life: To be loved and to love…. To know love and experience love…. To be filled and transcended by love…. Love is the reason I draw every breath.

"Evil has overtaken so much of the world; love can seem weak in comparison. It can seem like only an emotion—nothing more. But what love truly is survives. Love's reality is preserved upon the Other Shore; while love itself survives within all loving beings. At the center of us all exists love; we speak for it, progress it and we show its depths in what we do for one another." He was going to stop but he saw Maria's face beaming as she sat beside her husband, compelling him to go on, "Our belief in love brings forward what love can do; just as our belief in those we love can nurture them and help them realize what they can do. We were created from love and now we embody it, we preserve it. It defines us, and we define it." The man pulled back, feeling a twinge of pain for those he loves yet was without.

"Very poetic words," Ari said condescendingly. He had been covertly listening to the conversation from across the room. "But at the same time, your words are also very vague sir. You were so certain and specific in your ideas of evil, and yet you are so general in your ideas of this *divine love.*"

The man looked at Ari. He knew all too well the futileness of entering such a conversation yet for some reason he could not help but reply.

"I set out wanting to learn the workings of love," the man said in his defense, "yet came to know evil much more intimately. Not because evil interests me but because evil has surrounded me—hounded me and I had to understand what drove them to do what it is they do. Nevertheless, despite the fact that I have had to focus on evil for such a long period of time, there are some aspects of love of which I can speak as an authority: bonds and union being the sides of love I know best.

"You call my words vague. But to speak in specifics about what love is and what love is capable of is impossible—it is simply too narrow a scope, on too great a thing. I shall tell you what I know, rather, I shall tell you what I am able to convey in words yet the bulk of all that goes unsaid shall literally be *infinite*; for love is infinite. All those who wish to learn of love must accept that what they desire to learn of can never be fully understood—thus is the nature of any infinite thing.

"Humanity, in this age, finds it hard to grasp the infinite, we like to be able to master any subject we approach yet the mastery of love's knowledge can only be had by those who can accept that the progression of revelations will never end. The truths we learn concerning love are never the final truths; for love is ever-evolving and so the limits of our mind and sense of possibility must be as well.

"The whole of evil can be explained because evil is not infinite, it is structured—linear; whereas love is spherical and unbound. The nature of love is unchanging. Therefore, the core of what love is can be spoken of; however the extent of love and the workings of love cannot be taught. Love is a growing thing and so the believers of love must be as well. Yet for reasons beyond understanding most people like to settle at some point—halt their growth and entrench their mind, whether out of weariness, laziness, ignorance or loss of interest.

"All that being said, I cannot tell you *all* that love is—no one can. He who declares that he knows everything about any given subject knows absolutely nothing. I can only speak of what I have experienced and what I sense love to be capable of.

"Bonds and unions—I am knowledgeable of these aspects of love, not because of the revelations I have had concerning them but because of the people I am loved by and what loving them in return has taught me. I know what our love makes us capable of and I know the freedom their love gives me. I know what family is and I know what union is, as such I know two of the most intense aspects of love."

"When you speak of 'union' you are speaking of marriage?" Maria asked clarifying.

"Yes," the man said, giving his focus to this open-hearted woman, rather than debate with those who were adamantly deaf. "Although, I feel I should explain the difference between *marriage* and *union*.

"While one would propose that the definition of the word 'marriage' speaks of union and joining, it has been redefined over time and now concerns a legal union, not a genuine one. While some do indeed hold marriage to be the most sacred act a couple can make, in the end it has become meaningless—something easily entered into and easily left behind—a mockery of the nature of a true union. When you find the person you are meant to be with, the union between you and that person is already present; you do not create the union through ceremony, you simply awaken to it.

"Declaring those words 'I love you' or having another authority pronounce that you are joined to another does not create a union. We can easily deceive ourselves into believing we have found love and the pronouncements of others mean nothing.

"Fidelity, love, sharing—all these things that we swear to upon entering into a marriage are commitments that are already settled matters for those within a *true union*. A true union does not need vows to keep the two hearts in the relationship faithful to one another. A true union does not need to stipulate that they will be there for one another throughout all difficulty and unto death—such things are already granted.

"A *marriage* does not designate a *union*. A marriage is a legal partnership—a business partnership—not a bonding of hearts. A marriage can be performed by a minister of the law or of a certain faith, to any couple who applies, with no prerequisite that the two entering into the marriage know beyond a doubt that they are meant to be with each other or for that matter genuinely care for one another. Thus a marriage does not necessarily constitute a union; for a union is a joining that is carried out by Love itself, in a time before we were even born.

"Our union is made during our creation. When one soul is created within the Great Womb it is but one part of the whole; for one soul is actually composed of two Beings—each Being needing another half to complete them—one who we would call our union...our one love.

"Some call such a belief as this—two souls completing one another—a romantic notion; nonetheless, beneath the sentimentalized version of 'soulmates' lies the reality of two Beings sharing one soul.

"Some do not like the idea of their life's course being fated nor their love predestined—they reject such notions. Yet underneath such displays of fear and disbelief, even the critics want to believe they can have such a love as the one in which I speak.

"In entering into our life with the one we shall love already predestined, part of our freedom has not been taken from us," he explained. "Rather, our happiness and companionship in this life has been ensured.

"Over the centuries the sacred bond we have with our union has decayed into marriage, just as love has decayed into infatuation. As I said, a new reality with a belief in love removed, was formed and set in place. Marriage—a joining without the prerequisite of love—replaced union. When married, two people are joined in the eyes of the law yet whether there is a physical union of hearts already present may not be known and it is not required. The ceremony does not create the union between hearts; either the union was there before the ceremony or it never will be made."

Unable to keep quiet, Ari interjected, "You have a wife, do you not?" he asked bluntly, out of a desire to make a point.

The nameless man did not contradict.

"And you would have us believe that you did her the dishonor of never marrying her before the eyes of God?"

"Abiding by the laws of the land and the laws of the religion under which I was raised, I did 'marry' my wife but it was not the ceremony that bound us; we were already as one soul long before the ceremony, made so by the love that passed between us, not any vows taken. Had circumstances been different—had the ways of society not required the ceremony before the union was recognized—I would have seen no dishonor to my wife in forgoing the ceremony and neither would she; for I honored her in loving her and respecting her. Such sentiments are declared within a marriage—it is written into the script of the ceremony yet how often are these commitments met? A marriage will not hold us to good behavior, only our love for the one we are with will do so; thus the commonplace infidelity between couples seen throughout history.

"Within the old world when two people found their union there was indeed a wedding party to celebrate the love felt but there was no joining ceremony—no vows, no marriage license or other nonsense. There was simply the family— the community—celebrating the love between the two hearts. While in contrast, in this age, people feel free to move in and out of their marriages, knowing deep down that the ceremony means nothing if the love is not already present.

"Ari, you would declare that it dishonors a woman when a man wants to spend his life with her but does not marry her," the man said. Then posing the question, "Is it not a greater dishonor to enter into a marriage and declare the love to be lasting when deep down you are aware that it will not be?"

Waiting a moment for a response that did not come, the man continued, "Pretending that marriage equates union is the true dishonor.

"When we enter into a marriage, many of us delude ourselves into thinking that the one we are with is our one union. We deceive ourselves into thinking that we are 'in love,' maintaining our relationship through lies. And then on that inevitable day when the marriage ends, we tell ourselves that love is painful and temporary by nature; what's more, we begin to lose our belief that a real union of hearts even exists. When in actuality it was the illusion of a connection that we willfully took unto ourselves that was painful and temporary, not love. We wove the lie and then forgot we did so.

"When such things as this happen to us or happen between those around us—when we see marriages end or suffer the end of our own marriage—our belief in love is diminished, when in fact the bond between such peoples never should have been called 'love' at all. A madness of desperation, loneliness and lust has permeated humanity. Gripped by these feelings we are all eager to declare that we have found the one we are meant to be with, even when we know deep within ourselves that our union is not to be had with this person. By deluding ourselves into thinking we are loved or feel love for another, when in fact we do not, we belittle what love is and begin to believe that love is something that it is not.

"The rarity of our union—the fact that we have this bond with only one other within our entire existence, is what makes that one other person sacred to us. And yes, it can at the same time cause us distress when we do not believe that we will ever find the one other person we are meant to be with, among the billions of people now upon this Earth. But as I said in the beginning, our union was made before we were even born, it is not a matter of chance—the bond is destined, as is your meeting. Running along your parallel paths, your lives will converge. Until that day it is simply a matter of believing in love so you have the strength to wait for what is genuine.

"There was a poem written by those within my family, which I can recall from memory, that shows the emotions behind finding our union and what that means to our life."

The man's tone shifted, from a defensive one to that of prayer; as if he were recalling a psalm from his memory.

He began:

I breathe
but my heart shall not beat
until the arrival of you.

I shall dream
but only you can fulfill.
I shall call
but only you shall hear.

Only you shall know me
deeper than I know myself.

Only you can hear what I say,
that goes unsaid.

Only you hold all
that my heart needs.

Half of me was born within you—
we each were born to make the other whole.

I shall live,
but it is you
who will understand my life.

I shall act,
but only you can show me
the meaning in what I do.

I have a great depth inside me,
but only you can see it and cause it to rise.

My heart was made to gather what you give.
I live, but my heart beats within you.

I walk through this life,
but only you give me a bearing and a path.

I reach for the depths of love,
yet only you can help me touch them.

The life I was given is the love we have.
The world I live in is you.

My heart needs what only you can provide.
At night I try to rest,
but only you can give me
the peace I long for.

From across the distance I call you.
And through all obstacles
we come for one another.

I cannot die as long as you live.
My strength lies in you.
My reason, my hope and my belief—
all lie in you.

What we are together is who I am;
for we are united
and union is not a word
it is a state of being.

CHAPTER XII

The Divine

THERE WAS A MOMENT AFTER HE WAS FINISHED, during which all those listening let his words seep into them.

Samuel and Maria appeared deeply moved, looking as though they cherished each verse. The students were hesitant to react one way or the other. Ira and Aden returned from their outing, coming back to their father's side just in time for the review.

"Again with poetics," Ari said in a mock-exasperated voice. "You claim you know of love. You claim, in essence, that love is your God yet you cannot tell us clearly of love. You know evil so intimately," Ari stressed, as if caressing the word, once again trying to touch on any insecurities the man might have. "...so very intimately. And yet, you seem to know little of the goodness in this world. This leads me to question what kind of man you are, that you should be so preoccupied with the wicked that you do not know the slightest concerning virtue."

Slightly exasperated, the man answered. He tried to hold his voice steady, "You accuse me of ignorance concerning the divine. But who among us is not ignorant of the divine. You," the man said looking to Gideon, "tell me of your God. Tell me what he looks like. Tell me his history. Explain to me his reasoning—why he chooses not to act in times of crisis though he is capable."

Gideon looked overwhelmed. "I...a," he stammered. He had no answer.

The man turned back to Ari, "We are all ignorant of that which is boundless. What you do not take into account is the nature of that which I am trying to explain. When you speak of your idea of God do you not speak vaguely? Do you not find yourself unable to give specifics about a force beyond your full comprehension due to its vastness? It is the same when I speak to you of love.

"You discourage my use of verse but what is scripture if not verse? Be it Christian, Islamic, Judaic, Hindu or Buddhist. When attempting to describe a thing of infinite ability and beauty, somehow it is only right to speak in poetics. In giving you poems concerning love I am not being vague, I am simply describing love without limiting it.

"Evil can be seen, understood and laid out point for point, because evil is not infinite. It is what it is. And, while the greed, perversion and viciousness of those who choose evil is seemingly without end, evil's potential is not boundless, as love is. Thus, I need not poetics to describe evil, I can speak clearly of what I have come to realize about it," the man finished. Ari had nothing more to say. There was a period of awkward silence.

"Ari's question made me consider something," Asa spoke up. "Where is God in your beliefs? You say love is your God yet you told us the story of the first father and alluded to the fact that the myth of God was formed around him. Do you then propose that he—that first father—is God?"

"No," the man said slowly. Knowing he was once again going to have to explain something that was quite difficult to put into words. "It has long been known that all humans share a common ancestor—one father and one mother from who we all descend. The father I speak of was the *first* father—the first man. This first man was—is, more than simply a blood-relation to the generations to follow him; he is the father to all of us as well as the first heart to come to know the depths of love.

"He and his wife—the first mother—explored the workings and power of love. It was they who founded the old world that once flourished. The world based upon a belief in love was begun in their home and was expanded by the children their union brought forth. Over time there has been much myth built up about this exceptionally wise man but he is not a God; in fact the idea of a God that has been taught throughout the ages does not exist but for within man's mind."

"Blasphemy!" Aden hissed threateningly.

The man persisted. "The idea of God," he began stubbornly pressing on into this dangerous territory, "is a creation of mankind. The *character* of this all-powerful being is likewise, a creation of mankind.

"The God worshiped by many within this city and throughout the world is a judgmental one—vengeful, arrogant even. This divine being is painted as elusive and semi-indifferent to mankind's struggles—unfeeling even. He is portrayed as vain or even jealous—said to be one who loves mankind but who will spite those who do not worship him. This God we would worship, seems to possess all of mankind's faults, the difference being it is a sin for mankind to act in arrogance—to judge others and carrying out vengeance; while God has free reign to act in such a manner because it is said to be his place.

"Quite simply, God is not portrayed as a loving being. The God you would believe in does not act as an enlightened being—he does not act as a loving being. He acts as man would act, if he were free to reign."

"If God is a creation of mankind, then what of this?" Elijah said, holding up a leather bound copy of scripture; putting up proof that God is indeed more than the creation of man.

The man took the book. He looked at it. He had read it many times—he had once known it nearly word for word. When he was a child he believed that all the truth known of the divine was contained here within. But then, when he grew older, with each reading of it the feeling of excitement faded and the faith he had in the divine wisdom of the verse receded. Now, a lifetime later, after reading it with new eyes and after seeing the sea of blood brought about in its name, he had awoken to the realization that the book, like the persona of God, was a creation of man.

Despite how he now saw the book at present, the man could still recall how others saw it—how these eager young students would see it. He did not want to be the one to disillusion them but he also could not pretend to regard the book as the teachings of the divine. The man could sense this talk was going into an ever-more dangerous place. He would need to take great care in explaining his points—walking the balance of telling the truth without giving offence.

The man could sense the coming objections from Ari and his sons before they were even spoken; he felt them pacing like lions, ready to pounce on him when he spoke. "Works of many well-intended men are included in this book," he began, still holding the book in his hands. "There is much beautiful prose in these pages. However," he said, bracing for the inevitable backlash, "I do not believe this text to be a transcribed divine revelation. Having explored this text thoroughly, I believe it was written by mankind; what's more, it was written by mankind several generations ago and despairingly, has not been progressed since."

"It is the word of God and I will not listen to you insult it," Ari pronounced fanatically.

"I have no wish to debate your religion with you," the man replied. "I was asked to speak of what I believe and so I have my view. I have no intention to reexamine what it is you each believe."

It was clear that this would not do; the man was not going to be allowed to drop the point so easily. Realizing this, he proceeded to defend his pronounced conclusion, "I will say this," the man placed his hand upon the book and recalled from memory those passages that so accurately highlighted his point, "much of this book was written by those who looked down upon all but certain creeds, genders and races. I do not believe this is divinely inspired because I do not believe many of the thoughts in this book are those a divine being would have.

"In this book it is said that, if a woman is *accused* of being unchaste she may be taken out and stoned to death by all the men of the village. In this book," he said, laying a hand gently atop the cover—the skin of his palm sweaty against the faux leather, "it is stated that young women may be taken as spoils of war—that they may be taken as 'wives' by those who captured them and that if in time they do not please they may be turned out of the house and the divorce will not be a sin upon the man. In this book, it is stated that if a woman is raped then she and the attacker shall *both* be stoned to death. Or in some instances the raped woman must marry her attacker.

"Now, is it a divine being that would hold such prejudicial views of women or is it not man?

"In this book, there is little if any objection to slavery, even though possessing any living being is an immoral act. 'Slaves should be submissive to their masters in everything, and are to be well-pleasing and not talk back.' Tell me," he said, slightly indignant, "is this the will of a divine being or the desire of every slave owner?

"Even the beating of slaves is condoned. It is stated, in this text that the master should not beat the slave so severely that he or she die instantly; though later it is added that if the slave is wounded so badly that he or she succumbs to death within a few days of the beating, then there is no blame upon the slave owner.

"This book that proclaims the enlightened wisdom of 'an eye for an eye,' which only serves to perpetuate the unending cycle of inflictor and victim. Could a divine being reach such an ignorant conclusion? Would a god have no greater wisdom than spite for spite? No," he said, answering his own question. "Only mankind is so shortsighted."

The man took a breath. Clearly troubled by the conversation, he was reacting as though the name of someone beloved to him was being smeared. Gathering himself, the man pushed past his frustrations. "This book," he began slowly and gently, "has much wonderful prose within it. There are writings contained within that give hope and fortify belief in times of crisis. I have no doubt that many a wise man's words were folded into these pages. To dismiss the entire book outright is to prejudicially discard the insights of the genuine seekers who were included. I do not claim this entire book to be wrong, rather I simply believe that the work is not that of a divine being but of mankind. When I read this book I hear voices from both evil's movement of love's as it reveals both our dark desires of domination as well as our yearning to care and inspire.

"You might disagree with my interpretation of the text," he said in response to the ill looks he received. "I do not tell you what to think. I tell you only what I think, and my conclusion is that these are not the teachings of the divine being I have come to know—these are not the words of a loving being. The thoughts contained herein are the thoughts of man, veiled as the pronouncements of the divine. And whether this was done so out of ignorance, arrogance or a desire to sanctify what mankind wanted at the time by calling it the 'will of God' instead of their own will—a ploy carried out repeatedly over the ages—I do not know.

"In the beginning of this conversation I was asked who and what my God is and I stated that the character of the all-powerful being is one that has been made by man. This book," he stated as he handed the book back to Elijah with care, "is a book that reflects the thoughts and desires of the God you would believe in. But tell me, could an enlightened, divine being find no greater truths and solutions than those I have just stated?

"The divine does exist," he said consolingly. "There are those things that are sacred upon this Earth. And there is an all-powerful force. I am not an atheist. I do not reject the idea of an all-powerful being; I simply reject the characterization of that being as portrayed by those modern religions so predominant in this age. The divine is out there to be learned of but first one must be open to learning that the divine is something other than that which it has been called within that book and other texts like it. To gain knowledge of the divine one must leave behind all religion."

As he spoke the man saw fear in the eyes of the students and even in the eyes of Samuel and Maria, who were so open-minded. "It is frightening to contradict millennia of tradition, especially when it is said that if you do not believe in this doctrine you will face damnation. It is so absurd to think of God as a loving being, when he is portrayed as one who will punish you if you do not worship him—who will spite you if you do not adore him above all others. That is such a contradiction. The divine does not act this way. Loving beings do not act this way. Only evil acts this way. It is only those who would possess you rather than love you. Only they declare 'love me first and most above all others.'"

"But...." Elijah made to start. He was interrupted by the man, not violently but reasonably.

"No," the man said gently. "You asked me my view and I gave it. That is all I will say on the matter. I will not debate what it is you believe. I will simply tell you what it is I know, and in the end you can think as you wish." Many were not willing to let the issue be left there.

"I know you don't wish to discuss this further but I am not finished," Gideon said in a hostile voice. "You reject scripture and give only vague sources for the odd views you hold. If you are going to berate this book, which has been held as sacred by hundreds of generations, you should at least explain your reasoning better than you have."

"As I said before, we each can explore love—the divine. I did not dismiss the doctrines of religion easily. It was a slow progression towards the belief I hold now. As for how I came to believe what I do, I asked for truth and this is what I came to see.

"The names of those who taught me have been lost or forgotten. Each and everyone one of us have a connection to that wisdom held within the consciousness of love. We all have a connection to the collected wisdom and memory gathered over the course of history. It is through this connection that the knowledge of love has been perpetuated, regardless of the fact that the histories of the old world and its ways were erased and those who know the truth, suppressed.

"I gathered the understanding I have now through a variety of ways; the truths I have told you over these last days are not things that I learned alone. My family and I have been reaching out for answers for a very long time. We gathered our knowledge of evil through experience; while we gathered our knowledge of love through contemplation, sharing thoughts with each other and finally through the connection of which I have been speaking.

"Finding those who know the old ways has become difficult. Lacking a teacher within our community, we must turn to others who know the workings of that which we wish to understand. The information we seek is an ancient truth and so we turn to ancient sources. When we lack a teacher in our community we must turn to the teachers that dwell *elsewhere*—within that world which is a part of the Earth yet separate…the Other Shore. That world where the ancient still flourishes and the lost knowledge still lives in the memory of those who dwell there. I speak of those who are our ancestors, not in the sense of those who are a part of your direct bloodline, rather those who preceded us who we are kindred to and will remain ever-connected to. Through the direct connection we have with those who came before we can learn the knowledge that has been lost if we are willing to reach out, believe in what we receive and heed our heart above all else.

"Those who understand the truths that we now seek to learn of are out there, all we need do is seek them…all we need do is call for them. When we have searched among the people around us yet not found the guidance we need, we must widen our search," the man began to build a momentum; his voice was strong and had a sense of urgency. "…At times, those who hold the knowledge we need cannot be met by extending our hand but by extending our heart. We cannot meet them by leaving our homes and going out in the social places of our community but rather we must partly leave the place where our body resides and go within.

179

"We must leave behind the modern world that tells us such things are impossible. We must enter that in-between. We must commune, we must listen and we must believe in the connection. We must heed the inaudible whispers that reverberate through the unseen, across the distance to resound in our heart. We must open ourselves wide and absorb what we are imparted by love and by those who can still remember the old ways. We must set aside the logic we were taught by those who did not understand the workings of the unseen half of our world and who did not believe in a force that can bind us all.

"Part of the heart's ability is that of serving as a conduit—a connection. And we must take in the information that flows through our heart and awakens in the fiber of our Being. We must trust in the realness of what we experience within the unseen and use our connection to Love and to those who came before to learn all that we were never taught.

"We must recognize the realness of what takes place within and know that even something that takes place solely within us does, in every sense, actually take place. That which takes place in the world that lies within us is just as real as what takes place in the physically seen part of the world, if not more so; for something that takes place within has the potential to affect us on a deeper level than anything else.

"I learned the truths I know from my family as well as from those who were there in the beginning and endure on still, holding within them the lost knowledge of love's ways...."

Suddenly, the man's voice was drowned out. An explosion in the distance sharply cut across his serene reflection. The group scattered, hugging tight to the walls. The building

shook as if the bomb had detonated under its very foundation. Dust fell like fine snow on the ducking heads of all those
in the room. There was a surreal noise—a clash, the ringing
echo of a blast, screams and the thunder of falling rubble.

"There!" a voice shouted as the din started to fade. Looking up, blinded by the plaster dust, the man saw the outline
of Ari, Aden and Ira standing at the gaping window pointing
to the cloud of smoke issuing a block away.

"Enough of this nonsense!" Ari declared decisively. "We
must go find news...see where the lines have been drawn. We
are cowards to just sit here." Ari made to lead his sons down-
stairs. Aden and Ira eagerly leapt to his side yet Uri who sat
on the floor comforting his mother was not so quick to move.

"Come on Uri!" Ira said bullishly.

"He won't come," Aden said in a dismissing tone; regarding
his brother as a lost cause.

"Come on boys!" Ari commanded with a zealous seriousness. "Leave him." Aden and Ira turned, making their way
down the stairs behind their father; while Uri sat on the floor
defeated, looking ashamed as he wearily helped his mother to
her feet.

"We should leave the city," Yoseph declared, coughing as
he exhaled the plaster dust. He reached for his father who was
still sitting on the floor, reeling from the unexpected blast.

Their sweaty skin had been covered in the fine gray powder
that shook loose from the ceiling. Clearing his eyes, the man
looked into his son's face to see that his young son's hair had
been prematurely grayed by the same falling powder.

"No," Samuel said; staggering as he helped Maria to
her feet amid the chaos. "It is still not safe. We must hold

up here until the threat passes. The countryside will still be too dangerous."

"I think we should leave," Yoseph said bluntly; making his decision based entirely upon the fear bulging in his panicked heart.

"Just give me a moment," the man said in a pleading tone. He was still sitting on the gritty floor, trying to orient himself. He too felt the desire to leave the city but did not want to make a foolish mistake.

Though the bomb had not hit the building, it had felt dangerously close. The explosion had not hurt anyone physically but it had struck them all emotionally. For the man, the attack had hit on wounds that were already sensitive. He could take no more unexpected attacks.

Fighting the sense of unraveling, he sat, his back against the wall, trying to think of the best course of action. The tremors of the blast had rippled from the epicenter in the present all the way back into his violent past and all that had occurred on these very grounds a lifetime ago.

Would the attacks ever end? Would the scars ever heal? Would he always be the trembling traumatized animal cowering at any raised hand and jumping at every loud noise? Every fiber of his Being wanted to say, "We are leaving." But his heart knew, it was not yet time. The visit to this place had not yet served its purpose.

CHAPTER XIII

The Orphans

THEY ALL SAT QUIETLY FOR HOURS, too consumed in their own fears to converse with each other. The students along with Uri had left, following their curiosity out onto the dangerous streets after Ari.

Looking up from his own anxiety, the man saw that Maria looked burdened as she sat next to her husband.

"We will be fine," the man assured her consolingly. "The bombing was a ways from here. Things seem to be quieting down."

"I know," she replied in a voice that feigned strength. "It is not the bombings," she added, holding back tears. "My family lives in the city. I grew up here. This is where Samuel and I met. As strange as it sounds we've grown accustom to the daily attacks."

"If your family lives here, why don't you take refuge at their home?" Yoseph asked. "Why stay here?"

She looked pained by his question. Obviously she had been asking herself the same thing though, in a much harsher, self-judgmental manner. "I know I should have gone to them. We have not been back here in some time. We actually came back here at my mother's request," she continued in a resigned tone of voice. "Then the news came of the attacks and, I don't know.... We met you both and staying here just felt right," she finished, feeling guilty. "To be honest," she confessed slowly, "we have been dreading coming back. I don't have happy memories of my home here. Neither does Samuel." She laid her hand on his leg and gave him a weak smile. "We were coming back here because we had to; not because we desired to. After we were married we fought hard for our independence from my family. They were quite controlling. After a drawn out emotional battle with them, we moved away and have not returned since. It would seem we could not get far enough away," she added in a heavy tone.

"Forgive my bluntness but, something tells me your mother is not asking you to return because she misses you," the man said.

"How can you miss someone you never cared for?" Maria replied, her heart buckling under the weight of the sad reality. "My father has recently become ill and my mother wants us to move back. My parents, who could not have bothered with me when I was a child, now need me."

"They need *someone*," Samuel added, knowing the situation well. "Maria has always been the most caring of all the children. Her brothers and sisters are like her parents—too consumed in seeing to their own needs to worry about others. Up until now, Maria has always been teased for her good heart, as though it was her character flaw. Only now, when they need a nursemaid, do they see her caring as a virtue...or should I say an asset"

Maria said nothing to this; she knew Samuel was right. She sat there looking lost, then confided, "Today was the day we were meant to arrive. The family will be expecting us. This entire time I have been here I have felt the dread growing. I feel so torn."

"You don't want to return," the man said, "that is what your heart is telling you. But you feel obligated to do so. You feel guilty for not wanting to return. You fear that you are turning your back on your family."

By the way Samuel was nodding the man knew he had summarized the situation perfectly.

"Yes," Maria breathed. She wondered how he understood her plight so well.

"If she goes back it will be the end of her," Samuel said flatly. "They have always drained the life from her—beating her down, taking her self-worth, putting fear into her, making her beg for what they should have freely given. No," he said looking at her, "I do not care what obligations you feel you have. We should not go back."

The man listened to the couple's conversation, knowing it was one they had had several times over these last weeks. When at last Samuel was finished, the man spoke up, "I know your story good woman. Many of those who ultimately joined my family first lived the life you have."

"I would never have thought as much," she replied. "I have always gotten the impression that your family is very happy. In fact, that was what I was thinking of just before you spoke to me." The man looked at her questioningly, unsure of what she was referring to, having discussed a great many things. "When you spoke of your family's search for truths," she clarified, "it made me think how nice it would be to be a part of a group such as yours—part of a loving circle, reaching out together, learning together, encouraging one another.

"I know you have not said much about your family; all the same, I have this picture in my mind of what you all must be like and it is so different than that of my family. Not my husband of course," she added quickly, not wanting to be misunderstood. "Rather, my parents, brothers and sisters and even Samuel's family who, while different from my own, has been hurtful in their own way."

Upon hearing this, Samuel made no argument.

"My family is very close," the man replied gently. "But we came together in a different way—different than what you might think. We did not all start off together rather, we came together. In fact, there are a number of people within my own family who share your past." After thinking to himself for a moment the man proceeded, "Perhaps there is something else I should tell you before I go into my family's past. It has to do with what family is.

"You see, just as union has been belittled to equal only a legal bonding, so too the ties of family have been belittled— boiled down to the presence of a blood-relation; removing love from the equation.

"In the time before evil came into being, when a child was born unto their father and mother there was no doubt that the bond of family was genuine. Now however, everything has changed. Now a child can be born unto a man and a woman who are *not* that child's parents. As odd as it may sound to you, a child can be born to a woman who is not its mother and be put into the arms of a man who is not its father."

"I do not understand," Maria said. "If a woman bears a child she is that child's mother. If a man creates a child he is that child's father. How can it be any other way?"

"No, not always…not now," the man replied. "Forming a bond between parent and child is not a matter of *conception*; the genetics do *not* hold the bond. Shared blood does not create a bond. Parentage is decided solely upon the presence of love.

"Only those who do not believe in love, would disregard love as the defining element of family. In the old world it was different. *Love* created the bonds between people, shared blood was just a by-product of the creation of the physical body. But in a place that is devoid of love—that was founded upon an abandoning of a belief in love—a new method of denoting bonds had to be conceived of and it was the concept of shared blood that was fallen back upon.

"This idea of shared blood denoting a family bond is as absurd as thinking a priest pronouncing two people as married can forge a real union between them. The coursing blood does not bring love to the heart. The emotional bonds that create a family are not encoded within our DNA." The man paused; he still did not see comprehension in Maria's eyes, this was not surprising. It takes more than a few words to change a lifetime's way of thinking. Samuel likewise, was reaching to understand this idea.

He continued, "Blood can reveal shared genetics but nothing more; our blood does not dictate who we shall love or who shall love us, as such blood does not dictate who we have bonds with. Bonds are created from the presence of love. The depth of the bond is defined by the depth of the love felt. Family cannot be defined by the vein. It must be defined instead by the unseen substance that flows from the heart. We must define our family, not by who we share blood with, but by who we share love with."

"You would say then that a man and a woman who give birth to a child are not necessarily the parents of the child?" Maria said, recapping.

"A woman carrying a child in her womb and giving birth to the child does not make a woman a mother. I know this is a different way of thinking," the man said, understanding the difficultly they were having. "But in the end, my point is a simple one. The question is, what denotes parentage. I would ask you this: What is it to be a mother? Is the one and only prerequisite for becoming a child's mother the act of giving birth? Or is the woman not required to *love* the child she bears in order to be known as that child's mother? Is love secondary to genetics? Or are genetics secondary to love?

"A woman gives birth to a child, though, instead of nurturing the child she stifles it; instead of caring for the child she neglects it; instead of protecting the child she attacks it; instead of being that child's source of life she becomes a threat upon it—a drain and a plague.

"However, in time, as this child grows it meets another woman who does the opposite—who is loving, nurturing and cares unconditionally.

"Now, which woman is the child's mother? Which of the two women has fulfilled what it is to be a mother? Is it the first woman, whose only motherly act was that of giving birth, before in essence, abandoning the child? Or is it the second woman who, while having not given birth to the child, did help bring that child to life? What is it to be a mother? Is it a title that all women who have bore a child can adopt? Or is it not a bond made by the presence of love?

"If who our family is, is a matter of blood alone then the woman who tries to suppress her child, can be called the child's mother; for her's was the womb that brought the child forth—the two have shared blood and that is the only factor that is taken into consideration. Whereas the woman who would have loved and cared for the child could not be called the child's mother; for her blood is not the same as what runs through the child's veins. Do you begin to see the absurdity?" the man commented, at a loss as to how such a backward notion could be so widely accepted.

"If the title of mother and father solely belongs to those who share blood and is not determined by the presence of love, then the man who beats his child would have the same right to be called a father as the man who protects and provides honorably for his child.

"Is it not a contradiction to call a woman or man who hates their child, the mother and father of that child? Must one not embody what it is to be a mother or to be a father before they are allowed to be called such. Or is love not required and even the meanest, embittered, hurtful person, whose very presence is toxic to a child, can be given the sacred title of mother and father?

"Only in a world where love is not central would family be determined in such a cold way."

"I do not have a loving relationship with my family," Samuel shared. "They have not been as aggressive as Maria's family—they never slapped me down or sought to control me. They never hurt me per se but they also never gave me anything..." he stopped short.

Maria picked up his thought, "Not everyone has a loving mother and father. But what can be done about it? Regardless of it all, they are our family. Aren't they?" She asked.

"Abuse is not always what people do to us but what they don't do—the love that is withheld and the closeness that is never experienced hurts just as deep as the strike of the hand. Whether or not you meant to Maria, you just now summed up the belief that is instilled in us—the backward belief that makes those in abusive, loveless relationships resign themselves to stay in them forever.

"An unloving mother or unloving father is a contradiction in terms. We are led to believe that blood alone defines family, that when shared genetics are present, familial bonds are inalterable. Nevertheless, we all know deep within ourselves that a mother and father are meant to be loving and nurturing. This is why it hurts us so badly when they are the opposite. Blood determines *nothing*. When a person who has bore a child does not live up to what it is to be a parent they have lost their right of parentage.

"Define what it is to be a father? The father is the protector and the provider, he is the gentle strength, the steadiness—he is the guide. Define what is it to be a mother? The mother is the nurturer; she is the living womb—others develop and flourish under her care.

"Birth of a child and love of that child once went hand-in-hand. In the old world when a man and woman gave birth to a child they were the undisputed parents of that child; for in the old world, not loving your child was inconceivable. Here however, in the time since evil rose, things are different.

"Here children are born as a consequence of lust and loneliness; they are born as a mistake or miscalculation—outrageous terms to apply to one's child. And it is because a child can now be born unto loveless people, that a child can be born into the arms of those who are not their parents."

"I have never felt close to my parents," Maria confessed. "There were never, I love you's or I miss you's we have been together out of obligation and blood. I knew this was wrong—that things should be different in a family. But I simply thought, I did not have a loving family. Now I see the contradiction in those terms...that love equals family and where there is no love, there is no family.

"I don't know if I could simply leave them," Maria said, still struggling with guilt. "Regardless of what they have done it seems wrong to abandon them. I mean, even with all that they have done wrong, how can I break apart our family?" she asked, feeling as though she were going against the natural way of things.

"I feel the same way," Samuel reasoned. "My family was not loving but we also were never left to want. I would feel guilty to leave. I would be afraid to stand up to my parents regardless of how deeply they have hurt me."

"Fear and guilt—these are not things that bind a family.

"You say your family never hurt you but what you mean is that they never struck you. Because, in the end, if they did not give you love they did hurt you. It is a passive abuse, but depriving another of what they need to flourish, be it food or love or shelter, is abuse.

"I will not push you, I would simply suggest that you look at your relationship with those you call family and tell me if you do not believe family is meant to be more than what you have with them."

"In the past, I have thought that, perhaps I could talk with them? Point out what our relationship has been lacking and they would change," Samuel said, knowing he was deceiving himself. Maria said nothing to this; for she too knew it to be a desperate attempt to avoid a painful truth.

"I have found that those who love us—love us. And those who don't, do not," the man replied in a regrettable manner. He wished he could have simply agreed with Samuel's idea but he couldn't. "If you spoke up change might come but it would be only superficial and most-likely only temporary; for nothing has changed in their heart."

Samuel picked up Maria's hand, holding it tightly in his own. He knew the man was right. All their lives Samuel and Maria had known the truth, the man simply confirmed it.

"...you know what you each have with one another," the man reasoned in a heartfelt voice, trying to ease their heartache. "You know what your bond means to you both.... Don't you want that same depth of love from those you would call your parents?

"In the end," he said, "I know your story. You don't have to tell me all that you have been through for me to know the situation. The point to my sharing these truths with you was to free you from your misplaced obligations.

"You each must choose what you will do."

"If we were born to parents who never loved us," Maria asked in a sad voice, "does that mean, we will never have a family?"

"No," the man said in a consoling voice of imparted hope, "not at all."

CHAPTER XIV

The Fate

THE MAN, YOSEPH, MARIA AND SAMUEL SAT OFF to themselves absorbed in their conversation throughout the day. Time and again they were reminded of the violent events that had brought them together, as the eruption of automatic gunfire came in spurts from the direction of the Bank, carried on the wind into the room where they sat.

As the day progressed there finally came a point when Samuel and Maria could no longer speak of their family matters; they were too distracted by the sounds of war. The calm their small group had nurtured all day was all together brought to an end when, one by one the familiar faces trickled in, returning with accounts of the grizzly traumas suffered at the blast site and speculations concerning where the next attack might be.

Much to Ari's delight, the students were now gathered around him. After following him around the city all afternoon, the students had apparently come to look on him as a mentor.

As after any terrorist attack, there was a surge of patriotism. Zealots on the side that struck the blow felt a swell of unity; while the victims rallied in the wake of the devastation, clinging even tighter to the viewpoints being fought than they did the day before.

From what the man could tell, Ari's allegiance had been with the victims. The old man sat in front of the group of captivated students fervently regaling them with tales from his own military past. From his place across the room the man was slightly out of ear shot but he did hear snippets of the shouted manifesto. "We all must make sacrifices to combat the evils of this world!" and "It is God's will that we should thrive in this place!" were among the declarations that were overheard.

God's will, the man mused hopelessly. *During every war ever suffered the Gods have been invoked. Where did the allegiance of the ancient one actually lie?* he thought to himself. The answer rose in his mind, *On the side of those protecting what is genuinely sacred—first and foremost, their innocence.*

The man did not hold the political preference of Ari but in the end the titles did not matter. The story was, at its root, the same no matter the difference of rhetoric. It was the same power-play that had been looping for millennia. The names of the sides changed but the intentions of the leaders and the methods by which they carried out their agenda were the same.

The man rose.

"What, you do not want to hear the news of the day?" Samuel asked in a slightly wearied tone.

"I already know the story," the man replied solemnly. "I heard it a long time ago." He motion for everyone to follow him as he retreated to Yoseph and he's isolated corner.

From there they stared wordlessly at the spectacle. The four of them sat transfixed by the commanding hand motions Ari displayed as he spoke to the onlooking young men. Strangely enough, Uri was sitting by his father's side. Every now and again, in the middle of his declaration, Ari would lay a hand of pride upon his son, making motions that insinuated that his son should be pointed out as an example. Uri, finally happy to be of consequence to the man he wanted to be loved by, sat smiling yet held a slightly worn look about his eyes, hinting at what the cost of this paternal acceptance had been.

"Does it bother you?" Maria inquired. She was talking to the man but her eyes remained on Ari. There was a crease in her forehead, right between her eye-brows; she gave a look that was both confused and pitying.

The man turned to her, unsure as to what she meant.

She turned to face him. "The fact that, after days of explaining what it is you believe, they seem to have lost interest. What I mean to say," she clarified, "is that, the students asked you to speak—they practically forced you to. And now, after all the effort you have given, they have lost interest so easily. I would be hurt...frustrated."

The man gave a little smile that seemed more a twinge of pain.

"I am sorry," Maria said, fearing she had been insensitive.

"It's alright," the man reassured her. "I knew when I began that this would most likely be the outcome. In the beginning, when I first began speaking as a young man, it hurt a great deal when all that I shared was disregarded. It is a sacred act—passing on the truths we have gathered. These thoughts I share come to me in intimate moments or through arduous experience.

"It does hurt of course. It would be a lie to say otherwise. As expected as it is, indifference always hurts. But," he said resolutely, "I had decided days ago when, we began, that this time I would speak for myself alone. I have all but lost my hope of reaching others. For them," he said motioning to the students who were now listening to Ari's violent rhetoric, "it was an exercise in debate. Like a lecture they would attend in a classroom. They explored my thoughts in theory with little intention of applying them in life.

"Inwardly they sensed that the truths I spoke, if believed, would present a hard path. They chose instead to turn to an easier perspective."

"We did not see these last days as an exercise in debate," Samuel said, pulling his eyes away from Ari's display. He sunk into his own reflection for a moment as he searched for the words. "Every night when we are done talking, Maria and I sit to ourselves and discuss the meaning of it all. We feel our view of the world changing with each reflection you share.

"Earlier today we came to the conclusion that our perspective has now changed so much that we do not even know where to go from here. Especially after the talk we had concerning family. There is no going back to our old life.

We cannot go live with her parents, no matter the guilt we feel compelling us to do so. There is no viewing the world differently than how you have taught us to. So tell us," Samuel continued solemnly, "what happens now? Where do we go? How do we live? You have awoken us to many truths but how do we live with what we know? Are we simply to be outcasts—different from all others here?" He paused for a moment as the breadth of his questions widened from his life and his fate—to the fate of all those like him. "You tell us of the evil that surrounds and the plight of those who are loving, so what is to become of us? What becomes of the loving? Are we condemned to be the prey of the deceitful ones in the world? And if so, what kind of life can a loving heart have while surrounded by the hurtful? What is the fate of those who are not evil but who live in a world driven by them?" he finished, unable to hide the imperative nature of his plea.

With a heavy sigh the man replied, "Was it unfair of me to wake you into such a life? Perhaps. Years ago I asked all the questions that you do now—all those in my family have. And for many years no answers came.

"A very real hopelessness is fought. There was a time when we all felt that, no matter where we went, we would never be rid of the plague that is evil. Persecuted, we left this country and moved across the seas. As foolish as it is, we thought that, if we moved from this land where we had endured so much betrayal, we might be able to find a place where deceit did not exist. Of course, we found we could not travel far enough to ever escape the evil. No matter how many times we moved away from those who pained us and began a new life, we would eventually relive the same unending cycle;

encountering a new presence eager to destroy all we had worked to rebuild.

"Surviving under such circumstances for decades, we felt little hope for our future happiness or that of our children's. But then, years after sending out these questions unto the Fates, one afternoon, a man and woman came to our home, bringing with them new hope. This man and woman were different than any other people we had ever known. They possessed knowledge lost to most people in this age. One night while sitting with them I asked, what the fate of love would be—I asked if there was a way to bring the struggle with evil to an end. ...I asked them how this all began and how this would all end.

"They sat with us, just as I sit with you now. They poured out all they knew to us, just as I pour out all that I know to you.

"Having always been one for transcribing the most important realizations to come over the years, I chose to write down the account the couple gave unto my family in a journal I keep for us. I will share that entry with you tonight. I would have shared it sooner but you would not have understood. It is a simple story but you needed the background knowledge that you now have after these last days of our talking."

From within the depths of his personal bag the man withdrew a great bound book. The stiff spine cracked along the hinge of the leather joint as he opened it. He turned through the thick pages that had long been discolored with age, coming to pause at a particular entry written out in a language unfamiliar to both Samuel and Maria; the ink had been faded by exposure to the light of countless days. Continuing to flip through the great tome, the man came to the very back where the ink was vivid and the transcription was now written in English. For a moment he said nothing, he simply stared at the pages that turned, as though he was flipping through a treasured family album that, though being in his possession, he had not glanced at for some time. Then, quite suddenly, he halted and looked up from his inner-reminiscing and spoke.

"This story told unto us by the couple is a firsthand account; as such know that the history you hear is written from their perspective and had not been distorted with time. Some truths discussed herein you will already have heard me speak of, so it will be a bit repetitive in certain places; nonetheless, keep reading. This account takes all the pieces, brings them together and looks at what our fate will be." The man held out the book, offering it to Samuel. This act drew a look of surprise from Yoseph. "We never allow anyone, outside of family, to read this book. It is a sacred record for us; the truths within were hard-earned," the man explained. "We have suffered greatly simply for our awareness of what lies in this book. I want you to take it tonight, read this entry and see if you both do not gain something from it. We," he said motioning to himself and his son, "we'll be awake for a while longer; you may return it to us when you are finished."

Able to appreciate the trust it took to extend this book unto them, Samuel and Maria took the ancient journal respectfully. Settling in together they each read silently to themselves as their eyes passed over words that had been transcribed with care.

The text read:

The History and Future of Love

How can love live in Hell, among the evil? How can the innocent live among the perverse? How can the giving live among
the taking? How can the trusting live among the deceptive?
How can the feeling live among the manipulative? How can
the few loving hearts who remain live within a world overtaken by the loveless? —They cannot.

We are at a stand-off with those who have chosen evil.
We cannot coexist with them because their way of life is
contrary to all that we believe. We build and they destroy;
thus has been the unending cycle loving hearts have endured
while dwelling among those who choose evil. We want an end
to the pain—we want freedom.

Evil's answer to such a situation would be war. When
those who are evil want liberty they attack those who
would suppress them. When they want land, they defeat
those currently dwelling upon it. However, evil's solutions
would not work for us. Those who believe in love would
gain nothing through a war. All we want is safety and the
freedom to live as we would choose. Evil has committed many
egregious crimes against us yet we do not seek reparation,
only separation. Attempting to gain our freedom through
war would be fighting evil with evil—those loving hearts who
took part in the conflict would be lost, while the evil would
only be bolstered.

We can choose to spite anyone who makes the choice to
become evil, but we have not undone what compels them to
make such a choice, as such, the evil is immortal until brought
to an end by those who have chosen it. Lasting change in

the world only comes in the wake of a change of heart; realization, not wrath brings revolution. Evil lacks morality. We want them to change yet morality and caring cannot be reawakened by command or through a beating. Any loving heart who tries to end the struggle with evil within the arena of war shall lose themselves, even if they win the match.

Even if war was the answer we would not want it. Scarred and traumatized by previous attacks at their hands we still do not crave blood for blood. Evil need not suffer to satisfy the debt that is owed to us—a debt that was accumulated from the priceless value of each part of us damaged or stolen in the wake of each attack they carried out against us. …a debt which can never be repaid. …a debt we simply desire nothing more from our precious life be added to. We do not seek reparation. We seek a separation and with it a place to heal. We seek a sheltered place to live within where we may be apart from all that evil built and beyond their reach forever.

We who are loving seek the end of our battle with evil. But by what means can this end come? Some would propose we bring about this end by coming to terms with evil—a truce. But if those who are evil could bring themselves to respect what it is we desire, they would not be evil. No matter what we give them to spare us they will always take more, until we have nothing left. When there is no profit in the peace the terms would be ignored. Since they see no value in our life, they shall not care if it is destroyed.

For generations evil has persecuted the loving and when at all possible we have fled. However, there does come a time when there is no place left to go; when no matter the distance crossed, safety is still not achieved. We have gone to the ends of the known world and still the evil looms into view. Those who are loving ask what is to be done? Where can we go? How will this all end?

For generations—millennia, this unending conflict has drawn-out, producing victim after victim. We have been forced to leave behind all that we built in order to flee the threat we could not withstand. And having lived in this inescapable cycle for so long we know with all certainty that evil will come again and again. A branch can be severed from the black diseased growth but still the root survives to sprout a new vine that ensnares us and eventually grows to strangling lengths.

We want only to live—to live. We cannot bring about the end of the evil. Evil has covered the face of the Earth—no shore left undiscovered, no hiding place left unfound, no sacred place left untouched. ...Or is there still one?

With our backs against the edge of the world and the frontline of evil advancing towards us we searched for an answer. We raised our hands—reaching for Love's deliverance. We released from our hearts the echo of a plea to pass around the globe, willing it to reach the ears of the being of love's embodiment who could guide us and protect us.

THE ANSWER

The Earth was once a world where dwelled the loving. It was not always a place of danger. It was not always a house divided. It was not always a trough filled with evil's ways. It was once pure, untouched, undefiled.

Evil has taken over this Earth. We cannot cleanse the perversion with blood, or win back the lands taken in a war; purity cannot be restored through savageness. And yet we can neither co-exist with the evil nor give up our dream of a full, unthreatened life.

We cannot concede the life we want simply because the majority has chosen another way. One cannot say that what is right should be abandoned simply because what is wrong has come to reign. And so, in our need, we turned to Love seeking the answer. And we were led to our answer—to the enduring Other Shore.

We learned that the Earth has preserved part of herself. A sanctuary has been hidden away, which can provide the freedom and safety loving hearts seek. All those who believe in love have a place upon the Other Shore. At this time love is preparing to leave behind this world evil has created. We are preparing to make a journey out of this world—this old life—so to claim our new beginning upon the Other Shore.

There will be a journey out of evil for each loving heart. This journey will be divided into two legs. The first half of the journey is a process of gathering the means to be able to leave evil behind; while the second half is the breaking from the old life that we have had here—moving from Hell and back into the old world to reach our new life. The journey is an exodus of the loving hearts who have survived. It is our departure from this world we no longer have a place within. And it is through this exodus—this parting of ways—that love moves on. This journey is the next step for all those loving hearts who have awoken to the evil.

Some will say that this parting of ways should have come long ago. But we were trapped beside those who have become evil; for these same ones who hurt us were once those who brought us joy. ...they were once our family. The lines between those who choose evil and those who believe in love are clear but the emotional aspect of our conflict with evil has made everything complicated.

How It Began

Heaven and Hell—they were once the same world—this living Earth. Before the creation of evil there was but one world with no lines of division within it—not along the land or within the hearts of the people. The boundary running along the edge of these two worlds being that of choice. When the people began dividing into two—those evil and those of love—the Earth itself was divided as well.

At first it was one man—the first son of the first father—revolting against love. He portrayed his newfound ambitions as a revolution rather than a digression. And over time, the one became many, as he persuaded others to join him. The choices that were made by these few lost ones were incomprehensible to those of us who remained loving. As was the change that would soon overturn the only world—the only way of life—we had ever known.

The family of humanity grew, as did the number of those choosing this unnatural movement, creating a divide in the original family. The few became the many and over the course of the ages, the many swelled to the majority. It was at this time that the balance tipped. The old world of family, love, community and giving was over-turned and evil built the world they envisioned atop it—a world that was christened in mythology as Hell. It is quite literally an underworld—a culture existing morally below baseline human behavior.

All were once loving. Humanity once existed as one bonded family. Yet some within our family began to change they became driven to fulfill self-serving ambitions at detriment to the well-being of all others. They were no longer fulfilled by giving what was in their heart or the love they were given by the hearts around them. No, they were now drawn to a different idea of power. Given satisfaction by what they could sway and what they could possess; whereas once they were fulfilled by what they could help nurture into fruition and bring forth from within themselves to give.

Whereas once love was held to be all-powerful, evil had conceived of this pedestal—a place upon which one all-powerful person could reside above all others. And in their hunger to reach the top of this pedestal, they betrayed all, spited all, exploited all, overturned all...forsook all.

They seem driven into madness by their obsession to dominate—to be the one all-powerful. And to achieve this position they conceived of methods never before fathomed within the old world: war and deception, exploitation, theft and murder. In their fever to possess they took and hoarded the natural abundance of the landscape, bringing into being hunger and want; creating in the wake of their greed: poverty and crime, desperation and sacrifice.

The very existence of evil became detrimental to any and all creatures who wanted life; especially those who remained faithful to the old ways and chose to keep their belief in love. Nevertheless, in the beginning love did not flee the

Homelands or did we turn our backs on those who changed; we did all we could to help them awaken to the consequences of their choices.

In the beginning, those who were becoming evil were the very same hearts we had once been so close with. We could remember a time when they were caring. They were our family: our husbands and wives, mothers and fathers, brothers and sisters…our children.

Even when their choices betrayed all that we as a family had ever believed in, we let them stay. Even when the words they spoke and their every action shredded our hearts, we let them stay. We remained at their side, because we never conceived that these bonds could be broken. We loved them, and at the core of any love is an unwavering fidelity.

Torn apart, confused—sent reeling into the chaos as what shouldn't have ended, came to its end—we stayed with them, unable to let go of the people we once knew. They looked the same to our eyes but they were not the same. Their bodies had not given out but a rebirth had nonetheless taken place, it had occurred inside them. They had become someone else.

Unable to accept that the ones we had loved were dead— unable to understand that the person they once were had been the sacrifice at the birth of the evil—we stayed with them. Yet as evil swelled within them, more love drained from them. They became more potent in their viciousness and became capable of new atrocities never before seen. And when this happened, we were forced to flee.

✦

Unable to co-exist with those who were willing to attack and manipulate, we were forced to part ways with them, until a day when they returned to their original beliefs. Families broke apart as members twisted themselves. The one family of humanity divided and all changed. Eventually, the gorged boundaries of Hell encroached upon the borders of the Homelands and we were all forced to flee—abandon everything we had built to avoid the malice being projected upon us.

We were all unsure as to what had occurred and why. We did not know how evil had come about or what evil was. We knew nothing. Yet had not the time to seek out answers from those who were lost; we had to flee the unleashed spite—a force that likewise, up until this moment in time, had never before been witnessed.

It was during this time of the initial break, all loving hearts suffered their first wound. And it is in that first attack that we became trapped. We broke with them. We fled their rage—refusing to engage in a war with them. We surrendered the Homelands and wandered for a great many years until at last the revelation of the Other Shore came. We discovered this place set apart and settled there. It is a place open to all those who believe in love and beyond the reach of all those who do not. We know now that all we can do is go to the Other Shore and attempt to find enough peace to make a new beginning. This new beginning is not easily had but it is what we now endeavor to achieve.

Chapter XV

The Journey

"There are so many things that I do not understand. I don't even know all my questions," Samuel said, passing the book back to the man. It was late but for Samuel and Maria there was no sleep to be had until after their questions were asked.

"What part do you want to discuss further?" the man asked patiently, willing to do anything he could to help bridge the gap in understanding.

"Sometimes, when you speak of 'the Other Shore' I am confused. In some instances it seems a real place and at other times it sounds like a mental state we achieve. So, I suppose my first question is: When you speak of 'the Other Shore' are you speaking of a place that physically exists or is it a term used for a state of mind, reminiscent of the Eastern faiths?" Samuel continued, determined to understand. "I am wondering as to whether 'the journey' that was spoken of takes place over the inner-landscape or the outer? Is this journey we make to break from evil's world, meant physically or metaphorically?"

The man nodded slightly. He understood Samuel's concern. "The Other Shore is a physical place not a mental state. It is a community composed of loving people—a balanced world of rolling green, protected by the ancient consciousness alive in the unseen. In the Eastern faiths you speak of there is, Shambhala—the heart of the Earth. Shambhala is a place that indeed lies within the individual yet is also a physical one upon the Earth inaccessible but to a few souls who know where it is and how to penetrate its wild terrain. Such is the Other Shore.

"The Other Shore is an untouched part of the Earth, upon which those who believe in love dwell protected. In many senses it is the last foothold—the last foothold for a natural Earth that has been industrialized and polluted, as well as the last foothold for a people who have been persecuted and have no place in this hostile world."

"And this *journey* that is spoken of...?" Samuel said, moving on to the other topic he wanted to discuss. "I suppose, I am having trouble understanding why, if there is the Other Shore—a physical place where loving hearts can live unthreatened—why are all good hearts not simply brought there, right now?" Samuel asked awkwardly; having trouble knowing exactly what his question was.

Leaving the book in front of him, the man went about trying to answer Samuel's question, knowing full-well that it would take more than this one conversation to give the man clarity.

"You want to know why those who are a part of love cannot simply be taken away from this backward place and brought to the Other Shore right this moment?" the man proceeded slowly. "I wish the situation were as simple as picking up and moving but sadly it is quite involved. It is not simply a matter of journeying to the Other Shore—taking a boat and being done with it. It is a matter of being able to fully leave behind the evil—all that it has taught you and all the acts it has committed against you. It is a matter of coming to terms with the old before you can enter the new. Doing all this is more involved than one may think. It means making a separate journey to achieve resolve.

"Before we can leave the life we have had here and begin a new life on the Other Shore, we each must resolve ourselves with all that has happened here. This means all our nagging questions must be answered, all our wounds must be closed, all our past relationships must be reconciled—and all that has tormented us must be put to rest. Only then can we put away the old life completely and move on into a new life. There is a proverb passed down among those who have made the journey: 'We must settle the past if there is to be a future.'

"Wanting to travel yet unable to make the journey," the man said poetically, as if quoting a classic book that neither Maria nor Samuel were familiar with. "Trapped in evil, all loving hearts desire to leave the world created by those who have chosen evil; however, we have not had the means to do this.

"Unable to depart for our future until the plaguing parts of the past are settled, we must make *a journey* over the course of which we will gather our needed answers. Each of us who would make a new life on the Other Shore must make such a journey before we can have our beginning. This journey must be made here—in the part of the world evil has shaped. This journey is composed of two halves. The first half of the journey finishes the past; while the second half of the journey opens our mind to prepare us for our future."

A puzzled look moved across the faces of Samuel and Maria.

"For now we shall focus on the first leg of the journey—finishing the past," the man said, limiting the topic in response to their bewildered looks. "I know how nonsensical it sounds when I say that, in order to leave behind the evil, we must make a journey through its world.

"When at last my family reached the Other Shore, accompanied by the very ones who gave us the account you just read," the man said, laying a hand upon the journal before him, "we did not find peace. We were in a sanctuary, quite removed from this world," he said, glancing around. "However, a part of us was stuck here and we simply could not move on. While on the Other Shore we kept looping the same painful memories and reeling in the incomprehension of it all. Finally a day came when we were told that, if we wanted to be free to begin a new life on the Other Shore, we first needed to make a journey to gather all that we required to be capable of fully leaving evil behind.

"What we required was simple: the truth. We needed the truth concerning the attacks carried out on us by those we had once regarded as friends and even family but who in the end were a part of evil. It was explained to us that the only way to get this needed truth was to go back into evil's part of the world and see it—to make a journey of learning that would lead us behind all the illusions those who are evil project.

"The truth is the material needed for the formation of resolve. The hardest part about reaching the Other Shore is not crossing the miles; it is achieving the freedom to begin a new life there. *Resolve* is that freedom. I had reached the Other Shore but did not have resolve concerning my past here; thus I had to come back."

"That must have been difficult. ...making it there, thinking you were done, only to have to return," Maria said sympathetically.

The man stared off into his thoughts; his gaze became unfocused as he sat pensively recalling a memory of which neither Maria nor Samuel knew.

Finally he spoke in a low voice, still staring into his past, "I cannot tell you how difficult it was." Another moment and his eyes refocused, signaling his return from his reflection. "Not many go about their journey in such a way—going to the Other Shore, only to be asked to return here once more," he clarified. "Most make their journey before reaching the Shore. I think we were all brought there because we were hunted so relentlessly and needed time to regather strength and security if we were going to be able to attempt such a journey." The man moved away from his personal story, unable to continue retelling it. "Regardless of how difficult it was to return and how grueling the journey has been, I understand the need for resolve. Resolve is the means to leave behind the evil—to exit evil's part of the world and have no lingering ties to it. Before we are able to depart this place *physically* we must be able to depart it *emotionally and mentally*. To begin our new life we first need the full truth of the world in which we have thus far lived as well as the people within this world who we have become bound to through pain."

Maria looked at him curiously.

"Love binds us together, yet we can also become bound to one who causes us great pains," he explained. "We do not have a 'bond' with them, rather we are *tied* to them until we are able to come to terms with what they have done to us. And the only thing that allows us to come to terms is truth. Not fragments or surface truths, but the truths that lie at the root of it all. Lasting resolve can only be achieved by having the final truths, which, when dealing with a group of people who hide and lie, is no easy thing to reach."

"While I am heartened to know that such a place exists as the Other Shore, I find it disappointing to think that we must pass back through evil's world before we can begin our new life there," Maria said, showing her exhaustion.

"Perhaps you have already made the first leg of your journey and we are just now putting together the truths that you gathered," the man offered insightfully; trying to impart a hope.

His words brought a wordless stare of dawning comprehension across the face of both Samuel and Maria. The couple took a long moment of silence, as the years behind them were redefined by the ripple of this new piece of context given unto them.

"Goodness knows the last years have not been easy ones," Maria said. It was clear in her tone of voice that the offhanded remark was an understatement. New comprehension spread throughout her mind; all that was senseless wandering only a moment before now had meaning. "It would be a comfort to know that all that we have gone through the last years happened because we have been preparing for a new life elsewhere." She went on, "For years now we have become increasing more disturbed by what we see in the world; as though we have become ultra-sensitive to any ill-element around us. And more than this heightened sensitivity we have felt very alienated.

"Over the last years we have come to see how wrong this world is; as if we knew somewhere within how the world should be. We simply could not believe that the world could actually be what we thought—that the world could be as bad as it seemed or that people could be as hurtful and cold as we thought. Yet deep down we knew it to be true. We simply did not have a name for it until we met you and you began to speak of the evil."

"You very well could have been making the first leg of your journey. I do not know the specifics of what you have endured but what you describe—the awakening, the hypersensitivity and alienation—these things occur at the end of one's journey. You see, at the end of the first leg we begin to see this culture for what it is: evil, and then we come to realize that we are not a part of it; thus the alienation.

"The hypersensitivity comes from our reconnecting with Love. We feel our connection to the wholesome, innocence in the world and so are repelled when we encounter any perversions or foulness. A great many in this world have become slowly desensitized to the perversion they are surrounded by, either because they have accepted it as normal or have been told to do so by society. As we pull out of evil's culture over the course of our journey we reject what their society tells us and come instead to listen to our heart, and in our heart, we know that how mankind lives here in this place is wrong.

"If you want to know whether or not you have already begun your journey," the man said reflectively, "look back. When I look back over my journey, I know that it was in fact a journey because it *felt* like one. Looking back on these last years of your life did you feel as though you were settled in this part of the world or did you feel as though you were passing through it—moving from person to person, situation to situation gathering some truth or insight and then moving on to the next? If you did feel this, it points to the fact that you have been on your journey."

"We went through so much—more than I can ever convey. And it did feel like a journey, I think," Maria said slowly as she thought back.

"Yes," Samuel said, in a fatigued tone. "It is a comfort to know that all our suffering was for something but that does not completely take away the pain of what we went through. You have told us so much but now I beg you to tell me: why? Why did we have to go through so many hard and lonely years?

"One after another the hard truths came, like a beating. One situation after another we were forced into difficult choices. We have walked away from so much these last years and now you tell me it is because we were slowly breaking from the evil around us. Now more than ever, I need to know why we simply could not have been told of this Other Shore years ago when we first felt the longing for a new start? We were ready to leave all this behind years ago. Why couldn't it all be done with then?" Samuel's tone was both desperate and demanding. He was not angry; he was simply hurt and in need of answers.

"Because, as I said, it is not just about leaving," the man replied, identifying with Samuel's confusion having once demanded an answer to the very same questions, "it is about *taking all of yourself* with you when you finally cross that divide between worlds. While you wanted to leave most-likely you were not prepared within to do so.

"It is about, not only leaving this world in body, but breaking from it in your mind and heart. It is about leaving in such a way that you *never* have to come back to free a part of yourself that remains ensnared.

"Reaching the Other Shore is not merely a matter of crossing the miles between this place and that place. The full life to be had there is contingent on reaching a certain mental state and emotional state first, which through the journey we come to."

"What mental state do you speak of? A heightened awareness?" Samuel asked, showing hints that his own path had passed through the various faiths of the world.

"Yes," the man replied, his voice climbing slightly, "and no," he added; his voice descending. "Heightened awareness is the road but not the destination—it leads to the end state of mind needed to start a new life but it is not the final goal. No, the state of mind we need before we are free to live upon the Other Shore is utter *openness*. Openness to learn of an entirely new, boundless reality, which is only possible if we can mentally reject the false, limited reality we have been force-fed here since infancy. This is where the second leg of the journey takes us—through a process of opening our minds and removing the limits placed on us by the teachers we have thus far had." The man knew he was venturing into a new point, one that he had already decided he was going to stay away from for now. He wanted to keep things simple but he had to let the conversation take its natural course. "If you want to move to a place that exists under a different reality, you must be willing to let go of all you have ever been taught to be true—to let go of the reality that you know. Being ready to undergo such a complete reeducation takes more than a mere nod of the head—a: 'Yes, I am willing.' Realizing that all you have ever been taught is false is ultimately liberating yet in the beginning the revelation of the extent of the lies told is a shockwave that sends us reeling unto the fringes of madness.

"While taking the journey we see the hidden truth concerning this world—any virtue we thought this society had fades when the blunt wrongfulness of it comes into view. Over the course of the first leg of the journey you undergo an all-encompassing disillusionment, during which you may lose everything you have ever trusted to be true—from your family bonds, to your knowledge of God, to your own identity, to the baseline abilities of the human being itself. *Everything* you have been taught will be swept away in a storm of revelation. And, when the storm is over, you will wake to find that what has always been genuinely true in your life still remains; while all that was composed of lie and illusion is gone.

"A stark, barren plain—that is the world we wake to while making the journey. Our religion, our society, our knowledge of the world—it all withers and we find our self in a desert of harsh truths. Yet if you can keep yourself above the madness of seeing such a bleak world—if you can survive the collapse of all you have ever trusted to be true, and with no preconceived notions ask to learn the genuine reality of this world, then you have reached the proper mental state needed to leave this backward world and go on to the Other Shore to start a new."

There was a moment of silence. Samuel looked defeated.

"And the emotional state is the process of finding resolve?" Maria followed up, continuing the conversation as Samuel regrouped. She felt that, after a lifetime of building questions, everything had led to this moment where she finally had someone in front of her with the answers. She would not let a moment be wasted.

"Yes," the man said, catching up with the woman. "The emotional state is more about finding *resolve*—a coming to terms with the nagging paradoxes of your life, created by the attacks those who are evil have carried out upon you.

"As we live here, in this place, amongst a hurtful people, we inevitably accumulate scars. Some are on our bodies, others are on our hearts. And before we can leave behind our life here to start a new we have to sooth those wounds. As one who bears his share of scars, I can vouch for the need for resolve. The questions we each need to resolve are ever-varying, dependent upon the individual circumstances. These pressing questions can pile up to the point that they weigh down the momentum of our life to a crawl—to a halt—and keep us in the same agonizing place for decades on end.

"Resolve," he said reflectively, "it is the difference between being able to start anew or lingering on in torment. Without resolve it ends but it doesn't end—you walk-away, but you cannot walk-away; you must let go, but you cannot let go. Resolve brings a lasting end, and in doing so allows us to have a new beginning.

"Resolve solidifies our life-altering choices, making them permanent—never having to be revisited and incapable of being broken or shaken when we are pelted by one who is trying to cause us to doubt ourselves. Without resolve the path goes on but a part of us remains tied to what is still unfinished.

"Without resolve we cannot go forward, so instead, we linger on in an in-between, wasting away as the wounds continuously seep—trapped in the emptiness and crippled by torments—unable to move on from what has ended because for our heart it is not over," he finished heavily.

"I know it is getting very late, so late in fact that morning is not far off," Samuel said, trying to rally himself. "No matter how tired my body is, the rest of me is awake with questions. I don't even know where to begin," Samuel spoke, voicing Maria's thoughts as well. Both of them now viewed their past from a completely different perspective.

"Both of you need to remember that, while you may feel rushed to ask all your questions this night, there is tomorrow," the man reassured. "I do not know exactly what horrors and trials these past years have held for you but I have some appreciation for what you have been through. I have heard your story a dozen times. In hearing your story I hear my own. My questions are yours' and yours' are mine," the man said lovingly.

The man's words made Samuel and Maria beam as they never had before. As though they both had waited their entire lives to feel they belonged and not until this moment, with this man, had they felt that accepting embrace.

"Our life has been so very difficult. As Samuel told you, we have been ready to move on for some time now. We knew years ago that things here weren't as they should be. And, if indeed these years have been our journey, I am left with only one nagging question: *why*. Wasn't there another way?" Maria said in a serious voice, attempting to hold back tears. She felt the same hurt as Samuel.

"That is indeed the final question good woman. That is 'the why' that all of us who have taken the journey face. The short answer is: there is no leaving this place until we have the whole truth and there is no other way to have the truth than to see all of it for what it is. There is no easy way to stare into the face of evil."

"But we never spoke to anyone about any of this. We were never confronted by someone like you—someone who knew the greater picture—evil and love. How could we make such a journey? No one approached us to tell us of such an undertaking. We never knew the significance in what we were doing these last years, until we met you," Maria reasoned.

"Setting out on the journey is not always a formal affair wherein someone takes you by the hand and tells you what need be done. It was for my family but for most it is not. Setting out on the journey is as simple as making a declaration *within* that you want the truth and you want to practice a loving way of life. Make this declaration within yourself and your journey begins. Somewhere, sometime, both of you made the choice to not take part in all this," he said, waving his hand, encompassing all the shallowness of the present culture with the one motion. "You made a choice to leave all this. Both of you sensed the extent of the lies and the wrongfulness of what surrounded you and within yourselves you asked for the truth. That is where the journey begins; that is *how* it begins.

"There is a saying among those of us who have traversed Hell, 'Your heart makes the declaration and Love sets the path.' What this means is: What we say within our heart is heard by more than just ourselves. The declarations we make within are just as strong, if not stronger, than those we make with our voice. Love—the ancient consciousness in the unseen—as well as those on the Shore hear what we declare in our heart. And once we declare our preference—once we make the choice, once we decide that we want the truth—the path is set. Taking us by the hand the unseen leads us along a path of revelation. We need not think about it, we need not guide it, we need not even be fully aware that it is happening; all we need do is survive the *extreme* that we are taken to."

"And as to the question: 'Was there an easier way?' no, there isn't," he said regretfully. "I wish with every fiber of my Being that there was another way but there isn't. The journey goes as long as it must for our heart to gather the needed resolve. We will remain bound to this world and the evil that dwells here until our heart finds the means to let go."

"Has it happened for you?" Maria asked timidly; a bit fearful to ask him something so personal, not wanting to trigger a pain for him.

"I fear that hearing my story will not give you hope of a speedy resolve," he said with a faint laugh; having to laugh so as to stave off the heartache. "My journey has lasted longer than I ever thought it could. The deeper the wounds, the more questions there are to answer and the more miles there are to traverse before one becomes ready to move on."

"But if the object of the journey is to learn the truth, surely you must be ready to move on. I mean, you know the truth. You know more than any man I have ever met," Samuel reasoned, as if appealing to the Fates on the man's behalf that he had been through enough and should be allowed to put down his bag and return home.

"Logically, I should have already seen enough to have found my resolve. I have seen those who have become evil bare-faced. I have seen this world that they have built for what it is. I know what those who attacked me years ago, injured in me. Yet it is still not enough. Many times we can have seen enough of the truth about a person or an incident in our life to have what we logically need to put together the resolve we need to settle the issue within us. Yet the heart obeys no such logic. In our heart we can remain unresolved with parts of our past, even though, we might have seen and heard enough to satisfy our nagging questions; nonetheless many times, the heart needs not only the truth, but a final extra realization that will help to make the resolve lasting.

"We can have all the evidence yet still not have that final piece that our heart needs to allow for the most complete resolve to form. At the very end—after we have seen what we needed to see, heard what we needed to hear and said what we needed to say, there is one last thing needed for the heart to let go. It is an x-factor, in that, it cannot be defined. It happens when it happens and for myself, it has not yet come," he finished mournfully, bringing the long day of conversation to its conclusion.

Chapter XVI

The Third Night

S POKESMAN FOR SOMETHING THAT HE HIMSELF COULD *not understand, the man thought ironically to himself.* He laid upon his thin bedroll, sprawled out upon the hard floor, blanket pushed to the side, staring out blindly into the darkness. Absorbed in his thoughts, he was deaf to the street noise. Yoseph lie sleeping beside him. Maria and Samuel had long since gone to their own beds, setting aside their abounding questions for another day; however the man could not set aside his own questions quite so easily. On this night the questions of the present had recalled those asked many years ago. They sounded in his mind long after the end of the conversation—calling him back into his past, to relive the moment when he once demanded the same answers as Samuel and Maria.

It was a small room, warm and inviting. It was a bright and clean space compared to the filthy decay of the room he had been sequestered in these last three days. There were flowing green plants potted cozily in clay bowls. He was surrounded by aged wooden furniture. Tables scrolled with ornate carvings. Hand-sewn tapestries draped on the halls of the cottage. Food was laid out in abundance on a table set against the far side of the room, offering ripened fruits, crusty breads, freshly squeezed juice and stream-drawn water to any who entered.

Spread out just beyond the threshold of the open door was a rolling, lush, untarnished green landscape. The wind carried the aromas of the churning brine from a nearby sea. The faintest thunder of crashing waves echoed as they swept into the rocky coves that scalloped the edge of the island. Not a single industrial mark besmirched the masterpiece of the natural landscape. Whole, full and vibrant it towered, reminding the community of their central yet nonetheless small place in the greater lifespan of the Earth.

Within this sacred setting, in the living-room of this cottage, an intimate group of three people sat across from the nameless man, who seemingly appeared to be the same in age as he was in the present. One of the three was a man who looking to be in his late thirties, average height, clean shaven, with short dull-brown hair swept to one side, as if he had just stepped in from a rather violent windstorm. He had a young yet nonetheless learned air about him. He possessed piercing hazel eyes, a long nose and a strong jaw. The woman who sat next to him was resting her hand upon his knee in the loving manner. She too looked to be in her late thirties. She had long thick dark hair that fell at her waist and a kind, steadiness about her.

Finally, sitting beside the couple, taking the brunt of the nameless man's outrage, was a middle-aged man who looked young but at the same time very old. He looked to be a man in his late-forties who had been prematurely aged by a prolonged period of tremendous strain. He had the same look as those young people who are left pale and drained after a long bout with serious illness. The man had a full, neatly trimmed beard, a thick head of the same dull brown hair as the younger man sitting beside him only semi-streaked with gray.

Everyone in the room, including the man, was dressed in layered robes of hand-spun wools that had been dyed shades of muted earth-tones. Upon their feet they donned sheep-skin boots, which had been slightly dirtied along the bottom edges over the course of the daily chores.

Surrounded by beauty, the man was ever-aware of the sacred nature of this sanctuary but at this very moment, grief-stricken as he was by what he had been told, he was blind to it all.

"Why?" he asked, heartbroken. "We made it here," he went on, his voice steadily rising as the full weight of what he was being asked to do penetrated him. "We made it here after surviving all that was done to us and now you say the only way to heal from those attacks is to go back! It's madness!" his voice had intensified to one of outraged frustration.

The conversation had been carrying on for hours in circles.

Rising to his feet, he—a man of pacifist character—stood formidably before the three onlookers. "If this is the extent of wisdom held here, then I have misplaced my trust," the man said bitterly, reeling in hurt. "You say I need to 'understand those who are evil and learn the truth of it all.' But you already know—you know what the evil is, you know what it has done to us and why.

You know the truth that has eluded us. All you need do is explain it in such a way that we will understand. And yet, you would have me believe that you cannot explain it to us. That instead, we have to go back into that place and discover the truth for ourselves. It is madness," he repeated, shaking his head. *"Being there is what scarred us in the beginning. Going-back-cannot-be-the-answer,"* he added pointedly. *"We survived it all. We were brought here, to this place where we thought we may at last find peace, only to be told now that we must go back."* He shook his head again as though declining to accept this hardest of truth. *"This place—this sanctuary—has been our one hope for a new life and now you tell me our only hope for a healing lies elsewhere. You would have us go back after all that we endured there? Is it only me that sees how insane this is?"* the man said, continuing his rant, he knew he was reeling; he could feel himself unraveling. He felt utterly lost.

The middle-aged man—the most learned man upon that Other Shore addressed him, *"There is nothing that I could say or do that would give you the resolve you need. You will only make peace with what has occurred back there—where it all began,"* the learned man said blunt yet compassionately. *"To think that we would advise you to return to a place where you have suffered so greatly on a whim is unfair. We have learned over generations of experience that this is the only way that the final resolve comes.*

"You can stay here. No one is telling you that you must leave. You asked me the question of, 'How do I and my family overcome the trauma of what we have been through?' And I am simply giving you the answer.

"You can stay," the learned man repeated reassuringly. *"However, you know what your life will be like. You and your*

family have been here for almost two years and yet you have not been wholly at peace even for a single day. You have confessed to me many a time that, even when you do find peace, it is fragile and fleeting—broken in a short time and you descend back into turmoil where you helplessly relive the trauma. And I know you are not the only one. Many in your family are suffering the same wearying circles. Like many others before, you and your family have not been able to fully let go of what those who are evil did to you. You have not been able to start a new life; it was this very realization that made you come to us asking what could be done to finish it.

"After decades of living incapacitated by your past wounds and watching those you love suffer the same tormented fate, you reached the limit of what could be borne and you came to me looking for the answer. You wanted to know how to heal what had been done to your family so that you each could reach a place of peace. You said you wanted to retain the wisdom you learned over the path behind you yet let go of the bad that occurred. You asked this of me as though wishing I could erase the individual memories that pain you. Only, I cannot," the learned man admitted in a tone of slight regret. He continued, "You say that seeing the evil was what traumatized you in the beginning, but it wasn't. The trauma came from the shock of it all—the fact that you did not see the evil and were left blind-sided by the betrayal of those you drew close to you. It was all that you could not see that left the wounds you have carried. You have not been reeling in all that you have seen but rather in your incomprehension.

"Despite all that you have already come to realize about those who betrayed you, there is a great deal you do not know—things that you would not be able to comprehend no matter how long *these conversations continued; for what those who are evil have become is beyond explanation. It must be witnessed," the learned man said regretfully. "That is the only way for understanding to come. And unfortunately to witness what we must, we need to be there—near them."*

"I have seen enough," the man said, feeling insulted. "—too much," he finished, visibly shaking in his emotional state.

"This is true—you have been though more than any man should," the learned man agreed without hesitation. "Yet despite the extensive attacks you have experienced, what you have been able to see of evil's true face is limited. You can sense this—you know that there are huge pieces of truth that remain elusive. That is why you are plagued so," he gently added.

"This makes no sense to me," the nameless man stated, shaking his head again. "None," he added, holding back tears. "We need to have more conversations. We need explanations," he said desperately, "not more years spent surrounded by hurtful people. This simply makes no sense," he distraughtly repeated again.

"I cannot explain what evil is to you," the learned man replied, desperately sorry. "I so wish I could. But it is not the way it works. You must witness it. All I can do is assure you that you will not be going back there to endure senseless suffering," he emphasized. "You are going back to find the truth of it all."

"Going back to wander," the man replied; rejecting the learned man's assurances. "Just as we did all those years we were there— wandering from place to place, hunted and misunderstood."

"You will not be wandering," the learned man said plainly, forgiving the man's anger, knowing it stemmed, not from hatred but from hurt. "You will not be wandering," he repeated as if consoling a child. "You will be guided by Love. There are people

here who have suffered as you have who, after having made the journey we speak of now, returned home to this Shore at peace in themselves. All of us in this room have made such a journey."

"Explain this journey to me again," the man asked begrudgingly; his voice taut with frustration.

"The journey's path leads you to a situation wherein those who are evil will eventually discard their façade. The journey is a long path to a point in time where they will drop their illusions. Incidentally, this moment of candor is usually had at what is your darkest time, wherein those who are evil feel that they have absolute control over you and, in their over-confident triumph, they drop all pretense and show you their true face.

"It is a journey unto a moment of honesty. It takes a very long time to experience a moment of candidness with those who are evil. But when it at last happens you will understand what they are and what they have done to you, and in this moment you will be forever changed by what occurs. —This is the journey."

The learned man paused for a moment, as though waiting for some response or further question. When none came, he moved on in a sad tone, "You say you need conversation and explanations but, even after my life of reflection, I can give you no words that will put your past to rest for you. You will not find resolve through conversation. No, if we are to find the root of it all, we must go to the extreme—we must go behind the illusions and see the truth with our own eyes, and from that place of clarity gather the insights we need.

"If you take this journey you will not wander. A path will be laid out for you. This path will be laid out in such a way that all the unresolved questions in you will be answered as you move from situation to situation, place to place, encounter to encounter learning all that you need to ultimately find resolve.

"You go, you see what lies behind the illusions, you gather the truth you have been deprived of and then you come home—your journey leads back here to this Shore. And while you are on your path back home all the insights you have gathered over the course of your journey come together to form the greater truth that you have always needed.

"In seeing the extent of the influence those who are evil have, you will see how their presence has affected your development and, at the end of the path, you will come to know your 'original self.' You will regain the part of you that they took. You will be healed of the wounds they left on you. But more than that, you will come to know the limitlessness you are a part of, causing the world and your own heart to open their secrets to you."

Despite the learned man's insightful answer the nameless man looked unsatisfied. "All this to see what was behind evil's lies? I have always wondered," the man began in a tone of irony, "why those who are evil even bother with the illusions at all. They are so ostentatious, so self-righteous why aren't they more forthright about their plans for us?"

"Strangely enough," the learned man replied, "while they are proud of what they have become and see nothing wrong with their acts, many who are evil still conceal themselves behind the mask of a loving heart; for as you know all too well, under the guise of a friend they are able to get closer to those they would extort.

"You should know that, even if you make the journey, those who have become evil will deny their nature right up to the end. When at last you do see their true face, they will attempt to discredit you if you speak of what you glimpsed behind their veil. When at last you see them—when, in a moment of candor their pretenses and masks fall—they will try to confuse you to cause you

to forget what you witnessed. You must hold tight to what you realized in that split second when you see them for what they are."

"I may have a great deal more to learn but I have seen enough to know that many times, if not all, those who are evil will not come forward and simply declare themselves. They will not acknowledge their guilt and admit what they have done to us. So what good does it do to return? I have been there for a lifetime and by your own estimation the greater truth of them still eludes me."

"You would be making a planned journey for the purpose of learning. That would be the difference. You would be led—inner-guided—to the places and people you need to meet in order to gain the truth you lack. This journey would not be about getting those who are evil to admit what they are. It is about your seeing them and taking the knowledge of what you have seen to heart, to answer your nagging questions."

Driven unto the distressed edges of sanity after years of crisis—traveling in maddening mental circles—the man was left devastated by the solution he was given. The look upon his creased, bearded face was one of utter horror. He knew nothing for certain. Every time he found certainty within himself it was decimated by some unforeseen attack. Every time he began to trust those feelings that told him good was coming, he found he was made the fool as further hardship befell he and his family.

He knew that he had indeed become his wounds. He traveled through each day certain of nothing, believing nothing and trusting nothing—neither his own feelings nor anyone outside his family. "Even if," the man said in a meek, strained voice, "even if, I were to go—if we all were to go—how do I know this *would be the end of it? We have already been through so much... seen so much, heard so much and spend the better part of our lives reflecting on it all and still, we have no understanding of what occurred. After everything that we have been through, I don't even know if this," the man said, raising his arms to encompass his vast torment, "can be brought to an end."*

"Resolve is elusive because that which we seek to settle ourselves about is elusive," the learned man said in his gentle voice, heavy with wisdom. "When it comes to those who have become evil, gaining resolve is hard and slow because their moments of candidness are few and far between. In fact, it only happens once over the course of decades. When one who thrives behind a veil of lies realizes that we have seen its true face, when in a lax moment of over-confidence they let their true nature show, they will never again let the smallest sliver of truth show through their disguise. They will never again yield the slightest hint of the vile thing they have become within. You will never be able to confront the evil or to demand answers of it. You simply have to see it and know. It is unfair," the learned man admitted. "We are left to reach that final resolve, without a moment of open conversation with those who hurt us. ...without ever receiving an apology for what they did. With all their self-righteousness and brazenness, those who are evil have become cowards. Resolve is hard to reach. After an attack, we are left having seen the evil in certain people near us yet unable to speak directly to them through the façades that act as a partition. We are left searching within ourselves for that final clarity that reveals their intentions yet unable to get to the truth of the situation, lost amid the lies they have draped around us.

"However, regardless of all they deny us, we must find that final resolve," the learned man stated clearly. "All of us have

wanted to have a moment of unfettered truth with the evil—one blunt conversation about all that has taken place. But we must accept that this will never happen. One hard fact every victim of evil must come to terms with is that most inflictors will never confess their crimes. You have lived suspended in your pain because of this hard fact. Knowing that this is how it must be when dealing with evil, we go and we see all that we need to see and gain our understanding without that candid conversation.

"I know that you feel going back will serve no purpose," the learned man said slowly, emphasizing each word as he pushed back the man's weighty doubts. "I know you feel that your time will be filled with the same senseless attacks you have already suffered. But it will be different this time. You will not be as helpless as you think you are."

"Why?" the man asked, "what will change?"

"You will see those who have chosen evil for the desperate, empty things they have become. You will see through their façades, which put them off as powerful, to their true weak and sickly inner-state. In this moment, any power that you think they have over you will begin to dissolve. The only power they have over you is the power they lead you to believe they have. Right now, you see them as a menacing force but your perception will adjust when you see behind their illusions."

Regardless of the logic in the answers he received, the man continued to struggle. "So you would send my family on this journey, which you yourselves say is an extreme?" the man asked at a loss.

"Taking the journey does mean going to an extreme. Nonetheless, we must go," the learned man replied. "Those who are evil put us through one emotional extreme after the next, breaking us

down until that last breakdown. And when we are there—when we are at our extreme—those who are evil, feeling secure in their victory, will show themselves. After seeing this—after going to the extreme—though we be broke, we will rise up strong enough to leave the evil behind. After years of waiting to know what was at the heart of it all, seeing the truth will empower us even though we be at the edge of death. This is the path of the journey. This is the process of resolving all that is plaguing you," he finished, seemingly not knowing what else to say to calm the man.

The woman spoke up for the first time, picking up where the learned man's thought left off trying to give her insights to console the reeling man. "We are willing to go to such lengths in order to be healed. Right now, knowing how sick you are of watching those you love suffer, I know you would be willing to do anything to see your loved ones healed. Even if it means going on such a journey.

"Try as you may to heal, you are still bound to the evil who hurt you. Sadly, that is how it has been for many of us. We are each bound to a specific group of evil people—those who were the first to harm us. Evil has scarred almost every heart within your family and since you each received your initial wound you all have been tied to that specific evil person or people—held back from life—unable to go on. Disabled by your confusion; reeling in incomprehension you have been left confused and blinded by the lies they told. You have come to realize that there is no going on until the truth of the matter is at last had. That is why you came to us. But we cannot give you the truth you need.

"We each have to gather our own understanding. We each must witness the evil to comprehend it. Truth," she said consolingly, "after intimate betrayal all we seek is truth. After a lifetime of being sent in circles by the lies of others we seek truth. After sensing that the world around us is not what it appears to be, we seek truth—we need it. We come to the point where there is no going on without it. No healing, no peace…no future, no present—no life, until our wounds are resolved.

"It is when we come to this point—the limit of what can be borne—that we are willing to go on such a journey, regardless of where it leads or what it entails. We are in need of truth and unfortunately the path of revelation leads us through an extreme.

"We have all asked the questions you are asking now," she said, speaking from her heart. "All that we have been through feels like only senseless suffering. It is not until we are on the other side of the journey that we begin to see the purpose of all that we endured. For many in your position is not until the end of the path that you realize there was a path at all.

"We are all aware that, when we speak of going on this journey, we are proposing a very drastic idea. The whole notion of setting out on such a journey seems like taking the matter to an extreme. But we have learned that we must go to this extreme if we are to be free from the pains that hold us back from living," she finished.

There was a time of silence after she spoke. Her voice had been even-toned, soothing and gentle yet the truths she spoke of were hard. "I have never in my life understood why we must learn through pain," the man said plainly. "When I was younger I was taught of a divine being who, while all-knowing, chose to use pain as a teacher. It always seems so backward and for me, this seems to be the same issue. How can a loving person find their freedom by going deeper into the evil? How can victims of evil find their peace by enduring more time with their inflictor?" the man asked helplessly.

"I know," the learned man said, in an understanding voice. "I know your questions.... I have had these same thoughts and I agree with you wholeheartedly. A loving being should not teach through pain but at the same time," he conceded, "I cannot deny the clarity and the courage that we possess when we return from the extreme." His rhythm of speaking began to build, as though he were about to give a great speech, wherein the final truth of the matter would be laid out. "We go to the extreme—we traverse Hell; we endure the pinnacle of it and it is from all this, that we achieve our liberation. Learning of this process, we cannot help but ask why—why is this suffering necessary? Why does the path to a new life pass first through death?

"The path leads through the extreme because when we go to the extreme and survive, we come back with all that we need to bring the unending struggle to a close. After surviving the extreme we are fearless—there is no threat that can be put to us that could make us stop heading down our path; for we have after all, survived the worst.

"When we are at the extreme, all that the evil has cast upon us to cloud our perception, clears in an instant. The important and the unimportant, what is vital and what is trivial, what is right and what is wrong, who is true and who is false—all these things separate and the chaos within us settles.

"We come back from the extreme with a new appreciation for what we know within and a belief that can withstand any attack. At the extreme belief either solidifies or breaks apart; the extreme is the furnace that either dissolves the bonds we have to our faith or forges them into an unbreakable substance. As we hit the extreme everything that has ever been permanent within us breaks apart and either reforms through faith or is left behind in

exhaustion and renouncement. If, when at the extreme, we can still find it in us to believe we shall be able to hold onto that belief throughout any circumstances that may come after.

"At the extreme, we learn who has loved us and who has lied to us. Words are put to the test and the true regard of each heart is shown. In this the lies that have been hidden come forward; while what has always been genuine is affirmed—making it even stronger.

"We return from the extreme with conviction in what the heart knows; for it was our heart that led us through the extreme and we have come to trust our instincts above anything else we may hold as fact. All the restraints put on us as well as those we have put upon ourselves fall away as insignificant and we emerge unafraid.

"While love does not teach through pain, it is a fact that, when we have faced the worst we no longer fear the worst. When we have existed upon that precarious edge of life and death, we return with the deepest appreciation for life and as such we are prepared to fight for it—to stand up for our life and confront any presence who tries to hold us back from living. At the extreme is where we find our liberation from fear, doubt and all other inhibitions. And with this new freedom we have the means to do what we must.

"At the extreme, we bind our fate to the fate of our belief— refusing to abandon our beliefs even in the face of the prolonged pain. Over the journey our belief and soul meld into one, bringing about an embodiment of irrepressible life. The extreme pushes us far yet our belief in the renewal brings us beyond all.

"We return from the extreme with the belief that can sustain us. The evil breaks our confidence, yet at the extreme—

when it pushes us farther than we can go—it pushes us farther than it should dare to; for when a loving heart is struck it does not weaken, it grows stronger. We return from our near death with the desire to live burning intensely within us and we are willing to endure whatever we must—to confront whoever and overcome whatever tries to hinder us in reaching that life. So, while pain should never be our teacher and the nature of love is to teach through growth, as I said, I cannot deny the realizations, affirmations and clarity that come when we stand on the brink.

"We make this journey, we go beyond our limits, we gather all the truth we need and in the end all that we have done converges with all that we have learned and at long last...we are free."

The conversation faded and the man was brought back to the present, having experienced one of those moments where the gathered truth, insight and realization were at last coming together, as those in that room, so long ago, said they would.

CHAPTER XVII

The Convergence

THE CITY WAS EERILY CALM. All in the room slept as
he alone lay awake—eyes closed, mind turning.
*Clarity had upon the brink.... Reasons why we
are willing to make the journey...*he thought to himself. He
realized in that moment that his stance on the journey had
come full-circle. When speaking to Samuel, he had taken the
views the learned man had once given him. He knew at that
moment wherever the learned man was, a little smile must
have undoubtedly crossed his face.

I asked you why you brought me here, he spoke through his
heart unto the ear of the ancient one connected to him. *As
if forgetting I am on a journey to resolve my past, blind not to
anticipate the inevitable day, wherein the path you have led me
on would cross through this pivotal place.*

Is that why you brought me here? his pondering heart asked. *I tried today to give them an example of going on the journey to settle the past, all the while unable to give them the example of my being brought here out of a need to resolve my own initial wound. ...Here—to this city—which is for me, the extreme.*

I have been mulling over the precarious nature of all that I hold dear. Cowering in front of a movement that seems unstoppable. I was so foolish, he thought to himself, *I had come to perceive them in exactly the manner they desired—all-powerful, and myself just as they would have me—helpless. Caught in this perspective, I have lived in fear of them—traumatized by what has been and terrified of what will be. As the fear gripped me, I grasped more tightly to all I care about. My trust in you shaken, I wrenched my life out of your hands, thinking that I was a better judge of my circumstances than you. As though perceiving that all the bad to befall me happened as a result of your negligence rather than the deceptive evil. But no more.*

The renewal of trust happens now. No, I shall not leap fearlessly as I did when in my impassioned youth. The time of such blind action has passed; the excitement of faith bled from me when the wounds were inflicted. I return to you now, subdued but steady; possessing a silent reverence of you and solemn acceptance of who I am and shall choose to remain.

I give myself over to you with a hope that the future will be kind. I know you do not require my surrender before you embrace me but I give it nonetheless, as a show of my renewed faith in you. I surrender because I cannot see how all this will end but I believe now that you can.

I could not have planned the path behind me; I could not have laid out this journey in such a way that every question would be answered and every demon be faced; I have not the multi-tracked mind that you do. In vain I have tried to prepare for any contingency but still I am blind-sided. We shall do this together...in truth, we have always done this together. I blamed you for what they did, thinking somehow that you could have stopped it, only you couldn't; for you are not a God. You are all powerful—all enduring but you cannot swoop in and shield us. All you can do, in the end, is help us to endure and lead us safely home.

I shall once again make the choices of my life with you, rather than regardless of you. You and I shall come to terms—I no longer blaming you and you helping me to forgive myself.

All states are impermanent. All kingdoms, it would seem, rise only to fall. Yet one force is enduring. At this time their movement is prominent, yet just as they swept away the old culture so too shall a force come to sweep away what they have built. Not a violent front but a change of heart. I know not what will cause it but one day it will come. I have done what I can to bring it about; I have added all that I am to this building force and now I depart for safety with those I hold dear. I can rest at ease knowing the natural balance shall return and the one natural—immortal force shall endure.

The inner-dialogue at an end, his eyes opened—sharp, wide and clear. The room was quiet—no conversations, no war-cries, no debates. For once even Yoseph was in a deep sleep.

Rising quietly in the dark, drawing his shawl around him and taking his staff in-hand he closed the distance of the bare room and moved swiftly down the hall—rounding the stairs, moving down unto ground level and out into the still night air.

*If I am here.... If this all can actually be resolved, then let it
be so. I have lingered on in this death too long. Since that scarring
day I have been alone—apart from you and from my family—
isolated in my pain, grappling with the same ghosts, reliving the
same moments and struggling against the same unchanging facts.
I don't want to lose another day to this torment.*

⁓

He moved silently through the night, passing along the
narrow streets and underneath the arched doorways of the
old city. In comparison to what it had once been, the city was
unrecognizable. Small remnants of the ancient place looked
familiar beneath the modern alterations, but they were few
and far between. Thankfully he was not taking his directions
from recognizable markers. His heart was leading him instinc-
tively to the *pivotal place*—not the place recorded in history
but the *true* place.

He could remember the city the way it was, in truth it was
the one thing he could not forget. Much to his dislike, what
took place here had been driven deeper than any other memory to occur in his life. The attack had become the center of
his existence—above his family, above his children and above
his own faith. His miraculous life, which could so easily be
defined by his extraordinary communion with the divine and
the immense love of his family, had come to revolve around
the encounter with the evil he had in this place. This place had
become the axis upon which his Being revolved and because
of this, he had lost himself.

He had become his wounds. Long ago he had learned
that the only way to regain himself once more was to heal the

wounds. It was painfully ironic that, while others found his insights helpful, he could not heal himself. Clarity is so easily had when looking outward than when looking within. He understood the sufferings of others with such ease, finding the root of the pain that they could not; while the end of his own pain was ever-elusive.

For so many nights he had let the memories overwhelm him and rob him of his sleep. But on this night, he had crossed that line—moving beyond exhaustion to that point where he was too tired to let things go on how they had been; tired of cowering, tired of hiding, *tired* of begging within himself that nothing more happen.

Since that moment, on that infamous night all those years ago, when he stood before the council betrayed. Since that moment, he had been attempting to return to who he was before the attack—before they had come for him and the myths about him had been spun. He had trusted his heart back then—heeding his inner-voice in the face of death and torture. Yet at the same time, he could not help but think the man that he was then was only a child—unknowing and idealistic.

He wanted to again be who he once was yet, at the same time, he had come to hate who he was. Over the intervening years since the night when judgment was passed upon him, he had become his harshest accuser, blaming his own blindness as his downfall more so than the actions of those who betrayed him.

Haunted by regret and frayed by doubt, nothing had been certain in him since that night...since this city. Within the walls of this city he had lost himself. Would it be that within these walls he would find himself?

He felt words flow through him as he walked; it felt as though another walked with him, leading him down the path: *We must believe in our healing if we are to allow ourselves to be healed. We must stop punishing ourselves if we are to escape our pain. We must place blame where it is due, whether upon ourselves or upon others and then we must accept that what has passed, cannot be changed. We mustn't live in regret. We must be ever-growing.*

✻

He had not noticed the time when he left the building. Oblivious to the descending moon, he finally became aware of the approaching dawn as golden twilight hues began to fill the air. He was entering that *thin time* during which the veil between worlds parts and one can walk in the in-between. That time when the years behind us blur, the present dissolves and our entire life exists in one moment—all the years behind us and ahead of us converge and breathe as one.

Of course it was near dawn, he thought to himself, remembering back to his youth when he used to go out just before sunrise to walk among the hills.

Of course it would happen now, his heart whispered unto the unseen, once more acknowledging the keen sense of synchronicity that the Fates possess.

Turning his downcast gaze upward, he took in the scene of the narrow streets ahead of him. The modern city faded as the memory of how the city once had been intensified. He was treading a surreal path; he did not know where he was going and yet at the same time he knew that, within this city, there was but *one place* he must end up.

The man moved swiftly down the narrow streets. He drew his shawl over his head. His stride was too fast for him to use his staff so he carried it—from time to time, the end dragging along the surface of the stone pathways.

As he passed by, the vendors were opening their shops, pilgrims were entering the streets and the call for Morning Prayer resounded throughout the Quarters—a haunting, Bedouin voice cried out, summoning all to submit unto God.

Crossing back and forth between the present and the past, as he walked the streets he returned with a sharp push to the past—to a violent moment when he was pulled down the pathways of the old city, driven unto the council that was to judge him. Herded along by the bullies on his heels, he could feel once more the jabs to his ribs dealt by those wielding wooden bats. Shoved to the ground, then kicked as he tried to rise, he could once more feel the burn of the skin peeling away from his palms as it did that night when, hands out-stretched, he braced himself each time he was thrown down to the gritty floor of the earth. The core of his body felt sore as it had that night—the soft organs within bruised by the hard blows.

But then, suddenly, the man was pulled from the past back into the present by the obnoxious call of an eager merchant pointing to a painting depicting the scenes of the crucifixion—a tapestry woven of both myth and hard reality. Unable to comprehend the madness of it all, the man felt a grinding shock resound through his already reeling mind.

Plunged back into the past, he recalled being pushed forcefully through the heavy doors of the Temple, as they marched him before the council—that night they were to play the role of the puppets to those who sought to make a new church of their own. He faced the questions hurled at him over the inquisition. Time and deliberation compressed in this regression; no sooner than he was pushed through the doors did the lethal verdict come: "Blasphemer!"

In the space of a breath, he was pulled once more from the past, back into the present. Waking to find himself wading claustrophobically into a crowd of morning market-goers choking the narrow corridor.

Violently thrust back into the past, he found himself helpless and unarmed among a group of men. He felt the perverse amusement they derived from his fear. They were thrilled by the power they could exert over him—enthralled, like so many in their movement, to play the role of God.

Pulled from his past, he felt a stranger's hand grasp his arm; it was yet another merchant enthusiastically trying to sell him a faux crown of thorns. Lining the shelves of the merchant's shop were hollow plastic idols and figurines. His eyes continued down the length of the open shop; his jaw went lax in horror. There were a series of framed pictures in succession hanging along a makeshift wall composed of whitewashed pegboard. It was a portrait size image of a man—a man known to the world. It was the portrait of the ghost who had haunted his life. The man in the picture was exaggerated to the point where he lost his human quality. The colors chosen by the painter were primary and neon—utterly unnatural. The crown of thorns sat atop his head. Beads of blood gathered where the thorns cut into him. His complexion was pale, thin and sickly. His sapphire blue eyes were turned upward—nearly rolling back into his head looking to some divine presence not depicted. The nameless man gazed deeply into the picture in front of him. He saw his own reflection appear against the glass of the portrait. The two men blurred together for a moment, they were nothing alike yet were inseparable. His full face, contrasted the drawn out figure's. His dark, tanned skin reflected against the figure's pale complexion. His dark brown eyes stared into the figure's blue ones.

In that instant the man felt as though he had been struck swiftly in the back of the head by some invisible attacker. His perception was jolted, as though an earthquake had tilted the horizon. He was leveled by the madness of it—by the mockery, by the myth, by the belittled pain, by the lost truth and by the epic lie his simple life had been contorted into. He recoiled at the very thought of it—driven unto the edge of what his mind could comprehend as fate brought him to this perverse full-circle of events.

Breaking the grip the memories had upon him, he charged forward down the path, running through the gate and out into the hills, away from the inescapable events until, hoarse and out of breath, he came to the end of the path to see it looming before him—the place where the journey ended once and would again.

Pulled back into the past by a sharp pain cutting into him with such ferocity that the breath was pushed from his chest, the man found himself back with the armed mob, tied down—his pure body made a spattered mural of evil's hatred. Feeling that incomparable terror that comes when the fate of your body is in the hands of the immoral, blow after blow the memories of each lash coincided with each step bringing him along the path up the rocky mount.

The further we went the heavier the weight upon his heart grew. Lost in-between his past and present, one step was made upon the modern inlaid stone road while the next was made upon the dry dirt pathway of the past. He was pulled from his past by a holy man speaking words he could not understand he looked up to see a staff with a crucifix atop it raised before him, held by a priest who offered a blessing unto him. The man stared fixedly at the deathly figure set against the cross writhing in pain. It was a moment of agonizing horror frozen in time—hung on the walls of millions of followers. The aged cleric stared blankly at him, as he moved his withered hands—up and down, side to side—outlining the burden that the man had borne, which in turn had perversely become the symbol of the church that had been built. After making that shape that had outlined the years of the man's life, the priest walked on, reciting a prayer over and over again, as if in a trance.

Brought back into his past by a joint-severing pain, it felt as though the heaviness of the memory had dropped upon him. He fell to the ground. His knee dug into the dry gravel of the hillside; the force of the strike had embedded small stones into his open wounds.

On that day, as he traveled the path to the site, there had been those who followed him distraught and those who had followed him spouting damnation. In the past when he had collapsed under the weight of his burden there had been those who rushed to his aid, held back by the outstretched lance of the centurions and then there had been those who had rushed to kick him while he lay helpless, pelting insults after pitching rocks at his exposed back. The stones cast at him while he waked this path had embedded themselves in his life. The gravel of these streets had gathered in the intersections of the gashes splattered across his back and though the rocks had been physically removed in the days following the attack, fragments of these streets remained logged in the scar tissue still, preventing the full closure of the wounds.

Pulled from his past back into the present, he felt the sweat running down his brow—sweat not from the heat but from the exertion of the march. Pushing himself onward, his head spun and his heart swelled with pain, beating harshly against his ribs…the gripping memories playing out within him strangling him.

Blind to the pilgrims who thought him possessed, the man looked up to the path ahead of him—staring into his past where he saw once more the procession of the onlookers. The figures were dressed in robes, the women donning veils. All of them were shouting words he could not hear above his wailing heart. But then, sharply, the scene shifted once more and he saw a few early morning pilgrims walking ahead in suits and denim jeans. The path leading to the site had been worn down over the ages by those who sought to stand in that place where the life he had once lived had ended—the place he had been unable to escape since that day.

He could feel the weight of memory he was dragging up the hill. The voices of the ghosts grew loud in his mind, he could not hear their calls clearly back then—as he walked the path those many years ago but he could hear them clearly now. He could not feel the rocks they threw strike him those many years ago or the dirt they kick upon him as he passed by;

however he could feel it now, and in the revelation of the hatred projected upon him the pain was forced deeper.

Falling as the gravel shifted beneath his feet, he struck the ground and inhaled a lung full of dust. His sweat-soaked face, now stained with dirt, was tattooed with a blooming bruise. He coughed violently—tears streaked the dirt on his cheek. And when at last his eyes cleared, he saw a sight he did not expect. Standing before him in the distance were the outlines of those quite familiar. Standing ahead of him he saw his mother, his father and his wife. He saw them all hysterical, helplessly watching the events play out, just as he was helplessly enduring it all.

For him it was a nightmare beyond comprehension but it was even more torturous to witness what he was going through reflected in their eyes. Beneath the ridge of his swollen brow and through the blood and dust he watched them breakdown—the whole family descending into madness.

But then quite suddenly, everything around him faded and *her* face was brought into sharp relief. It had been so long since he had seen her face, over the course of their separate journeys they had been painfully apart but for the briefest moment when their paths drew close and they could almost touch.

For years he had reached back into his memory nightly for a clear image of her face—reaching for a memory that might invoke her strongly, so to make him feel as though she was near. The memory of the evil had drown out all else— like a thick murky tar weighing down all bright memories within him. Yet it was now that he could see her clearest— hysterical, distraught, enraged, struggling against his father's arms—trying to reach him, trying to stop that which she did not have the power to end.

Returned to the present the landscape of the past faded but for her, the translucent figure of her lie ahead of him like a ghost displaced from her time—this revenant of light and love bound in a skin of memory and longing called to him. He rose again; the clear image of her face had lifted him from the ground—pulling him out from underneath the crushing heartache.

Following the image of her afire on the horizon he continued up the hill, chasing her. ...desiring only to be with her. In his fever he forgot that what he saw was only an embodiment of his love and memory; while the real woman was elsewhere gathering her resolve just as he was gathering his.

Reaching for the memory of her, he was reaching for the end of the pain. Needing sanity he walked, his hand outstretched towards the fading image. And it was as the face of his beloved diffused in the dawning light that he woke from his fever of memories to find himself at the top of the mount alone—upon that place looking out over that city, surprisingly feeling clearheaded—alive and free rather than dead and stranded—ready to overcome.

Drawing his shawl back to let the sunlight wash over him, he stood exposed yet unflinching. He was free of the terror that drove him into hiding and forced him to cower. Once more he stood a proud son with the sun upon his face.

He looked out across the valley—standing before the looming city looking it full in the face without fear. He had at last conquered that which conquered him. Having willingly relived the attack, he would no longer live under the threat of its return. In reliving it he had proven to himself that he was not as weak as he had come to believe or was he as broken as he felt. And standing there—his feet in the very dirt upon which his blood ran—the ineffable meaning in what he had done settling within him. He had reached a place where he could see beyond what had been done to him; the brightest memories now being what he had done in the face of it all.

Refortified, he stood there, steady and clear. His piercing gaze sweeping the valley as the sun ascended. He inhaled, feeling new strength cycle through him as he re-expanded his lungs that had been squeezed tight by the strangulating burden of memory he had borne. Released from his past he could at last see his future. No longer seeing his wounds but rather himself.

⚬

Descending from the hill all was different. He was no longer defined by his pain he was defined by his *survival*. He was no longer defined by the evil that had risen *against* him but by the love that had risen for him. No longer defined by those who had betrayed him but by the love of those who enabled him to survive what should have killed him.

The last time he had stood upon that ground he had died—that was what everyone had been left believing. And from that day he had lived ever-more as *the nameless man*. Bound in a fear-induced silence, since that day he had been unable to speak as openly as he once did—allowing the realizations that flowed from the unseen to be passed along to the communities. No, he had been forced to retreat into himself so deeply, that even he seldom saw or heard from his original self. Long ago, evil had taken his voice yet on this day he had regained it. *Silence allows lies to spread. Inaction allows for negative action. But no more,* he thought to himself. His feet were planted steady as he took each step on the shifting terrain until he reached the base of the hillside.

Everything had been taken from him—his words had been taken and twisted to suit the agenda of those who sought power over their fellows. His name had been taken and given to the lead character in the fiction that had become the foundation for a church around which the greedy gather those who are desperate and able to be extorted. The sanctity of his body had been violated, his sacred realizations had been warped—his very life had been taken.

No, he had not died that day, while stretched out upon that ground—laid out upon that wood—but neither had he lived a single day since. Yet over these last days he had done all that he was never again to do: he had returned to the place he was to never return to. He had spoken those teachings he was never to speak. And despite the fact that he did not have a name to give or a personal history he could share, he had been himself.

No, it was true, he was not the impassioned idealistic youth he once had been. So long had he sought to return to what he was before the attack but the final truth was: there was no going back; for the youth, while eager and devout, was unknowing of the evil. He would go forward from this place and become the *matured idealist*—the believer who had recovered from doubt; the reunified one who has recovered from torment. He would be different than he was; he would of course be changed by all that had happened yet at the same time he would be familiar.

He walked through the gate once again. As the realizations rippled out within him—progressing his recovery—he felt the residual fear lingering as he emerged into the crowds of daily pilgrims. For a moment he braced—afraid of the crowd. Yet almost at the same time the fear rose, he could feel a surge of defiance. He would live in hiding no longer. He would no longer cower in the shadow of evil's unspoken threats. He could once again recall the greater force that he was a part of no longer dwelling on the numbers of those lined up against him but of the strength of those lined up behind him.

Passing back through the streets where the worst night of his life had publicly played out, he did not recoil in an assault of memory as he had so many times before. Instead he walked calmly, with a serene resolve circulating through him, his head high and his eyes wide. He walked at an easy, determined pace; his staff following his lengthy stride. He heard everything that went on around him and yet he heard nothing. He took in everything occurring and yet he was thinking of only one thing.

The merchants did not approach as they had only a few hours before; he made his way back through the market undisturbed, as though something in his gait and demeanor made them ashamed to solicit him for sales.

The call for afternoon prayer now resounded through the four Quarters. The cry did not speak to his faith, it did not move him to turn to the East and submit, but at the same time the throated cry, sung with his soul as a counterpoint—reverberating in twin tones—as he let out his call of rejoicing freedom.

Continuing back to the building, the streets roared with news—groups of people talking of the latest events. Yet he did not need them to tell him what had occurred, in his heart he could already feel it—the threat had passed. It was safe for them to leave.

Rounding the final corner he walked down the narrow side street, across the threshold and up the stairs that led to the second level of the abandoned building that had been their refuge these last days.

He came through the door to see the face of his son looking frantic. Yet Yoseph's worry faded instantly; the boy could tell that something had happened to his father, something strengthening.

"Gather your things," he told Yoseph when he reached him.

Reading his father's tone Yoseph knew they were not leaving in a rush out of some new threat but rather, because the time had indeed come to depart; whatever had needed to be done here over the course of their journey, had been done.

Noticing the events, the others in the room approached.

"It is safe to leave," the man said, answering the question everyone was about to ask. "My son and I will be resuming our journey."

Hearing this news, Samuel and Maria looked stricken. They were sad to part ways with the man at what seemed like only the beginning of their friendship. Their moment of their choice had come.

There was general disarray as those in the room busied themselves, hastily leaving. The farmer, his wife and daughter, who had said very little to anyone, immediately gathered themselves and departed, hoping their home was still standing. Ari, his wife and sons, likewise made to depart without any kind of farewell or the slightest acknowledgment of what had passed between then all over the last days; the silence itself underlining the unspoken things that had taken place behind the vocal debates. Ari passed down the stairwell without a glance at the man. The only hint of care came from the youngest son Uri who, for the briefest of moments, looked as though he wanted to say something. He stopped, looked at the man, opened his mouth and then hesitated. Ari called to him; he set aside the fleeting longing and obeyed. They all passed through the doorway and shuffled down the stairs, followed by the students, who ultimately found Ari's war-cries of more consequence than the man's beliefs in love.

Samuel and Maria lingered, standing beside Yoseph, watching as the man gathered himself across the room, preparing to leave.

"I do not understand how they can simply walk away," Maria said in disbelief, watching the students pass over the threshold. "How they can go on with their lives—unmoved by all that has passed here. As the conversation progressed, I expected some dramatic change to sweep through the people here. This was all so very important. Your father," she said, struggling for words, "he is unlike anyone I have ever met. He is the answer we have been searching for."

Yoseph listened to the footfalls hitting each stair as the last refugees left the building.

"The greater choice is held within the smaller choices," Yoseph replied plainly. "The pivotal moments of our lives do not announce themselves. The divine does not reach out to us in dramatic display. It is all very subtle yet it is clear enough for those who wish to see it. Sadly, it is also subtle enough to be dismissed by those who do not wish to see it."

The last footsteps faded. A door opened. A door closed. The group emerged out onto the city streets, where they joined the flow of the mob.

Belongings gathered and staff in hand, the man joined his son. The man, Yoseph, Samuel and Maria all stood alone within the now empty room. So much had been shared between everyone who had dwelt there over those days. All the others who had resided here were willing to dismiss the meaning of the words that had been spoken in this space and continue on with their lives, as if nothing had occurred.

The man had seen it many times before. Days ago, when the conversations began, he had opened his mouth knowing that perhaps a few but probably none would actually hear him. The fact that he had formed a friendship with two of the hearts present had been more than he had ever expected.

Sensing the couple's hesitation the man spoke, "You may come, if you wish."

The look of relief that instantly passed over both Samuel and Maria's face gave the man his answer. They all would set out together, the couple following the man and his son as they made their way back to their old homelands just north of the city, to finish the pilgrimage they had originally wanted to make.

The man laid a hand on his son's back, directing him to lead the way for the couple. Samuel and Maria passed down the stairs after him. Then, with one last glance at the horizon set beyond the gapping window, the man swept down the stairs. The tails of his shawl flickered—trailing behind him. The room was at last silent.

CHAPTER XVIII

The Limit of
What Can Be Borne

AS THE SMALL GROUP WALKED, the silhouette of the ancient city grew smaller behind them. Everyone remained silent over the first few miles; it was clear in his demeanor that something had happened to change the man. He had not gone into detail about the events of the early morning. Samuel and Maria knew that later, once the man and Yoseph had time to themselves, Yoseph would undoubtedly be told the story of what had occurred during those twilight hours the man was gone. But for now, as they walked, no one felt the need to pry.

During this time gratitude was central within the heart of Samuel and Maria. When the man extended his invitation the couple felt a renewed sense of possibility. For the first time in their lives they felt they had a genuine reason to believe that lasting change had come to their discouraging daily circumstances. Yes, many questions lingered; answers had been given yet new holes in their understanding had also been created. However, unlike before, the unknown did not dominate their thoughts. Walking with the man they felt assured that more answers would come to bring them beyond the oft-repeated questions.

The couple had grown accustomed to wandering without a bearing. For years they sought answers to 'the why's' in books—riffling through arcane sacred texts to find an answer to their present paradoxes. Yet none of the answers gleaned ever felt permanent. The various religions they explored were like temporary refuges; all the teaching they had clung to seemed makeshift—flimsy explanations put together in haste that they could make do with until the materials of a solid, complete explanation were found and they had the means to build concrete conclusions.

⁂

Descending the slope of a hill, the city was about to fall out of sight for good, sensing this the man came to a halt and turned, for the first time since they departed he chose to look back at what was left behind. For a long moment he stood there staring down the beast that had followed him for so long. Any thoughts he had he kept to himself. He simply stood there quietly staring for a time before at last turning forward looking toward all that awaited him.

The journey north back to the site of his old homelands was a full day's walk. To pass the time Samuel thought it acceptable to resume the conversation from the night before.

"I still do not understand how anyone could find it in them to make such a journey as you describe. I do not think I will ever understand why it would be necessary. I know what my wife and I have endured and I don't see how anyone could be asked to voluntarily endure the hardship and alienation that we have," Samuel said, posing one of the questions that lingered with him from the last talk.

Open to continuing the conversation, the man had a new enthusiasm rising in him since his emotional morning. The fear that had gagged him was no longer present. Samuel and Maria would not twist the meaning of his words, he knew this—he knew they were good people, and for the first time in a long time, he trusted his instincts.

"One reason we are willing to go to such an extreme to find resolution is because the evil has already brought us to an extreme. We are willing to endure the extreme—to make a journey such as this, because we reach a limit. We become so tired of going around and around in our mind—asking the same questions, reliving the same moments, replaying the same conversations—that we become willing to do anything and go anywhere if it means ending the unending cycle of torments. The evil pushes us to the limit of what can be borne and it is there that we become willing to do whatever it takes to restore our inner-balance.

"Human beings have an inner-balance. When the things we are confused about outnumber the things we understand.... When the parts of ourselves that we are insecure about outnumber the parts of ourselves we are confident of, the inner-balance tips and who we are goes into chaos. We become incapacitated by our confusion and lost in our inability to understand the incidents within our own life. The deeper the trauma, the deeper the loss; the more numerous the questions, the more incapacitated the person becomes. One can live in this stranded state for *decades*," he stressed, understating the truth, "however, every scarred person eventually comes to a point within their lives when they are willing to do *whatever it takes* in order to be healed. They reach what some of us call: *The limit of what can be borne.*

"At this limit, any fear we feel concerning what must be faced and any weariness holding our feet in place becomes nothing; the need for resolve is paramount, overtaking all such inhibitions. Courage has not been found; the fears that have held us back from the hard but necessary path simply become nothing; for we know that the fate we fear the most is the one we have been living."

"I understand," Maria said. "The need for change becomes so pressing that we are willing to do what once frightened us." Samuel took her hand as they walked. He knew the deeper significance of her words. "This, right now," she confessed, "leaving the city—listening to my heart rather than any guilt I feel—this was once impossible. I was trapped for the first thirty-five years of my life. I know I could not survive another thirty-five. I reached the limit you speak of years ago. Today I finally feel free. The only twinge of regret I feel is in the knowledge of all the upheaval my choice is making. I know what it will be like in my parent's house today and in the weeks to come. I do not want to hurt anyone but I also know," she finished, her eyes sad, "it could not have been any other way."

The man stopped walking. He turned to Maria, "My choices have likewise caused a great deal of upheaval, even pain. You, like me, never set out to hurt anyone. You did what you did to be free from those who would control you. We cannot worry about hurting the illusions of others, we must be concerned with our well-being—our life. From what you have told me it sounds as though your 'family' was living under the illusion that you all were close and happy, when in fact you were not. You chose to walk away from this illusion, knowing that living with it for the rest of your life would be unbearable. I know you are worried about the backlash from the choices you have made today. Your leaving will create a hole in the illusion your 'parents' have lived with, but any pain they feel because of this is not your fault. They chose to live with the lie; it was going to unravel one day, no matter what you did. You are not responsible for the pain they will suffer as their illusions fall."

Maria nodded her head. A tear streaked down her round cheek. "I do feel regret," she confessed as she wiped the tear away. "Not in the choice I have made," she clarified, "but that it had come to this at all...that the illusions could not have been done away with long before and we all sat down and been sincere with one another. I tried. I tried so many times. But my openness was always exploited, never reciprocated. They could never set aside their aims and just talk about what they felt."

"I know," the man assured. He slowly began walking again. The glaring sun pushed them onward. He walked beside her. "Regretfully, this is often what seeking the truth means.

"We ask for truth, not knowing what shall come or what the cost shall be. All we know is there is no going on without it. We know we cannot survive as we are: distraught, self-doubting, trapped. Our life has come to a halt and all that was stone in us has tuned to quicksand. Lost to ourselves, we know the only thing that shall restore us is *truth* and so we invoke our right to be shown the missing pieces and unfortunately the path of discovering truth leads us to some disturbing places and a great deal is overturned in the wake of revelation.

"Truth—it can be uplifting and it can also be devastating," he said in a haunting voice; speaking of an untold past behind him, which both Samuel and Maria were gaining an appreciation for as the minutes passed. "Yet even when learning a truth takes out the heart of us, we are still more with it than we were without it; for with the truth we cannot be enslaved by lies or manipulated by those who spin them. With the truth we can cease the circles of confusion and move forward whole and focused, following our heart."

Turning to Samuel as they walked the dusty path the man spoke with an ever-more candid tone, "You said that you could not understand how taking this journey could help; thinking it would seem to only cause more harm. But here is what this matter comes to in the end: At times it can seem like learning the truth leaves more scars upon us than we had when we began. Yet any sting felt when learning a hard truth will subside in time and we will be left with the facts alone, and with that knowledge, freedom. Awareness liberates us from the hold those who weave illusions can have on us. While truth delivers us from the debilitating confusion surrounding the most traumatic moments of our lives; for truth can bring resolve and resolve helps us in reuniting ourselves. Truth can bind back together what vicious lies and intimate deceit have torn apart.

"We do all this—we go to the extreme in order to gain *resolve*, which is at once both a needed and an elusive thing," the man said darkly emphasizing his words to insinuate that he too, like Samuel, had struggled with this point.

The man continued walking as he talked. He no longer shied away from the sun. The fear was gone from him and the certainty that had risen drew in everyone around him. Samuel and Maria's full attention turned toward him as they too walked the open lands. Likewise Yoseph too listened, not necessarily concerned with the words his father was saying but the open, self-certain manner in which he said them; for it had been a great while, if ever, that he had seen such strength emanating from within his father.

"When, in our *mind*, we need to know an answer we simply ask a question yet when we need to know something in our *heart* it is very different. There is not always a clear question to be asked, only a clear need. There is seldom a tangible idea of where to find the missing truths concerning our life, instead there is only the piece missing in our own understanding—a festering hole in our own heart and life, which has kept us from knowing what happened to us to leave us so hurt and crippled.

"When we seek understanding we seek a realization, though about *what* or *who* we cannot always say. All we know is that we need to see something, we need an explanation— we need the truth concerning what has happened behind the scenes in our own life—what evil has been doing *to* us and what love has been doing *for* us.

"What we seek is this: the departure from evil's world, the healing from all that they have done to us and the beginning of a new life in a world where loving hearts are still in majority and thus the way of living is one of authentic community. However before we can leave this place we were born—this place where evil reigns—to begin a completely new life there are preparations to be made. If we want our departure to be *final*—requiring no trip back to retrieve a part of ourselves that the evil took, or to gain vital clarification concerning who they are and what they did to us—we must finish the old. If we are to be free to begin a life elsewhere, we must sever all ties we have to the evil here; an evil who, like it or not, we are bound to whether because they are our inflictor or because we once loved them in some way and have yet to resolve those feelings. We are bound to those who are evil because at some point in our lives we loved them, were taught by them or were attacked by them, and before we can move on our feelings concerning them must be resolved.

"The first half of the journey—the gathering—is the collecting of all that shall be needed in order to leave this world behind forever. The first leg of the journey is the assembling of resolve," the man said, continuing into a new topic, fully holding Maria and Samuel's attention.

"Before we can escape Hell each of us must escape the moment of attack we have been trapped and reeling in—that moment when the *initial wound* was received. The initial wound is the attack that hurts us the deepest—the attack on us that neither our heart nor our mind could work through. It is that attack that we could not move forward from—unable to escape the impact-crater, for the sheer walls of it were too steep. For years—decades, you tried to climb out of that traumatizing moment" He went on speaking in a personal tone, "...and there are times, when you think you have found the answers—that you think you have escaped the wake. However, the explanations you came to were never complete; they were only ever the surface truths and with the evil the surface truths are nothing—nothing. The *surface truths* are misleading; they never fully connect you to the inconceivable, unexplainable truth of those who have become evil, which lies beneath the surface of their façades.

"Comprehensive understanding is the wounded soul's path forward out of devastation. Each thought had in which something is comprehended brings us forward and in this instance brings us out of Hell and closer to a new life beyond this backward place. The first leg of the journey is the one in which we gather all that is needed for a final resolve and thus for a complete severing from the evil.

"There are many wounded souls on such journeys; bring all those journeys together and you have the greater exodus taking place, as loving hearts leave the ones who choose evil and lend themselves to the preservation of the old ways upon the Other Shore."

"You have spoken to us of the first leg of this journey but what is the second half?" Maria asked, a little hesitantly. Part of her feared the answer.

"After all the truth is gathered there comes the time of assembly. This is a period of contemplation during which all that we have gathered shall come together to form a clear picture of the beast—what an evil person is, and what they want, what they have done to us and the world that they have built. The truths we gathered on the journey shall unite during this time into tremendous and powerful realizations, which act as a stimulant waking us to the true state of things. Both the true state of the world we live in, which the evil has shaped, and the true state of ourselves after living in that world— repressed, brainwashed and incapacitated.

"Each loving heart to be born into evil's culture—their world—has been entangled within it. We have been en- trapped by the evil people around us who we perceived to be our family, our friends, our mentors and peers; imprisoned within the reality those who have chosen evil have imposed upon us since a young age. Yet once the truth is gathered resolve, at last, begins to form; the waking takes place, the pulling away begins, and the journey continues as we move through the barrier of one world and into another. This final portion of the journey brings us through the transition between the end of one life and the rebirth into another. The part of the journey that is the departure from this shore and the homecoming to the *Other*."

"I have a question," Samuel interjected when it seemed as though the man had finished his thought. The long road to the lands up North was passing quickly with the flowing conver- sation. "You have told us that the only way to gather the truth about those who are evil is stay here in their world and make the journey. And yet you have also told us that you have met others who remember all that has transpired between love and evil—that there are those who know the 'whole history' right from the very beginning. So, if there are those who know the truth about the evil, why must those of us who wish to leave be forced to stay and confront evil in order to learn about it? Why can't all those who believe in love be guided out of evil's world now, brought to the Other Shore and then taught the truth once we are there? Why must we linger here?" he asked helplessly. Still struggling with the justification for the prolonged suffering he and Maria endured. "I realize that we each must find resolve with all our personal pains but why can't those who know about the evil simply help us understand what happened to us?"

The nameless man laughed softly to himself. "The short answer is: For the simple reason that some things must be seen to be believed." Knowing that Samuel's questions, like his own, would not be satisfied with the short answer, he continued, "The truth of those who have chosen evil cannot be *taught* to us. The mindset of one who has become evil—their desires, their methods cannot be *explained;* for what they are is incomprehensible to any who has not *witnessed* them. And even after having witnessed those who are evil in their full horror, it is hard to grasp what we have actually seen—to give the name 'evil' to the act…to the person.

"No, sadly to understand the evil, it must be seen. There are some truths we can take secondhand and some we must experience for ourselves. This is why the journey has to be made; for upon our return having witnessed the methods and heard the evil's great plans and true regard from its own mouth; having seen behind the veil and recoiled at the ugliness of the beast's heart, we have the truth, we have witnessed the inconceivable and therefore can understand it."

"Even with the wisest of teachers, we could not comprehend what they have become or the world they have built upon this Earth without seeing it with our own eyes. Explanations cannot fully convey what those who have chosen evil have made themselves to be, their methods and goals make no sense. The choices of those in evil's movement cannot be understood *logically*. They can only be understood through observation—we *see* what they want, what they do, what they believe and we come to accept that, while logically it makes no sense for a person to be what they have become and to follow a path that is leading to death, they have. In many ways those who have chosen evil are insane, and there is no comprehending the mind of a mad man, one must simply accept what they have become.

"I can understand your wanting a different, less painful, way of awakening to the truth. But, unfortunately, there is no other way. We must go and pull back the curtain and see them for what they are—see the world they have made, even though we may be disturbed by what we find and alienated while dwelling here. And, if we can recover from this devastating realization of what those who are evil are—if we can pull ourselves back from the reeling shock and while staring at the evil and the perverse world they have made, reaffirm that we do indeed have the right and the ability to break from them, then we are able to sever all ties to it and begin a new life apart from them."

The path led on. The nameless man continued, he now voiced the truths of the learned man to Samuel just as they had once been conveyed to him. The circle taking a full turn.

CHAPTER XIX

The History of the Lie

"THE PATH OUT OF THIS BACKWARD WORLD IS involved," the man said. In that moment the sunlight struck him full in the face. He raised a hand to shade his eyes. Squinting past the blinding glare, he continued walking; trusting his instincts to help him keep his footing on the loose gravel path. When he spoke there was the slightest hint of fatigue in his voice but it melted into a solemn tone as he pressed on. "We must leave behind our past life lived in this world and resolve all that occurred between us and the harmful ones we have encountered; thus the first leg of the journey—the firsthand gathering of truth. During this part of the journey our *heart* begins to transition from one life to the next. During the second half of the journey our *mind* begins to transition from one reality to the next. We untangle ourselves from the false teachings that structure our mind.

"I know that you have trouble reconciling yourself Samuel, as to why any loving force would ask us to confront the evil who has harmed us as a means of healing. Believe me, I have struggled with the same paradox. Yet as I come to the end of my own journey, I cannot dispute the volume of truth gathered. Yes, after making the journey I bear a few more wounds than I did before setting out. Dwelling amongst those who are evil we witness horrible things, harsh, blunt truth that is needed for our healing, but at the same time is damaging to behold.

"Before the journey I saw the truth yet had no context for it. There were moments within my daily life when, staring into the face of one who I thought I knew, I saw the face of someone inhuman—obscene and conceited. Yet when this occurred I did not know what I had actually seen. I did not know that, in that moment, I saw 'evil.' I knew the ancient word 'evil' yet its actual meaning remained unknown to me. I was taught the myths of evil—told the stories of demons and devils yet I had no idea as to the reality of evil. I had not yet matched what I had seen behind the veil of feigned compassion and brotherhood with the ancient word.

"The majority have joined to the movement of evil. Throughout our impressionable years we are folded into evil's culture—taught that movement's priorities, its customs, its versions of history, its gods, its values and so on. At times we sense the wrongness of what we are being told yet we seldom reject the ways we are taught. Brought into their culture, we are taught ways that we know in our heart to be wrong yet many of us choose to disregard what our heart is telling us and accept the backward ways."

"Why?" Maria interjected, needing an answer. "Why don't we listen?" she repeated again, needing an explanation;

not only of the behavior of those in the world but for her own betrayal of self that had taken place throughout the years of inaction.

Squinting in the mid-day sun the man turned to her. "Some of us are afraid to follow our heart and go against the mob. Some are too lazy to delve deeper. Some are simply uncertain. ...We look around us to see that, what we may deem to be wrong or backward, is perfectly acceptable to everyone else and so we ignore these instinctual hints pointing to the nature of the place we are in. Years pass, we ignore the signs that speak of the loveless relationships we are in. We try to brush off the nagging feeling that there is something profoundly wrong with the world as it is. We cannot get to the root of it. The feeling fades only to rear up again in time. The questions go into remission only to return and plague us anew.

"Some of us come to a point wherein we try to silence these whispers because we fear that all 'the wrongs' will add up to a hopeless situation. Many are afraid to leave what is empty, be it a relationship or a religion or an environment, or a cycle of habitual behavior; if it is the only thing they have ever known. Because, while it is detrimental to them, they *know* it and do not wish to change—shying away from the hard emotional and mental work that would come with overturning all that is false or harmful and setting out in search of what is fulfilling.

"These instinctual whispers of the heart speak to us of the greater wrong that we are entangled in. It is our heart's way of prodding us into action to secure a better future for ourselves. While living our lives in this culture there comes a time when we begin to sense that something is backward. We begin to see that mankind has become something we are not meant to be yet we do not know what we are seeing is 'evil.' Yet the moment does at last come when we realize that evil has no horns—it has a human, and all too familiar, face.

"In this moment of clarity, while we do not understand what has happened or how those around us could be evil, those who want the truth are guided on a journey out of evil. While on our journey we are led into situations wherein we are able to see beyond the flesh—into the heart and realize that certain people are not what they appear—they have become something perverse, dark...evil. In this moment, the myths of evil fall away. Disillusioned we wake to the reality of evil—to the true state of the world and to our place within the epic story of the struggle occurring between the two beliefs at work. And while the time spent witnessing the reality behind the veil is grueling—difficult beyond words—it is somehow begrudgingly worth it in the end, if it means solving the maddening mystery of the unanswered questions and resolving the stalemated dilemmas within ourselves that have kept us bound to a negative way of life.

"On the journey we go to the extreme where we bear witness and glimpse the stomach-turning reality. We fill ourselves with truth—truth that is gleaned from cold fact. And it is as the meaning of these truths comes forward a piece at a time that we slowly make the transition from the old and into the new. We break from all that is false, making our way forward, towards a rebirth.

"The journey out of this backward world is involved; for we must withdraw from one reality if we are to be free to enter another, as well as withdraw from one life so as to be free to enter a new. For each individual the two transitions between worlds and lives happens simultaneously, creating their 'journey out.' Pulling our perspectives back we can see the larger journey taking place across the Earth by all those sickened by this world who are in search of what is genuine...all our separate paths entwined together to create the *exodus of love.*"

"Speak more about this transition between worlds," Maria asked, wanting to know what this journey was leading up to.

"The first leg of the journey was the heart's path out. Second leg of the journey is the mind's path out.

"While the transitions of the heart and mind take place together there are two distinct things occurring within us— the mind's transition between worlds and the heart's transition between lives. As I have said before, this journey is not a matter of crossing physical distances alone; for our mind it is a matter of transitioning from one reality and into another. The second part of the journey is focused on breaking our mind out of the confines placed upon it so that we may accept the unlimited workings of our true reality.

"You see, when we are born our mind is a free-form, having not yet been structured by any teachings. Of course we do not remain a free-form thinker; from the moment we are born we are inundated with information—some of the teachings we are given are correct but sadly, in this world, most of the information we are given is more hurtful then helpful.

"Knowledge is meant to expand the borders of our world, our perception and our thinking. The teachings we are given by a people who do not believe in a limitless force narrow our world, our perception and our thinking. Things that are normal in love's reality are classified as 'impossible' here and when these impossible acts are carried out they are called *miracles*—something impossible but for one who is divine.

"When we are children we are free-form thinkers—able to take in the great scope of the world of possibility we live in. Yet by the time we are grown we have become narrow-thinkers; that is, if we are still able to think for ourselves at all. Our once boundless mind is now rigidly structured to that of a narrow corridor where few things are possible and the landscape of the vast world we are a part of cannot be seen.

"The transition of the mind from one world to another is a matter of breaking down the teachings instilled in us, which narrow our thinking, so we can once again have that free-form mind. In leaving this culture and going to the Other Shore, we will be moving away from the disbelieving perspective, where little is possible and going into a reality of boundlessness. Our mind must be ready to accept limitless possibilities.

"Our mind must be led into this new reality—the ancient reality, the workings of which been present on this Earth since long before evil came into being. The genuine reality, the roots of which penetrate down into the soul of the Earth. Unlike evil's reality, which is a construct of lies that sits atop a bedrock of betrayals, with no roots to speak of—a dead thing that has been superimposed over that which lives."

As the man finished he could not help but notice that Samuel looked strained. "What's wrong?" the man asked.

Samuel tried to find the words. "I can understand needing to resolve any lingering pains but now you are talking about moving from one reality to another…I do not understand. Evil may have taught us things that were not true but the lies can only go so far. I mean, they cannot change the nature of the world. Some things are what they are. They cannot change reality," he said with certainty. Adding helplessly, "Can they?"

The man paused along the dusty path, everyone paused with him. He wet his parched mouth with a swig of water, then wiped his brow with the back of his hand. He turned to Samuel. "One would think that reality is reality—that it is one of the few things that is unalterable; however this is not true. While the 'genuine reality' of this world does always endure on under the lies that have been superimposed, another reality—another set of workings for the world can and have been put into place.

"Now you might ask how such a thing is possible. How can evil—how can mankind—alter reality and rearrange fixed truths? The answer is: By turning the power of the mind against itself."

Putting the lid back on his water jug, the man waited until everyone else had their fill and then they all continued on, talking the long miles away.

"If the mind can be convinced of the realness of a lie, then that lie becomes a truth within the life of the one who believes it. If the mind can be convinced of the existence of a boundary, then that boundary shall become a limit within the life of the one who believes it. If the mind can be convinced that something that is false is actually true or that what is wrong is actually right, then it is possible for a lie to supplant the truth; for even if it be a lie the mind shall reinforce the lie with the unparalleled force of *absolute belief* and in doing so use its natural power to make the false working an actuality.

"Anything that our mind believes to be true holds power in our life, even if it is a lie. The mind has the power to make a thought real in the life and body that it governs. For example…" he said speaking directly to Samuel. "If in your mind, you are convinced by a doctor that you have a life threatening illness, which will in time kill you, you shall watch as your health drains from you. Not because the illness was a reality or because your death was imminent but because the absolute belief that your mind held concerning the illness made the sickness real and your life was effected by it—yielded to it.

"The force of the mind can be put behind a lie or behind what is real—behind limitations or possibilities. Our ability to make concepts real through the certainty of the mind is a natural power we hold. It is the natural ability of all beings. An ability that is very useful and amazing, yet also extremely dangerous. It is meant to aid us in bringing to fruition new possibilities from the boundless reality of love. The ability of the mind to make things real is meant to be a gift that helps us reach for a new depth of love and then bring it to manifest. It is how we actualize what we have never seen before but have learned to be possible.

"Those who became evil erased the truth to establish their lies. This is how one goes about birthing a false reality.

"Born into evil's version of truth many know only evil's explanations, evil's beliefs and their histories. We have been taught what the world would be were it not based upon and moved by the boundless reality of love. We have been taught to reason within the limited confines of the reality the past generations of evil have placed on us. Just as our children shall be confined to the reality the present evil teaches to us and we unknowingly pass onto them. We bring our children into the reality according evil, passing onto them the lies we were taught, unaware that all we perceive to be fact is indeed false. We were taught the lies as truth and we teach our children the same lies, as though passing on a disease to them before learning we are infected. However those children who have an open-hearted presence in their life have hope; for while we teach them all we were taught of the false reality we also can pass on to them our belief in the limitless possibilities of love. We can instill in them an antibody that can help them survive the downfall of the lies and live to know the truth. That antibody, which combats the diseased reality, is our *open-mindedness*.

"All those born after evil became the majority have been force-fed evil's version of all things. The movement of evil has given us the explanations for all that occurs: they have told us what we can accomplish and what we cannot, what is right and what is wrong, what is natural and what is unnatural—in every way that a person can be dictated to, we have been.

"Those who became evil stopped believing love to be all-power, all-important and all-fulfilling. And so when the time came to define what was possible and impossible, right, wrong and so forth, they taught the next generation of a world with love removed—a world with false limits and corrupt values. They raised the generation to come within a world without all the possibilities that love brings. They raised the generation within a reality where possession, perversion, and the pursuit of power are central instead of inherently wrong.

"The wisdom of the old culture was lost because it was not passed on; those who became evil bred out the knowledge of love and the workings of the old world. As the generations passed and those who recalled the old ways converted to evil's movement, they consented to take 'the new truth' and let the old wisdom die. While those few who were left from the old world, who never converted, suffered having their voices drown-out and being discredited as their deeply-held beliefs went out of fashion in an age of predominant evil.

"Those who were not there when the great lie—the new truth—was agreed upon have been taught its doctrine as truth and whether by ignorance or preference have accepted a false reality as the only reality.

"What it really comes down to," he said, wiping his brow again with the edge of his tattered shawl, "is the fact that it is human nature to accept what is being accepted by those around us and to believe what we are taught by those we regard as our teachers and parents. Using these human traits to their advantage, evil could instill the reality they designed within the new generations who, like every person born before them, came forth into this life open to learn and trusting of those who surround them. In feeding the new generations the agreed upon lies, those who became evil could rid themselves of the old world, which viewed their choices as wrong, and be free to create a world where their backward way was the one true way of living.

"What we take into our mind is either rejected—cast out as impossible and unnatural. Or it is accepted—allowed to take root in our mind and put into place as reality, and is subsequently reinforced as truth by the force of the mind's certainty. Through this process, as the lies become the reality within the life of the one who believes it, a false reality can be made. And when the lie has been accepted so extensively that the truth has been utterly lost but for the few who refuse to convert. The result is the world we now live in…" he said raising his arm slightly, his finger denoting a small outcropping of land chard black by a recent mortar shell. "…where it is as if the old world never was."

"None of the generations born after evil founded their world knew the whole truth concerning the old world? What of those who became evil back in the beginning? They still knew the truth?" Maria inquired.

"Denial is strong," the man said flatly. "Those who rejected the old truth are fanatics, believing that the new ways embodied by the movement of evil are better. Now I know how twisted this reasoning is and I do not want to enter a conversation about why those who are evil choose what they do. They simply do. They viewed their transition into their new philosophy like we view converting from one religion to another. They liked the new doctrine of possession and power, as opposed to the old one of community and love. So they abandoned the old and went full-force into their new faith with the same blind fervor as any zealot.

"Those founders of evil who were there when the lie was agreed upon, of course, recall the true reality. They were there when the old world flourished. They were raised within the old ways. They have simply convinced themselves that what they put into place is more desirable. If the liar repeats his lie enough, he can even convince himself that it is true.

"They have justified the atrocity by telling themselves that, while it was not the first reality it is the 'rightful way.' Yet despite all the propaganda, I think that, under the layers of self-deception, justification and vain reasoning, they know the hollowness of what they have built. They know that they buried the truth as a means to bury the crimes they committed. Regardless of the doctrines they wrote and repeat again and again to themselves, they can never fully drive-out what they know in their heart. Denial pushes down truth but it does not dissolve it," he finished.

The magnitude of what had occurred between love and those who chose to become evil brought Samuel and Maria to speechlessness. A mile of silence passed as the words that were spoken sunk in. Finally Maria spoke. Her voice shook with disbelief, "There must be some fragments—some remnants of the world before this, I mean," she said, coming up short, "even a civilization that has been wiped out leaves some remnant of their former glory. Stories, songs, artifacts," she reasoned. Half expecting that, somewhere on the earth, stone tablets containing love's history were waiting to be unearthed.

"You have held in your hands a book containing the wisdom my family has gathered. We have only a fraction of the greater story. The history of that old world was mostly handed down in an oral tradition; as such it was easily erased. The few fragments of truth that managed to remain were taken up and entwined in the mythos and folklore of the new world—no longer recognizable as remnants from that loving way of life now gone. Generations of loving hearts had gathered a comprehensive understanding of the reality upon which the world exists, as well as the capabilities of human beings themselves.

"Reaching out into the unseen bringing forth all that was there to be known—delving into love itself—they ventured into the gulf between worlds returning with insights, which were later woven into parables for the next generation to understand and pass on. Yet sadly the old wisdom was lost when those who once treasured it abandoned it for 'the new truth.'

"The old world has all but died out. It lives in those few who have rekindled the old ways. Its record is not to be found in the history books of this world. Within this present age we look to the written archives to know the world of the past. Yet only a thin shard of the past has been chronicled and, depending on the scribe, the accounts recorded vary. The stories of the old world live on in those who dwell upon the Other Shore and in people like you who work to discover the truth.

"And even if every single person abandoned the truth," he said defiantly, "it would still endure; for when a truth is lost or cast away it does not dissolve into non-being it returns to the place from whence all wisdom flows. There it waits to be tapped into by one who is willing to reach—one courageous enough to break through the barrier of lies and delve into all that exists underneath the false reality, waiting to be known.

"The truth can live on under all the lies. The abandoned wisdom gathers at the heart of this world where love's consciousness lives eternal and from there the truths are able to flow directly into the heart of one who seeks awareness of them. The truth endures on under the foundations of evil's world, lying there waiting to be unearthed by one who is willing to open themselves up to another explanation.

"The desire for truth at all costs, is the doorway into genuine reality. Openness, belief and fortitude—all these meld together to form the will necessary to defy the illusions and find truth. To exit evil's reality the pathways of reasoning must be reformed—all that is known must be opened to redefinition."

"I do not know if I can forget everything I have been taught," Samuel confessed, as they all sat down for a moment on the side of the road to rest. "How can we forget all that we have ever been taught to be fact when the knowledge has become nature to us—gone to without a second thought? If what you say is true, then for the past forty or so years I have been taught nothing but lies. How do I even go about sorting through such an entangled mess?" he asked, daunted by the seemingly impossible task.

"One thought at a time," the man said, simply.

CHAPTER XX

The Reeducation

"THESE LAST DAYS.... These conversations," Maria began in dawning comprehension, "this has been in a way our reeducation, hasn't it? We came to a point in our lives when we were open to learn of a new way and then our path led us to you. This is all part of our journey, isn't it? You voice your thoughts and in doing so give us a new perspective on matters."

"Everything that happens in our lives happens for many reasons. I was meant to go into the city to resolve my own questions but, as it would seem, I was also meant to meet you both. I think we will find that our paths are all intertwined." His words came easy. There was no burden upon him. He walked down the path, his head high, eyes forward. His shawl covered only the crown of his head and his staff was no longer propping him up, rather it glided beside him, moving in stride with the rhythm of his gait. "Mind you," he said, the hint of a smile upon his face, "the transition of our mind is meant to happen a little more gradually than it has these last few days."

"What do you mean?" Samuel asked.

"We have packed a great deal into each of the talks we have had. I have presented you with an entirely new reality in the course of only a few days. In fact, submerging you in this new way of perceiving, when ideally one is meant to be eased in."

"We have been alright," Samuel insisted. He looked to Maria for agreement but she could not give it.

"It has been hard at times," she said, silently reminding Samuel of his own struggles to understand the vast information discussed. "We both have been thrilled by these conversations but it would be a lie to say it has been easy to take it all in. I feel exhausted sometimes—mentally strained—as though I am exerting my mind on this journey more than any other part of myself."

"It is true. You feel mentally strained because you are exerting yourself. The mind is complex thing. Our mind desires security; it takes comfort in knowledge that need never be questioned. Our mind needs routine and the ability to trust in its surroundings or else it becomes unbalanced.

"New realizations, especially of this nature, should be taken slowly to give the mind a chance to adjust. Over the course of the journey, to help the mind make what can be a difficult transition, the truth comes slowly at first; in an attempt to ease us out of the lie gradually. The shock of extensive lies can be damaging to one's psyche. The path progresses as fast as it can; that is, we are given as much truth as we can take without our mind recoiling in disbelief or unraveling in shock.

"The boundless reality thriving on the Other Shore is good for us yet it is also different than what we have thus far known and the mind can have difficulty with such radical change. Sometimes the truth, when it comes too fast, can do more harm than good. Even with the gentlest progression we will experience bouts of anguish where we lose hold. They subside over time; once we realize we can trust the new truth we have learned. But until then, we feel the mental strain; for there is no easy way to learn that most all that we have been taught is a lie."

"It is mind-blowing," Maria commented. "I know it is all true but still, part of it is...unbelievable."

"I know it is," the man replied. "Remember, I was once in your position struggling with the same truths. And regardless of all I have learned, I struggle still," he offered candidly. "During this final transition, the mind is cast into a churning sea of colliding swells—new truth colliding against all that we thought to be true. During the transition of perspective it can feel as though we must struggle daily to keep from being dragged to the depths of insanity. But there will come a moment when the mental strain lessens. There will come a turning point when the force of the new truths we have learned overtakes the lies, causing the current of our thought processes to shift, taking us gently in a new direction—into a new reality.

"We want to learn and so, as hard as some of these truths can be to take in, we will gradually integrate them into our lives. Willingness to learn and consider ideas beyond what you have been taught is crucial. This seems like a desire that many would hold but it isn't. Many fear the truth or are indifferent to it, giving it little priority in their daily lives.

"We are led out of lie by following the traces of truth regardless of where our journey might bring us. We are led out of illusion by picking up the thread of what we sense to be genuine, among all that is starting to seem wrong and following it, until it brings us to what is right. We are led out of the lie by not clinging to what we inwardly know to be false. Mental laziness, denial, closed-mindedness, fear—these things anchor our mind in this false reality," the man's tone shifted; he suddenly became reminiscent, as though he were about to tell a story from his own past. "When we are young children we are taught the workings of this world one thought at a time. We are taught how to view our reality and perceive our own capabilities one thought at a time. Our mind is twisted one lie at a time and it must be untwisted one truth at a time.

"One thought at a time, a bent perspective can be straightened. The truth may flow in the opposite direction than the way we have been taught to think. Nevertheless, as the truth continues to flow unhindered by denial, slow at first and then stronger, our thought process gradually begins to flow towards the infinite rather than the forgone. Until finally the current changes completely and we find ourselves perceiving our reality without boundaries.

"Through opening ourselves to the workings of a new reality and following what our heart tells us above all other reasoning we enter a new life in a wider world; wherein we reawaken to our true identity, our true history, our true potential and our true family."

"Why did everyone else reject all this?" Maria said, coming to a halt. "In the room," she added, "during the conversations.... Why did everyone else reject your ideas?"

Everyone stopped to listen to her.

"I have waited all my life for such truth and as I walk down this road I cannot help but think about those who chose to reject everything that we spoke of. It is beyond me why anyone would resist insights that could potentially give their empty lives meaning."

The man's mouth showed a slight consoling smile, as though to say, he understood her questions all too well. "Once, a long time ago, I went unto the people and shared openly all the reflections I have collected over my years of pondering and reaching. I did this out of a desire to share the meaning that my life had been given with those in my community who I saw suffering daily. Many rejected what I shared because it went against centuries of tradition. I—a young man of no consequence—who was I to bring word that the divine was not to be feared but rather embraced? The message of my words went overlooked by most. The politics of what I was saying seemed to dominate. In the end, I learned that there are those who reject aid because, as incomprehensible as it is, they have no desire to end their suffering. They have chosen suffering as a way of life; capitulated to their circumstances, they resolutely believe no change can come. While others have resolved themselves not to delve deeper; letting all that is trivial become central in their life. While still others give truth no priority in the grand scheme of their pursuits.

"As I just said, to make the transition from lie to truth," he said, beginning to walk slowly onward, "one must be open to the truth. We must be open to the possibility of learning that long-held beliefs are false. We must be willing to let the world we know fall. We must not fear the devastation. We must be strong enough to stand within the ruins of the only world we know. We must not lose faith when everything we have ever known is poured from us, during a time of the Great Emptying when all lies are left behind and we find ourselves existing in a void, in the time before the actual truth has yet to refill the vacuum left by all that has been removed.

"It is easy to speak of making such a transition but it is infinitely more difficult to experience," he frankly added. "If we are not willing to let the false world fall, if we cower and resist the transition—clinging to the lies, even though they are harmful—we shall hold up the false world with our own denial.

"The person who wants to make the journey must be open to seeing what they have not seen—be it the disturbing revelation of evil's presence and their lifelong deceptions, or the brilliant revelations of what is possible through love. If a person is sincerely willing to learn the truth, the cemented lies can be broken apart—overturned, thus allowing for the laying of a new foundation, or rather the unearthing of the old one.

"When the heart is open to the truth...., When the eyes are willing to see.... When the mind is willing to brave redefinition.... When we want the truth—all the truth, no matter the cost—the departure, can commence. In the end, it is simple. The entire journey begins with the desire to know the truth. You ask the question and Love sets the path. With all your heart you make the statement: 'I want to know the truth,' and Love sets the path of revelation, which is the same path that leads out of lie—out of the world of evil's construct. It is the path that leads you home, to the place you have always belonged. It is the path," he concluded, "that leads you back to your original self."

"We have always wanted the truth," Samuel replied. "We simply did not know where to find it. The truth was merely a vague concept, something that we could seek but never touch. My life is proof. I am a student of many different faiths," he shared. "I have gone from one doctrine to the next searching. I never knew what the truth was but as I read the texts and listened to the different teachers, I knew what is wasn't. I feel like I have been stumbling around, wandering without compass or guide until now."

"We all feel as though we wander until at last we find ourselves at the destination. Truth is elusive. It is not meant to be so. It simply is because it is lost within a mob of imitations. All we can do is become aware enough to know it when we see it," the man replied. "We must rise above the desperation that causes us to accept any messenger that comes down the road. Desperation blinds and we become willing to accept the peddler of lies as long as he tells us what we need to hear.

"I know you felt as though you were stumbling through your search but you weren't. That is simply how it is done here. We wade forward into the information presented to us and use our inner-senses to determine its authenticity. When presented with a piece of information, be it in a conversation or in a book we read, we must take it into ourselves and before accepting it we must sift it through our heart and ask ourselves: Does it feel right? Does it feel wrong? Does it feel like a truth or is there something about it that seems 'off?'

"During your search, while on your journey, you have found truths Samuel. And not just over the course of your studies but within yourself. What you would like Samuel, is what we all desire: a guide—someone who can take you by the hand, affirm your every realization and tie in the purpose to your every step."

Samuel nodded, agreeing that this was exactly what he wanted.

"All those making the journey long for this. We expect it," the man said; his voice rising to a place of lightness and humor. "We are brought up reading these old mythic tales of heroes who take upon themselves a quest. And unfailingly, in such stories, there is one all-knowing character giving our hero the answers that reveal what part his actions play in the greater story. Sadly, there is no such sagely character striding beside us as we walk the long path. I know you both think I have all the answers you need," he said; looking to both of them with a slight smile. Knowing just how far from all-knowing he was. "I know you believe I could be the guide you seek but you will learn in time that I cannot. We all seek the one with insights to relieve our sense of wandering. Having so little faith in ourselves, we turn to the outside world to find a reason to trust in what we have always known. We go outside ourselves, searching for what is already within."

Samuel looked sideways at the man, wordlessly asking the man his meaning. His eyes wide now. The sun had begun its descent.

"The guide we seek is not an omnipotent person. The needed guide beats within our own chest. —It is our heart," the man said pointing to the center of Samuel chest, leaving him breathless at the realization. "It is your heart.

Through the labyrinth
and across the distance,
she is the guide.

She is the one who can sense
what our eyes cannot see.

She is the one who can hear
what our ears cannot.

She possesses the oldest part of us
whose memory goes back further
than that of our mind.

She is the one who is connected to those
who our life is bound to,
even when they are afar.

She is the one who receives the whispers of truth
from the place at the center of existence,
wherein all that has been lost still endures
and all that has yet to be discovered
waits to be called forward back into being.

He finished.

"Where is that from?" Maria asked, looking tired after the day's walk but nonetheless, interested.

"From the book you read," he replied, laying a hand on the bag slung at his side.

"You wrote it?" she asked.

"A long time ago, when I was in Samuel's place," he replied. Samuel smiled, feeling a swell of brotherly affection.

"Brought into a cannibalistic society where one crawls over their own brother to achieve their goals, we are never taught our self-worth let alone the ability of our heart. As such we feel compelled to look beyond ourselves for answers.

"Our heart is the part of us connected to the love that has survived. The part of us connected to those who were there at the beginning and recall the truth. Our heart is the part of us connected to those who are the Mother and Father of us all, who are at this moment calling the children of love home. Leading us all from afar, they tell us to follow the voice echoing through our own heart across this barren terrain and to the Other Shore, where home awaits," the man grew silent. Something happened.

"Samuel," he said directly. A thought occurring to him. Samuel looked up from the dusty road and into the man's eyes. A moment of still anticipation stretched. "You have asked me many times over the last days, what would make a person be willing to endure the extreme of the journey. And I have spoken of our desire to bring an end to the suffering that has carried out within us. And that is true, but there is another side—another reason why we are willing to endure so much to resolve the old. We do all this out of a desire to heal but also out of a desire to *live*," he said slowly. His voice was deep, steady and calm. "Our longing for life is so strong within us that we are willing to do whatever we must in order to escape this death.

"We want to live without the looming threats that overshadow us when we are surrounded by those who have become evil. We want to build something lasting. We want to grow untainted, unharmed and without influence. We want to be free to know of love's ways and explore love's workings without ridicule. We want to be free to voice our heart without invoking evil's wrath. We all know this will never happen within a world inhabited by those who have become evil.

"Those who have become evil have renounced love's ways yet still they fear love's presence. They fear one who is empowered by love; for they fear what they cannot sway. They fear those who they cannot buy or threaten; for they have no means of controlling such a heart and they need control at all times to feel satisfied.

"Those who have become evil fear and resent those who remain loving. They hate to see the ways of love resurrected; for it reminds them of what they betrayed. A presence of one who is just, naturally makes those who are immoral all the more obvious. The presence of one who is innocent-minded naturally makes those who are perverse all the more obvious. It is a simple contrast. Our presence threatens their walls of denial and the integrity of their self-righteous illusions of guiltlessness. The presence of someone honest shows by contrast the presence of underhandedness. When one who has become evil stands beside a loving heart, their corruption is more noticeable; while if one who is evil is standing beside another who is evil the corruption is negated, appearing common. And so they want no one who follows the old ways in their society. ...One more reason why we will never thrive among those who choose evil.

"Every loving heart who has ever risen in their society has been discredited, discouraged or simply assassinated," he said bluntly. For the briefest of moments he sounded strained with frustration but then his taut tone relaxed into resolve and he spoke with the peace of a man who had come to terms. "We go through all that we do because we want to be free, to be safe and to live.

"We endure the journey because it is our only hope for a full life. Ever-hunted, ever-judged, ever-hindered, ever-influenced, ever-exploited we are willing to bring to an end one life if it means severing all ties to the surrounding evil. ...if it means overcoming the pains of the old life we lived among them and relieve ourselves of the burdens we have been forced to live under. We are willing to undergo the Great Emptying—to endure this transition...this death—if it means finally being filled with what is genuine so that we might at last know joy.

"It is in the lengths to which we are willing to go that we show how much having the life we have always dreamt of means to us. The revulsion felt when we wake to discover that the society we live in is a manifestation of an evil movement sickens the soul. The extent of the lie fractures the mind—splitting to the psyche and disorienting to our very footing upon this Earth. The emotional agony of waking to the true faces of those who surround is devastating. Waking to find that, in our innocence, we have been mutilated, violated, exploited and suppressed by those who we trusted is heartbreaking—the shock of it stops the heart and the truth impales our very Being. In this time all trust is broken into pieces too small to seemingly ever be put back together. But even with all the trauma the waking brings, we wake."

"We had no other choice," Samuel added.

"No, we always have the choice," the man corrected Samuel politely. "We all can choose how to spend our existence. We can wake," he said, highlighting the one side. "Or," he began, watching a group of uniformed soldiers being ferried in a utility truck along a parallel road, "we can remain ignorant."

"We chose to wake. The death of the old life, while painful, is the only way to break the connection and purge the evil. The journey, while arduous, is the only way to gather the means to move on to a full life," he finished calmly.

"I have a question. What do you mean by death?" Samuel asked almost immediately after the man finished. The word had stood out to him. "Do we have to die to escape the evil? Are we physically born onto the Other Shore, like an afterlife?"

"When I say death, I do not mean physical death. Rather, a part of us dies," the man said, trying to explain, "the part of us that could have stayed here and made a life here is the part that dies. When I say that our old life dies, I do not mean to say that we must end our existence to escape this place. I mean death in other terms."

"I did not know there was any other way to think about death, other than to perish. The end of this body," Samuel said, grasping at a handful of his shirt along his chest, as though in his mind it were the skin of his body.

"Death is but one more concept that we have been taught to think of in narrow terms. One thought at a time we expand our mind. So, what is it to die?" the man said pensively, expanding the meaning of the word. "It is not the withering of the body; for nothing ends with the withering of the body, a different transition simply takes place. No, death is a brought end. To suffer a death is to suffer the end of something.

"To be free of the evil we had to bring to an end the life that was tied to them—the life that we lived here in the world they constructed. We needed to separate who we truly are from who they tried to shape us to be—to filter them from our blood and restore the purity of self. In this process the entirety of our Being has to be stripped down, dismantled and any fate had beside them brought to an end so that our original self can be reassembled and given a chance at a new life.

"The end of the old life—the death of which I speak—has nothing to do with a physical death. The body can go on yet lifetimes can end and begin again. Our feet can travel the same paths each day yet immeasurable distance can be crossed. The physical measures of miles and years exist, yet the internal measures are what truly define what has been. Eventually the measurements imposed by man are too limited and only the heart can define what has been endured, what has been accomplished, the distance traveled and how many lives have been lived.

"Within the span of this body, I may live several lives; for the distinction between lives is made, not by the taking of another body but by the end of and beginning of a new life within my heart....

CHAPTER XXI

The Transition
of the Heart

"IT IS TRUE," the man said, trying to ground this concept of death and rebirth in reality. "One life can end. All ties to that life, resolved. All questions accumulated over that life, answered. All ways of living, changed.

"Some will live only one life, choosing to remain stationary—the same person now that they were decades ago. Yet those who seek and learn and grow shall inevitably live several lives over the course of their existence.

"We need not die in body for a defining distinction to be made. We pass over a divide—an event that draws a line. The memories of the old life fade—washed out by the sun over the long distances we travel. We come to a place wherein, we look back at what we once were—at where we once were—and it seems a dream...hazy and scarcely possible.

"Old acquaintances will revisit us like ghosts from the grave. They will come to us, drawn to a face of one they recognize. They will approach us looking for reunion only to greet a stranger; for, while our image is the same, the soul of us has evolved. Reborn again and again, we shed the skin of the old life as we progress; for it is too small to contain the evolving soul.

"And in the end," he said, his voice deep now with unspoken context, "even the name we have lived under can be left behind if we so desire. Regardless, if we choose to keep it, it will be redefined, as we are reborn." The pace of the man's thoughts slowed. He took a breath then picked up the conversation. "We have spoken a great deal about gathering truth but these insights we accumulate build into a metamorphosis. We are redefined as our world is redefined. Surviving this journey of harsh revelation strains us past all extremes precisely because it is a death. The death of what once was, so that we might at last become what we can and should be.

"Part of us dies during the second leg of the journey," he said meditatively. Speaking as a man who had, only hours before, experienced the end of which he spoke. "Dreams, hopes, love—all that is immortal in us survives the death of the old life, seeing us into the next. One could say these immortal parts of us, when combined, create our soul—the unchanging core of us that leaves the dying life and moves onto the next."

His words were soothing. He spoke with the peaceful resolve of one who had come to terms. The wake of his insights stretched out into a long silence. No one thought to speak. Everyone walked quietly across the landscape; each mind engulfed in the present moment of reflection.

For a long piece there was only the sun and the wind and the sound of footfalls along the gritty path. A faint breeze began to drift in from the west, breaking across the sweaty brow of each walker.

"I know you are afraid," the man said in a soft voice, "...afraid of the changes coming to your life, even though they are long-awaited. Strangely enough, I have found that the death of the old life happens gradually over years, even decades yet it also happens sharply, abruptly—the present becomes the past. Part of us sensed that it would end, part of us even knew that it needed to; nonetheless when it happens there is shock." The man's sharp gaze went out of focus as he lapsed into a more personal inflection. Suddenly everyone could sense he was no longer discussing general concepts but personal truth. "Exhausted after the prolonged difficultly, we think the old life, with all its suffering, will never end. Yet one day we become aware of the distance between where we were and where we are and realize we moved into another life.

"We cross over the extreme and find on the other side a calm. We do not find ourselves back where we began in our youth, as I thought we might, but rather, re-strengthened with a new path before us, which we never thought we could dare tread." The man receded even deeper into himself, speaking now to his own fading demons. "I wish it all could have happened sooner," he whispered regretfully. "Goodness how I wish it could have happened all those years ago. Then we wouldn't have had to come back," the man's whispers were loud enough for all to hear. Samuel and Maria had some vague hold of what he was speaking of but did not ask questions. Instead they just let him talk—let him say what he needed to.

Yoseph of course, knew exactly of what his father spoke; for he lived the same life and walked the same path.

"I wish we had not needed to come back. But I know," he conceded peacefully, "that there was so much to rid ourselves of." The man went on, "It all went on so long I began to think I would never reclaim myself but I did—we can. We can assert our right of choice and break free.

"There were so many lies...so-many-illusions. They told me.... They told me what would happen then. I simply did not hear them," he said vaguely. His voice trailed off.

"Father?" Yoseph inquired. He stopped and stood in front of his father.

Samuel and Maria remained quiet.

"Before we came..." the man replied. He looked into his son's eyes. "During those days of long conversations before we left..." the man added meaningfully. He spoke freely, as though he and Yoseph were alone. "I remember it so clearly. They said: 'The revelation of so much falseness called for the testing of all that we hold to be true. All that we have ever been certain of needed to be put to the test so that only what is true would survive...only those who are genuine would retain their right to a place in our life.'

"He said, 'Against the world of lies a force comes. A force that is unleashed when, no matter the consequences, we demand the truth. The ripple of this declaration passes through all that is known, all that is taught, all that is believed and all who are near us, causing what lays in the shadows to be revealed, whether it is willing to be or not. All that has gone unspoken will be heard. True intentions will be linked to the acts that have taken place and in this the choices made by each surrounding heart will be known; distinguishing loving and true, from evil and conceited.'"

The man kept speaking as though he could not stop the flow of the words. At times his tone was one of a sorrowful awe; while still at others he verged on the confessional. He had started walking again as he slowly rose from his own consuming thoughts. Yoseph drew closer to him as they continued down the path, the long miles behind them converging into one moment of synced clarity.

"The death of the old life comes," the man repeated, new meaning now held in the words. "During the beginning of my own transition, when I saw what would be the first of many illusions fall, I was impaled by the truth," his voice convulsed, "for at the tip of it was the betrayal of all those I had entrusted myself to—opened myself to and called my brothers. I could not see that there would be any life after that gauntlet of brutal revelation. There was only what had been done, no room left for what I still dreamt of doing. And that is all I ever thought there would be—I thought I would dwell in this in-between forever—unwilling to die yet unable to live." The man was now speaking directly to Yoseph. Samuel and Maria kept quiet, sensing how long this talk had been building. "For years I teetered upon the edge of sanity and madness. Seeing the evil come forward and the world I thought I knew disappear, the lines of reality blurred. I could no longer tell what was real and what was an illusion. I had felt certain of my reality once but that was before the revelation of lie; I had faith in people once but that was before the betrayal.

"They took who I am," his voice trembled. "After the end-game was played out and I finally saw them for who they were I was certain of nothing—not who I was, not what was real—nothing. I lay there dying; able to be brought back to life by just one, single, loving touch...so rare among the mobs of indifferent. Thankfully, you were all there," he said, taking up his son's hand.

The man pulled out of his haunting recitation. "I am sorry," he said suddenly coming to a stop.

"It's fine," Yoseph said supportively. "You're fine."

"A great deal just suddenly made sense to me," he explained.

"That's good," Yoseph reasoned. "Here," he said, unscrewing the lid to his water bottle and handing it to his father.

The man drank, regrouping himself. He poured a bit of water into his palm and ran it over his face, leaving a webbing of dew over his cheeks.

Extending his staff the man began walking, slowly getting back to his normal pace. He still seemed a bit disoriented.

"I am sorry," he said again, looking over to Samuel and Maria as they all continued down the road. "We all have questions that need answers. I have mine just as you have yours. I think you will find that, sometimes we are given the answers only we don't understand their full meaning until later."

"We understand," Maria assured him.

"Where were we before I went off on my own?" he asked with a laugh.

"It's fine," Samuel replied shaking his head. "We can just walk for a bit. We don't have to talk."

"No," the man replied. "I want to answer your question. I know I have scared you a bit with this talk of death." He laughed again, trying to lighten the tone.

"I suppose," he said, finding his footing. "In the end, I want you to be assured of this: Yes, in our pursuit of the truth, we are pushed beyond the limits of what we can bear—of what we can understand and of what we can survive. And when you reach the point when it seems as though there shall be nothing more—that all life has come to its end and now there is only the pain of what should have been but was never able to be, I tell you this: it is not the end of your life. It will pass. There will come a moment when we can finally surrender the old life, reenter the womb and restore our original self.

"Our torn body can be rewoven. The shattered mind can be pieced back together. The broken trust can be reset and refortified. The gashes upon the heart can be sewn and the scars can disappear as new, unmarked flesh grows over the place they once bled. Any pieces of us left forsaken can be regathered; for after the death of the old life we do not simply linger on as we are. No, after the death of the old life we reenter the womb and start building towards a new life. That is the heart's transition from death," he said firmly. "And while in-between that transition from what *was* into what *shall be*, we reenter the womb in preparation for a rebirth."

"You have spoken of our original self a few times over these last days. What do you mean when you say that? Do you mean who we were when we were children before we were taught so many lies? When you say, over this journey we return to our original self? What do you mean by that?" Samuel asked.

"After we leave behind our past and reject all the lies we, in a way, start at the beginning again. We have the freedom to discover who we are without influences. During this time, after we have been emptied, we reenter the womb. This is an expression for a time of reformation, growth, innocence and definition.

"There is a time after death but before the next life when we have been emptied of the old but have yet to be refilled by the new. This in-between is defined by the reforming of our identity—the re-emergence of our original identity, which we once held for a fraction of a second after our birth, before our indoctrination and integration into the faceless mob.

"During this time of reformation, who we are shall change but, at the same time, not change. The reformation is not an altering of self but a purification of self—a rebuilding of self, a healing and freeing of self. During which, who we are will seem to change from who we *were* but in truth we *are* becoming who we always have been at our deepest level—we are becoming our original self.

"There is a great deal that occurs during the second part of the journey," the man said as he took another sip from Yoseph's water bottle. "While the first part of the path focuses on seeing what is around us, the second part entails seeing what is within us. We strip off what was placed upon us. We separate who we were swayed to be, from who we are. We untwist the part of us that was corrupted. We reclaim the part of us stolen. We cleanse the part of us dirtied. We find the person who lies under the scars, reconnect to them and bring them forward.

"Sadly, most of us hardly know who we are. Submerged in a world of strong influences, we have only ever seen fleeting glimpses of who we would be if left to ourselves. Moments when the mob's influence is pushed back and our own thoughts come forward—emerging from underneath all that the evil put upon us.

"Each time we are force-fed lies or molded to be what we are not we suffer an attack upon our identity. To restore our original self we must not only recover parts of ourselves but reaffirm the parts of us damaged during the attacks we suffered. We discover parts of us that have never before been allowed to come to light, having always been suppressed by the dominating presence of evil.

"After having lost hold of the center of our self as a result of evil's bombardment we are reoriented by discovering the personal truths revolving at the center of our Being. The body of our identity can be re-fortified by the time spent within the womb of redefinition and exploration of self." He wiped the water from his beard with the back of his hand. Screwed the lid to the bottle back on, then passed it back to his son. His gaze turned to the path ahead. "We are now entering a time where we are going to be able to come to know who we are, what we believe and what we want without evil's interference. We are entering a time of re-connection; wherein we will be able to listen calmly for the voice within as it begins to breakthrough all the barriers of suppression that have been instilled within us. The voice of our original self is a voice that we may not even recognize at first but one whose tones and thoughts we must not fear. The suppressed voice shall awaken, emanating from deep within and shall slowly and naturally merge with who we know ourselves to be. Until at last we find we have come back into our true selves."

"So this final leg of the path...we four are experiencing now?" Maria asked.

"Yes," he replied with certainty.

Her face relaxed upon hearing his words. A sense of stress hanging upon her seemed to lift. She was consoled by the knowledge that she and Samuel were not alone.

He continued, bringing his point to its end, "We shall be disconnected from the person we knew ourselves to be in the past life and we shall begin again. We shall rebuild ourselves one truth, one thought, one belief, one dream at a time, until we have recomposed the body of our identity within its pure form.

"To be stripped down is a painful process and to be built back up is a slow one. A return to the womb does not end after nine months; the transition between the end and the new beginning can take years. Yet when our true identity finally has been restored and reemerges in rebirth.... When at last the full meaning contained in the truths we gathered on our journey comes together to form the greater understanding.... When at last we have broken through the barrier instilled within our mind and lay completely open to the workings of an old world, we find we have made the journey out of Hell. Having left evil's lies behind along with the pain that they caused us, we come to find that we have left their world behind and we have at last reached its outer most boundaries. For a time we must try to survive, on these outskirts, we must try to holdout, living obscurely—not a part of evil's world but not yet entirely clear of it. And it is here on the outskirts of evil's society that we shall wait for the boat to come to carry us to the Other Shore. It is here that we shall wait for the arrival of one who knows how to physically reach the Other Shore to come for us and bring us home to that untouched place that has been preserved."

CHAPTER XXII

The Parting of Ways

WELL PAST MID-DAY THE SMALL GROUP OF travelers were coming to the end of the long road. "We are almost there," the man said. He held no map or compass, he simply knew. Though the lands had been shifted with time and black roads now cut through the landscape disorienting him, he could still feel his former home drawing near.

With the promise of rest ahead, everyone felt an upsurge in energy.

"We could have driven," Samuel said, watching a car pass swiftly down a road in the distance, a touch of yearning in his eyes after the long day's march.

"I am not one for driving," the man replied. "Besides, taking these modern roads, I would not know how to go about getting home. I have only ever walked this land. It would not feel right to drive. I came here to connect with my former homeland for me to do this my feet must touch this ground. I must go slowly over it, breath in the wind and feel the touch of the grass. Driving has its uses I suppose, in certain situations. But when one's intention is to connect with the land being passed over, walking is the only course."

Yoseph smiled at his father, thinking back to how many miles he had walked by his side.

The four walked quietly for a time. The back hem of Maria's skirt brushed the red dirt road in rhythm with each step she took. Her long hair tucked away in a fold of the cloth veil covering her head. "How long has it been since you were last here?" she asked.

The man looked at her and smiled, "Several lifetimes."

"You left here to go to the Other Shore?" she asked.

"We left these lands because we had to. There were certain people who lived here who were never going to leave us be. So we took a boat across the sea and made a home in the green lands to the north. For a time we dwelt there; it wasn't until later that they came to guide us to the Other Shore.

"If we are to reach the Other Shore we need someone to come for us?" Maria inquired.

"Yes," the man explained. "There are a few different ways to reach the Other Shore, one of which is to have a guide," the man laughed to himself. "I guess I was not completely correct Samuel. We will have a guide at some point."

Samuel laughed. His bearded cheeks pushed back into a round smile.

"As I have said," the man explained. "The Other Shore is a part of the Earth but at the same time it is 'set apart' so that it can be safe from the ever-greedy hands of evil. If one seeks to go to the Other Shore, there is a veil of sorts that must be lifted before we can enter. I know this all sounds rather otherworldly," he commented with a smile. "But some of love's workings are beyond imagining.

"Evil has constructed this corrupt, offensive, toxic world, in essence converting Paradise into Hell. They were able to do this with the consent of the increasing number of peoples who desire evil's ways. ...We have spoken of how the balance was tipped, when suddenly there were more evil than loving," the man said in a questioning tone; wondering if Samuel and Maria could recall this point among all the other matters that had been discussed. The couple nodded, allowing him to proceed. "The new majority took up its place of authority, changing the world mankind was building to suit its foul tastes and within this epoch the feel of the Earth changed. Yet the heart of the Earth remains untouched—preserved; for the Earth itself was never evil. The Other Shore is, in many senses, that soul of the Earth that was kept safe for the loving hearts that remained. Like an impoverished mother saving all she has left for her children, the ancient consciousness set apart this protected place for we who honor the old ways, so that we might have a chance at a better life. This hidden shore—this protected sanctuary—is a place where no evil is allowed to dwell. As evil spread, consuming all and driving out the innocence from the Earth, a line was drawn. We are told that the ancient one said, 'Enough, you shall take no more' creating the divide between what evil can touch and what it cannot—what it can alter and what cannot be changed.

"The Earth yielded a piece of itself to act as a sanctuary. I know that it is hard to accept this as real, being as it is so beyond our comprehension yet love holds abilities that we do not fully understand but that are nonetheless real. Belief acts as a temporary bridge when we learn of matters such as this— we believe in it and simply accept it until the time comes when at last we can understand it," the man finished. The miles had been crossed and the lands of the man's former home were drawing nearer, just as the end of this long in-depth conversation was drawing to its close. On the horizon the man could see the place where his family's home once stood.

It was a climactic moment. That low hilltop that they stood upon might as well have been a bluff overlooking the whole of the journey behind them. And as though she too could sense the greater significance, Maria asked a question, not just concerning her future but the future of all.

"How will this end?" Maria asked. The man turned to look at her as she continued. "You have spoken about going to the Other Shore, but what about all this? What about the people here? In a way, leaving here seems like we are choosing not to try to change the wrongness here. I feel a little guilty. Should we be trying to leave? Shouldn't we be trying to change this world rather than abandon it?"

The man frowned. He looked strained. "I don't think there has been a question more agonized over than the one you are asking. The original family that I spoke of—the first father and the first mother—lost their son and many of their other children to evil. They were never born into Hell; nevertheless they made a journey into this world all the same because they could not move on and begin a new life until they resolved this very question.

"I am a father. I have never suffered the loss of a child to evil but I know how hard it is to accept the loss of one I felt kindred to. Ever since the initial division in the original family, an internal struggle has been playing out in the hearts of those evil left in its wake. Over and over and over, love has been prey to those who have become evil. As we wait for them to change their ways—to come to their senses—we have been exploited and spited for our caring.

"When we look at one who has become evil, the first thing we see is who *they should be*, not what they have *chosen to be*. They are our family—nothing is more sacred to one who believes in love than the bonds that are shared. But they have changed—we have to come to terms with this.

"You ask me, how this will end. And the answer is: not easily. It will end sorrowfully and with much grief. Those who believe in love leave this world like a funeral procession, mourning those we have lost. Many of us have stayed here because we simply could not let go of the memory of those loved and lost. Nevertheless, after much agonizing and searching, we have all come to the conclusion that it is indeed time to leave."

The man looked pained, not by something within him but rather by the sympathy he held for the pains of others.

They all stood there, looking out over the horizon, feeling as though it where the whole world they were now gazing at in retrospect as they all spoke of the greater events.

The man went on, "There are some who think the end will come in Armageddon and judgment but this is not justice— it is not a loving solution. The end of the world has already come; this backward world is the post-Revelations world.

Some wait for the end to come, blind to the fact that the end has already come. The old world was overturned and it was evil that brought about the end, not any God. And now, after the end has come, justice will not be had through judgment but through freedom.

"The choice evil has made cannot be forcibly reversed, and few voluntarily take it back. All those who have chosen evil cannot be judged, sentence and isolated; for love does not settle differences through condemnation and eradication. Those who are evil have willfully chosen to become what they are and shall follow that path to its bitter end; as such we can do nothing more than let the descent run its course. As painful as it is," his voice wrenched, "we must let them travel the path—continuing in that ever-declining way of life; until eventually the final extremes are breached and evil comes to its own self-destructive conclusion.

"The world evil has built cannot be dismantled by outsiders; for evil protects it too viciously. This world has to be dismantled from within following a communal change of heart; however, this end is unlikely. The world evil has created shall continue on until another shift occurs. Only then might the natural world eventually be able to rise once more from beneath the ruined foundations and the old ways become the new.

"So we have come to a parting of the ways with them. Love is not a part of evil's fate. We shall not travel the road of descent with those who choose evil, as they go unto their apocalyptic end. We have not chosen this fate, we have not played a part in bringing about its outcome and it is not just that we should share in the repercussions of a crime we did not commit. Therefore those of the old ways shall completely withdraw from this part of the world dominated by evil. We shall leave behind this world that we have been hunted in and unable to flourished within. The transition of the heart and mind was but the path unto the final transition from one fate to another."

"Some say a shift is indeed occurring now," Samuel offered; staring at the man as he looked over the horizon. "A shift of consciousness," he clarified. "Perhaps there will soon be a spiritual reawakening?" Samuel concluded halfheartedly; as though wanting to believe such a wide-scale awakening to be possible, but not having much expectation of it coming to pass.

"Perhaps," the man replied; not discounting such a dramatic turn of events but, like Samuel, not expecting it to occur at this time. "In every age there has been a movement who thought that their generation would be the one to spur 'the awakening' and yet, every generation eventually falls victim to the same indifference, greed and laziness. Religious communities live with the expectation of one who will come to bring this awakening to the people—one single person with the ability to help people see all that they overlook. The hard truth is," he said solemnly, "most people see all that they need to; most people are aware, they simply do not care to change. On some level all people sense the emptiness in their lives and the wrongness in their actions but the machine keeps churning."

"You are right," Samuel admitted. "But isn't there an obligation for those who know the truth to stay and give it unto those who don't have it?"

"Giving truth, where truth is not wanted, leaves the situation unchanged and the one who brought the unwanted reminder, spited," the man replied morosely. "Like you, I use to believe that there was a magic truth that, when spoken aloud, would be a catalyst for a great revolution of consciousness that would reprioritize the skewed values of the people. I once sought this truth like a man in the desert seeks water—digging and digging. However, there is no such truth to be unearthed.

"People do not live as they do because they lack the truth; they are living as they do because they do not want the truth. If it were a matter of simply sharing truth with each other there would be a point to our staying here, but it isn't. People don't lack the opportunity to change, they simply do not want to. And so, we depart," he said somberly. "We cannot take responsibility for the choices of others. Each person must come to their own realization for there to be lasting changes. I once spoke to the crowds, sharing the realizations I came to, hoping for the transformation that occurred in me when I first learned of the truth, to be passed on to others. Yet, in the end, I learned that my answers are my own. My truth is meant for my life. A realization to me is many times, worthless to any other man.

"We each must come to understand the truth firsthand. We have little emotional resonance to a truth we learn second or third-hand. Our appreciation for any truth is formed over the progression leading up to its realization. A personal journey to the truth is necessary for the kind of penetrating understanding that spurs change.

"When I share with you a realization I have come to over the course of my own progression, I can share facts only. I cannot impart to you the context through which I have come to understand each truth; for that context stems from my own life—my personal experiences had while coming to each individual insight. The facts alone can help others who have taken it upon themselves to further their progression, such as you both," the man offered as an example. "Nevertheless, full comprehension comes through living it, not hearing it. Right now, over these last three days, I have been giving you all the facts—realizations that I have come to over my personal progression; however much of the information I have shared with you has not taken on its full meaning for you yet because you are taking it all secondhand and have no personal link to it. Only when you make your own path to the truths I have shared with you, will you fully understand what it is I have said. Knowledge must be achieved for it to become a part of us.

"If humanity is to change each individual must change their own self and their own life. We cannot change one another. We can only change ourselves. This backward world will be changed, not by one person who manages to miraculously shift the consciousness and perspective of all others, but by each individual making their own conscious effort to find the deeper meaning in living.

"The truth has been forgotten and in some instances erased but it has not been lost. Every living being is born with a connection to the ancient consciousness in whom the collective wisdom of the ages lives eternal. Those who want truth—those who desire to know the nature of their surroundings, will seek. We operate under the assumption that we need another person to wake us from our ignorance, when in actuality we have the ability to wake ourselves. Procrastination, not lack of aid, keeps many from reaching their potential. Those who want to learn will look and listen. Those who genuinely want, will act.

"The sad truth is most people are content with the agreed upon lies they are handed. Most people feel an inherent meaninglessness to their lives, yet they do not seek to actually make the needed changes to bring improvement. Most people in evil's movement sense the inevitable desolation their ways are leading to but they will not change their choice. We who choose to live reflectively cannot stay here preaching endlessly to those who do not feel the need to change; we will suffer and they will never change." The man took a breath, lifted his heavy tone and went on. "You would propose that those of us who know the truth have a responsibility to stay and share what we have learned. But even if all loving hearts depart this land the presence of the truth will remain; for the connection we each have to the ancient consciousness will ever-remain. Regardless of what choices those who join evil make to destroy themselves, their connection remains intact. By leaving this part of the world we are not abandoning those who will choose to stay, we are removing ourselves from harm; while leaving those who choose evil's ways to the life they want. Love itself—the ancient consciousness—will never leave behind anyone regardless of how much time has passed. Every living being, regardless of what they have turned themselves into, remains ever-connected to the ancient consciousness and when at last they do seek to restore themselves they will feel the wellspring of wisdom come up within them to lead them back to themselves. There are no victims being left behind. Those left here are the willing. While there are those who are born into this world, who are unaware of the nature of this backward place, the knowledge is there for those who desire it. Even if we are surrounded by evil, we may reach out to the mentors in the unseen to help in progressing our understanding.

"The decision to leave," the man finished resolutely, "was not made lightly. This parting of ways has been building for thousands of years."

Samuel looked defeated. "I feel the same frustration as you," he replied sympathetically. "I wish people would change but they simply won't. I use to have a belief in the goodness of people but now.... Just hearing you talk about all that evil has done and then looking back over my own life to see how I was manipulated and twisted, I cannot help but ask if those who have done so much wrong will ever be held accountable?" Samuel asked. He did not seek vengeance. He wanted a reassurance that evil would not be allowed to dominate the innocent forever.

"I understand your feelings," the man replied, having asked this question of the Fates many times himself. "And while I do not know if evil will be held accountable or not, there was something foretold a very long time ago by one of the original family...who was there in the beginning and saw evil's rise. It was said that there would be a moment of justice carried out, not through punishment but through choice, wherein each heart would get what they have chosen. This is what I mean when I say that the true justice is freedom.

"Loving hearts never chose evil's culture as our way of life yet we have been surrounded by evil's world—bombarded by it, lost within it and confined to it. We have had our choices stripped from us and another life—another fate—imposed upon us.

"Justice would not be vengeance. It would be freedom for all loving hearts to live as we have chosen and for those who choose evil to be left to the inevitable natural consequences of their choices. This freedom shall be the restoration of balance—evil shall be given the Hell they built, protect, perpetuate and prefer; while love shall be given its own place—a part of the world upon which we may flourish within a life built on our own ways, where we are safe and free.

"For millennia a profound injustice has been carried out upon the generations of loving hearts. We have been taxed, judged, condemned, imprisoned and ridiculed...deceived, exploited, denied and exiled. However this injustice shall at last, be set right as we make our choice, that choice is shielded from evil's displeasure and we finally depart for a place beyond the evil's reach. True justice is each heart getting the life they have chosen and no heart being able to subjugate another, robbing them of the ability to choose their own fate.

"Each shall have the world they have chosen. The movement of love shall leave this Hell in a collective and final exodus. All loving hearts shall come to the borders of Hell united as a new and at the same time ancient family, and in that moment the world shall divide, leaving two different peoples to stand upon two separate shores—one upon this corrupt creation and one upon the Other Shore. And in that moment there shall be a final parting of ways until, be it lifetimes later, evil's choices have reversed and they once again seek to return home."

"Do you think that day will come?" Maria asked; staring out to the horizon.

"Perhaps...one day," the man replied faintly. "As resolved as we are, I think all of us who are leaving hold hope for reunion. This dividing need not be a permanent one; for just as the heart can change so can the boundaries be redrawn or erased. Nonetheless, as long as evil exists the walls of love's sanctuary shall hold, unbreachable—unmovable—unyielding; for this heart of the Earth—this last foot of ground, shall not be compromised. It is all that we have and the very least that we deserve.

"The Other Shore...it is our past and our future."

CHAPTER XXIII

The Fourth Night

E HAD WALKED ALL DAY WITHOUT TIRING.
He felt inexhaustible while driven by the
surge of rising strength had in the wake of
his reclamation. He had not slept the night before but he
felt no fatigue; in fact he felt the opposite, he felt a sense of
heartening renewal, which no amount of sleep over the years
following the attack had ever brought him.

The distance between the man and the city was at last
growing. This time, as his feet walked away, his heart went
with him—no longer bound to the place. The memory of
what had occurred there remained within him, it always
would; nonetheless, the memories no longer controlled him.
His hope defined him now, not his fear.

*

It had been around dusk that the horizon slowly became familiar. Many houses and semi-modern structures had risen since he and his family had left. He had known the land here when it was young and wild, and could not help but feel a twinge of sadness at how it had been worn with old age.

Scanning the horizon, they found a bit of deserted land just beyond the village that seemed inviting to travelers. The old fire pits marking the encampment, confirmed the assumption that it was indeed frequented by those who chose to make a journey northward on foot. Strangely enough, the lands he chose to stay on—the lands he feared to be accused of trespassing upon—once belonged to his family.

They all could have stayed at an inn, but instead, if only for one night, the man wanted to lay his head down upon these grounds once more. These lands where he had been raised, and had in turn raised his own children.

Last time he had ventured into that city he had been smuggled back to these lands—hidden in the back of a cart, broken, stitched and nameless upon his deathbed. But now, after returning to the city to confront what had taken place, he wanted to return home to these lands strong, upright and renewed.

The evil had been able to chase him from his own house. They had falsely accused him of committing crimes against God; they had imprisoned him, degraded him, tortured him and attempted to kill him. Nevertheless, despite all that had been done to him, he had lived. Despite all that had been done to silence him he had returned to the city and spoke the truth once again. And now that it was done, he would take his rest upon his lands and sleep, unafraid of what surrounded him.

His words had been taken, twisted and laid as a foundation of a faith that was not his own. There was nothing he could do to clear his name; the lies were too fiercely protected—too widely accepted. The people did not want the truth; respecting that, he would leave them with the lie.

No—in the end, he could not clear his name but he could reclaim himself from the fear that held him hostage and the memories that had incapacitated him.

Finally making camp at the end of the long journey, the man realized that evil only wins when we let them stop us from living—when they are able to make us hold back or hesitate, whether out of fear or fatigue they celebrate a victory. For too many years the evil had been victorious over him; in his silence it had conquered him and in his fear it had subjugated him, but no more. On this day he had overcome.

＊

They made camp and directly after eating the man laid down upon his bedroll and fell into a deep sleep, the likes of which he had not experienced since before the attack. Yoseph was not tired, his father had yet to speak with him of the events in the city but the boy could sense that his father had overcome part, if not all, of the events that had occurred there so long ago. This was so momentous and long-awaited that Yoseph could not sleep out of sheer excitement.

The young man, with the old soul sat fireside, gazing around at the lands he had heard stories of for so long yet had never been able to see with his own eyes. Last time he was here he was inside his mother's womb; his feet had never walked these grounds and his eyes had never seen their old home. The house was gone, the family's gardens had long since withered—the fallen petals had turned to dust and been carried like ash to other lands. Nevertheless, despite the time elapsed, Yoseph could sense his family's presence upon these lands, as though the faint ghosts of each memory still dwelt here, playing out the past that had once taken place.

Their family had been imprinted upon the lands. Yoseph could sense his loved ones nearby. Sitting cross-legged, Yoseph placed his hand flat upon the cool dirt at his side, digging his fingers in—the earth compacted in his hand and gathered under his nails. He did not know if he was trying to anchor himself to this place or connect to the memories still alive in the land beneath him.

As they sat, a small fire burned in front of them, not for warmth but rather for light, Samuel and Maria watched Yoseph. They could tell that he was deep within his own thoughts. The couple felt they should leave the young man be, yet some open quality about his demeanor spoke of a willingness to talk. Over the last days the young man had been polite but reserved. Whether due to his private character or a protective mechanism he had developed as a result of his family's past, Yoseph kept his thoughts to himself. Tonight though, the walls were down and in time a conversation eventually began.

"You made one of these journeys?" Maria asked in a somewhat motherly tone.

"Yes," Yoseph replied.

A deepening look of disapproval shown on Maria's face. She looked as though she wanted to scold him for putting himself in danger.

"Would you tell us the story?" Samuel asked timidly. Maria still looked troubled.

Yoseph looked torn. Unconsciously he glanced over to his father who lay asleep. He then looked back to the fire. He sighed slightly. "What you are asking to know is simple but also, complicated," his voice had a strained quality. "Our reasons for taking this journey are simple but the actual process of rebirth and journeying between worlds can seem fantastical or complex to some. Therefore it makes for a difficult story to tell. I..." he hesitated. He was not as good with words as his father. He did not know where to begin. "As you know, my family lived in this region before. It was in another life...I mean that both figuratively and literally. While I have been told that there were years of happiness, I was born after the attack on my father, so my life was one in which we were outcast, alienated and hunted. We spent our days in exile. As my father said already, we fled this area and headed north, where we kept to ourselves, trying to heal from the wounds. Until the day when *they* came and we were brought to that Other Shore.

"Throughout the entirety of the first life my family hardly had a single day of peace, so many among us having been attacked early on and left emotionally crippled. The good days were so rare it was painful when they eventually did come because we knew they would not last. Working for years to try to resolve the trauma on our own yet having no success, we consoled ourselves with the assurance that the wounds received in this world would not pass with us into the Other Shore. Yet, to our great disappointment, the questions we struggled with here crossed the threshold with us, following us to the Other Shore, causing the suffering to draw out.

"We had crossed into a new land but we were not given the peace of a new life. Our attackers were not able to follow us to the Other Shore yet we carried a part of them with us. We could not heal from the wounds inflicted upon us and, after decades of attempting to overcome the traumas, we were left willing to do anything to heal. Anything—even take up a journey and consent to pass back into this dark part of the world. I know it seems like an outlandish thing—to be willing to leave the Other Shore and return to this Hell." Yoseph explained. "I heard you ask my father, what would be so horrible that we would be willing to undergo so much. It is simple...when it is a matter of saving those loved ones you have watched suffer for years on end, you are willing to do anything.

"When the well-being of those we love is compromised, everything changes—the weakling becomes the rock, the absent one becomes the companion, the doubter becomes the visionary and those who love us become our savior. When our loved ones are slipping from us, our true priorities come into sharp relief and we find the strength within ourselves to carry out tasks we thought far beyond our capability.

"For decades we watched each other unravel. There was a group of us who spent our childhood and youth helplessly witnessing the aftermath of attacks that we were never present for, carried out by villains we had never met but whose names were spoken with taboo and infamy.

"*The why's* undid the minds and faiths of those I love and until 'the why's' were answered no one would ever heal—no one would ever live.

"For most of our first life, we who had *not* been wounded, lived in a state of helplessness, having to watch daily as those we love went in circles, reeling in a pain we could not end. During this time we—my brothers, sisters and cousins—built a firm resolve within ourselves, vowing that, if we could do anything to heal those we loved, we would. And finally the day came when we were presented with an opportunity to make a journey the purpose of which would be to gather the cure needed to heal those we loved.

"We in the family, who were able enough in body and mind, came back here to confront the evil and gather the truths needed by those crippled among us, who could not heal from their wounds without certain understanding. We passed from the Other Shore back into this part of the world, which evil dominates, at which time we each were sent in a different direction, to find answers to different questions—to resolve a different wound for our different family members."

Yoseph turned to Samuel. "I heard you ask my father if there wasn't some other way of learning the truth we needed. But as he said, evil goes beyond logic, beyond imagination, beyond reason and so to grasp what it is one must see it. Sadly, in the end, the only way you truly learn of a people is to live among them for a time. This is a painful fact in the case of evil; nevertheless, be it a hard truth, submersion is the quickest way of learning.

"After living on the Other Shore for a time, it became clear to us that, despite coming to a new land, we were still struggling with the old life. My father in particular was still plagued. He went to the original family who lives there, and asked what could be done to bring the pain to an end. It was then that he was told of the journey. We were told not all in my family could survive such a task after all that had been done, so only the strongest would undertake the journey; while the severely wounded would stay on the Other Shore. I was among the generations that came after many of the most traumatizing attacks; as such I was stronger than many others and was among those chosen to take-up a journey."

"Were you forced to go?" Maria asked.

"No, I chose to go," Yoseph corrected. "I had lived my life watching my loved ones suffer. I had never seen my family at its full strength. I had never seen those I love before they were wounded. I had spent my whole life wanting to end their pain—wanting to be able to do something to ease them. But I was left helpless, able only to watch them struggle. Many among the later generations felt this same helplessness so, when we were presented with the solution, we were willing to do whatever it took.

"When the time came to prepare for the journey, we all took council with the original family—the first father and first mother—who were both there when the ways, workings and power of love were originally discovered.

"We were not the first nor would we be the last to undertake such a journey. Nearly all those who came to dwell upon the Other Shore had once lived bound to someone who chose to become evil or bore scars from an evil encountered. A few members of each family now settled upon the Other Shore have, at one time or another, made a journey to gather what was needed to relieve their family's suffering."

Samuel interrupted, "I do not understand how one person can gather the truth needed to heal another person, when evil is something that must be *seen* to be understood," he added, confused. "If you can make the journey and then simply return and tell someone what you saw, why then can't everyone simply be *told* what they need to know by one who has seen the evil and be spared the journey?"

"Because…" the young man began, "we do not pass on the truth through 'telling' our loved ones.

"We who are on journeys are to stay within this dark part of the world for however long it takes to gather all the truth needed. Guided from afar by the elders and by the omnipresent force of love, we are led from situation to situation, place to place, person to person, from which we are able to glean the truth we need. And once all the necessary truths have been found we begin the journey out of this place, bringing all that we have gathered with us back home to those who need it. Once home, all that has been gathered will be released to each loved one in a moment of transference that can only be had when the deepest love is present. Our hearts join to their hearts and the understanding they never had is transfused into them from we who made the journey. The kind of connection required for the transference of realizations is only had between the closest of family members—those who have witnessed our trials, who we love and have always trusted, and felt understood by."

Samuel and Maria felt they could accept Yoseph's answer. Knowing how deeply they were connected to each other.

Thinking over what the young man had said, Maria spoke, "So you left the safety of the Other Shore to come back here," she summed up. "How long has your journey lasted?"

329

"Time is a strange thing," Yoseph replied cryptically. "If you start counting when the attacks began, this journey has been a very long one."

"You are only what, twenty-five or thirty? How old were you when you left the Other Shore?" Samuel asked.

"Again," Yoseph said in a strained voice, "my family, like so many who reside on the Other Shore, are beyond traditional measures of time.

"When we went to leave the Other Shore we were led to the divide between worlds. It was then that we were told what to expect upon leaving the sanctuary."

Samuel and Maria looked expectantly at Yoseph. He hesitated again. "You won't believe it," he answered. "And I cannot explain to you how it all works, in a way that you will understand it. I don't even understand it. It simply, *is*."

"Maybe we won't understand what you are going to say," Maria replied. "There have been a great many things that your father has spoken of that I do not understand. All the same, I still believed what he said. ...I will believe what you say, no matter how outlandish it may seem because I believe in you and in your father."

Accepting this, Yoseph proceeded, "As inconceivable as you will think it, we were told that, during what had been no more than two years for us upon the Other Shore, more than *nineteen-hundred years* had passed for those within this part of the world."

Yoseph was right, both Maria and Samuel said nothing. All that he was saying seemed too far-fetched—fiction not reality.

"Time passes differently upon the Other Shore. It is literally an isle removed—set apart from the reality that evil has imposed here. As I said, I don't understand how it works. It just does." Pressing on despite the lack of understanding, Yoseph continued, "We learned just before departing the Other Shore that we would not be returning to the age we had left and the way of life we had once known.

"While this inconsistency of time, was—is, difficult to grasp it did quiet one of our main concerns. The worry being that, if we went on this journey, which can last a lifetime, we would miss crucial events in the lives of those we were leaving behind. But you see, because time moves differently on the Other Shore as compared to this part of the world, during the many years that those of us who are making journeys have been gone, it has only be a matter of weeks for the family who we had left behind. Weeks that no doubt are being spent in intense worry for our safety, but still only weeks, rather than a lifetime. The one comfort we who make the journey have, is that the slower passage of time insures that, while apart from our loved ones we have missed very little of that daily life we have with them, which we cherish so.

"Setting out I, like my family, knew very little concerning the truth of evil. I had only ever seen glimpses of a foulness the likes of which I could not conceive. I had only ever heard the stories of a people who seemed so cruel, it was difficult to imagine they were not fictional demons. At the beginning of this journey we knew nothing of the greater events taking place; however, now, many years later, the long-needed truth has begun to surface and we have begun to understand. We finally—at long last—have seen what needed to be seen and the journey out has begun." Yoseph stopped. Everyone stared deeply into the heart of the small fire; sparks drifted upward and the new thoughts sunk into their open minds. For Samuel and Maria the information did indeed seem surreal; had it come from anyone else they would not have believed it. However, there was something about the man and his son that made it all possible. The couple did not question whether or not they were being told a lie, they knew they were being given the truth. They simply wondered how it was all possible. What they had been told contradicted all that they had ever been taught. But regardless, in their heart; they knew it was all true and quietly, as they sat there accepting this contradiction, their minds made the transition between worlds.

Chapter XXIV

The Story

THE NIGHT HAD PASSED WITH A CERTAIN MAGIC to it. Yoseph lay for a long time staring up at the black sky musing over the wonder of the full circle turn that had at last taken place for his family. Did any of those who lie sleeping in the surrounding villages, sense the greater events taking place? Few, if any, might sense the presence of the native son who had returned to his birthland or the age-old events that had finally concluded after two millennia.

Yoseph's eyes slowly closed and the rhythm of his breathing became long and deep. A fleeting thought passed through his mind as he drifted off. *Silently, without being recognized for who they are, the loving walk their path. In the background of the insignificant, daily running about, the greater events play out.*

⤜

It had been a risk to make camp on open ground, given the instability of the area; however the man had felt assured of their safety. His certainty had been so strong it had an effect on those around him. Any doubts the others might have had concerning their exposed camp were muted by the man's resounding declaration that no harm would come to them. And indeed, over the long night, they had slept undisturbed.

The blazing sun rose and with it the nameless man. For a time he laid upon his bedroll, as night entered its transition into day, thinking of the last time he had slept upon these lands...how long ago it was.

When the others did at last rise, a plan was made to stay in this area for a few days. Firstly as a means of regrouping after the ordeal in the city and secondly, to give the man some time to reconnect with the strong part of himself that had once flourished upon these hills.

Throughout the morning the four of them sat quietly, taking in the breadth of the changes that had occurred. Gradually, as each of them came to the end of their personal pondering, another conversation was begun—one that would make the man share the truths he had locked away within himself.

"You have told us a great deal about evil and love," Maria started gently. "But now, I want to know your story. Tell us your name. You must know by now that you need not fear us." She looked him in the eyes. There was no deception in her gaze, only a genuine desire for closeness.

Hearing her request the man did not recoil as he once would have, but neither did he leap to spill out his history for all to see. Maria thought it was a matter of trust but actually it wasn't. While the man had conquered the evil that tried to conquer him, his name was still entwined with the fictions; as such, he had to be careful in what he chose to share.

Rubbing his bearded cheek gently as he thought solemnly to himself, the man looked torn. "What you now ask of me dear woman," he confessed, "is a greater request than wanting to know any truths I have learned about evil or God. Yes, speaking of my own beliefs leaves me open to the judgment of those who believe different than I; however, speaking of *myself*," the man said hesitantly, "leaves me open to the preconceived notions you already possess of who and what I am."

Samuel spoke up, "Surely you know how we regard you. The only notion we have formed over these last days is that you are the most insightful man we have ever met."

Never seeing himself as others did, the man left the praise unacknowledged as he moved on, "While in the beginning I might have held back my name and my story out of fear, I hesitate in telling you now, not because I distrust you, but rather because I value you as a friend and I do not wish to see our bond lost."

"It won't be!" Maria declared from her heart. "How could it be?" she added; positive that nothing could be revealed that would cause her or Samuel to regard the man any differently.

"Telling you my story leaves me vulnerable to your preconceived notions of who and what you already believe me to be," the man repeated.

"As Samuel said, we believe that you are a good man—a great man," Maria said, not understanding the man's reasoning.

Yoseph, who understood his father's meaning perfectly, said nothing. He waited silently, his eyes fixed upon his father, curious as to what he would decide to do.

The man began, speaking as if he were giving a hypothetical example, "As of right now, you know me for who I am. Yet if I were to speak my name and that name be familiar to you—a person whose life story you have been told—your perception of me would be altered by all that you already think of me."

Realizing that he was dancing around his point, the man gathered himself and continued on in a more direct manner, needing to walk the fine line of explaining himself without having to fully reveal the context of his words. "As hard as it is for you both to grasp, before we even met you were taught what to think of me. Before you ever spoke with me, you had a preconceived notion in your mind as to what I believe and what my life has been." The man cleared his throat in an effort to break the tension bearing down on him. Then said plainly, "My name is 'of note,' though, most all that you have been told of me has been distorted."

Maria and Samuel looked at him uncomprehendingly, forcing him to go on. "A lifetime ago, I withdrew from society after being persecuted for my beliefs. The quiet existence my anonymity now brings could be taken from me should I tell you my name. What's more, all that we have discussed over these last days will be tainted and our friendship changed when you hear my name; for your perspective of me will be altered, as you link me to the myth they have woven around me. Therefore," the man said a little sorrowfully, "while I will consent to tell you parts of my own life, I shall, for the time being, remain the nameless man."

The sun rose to mid-day, caravans moved across the swelter-
ing edge of the distant horizon and the couple waited, their
eyes fixed on the man as he prepared to call up the joyous and
sorrowful story of his past. He knew the couple had some idea
of his journey; he had been told of the conversation that took
place the night before. All the same, there was still so much
that had not been touched upon.

"It is hard to clearly remember what it was like in the
beginning," the man said awkwardly; out of practice when
it came to telling this particular story. "The memories of my
youth feel vague and distant; for so much has happened since.
Time," he said reflectively, "does not place distance between
us and our past, incidents do—the more that happens to
us, the further we are taken from where we began. For some
people, years pass and yet they do not move at all; for little
has happened to progress their life. Some grow from what
they were; while others degrade. Either way, none of us are
what we were. For myself, trying to recall life as it was in the
beginning, has always triggered an ache within me. When I
look back on the youthful, strong heart I was, all I feel is a
resounding sense of loss; for I am not that boy anymore. This
ache has begun to ease over the last day because, for the first
time since the attack, I have hope of regaining my former
strength of heart.

"Broken as I have been, there was a time when I was whole.
Frightened now, there was a time when I was fearless. Quiet
now, there was a time when my voice could be heard resounding upon these very lands." The man took a bracing breath.
"In the beginning I was like those idealistic young students in
the city—I was convinced of mankind's goodness and pious

with the traditions taught unto me. I bled with sympathy for those around me who suffered and fought for the stranger as if they were my brother or sister.

"When I was a young man—a mere boy, I started my exploration of the unseen. I wanted to learn something that could heal humanity. I was searching," he said, straining to explain, "for something that could relieve the inner-conflict I witnessed in those within my community. The first years of my life as a young man were defined by my belief in the goodness of people as well as the conviction that there was something—someone in the unseen to be met.

"I went unto the divine offering, not my reverence but my love. Years later, these actions would be condemned by the religious community as a lack of respect for God. I preached that God—the divine—was not the master of mankind but the parent. I removed the distance between humanity and the divine. I thought this realization would give people comfort... they would know they are loved by the divine and in this be heartened. But instead I was condemned. Painted as one who perceived himself to be the equal of God.

"When I was a young man, I simply wanted to embrace God. One morning, while walking these hills in the early hours, I reached out into the unseen and felt that embrace come. When it happened, I realized that everything we knew about 'God'—the one in the unseen—was wrong.

"I had been taught by my religion that God was one to be feared yet I learned that morning that the one in the unseen was not a Lord but rather a gentle soul to be loved. At that time humanity was regarded as the lesser creations of an awesome deity. It was taught that we were brought into existence by God to be governed. But that morning, while walking along these nearby hills, I learned that we are *children* of the divine not *subjects* to it.

"These ideas, while known today, were revolutionary at the time and anything revolutionary in this part of the world invariably draws condemnation and controversy. This new idea challenged the ways of the religion I was raised under, which was based upon the unreachable nature of God. For the most part, I shared my insights only with my family. But there eventually came a time, when I was older, when I was asked to share my insights. Unaware of the nature of what surrounded me, I consented to do so. In preaching these ideas, I was publicly challenging the long-held traditions of the central religion. Again," he said, pulling back from his recollection to commentate on the varying perceptions of the ages, "this sounds like a small thing given that, in this day and age, religions are challenged daily, but at that time and in that place, traditions were not to be deviated from; especially those doctrines that were laid down by the great prophets.

"While in the beginning I was sharing my ideas with only a handful of others who I believed to be my friends, I was eventually pushed onto a larger stage. Many people started to gather around me—some of whom genuinely sought to learn but many of whom were scheming and deceptive, seeking insights that they could peddle unto the masses as a means of bringing themselves celebrity, wealth and worship.

"Unbeknownst to me at the time, I had enemies mounting on several fronts. My belief in the inherent goodness of people had blinded me to the duplicitous creature a human being can become, which in turn meant that I would remain ignorant of the conspiracies constructed by the evil around me, until the very end, when I found myself at its mercy.

"My betrayers," he said seriously, "were ones I had taken into my home and regarded as brothers. I shared everything I knew with them. I brought them into my family. I had befriended them out of a desire to connect with like-minded people yet they had befriended me out of a desire to take what truths came through me and use them as a means of acquiring status among the people. Plainly put: they wanted to be prophets—Gods—yet in the end, when they went out unto the people, most of them sounded, not like wise men but salesmen, and so they needed the insights that came unto me to be able to play the part more convincingly.

"Mounting on another front were the leaders of the religion my views challenged; driven to keep their way of life intact. In the beginning, the truths I spoke were disregarded yet, over time a following began to gather of people who were seemingly open to a new perspective on matters. When I was asked to speak every person who came to listen to me was one less that attended the Temple. When my notoriety rose, I became a threat unto those there who drew their power from their flock's obedience.

"The truths I spoke then, differ from those truths I speak now; the revelations that came to me all those years ago have had a long time to progress. You know my views now, on God and the true greater force, but in the beginning, I was still semi-tied to the concepts of the religion I held. At that point in my life I had not totally stripped away the God-head. I was making a transition from the reality I was raised in, into the true reality. At that time, I knew only this much: God was not a ruler but rather a father. ...I knew that we were kindred with the one in the unseen. I knew that we each were connected to the divine—directly connected—and through that connection we could commune with the divine without the assistance of any ordained figure acting as an intermediary.

"While this was an exceedingly simple message, my words were not well received by the leaders of the old faith. Men whose power comes from being the intermediary for humanity and the divine, have little power when each person can connect with the divine themselves. The leaders declared that I was challenging the power of God, though in truth their grievance with me was that I was challenging their power. You see, I was preaching a message that compromised their place of influence among the people and I was hated for it. They feared me, or rather they feared the change that could potentially be triggered by the truth I brought. And so, when presented with the opportunity, they lashed out at me.

"And on the final front," he said in a heavy exhale, "there was an old evil—the ones who inflicted the initial wounds upon my family. They wanted our money, our home, our title, our compliance and ultimately our blood. This evil schemed behind the scenes during the years that I preached, using their influence in the political arena and in the religious altars to paint me the villain—the threat.

"In the end, it was my companions—those I regarded as my brothers—who betrayed me unto the leaders of the old faith and then this old enemy of my family stepped in, using their political influence to push for the maximum penalty, which, at that time, was death.

"Evil conspired around me playing their games and I was unaware of it all. Money was exchanged, ambitions came forward, lies were spun, truths were twisted and I found myself on trial."

"What were you charged with?" Maria asked in a strange tone. Some small part of her already knew the answer.

"Blasphemy," the man answered. Adding in a flat tone, "But the declared charge was secondary. The charge was an excuse for those who already disliked me to be free to lash out and for those who wanted to use my words for their own purposes to be rid of me."

"The trial took place in the city, didn't it?" Maria asked. Again, speaking as if she already knew it to be true but needed an affirmation as the final pieces fell into place.

He knew she was putting it all together. He could have stopped there and said nothing else. He looked at her—into her warm, genuine eyes and chose to continue. "I had come into the city on a personal matter. I was with a few members of my family when I was arrested and taken before the council of elders for trial."

"What happened?" Samuel asked in horror. "You're alive, so obviously you were not put to death."

Samuel did not yet grasp what Maria was beginning to suspect.

"I *was* put to death," the man said; sensing how close he was coming to linking himself to the myth that had robbed him of his true identity. "I had been taken near dusk," he said tremulously, "judgment was passed on me over the night, I was found guilty near dawn and then I was taken to be executed. I was put through a torture that kills *all* who endure it only, I didn't die. My body was utterly broken but I survived. Make no mistake," the man emphasized gravely. "Part of me did die that day. My physical wounds were of such an extent that I should have died.

"Rumors had been whispered in the city that I had died and I chose not to contradict them. Still hunted on all fronts, when I was well enough to travel, I was smuggled out of the city by my family. We abandoned our home, which stood nearby on these very lands and we fled.

"After I departed rumor and myth were built up around my name as well as around my death. My teachings were taken, distorted, repackaged and preached, and in time they were used as the foundation of a new religion—a religion that I neither gave birth to nor am a follower of." The man stopped. There were unspoken things coming together to form an answer that neither Samuel nor Maria dare speak aloud. The man could sense the realization building and braced for what would come next. Silence fell, as the identity of this nameless man became clear.

"You are...*him*," Maria asked breathlessly; not knowing how it was possible, only that it was.

Yoseph looked to his father, wide-eyed and fearful.

The man himself said nothing. He looked sick for a moment; he paled with panic. Then, strangely, after that fleeting moment of fear, he calmed. The strength he had reclaimed rose in him. "I am the man you have been speaking with. You could mean many things when you say, 'You are him.' And in the end, regardless of who you might mean, the answer we will come back to is: I am who I am, not who I would be made out to be by others. You have come to know who I am, even without a name.

"Much of my history was written by those who neither knew me nor fully understood me; tailored by men who feigned piety to gain the trust of those longing to connect to the divine. Men who fully understood mankind's need for forgiveness and communion, and foresaw the power they could have if they were seen as the ones with the power to connect man to God. When I would not found the church wherein man needs intermediaries to reach the divine, my 'brothers' spoke in my name. They created the myth and I was made into who and what they needed me to be.

"So I say unto you dear woman," he said, looking into Maria's full face, "if you think you have heard of me—if you think you know my name—I will tell you now: you do not."

The man did not want to be mean; he was not trying to be hurtful but he was slightly defensive. He did not like to be confused with that of the myth. In his mind, who he was and who he was made out to be in history, were two different men. "You can see now, can't you?" he said, holding his gaze. "Why, after having been used and betrayed so, I would hesitate to speak of my beliefs and my history with any who are not family."

Maria nodded. She knew what he was saying. She knew who he was but still, she was in shock. "You said money was exchanged…that you were betrayed," she said slowly; bringing new context to old words. "They betrayed you for thirty pieces of silver?" she added, speaking in a tone of both declaration and question. Samuel's eyes became wide as the truth became clear.

Knowing that, while his name had never been said, it was all the same known, the man dropped all pretense. "If only they had simply wanted thirty pieces of silver. If only their ambition had been that shallow…if only they had been satisfied so easily. But the greed of evil," he said slowly, "runs far deeper.

"The money my family inherited from the generations to come before had been what first drew evil's eye. My wife and I are both descended from a royal line many generations removed; as such we were never made to want. We were not nobles; our family had long since renounced the titles we inherited. Those in my family lived as farmers, herdsmen, carpenters and weavers. The money meant little to us. The land and each other—those were the only things of value to us. But the money meant a great deal to others. As did the insights that came from the unseen, which likewise could be peddled to any who sought help in a desperate hour.

"We were all so innocent," he said with regret. "…so unaware of what mankind has come to crave and the lengths to which they will go to acquire what they desire. It was the money that first drew the evil to us yet they soon discovered that the revelations those in my family came to were of far greater value.

"Evil does not seek coin in a desire to possess the metal with which it is made but rather, for the influence the coin has over the minds of others. They seek anything that holds sway in the minds of others. In this backward world, he with the most wealth rules all others; while he with the most wisdom is made to swallow the bitterness of his unlived dream—made a slave for the profits of others. The desire for amassed wealth is a manifestation of one's desire to possess—not objects but other people. The truth my family has been given—the intensity that truth brings and the presence it commands—were more appealing than the coin to those I had befriended. And so they betrayed me," the man sighed. "Once I opened my mouth and crowds gathered around me, just as you do now. In those gathering crowds I felt a building movement within humanity. Once before I was asked to speak of my beliefs, just as you asked me days ago. And I did speak—bursting with optimism and conviction I spoke. Only in time to be forsaken by these once-brothers…these apostates," he finished meaningfully; the words reverberated within the hearts of Samuel and Maria.

It was impossible, yet possible. It was unbelievable yet beyond a doubt, true. It was an inconceivable crossing-of-paths yet at the same time, for the couple, it was somehow a meeting that had been long-awaited.

"You died…" Samuel said in a disembodied voice; now fully aware of the truth his wife had come to moments before. "You died and then you…." Dazed, he could not speak the words.

"I should have died. My body was utterly broken but my heart…my heart was still bound to those here—my wife, my children. By their love I was pulled through. By my love for them and their love for me, I survived that which should have killed me," the man said. He looked to his son; a deep appreciation reflected in his eyes.

For the flicker of a moment Samuel looked at Yoseph—his eyes fixed, his face impassive, as though he was staring at a piece of contradictory evidence. "You were said to have…."

"…no family," the man finished, knowing the words that would come. "Myths made to suit an agenda," the man replied dismissively.

"What was true?" Samuel asked in a disillusioned voice. He was willing to take the truth and leave the lie, if only the man would give it to him. "Within all of it, what was true?"

"My name," the man said plainly, wiping all other preconceived ideas away from Samuel and Maria's mind in one clean pass, "…only, my name."

CHAPTER XXV

The End and the Beginning

THE MORNING AIR WAS COOL, his eyes opened and stared out into the lightening dark. He could have been in the old house, lying in bed next to her. It was surreal. He had woken up in an in-between. Drifting somewhere between the old life and the new, seeing faint memories play out against the mist. He could feel the young man that the evil had killed returning to him. That scar-less man, that fearless man—heart beaming, soul searching, every fiber of his Being, believing.

Basking in these warm feelings, he just laid there for a time, floating in the gulf between worlds waiting for the dream to recede just as it had so many times before when, for a moment, he felt healed and hopeful, only to come crashing back down into this oh so suffering world. However, night became day and the joy did not fade, it intensified. The moment of renewal drew out and encompassed him, suspending him in its womb.

Closing his eyes, he could almost feel her lying next to him. He could feel the warmth emanating from her body. He wanted to roll over and embrace her yet he did not dare reach out—he hardly even stirred; for deep down he knew there was no one there to hold. She was on her path, making her journey, just as he was on his. One day the two paths would converge but until that day he had only his longing.

He laid there, the exhaustion dissolving as the light around him grew brighter—filling him. He soaked in the morning, taking in the place he was at, the confrontations that lie behind him and the reunion that lie ahead of him.

The final insight that these last days amounted to had dropped into his turbulent mind like a touch of calm. The rejuvenation spread; swelling in his chest and traveling through his veins. The stress lines of the deep wear that were upon his heart were filled and the reservoir of strength was slowly deepened.

⁂

His life had not all been bad. No, there was a time of good—a time of union, children and home. Before the entanglement of religious debate and the politics there had been a simple life of ease and comfort.

These thoughts of how life had once been, always an ache to him, weren't today. No, on this day he was reminded that there are things beyond the evil. On this day his recollections reminded him that he was not his wounds; he was not the betrayal. For a time it was as though he had become the evil— not in that he had chosen evil but in that, he had become what they had done to him. But no more.

He had waited for someone or something—some hand of fate to make him the person he once was, but why couldn't he simply choose to hope as he once did? Choose to believe as he once did? Choose to act as he once did? Choose to be fearless as he once was?

Evil is a choice, he thought to himself, *and believing is one as well.* All this time he thought he had been waiting for belief to return to him, when in actuality he had been waiting for a reason to return to it—waiting for a reason to *choose* to believe.

Would these extensions of himself—faith, hope, belief— come alive again if he simply *chose* to indulge them? The difference between him now and the boy that he once was, was a matter of strength. Did he have the strength to believe—to go out into the unknown, unafraid and trusting? He had once trusted that he was safe, only to be blind-sided by betrayal. So why should he trust again? Wasn't it his blind trust that had led him into his vulnerable position those years ago?

He had the desire to be what he once was. But was desire enough? He drew back the single blanket that covered him, picked up his staff and rose from his bed. He faced the glow on the horizon where the rising sun would soon peak and he began walking.

❧

His contemplative life had begun here—upon this ground— on a morning such as this; while walking at dawn. One morning while pondering what lay in the unseen, he released a request from his heart that rippled out—defining all that was to come.

The tall straw-like grass parted around him as he walked the outskirts of the village now built where his home had once been. The morning wind broken upon his back, moving the tails of the shawl draped over his shoulders. He tried to look past the structures that had been erected and remember the land as it once had been, just as he was trying to remember the man he had been before the hand of mankind's dark ambitions had so violently attempted to reshaped him.

The fig trees that had once rooted around the land had long since been uprooted; he mourned for them as he would old friends. Nonetheless, despite its forced conversion to the modern era, the landscape still kept its ancient spirituality. He could feel the same old soul residing in the earth beneath him and air around him as he walked. The well-worn paths his twilight travels had once made through the landscape were long gone—overgrown and faded.

Removing his sandals he let the stiff, dry grass pass between his toes and the dry dirt gather on the soles of his feet, just as it did when he was a younger man. He wanted to immerse himself in the moment—give himself fully over to it and be renewed. He refused to let his mind wander; he would not let his worries hold his focus. He neither looked ahead of him nor behind him, he existed fully in the moment. He breathed with it and felt the re-birth of the part of him that had died— that part of him that had never recovered after the attack.

He had forgotten the fervor that had compelled the boy that he once was to come out at dawn to seek and reach. The pain had dominated him but the memory of what had taken place—the love, the trust, the intimacy—had lived on, enduring silently within the land beneath his feet and within his heart.

He harkened to the memories of how it all began. A wind of remembrance blew through the hallways of his soul and long-dead parts of him coursed with life. The heavy limbs of his belief—of his idealism and of his hope—tingled as his original self was resurrected. It had not been three days after the attack that this resurrection took place. It had not been so simple or so convenient; for it had never been a matter of reanimating this body but rather, of reviving his soul and renewing the self-certainty that had been stolen from him on that day.

Trauma ties us to a debilitating pain, trapping us within a moment, within a day, within a place and among a people who harmed a delicate, cherished part of us. Deep-seated fatigue puts the soul upon its deathbed; trapped in limbo we await that healing reason that can give us the power to rise up stronger than we once were. In this in-between he had dwelt—neither dead nor alive—waiting to be taken by the hand and risen up.

He had come back to this place where it had begun. Initially he had not known why he should return. He was following a nagging need to walk the old lands but for what reason he did not fully know, until now. He had come to renew the original choice he had made as a younger man. Having endured the wrath of the evil because of the choices he made, he now had to choose whether to make those choices again or abandon them. He had to go back to the moment that had begun it all—the moment where he chose to reach out to what lay beyond in the unseen—and then decide whether that had been a mistake or an achievement.

After the attack, he looked back at the trusting curious young man that he was and saw the fool. He had reached out into the *larger matters* without any appreciation for what he was entering. In his mind, it had been that morning when he first reached unto the unseen, that his life had taken a pivotal turn; passing into an altogether harder course. *Yet here I stand,* he thought to himself, *upon the same lands, at the same time just before dawn, one foot in the past, one in the present, with the choice to reach out to the unseen as I once did in the beginning or to instead choose to close myself off forever.*

Many times, while deep in his affliction, he had cursed himself for ever seeking, forever reaching out. Damning himself for his eagerness, for his curiosity and for his naivety. While he knew on some level that it had not been a mis-step of belief that had brought him into suffering but evil's hatred, he had punished himself rather than the evil for many years.

He knew he had not made a mistake in choosing to reach out to the unseen, even though he had lived to know regret in those most excruciating hours of unraveling. He knew that he had not made a mistake reaching out to the unseen or for that matter, to the people, even though he had suffered more pain than he could bear because of these choices.

So now, going back to where it began, after all that had happened he knew the choice he would make. He would reach once more and in doing so relieve the young man that he was of any guilt in the backlash that was suffered.

In that moment, as he stood there building to reach out, he came to terms with who he was—who he always would be—and found pride in his character rather than fault.

Thinking he would never be able to trust the one in the unseen again, the man realized it had not been his blind trust but rather, everything that evil had done to make him blind, that had led to the attack. ...A blindness that he no longer suffered from.

The morning wind blew in from the east. The sun rose and tremulously, his heart spoke, *I come to you, seeing the dangers that surround, trusting that you will be the one to guide us through. I trust you, not because I need to but because I want to. I surrender the final illusion of control, placing my family's fate in your hands.*

Guide me. Bring me where you will. I have no fear.

When the others woke the next morning, the place where the man had lain was empty and a path of footprints led away from their small encampment.

For a moment Yoseph was startled. He always braced for the worst-case scenario—a side-effect of his trauma. But this morning Yoseph felt the panic for only a moment before a calm began to spread in him. He felt as though a balm of reassurance had been soothingly spread upon his trembling heart.

The man had spent the morning out along the hills, walking the same paths he had as a child, long before he had been awoken to mankind's dark ambition. In returning to those hills, he returned to that simpler time. He renewed himself to the value of knowing the truth, regardless of the heartache that can come from being one who represents that truth.

When at last he returned from his walk, he gathered everyone around him. For the first time in four days it was he who began a conversation.

Samuel, Maria and Yoseph looked at the man intently. The change in him was noticeable he was relaxed and unguarded.

"Since we met, you have heard only the pains of my life. But I do not want you to think that this is who I am. I am not a person who focuses solely on the negative. I know it may seem this way but it is only because, after all the attacks carried out upon me, I was left with my pain alone. That is," he said, glancing at his son, "until this morning."

The man took a deep, calming breath and glanced up to take in the surround. "There was tremendous joy once," he said, needing to tell himself this as much as he did Maria and Samuel. "There was a time of optimism, trust and innocence. There was a time of warm contentment and embrace—a time defined solely by the depth of the love felt, no pains or plagues. So much of that time happened here—on this ground," he said, as he took in the scope of the landscape. Continuing, "It was because we knew this time of immense joy, that the time of suffering pained us so. It was because we once knew this complete fullness that the emptiness burned so.

"I have told you of the painful part of my life; I have told you of my encounters with the worst examples of mankind and how I learned what they are capable of. Yet I have not told you of the best examples of humanity I know, those who showed me what love is. I have spoken to you of those who left me scarred and afraid but not those who helped me grow strong and balanced.

"There was good once..." the man repeated with a slight laugh, as the long-overshadowed memories of happiness came forward in his mind. For the first time since meeting him, Samuel and Maria saw a smile cross the man's once resigned face. "I was born from a loving womb, brought forth into embracing arms, raised in a nurturing home, united to a woman with a beautiful heart, became father to four chil- dren.... No," he emphasized, "my joys certainly outweigh my sorrows—they always have. I was simply too tormented by the bad to remember the good.

"Pain alters our perspective. Pain is blinding, not only to the eyes but in terms of what the heart can recall. A strike is landed upon us and in that moment a shockwave passes through our mind dulling all other memories, leaving the pain prominent and the joy we felt only moments before, forgotten. I am so-very-grateful that my pain is finally lifting and I can see love once more," the man said, speaking with the utmost sincerity.

Sitting around the smoldering fire, the morning light flooding across the widening landscape as the story of the homestead that once flourished beneath their feet was told.

The fear was gone from the man. His voice, once tremu- lous, was now solid, clear and confident. The cowering man had risen, becoming the tower of strength he had once been. His confidence beamed from him, fortifying those around him. What he pronounced to be possible, was possible. His penetrating gaze drew them in. His renewal, renewed those near to him.

"Given everything that you both have been struggling with personally these last days, I feel there is something I should share with you. I was going to tell you this days ago, when we were speaking of what makes a family; however, I let my fear hold me back.

"I know you envy the closeness of my family. But you should know that my family is composed of orphans." Upon hearing this Samuel and Maria's focus sharpened. He continued, "Many of my loved ones, including my own mother and father, were born into families who never wanted them, loved them or cared to understand them. The first generation of my family liberated each other from loveless ones to which they were born and came together to form a true family.

"Our family," the man said, looking to his son and then back to Maria and Samuel, "began with two people—my wife's mother and father, who truly became the mother and father of our whole family.

"It would be around these two hearts that my family would form. They gathered the first generation, who would in turn bring forth the next. Leaving their childhood homes in the north of this country, they traveled south searching for the lands upon which they could found their home.

"My wife's father came from nobility; he was a descendant of a 'royal line' yet he was the third son, and so not of great consequence to his parents. He had met his future wife when he was a young boy, she having been a slave within his family's large estate. During his very lonely childhood, this young servant girl had been his saving grace and the single loving presence in his neglected existence. Playing together as children they were, even then, companions in this life. Some think that marriage is a bond that only comes forward in adulthood, but we can indeed meet our union when we are children. This, most-innocent, wholesome form of union, creates a precious foundation for those couples who are fortunate enough to experience it. My wife and I experienced it," he added. Freely sharing an intimate part of himself. "You see, we were raised together. The deepest love between a husband and a wife always lay between us, even at that young age; as though some part of us knew all that we destined to experience together. The union forms between the hearts of two children and evolves as the children grow, until at last the innocent-hearted companions become lovers.

"The friendship and love between my wife's mother and father had been forced to grow from a distance, seeing as his aristocratic mother would not allow him to associate with anyone 'below his status.' Nonetheless, despite being separated by his parent's prejudice, the young couple's care for one another steadily grew. When at last the boy became a man, he made the difficult choice to leave behind the family he had once hoped to be loved by, to set out in search of a place where he might start his own family and surround himself with those who were genuinely loving. As the boy had grown into a young man, so too had the girl grown to be a young woman. And when the time came to depart he took only his inheritance and her—his beloved.

"Together they journeyed south, eventually finding the land upon which they would build their home and begin their family," the man said, raising his hands, "this very land. For a long while it was only them and their children—they met no others who believed in the love that they did. During those early years, they worked the land, raised their children, cared for one another and dreamed of one day meeting like-minded people, who believed in the kind of bonds that they did. Bonds that interconnect souls, making a family more than a community bound by blood but one great soul bound by love.

"In time, there came a day when these two finally met two others who, like them, had been born unto loveless arms yet still longed to meet others with who they could have real bonds. These two kindred hearts were that of my mother and father.

"At the time my parents were not yet married, though they deeply wanted to be. My father loved my mother and had asked her parents if he might marry her but, in that time and place, the father was the head of the household and he alone decided who his daughter married. My mother's 'father' looked at my father and saw only a young man of meager wealth, which in his mind was unacceptable.

"My mother had only seen my father a few times—only spoken to him briefly; however it had been long enough for her to know that she wanted to be with only him.

"Upset by her father's immovable stance and hurt by his insensitivity, my mother could not bear the possibility that she might be forced into a marriage with another man who she did not love. One morning, overwhelmed by the hopelessness of her situation, my mother retreated to a secluded village garden, where she collapsed in tears. And it was there, while hysterical, that she was found by her rightful father.

"My wife's parents would, in a sense, become the father and mother of our entire family. They would become the long-needed parents to the many orphans and slaves who would be gathered in the coming years to create the branches of my family.

"My wife's father found my mother that day in the garden. He went unto this distraught young woman to see how he might help. Hearing her circumstance he went unto her 'family,' on my father's behalf and in the end, after many visits and much frustration, ended up making arrangements for the two to be married."

"How did he make her father accept your father?" Maria asked, looking slightly pained. She could feel the hopelessness his mother had experienced that day in the garden.

"He gave the man exactly what all such men want—money," the man replied plainly. Maria was not at all surprised by his response.

"And so the family grew..." he pressed on, not wanting to dwell on the evil his family had encountered but instead, the loving circle that had been gathered.

"My mother and father were wed and another branch grew on this family tree. Two more couples were gathered quickly after my mother and father, one being that of a friend of my father and mother and the other being that of a slave couple my wife's father met in the city and freed. And so it was that the first generation of our family was gathered—lain down like a foundation for all the generations to come, bringing my family into a time of affection, peace and growth.

"It was during this golden period that my brother and I were born, as well as many other children, one among them, my future wife." The man became quiet. His thoughts left the small group for a moment as, within his heart, he traveled across the current distance to her to bring forward the unparalleled love between them.

"Once we woke to our bond, my wife and I had our own golden years during which we grew into one another and came to realize how deep our union goes. We found we were not only joined in heart but were—are—one soul in two bodies. What was true then, is still true now. What I am, she makes me. What we accomplish, we do through one another—because of one another.

"We had warm days spent working at each other's side; long talks that inspired tremendous realizations; the sharing of dreams and in this, the intimacy of exposed hearts entrusting one another with the very reason they find in living. We had nights alone in the garden, underneath the fig trees, among the flowering bushes and the fragrant evening air." He paused again, his focus leaving them again for the briefest of moments, as he returned to that garden and the memory of her embrace. When he spoke again his voice was flowing, gentle and deep with emphasis. "Those years were more than 'golden,' they were blissful—a lifetime of an intense love and profound closeness; every day the two of us became more tightly entwined, defined by what we were together.

"With the birth of each child, we saw the embodiment of what we were together—an incarnation of an array of the different things we loved about one another. With the dawn of each day, we had the gift of more time to spend with one another and with the rising of each moon another night throughout which we might hold each other. With the passing of each season our love knew another period of growth. Our hearts overflowing with affection, we knew no stronger time, more confident time in our lives." His intense voice gradually softened and a shadow of longing crossed his face. "I have been too long without her. This journey has stretched on for far-too-long." Yoseph stared down at the ground, unable to look anyone in the eye as his father spoke. "It has been a lifetime since our last meeting, she on her journey and I on mine. Yet," he went on, trying to trust, "in the end, I try to remember that our love for one another has brought us through death—death," he stressed. "My love for her and her's for me, brought us through that which should have killed us. And so, I know our love shall bring us through all that we now endure, until we are once again able to return to those blissful days."

It was apparent to Samuel and Maria how sad the man and Yoseph were. As strong as the man was, in that moment he was utterly vulnerable. Maria felt an overwhelming urge to embrace them both—try to impart some small comfort. Yet, in the end, she knew there was little to do; for when we are without the ones we love, we do not want consolation or comfort we just want *them*.

Leaving his own story there for a time, the man rounded back to the greater story he was telling, returning his focus to his family as a whole.

"Yes," he said, struggling to clear his throat of the welling emotion, "the spring of our lives lasted a great many years— throughout my childhood and into my adulthood. I was married and saw the birth of the first two of my four children before the evil came for me. It was during this thirty year span that we all knew the most peace. I will not pretend that those years were perfect; evil had been met during those years. Many in our family had already begun accumulating wounds. Even then, the need for the journey was building on the horizon like a storm that would have to be endured; nonetheless, during that time we all were together, bound by our love, and did our best to help those who had been hurt manage their pain, unaware of the greater struggle of which we were all a part.

"It would not be until the birth of my third child drew near—the birth of the young man who sits next to me now," he said, laying a loving hand upon his son's knee as he gave him a warm smile, "that the attack would come. It was when he was in his mother's womb that the evil around me carried out its endgame and the time of greatest torment began. He and my daughter, who was born some years later, were born into the winter of our family's life—the hard years of the aftermath.

The gathering of kindred hearts slowed after the attack and in time seemingly came to an end, as encounters with loving hearts became rarer and bouts with evil more commonplace.

"The attack in the city, the abandoning of the home we had all built together on these grounds, the time of being hunted and terrorized...." He paused suddenly, he could feel the pull of the past pains, like an undertow trying to sweep him back under the dark waters from which he had only recently surfaced. He stole himself; he had given the past enough focus now was the time to focus on the love present.

"Seven years of feast and seven of famine...that is the proverb, but for my family it was not true. We had known decades of relative peace and another lifetime of sorrow, fear, isolation and separation. Nevertheless, it had been the golden years of peace, which we all remembered with such fondness, that made us willing to fight so hard for a lasting resolution—an eternal spring."

The man stopped, the fire had almost burned down to ash. They would add no further wood to it. Their time on these lands was coming to a close. The fire would burn down to ash, a mark would be left upon the land and in time, even the mark would fade, just as any trace of the old homestead had long-since faded.

Samuel and Maria could sense the end coming and mourned for it. They had dreaded the parting of ways since the very first day they met the pair. Alone in the world, the couple had longingly searched for kindred hearts. And throughout the breadth of their life they had never found any, except each other; until that is, Yoseph and this nameless yet familiar man entered their lives.

Listening as the man spoke of orphans being born into loveless arms, Samuel and Maria needed no help in understanding the plight of such children. The revelation that family is determined not by blood but by love, had freed them from their ties to those who gave them nothing but tried to take everything. He had given these orphans hope for a future.

For the whole of their lives both Samuel and Maria had lived in a reality where they had a family but were simply unloved and misunderstood by that family. Yet it had been this man that had liberated both of them from this despairing existence and shown them all that they deserved.

Over the last four days the couple had experienced the end of one life and now wondered when the next would begin. The man had affirmed for them that *no*—they did not belong in this world. But now they were left wondering how to reach that next place.

And, as though he could feel their thoughts flowing through his mind, the man looked at them both with a ponderous stare. He turned away to watch the last flickering flame of the fire recede into the burnt wood carcass. He looked up again, passing his gaze over the lands of the past life and thought to himself, *I thought this pilgrimage had been for me alone. I thought I had returned to these lands to achieve my own resolution. I thought I had been guided back to this city to confront my past and indeed, I was. However, there is never only one purpose to our actions. Lives intertwine, paths run parallel and the actions of one effect many.* His eyes came to rest on Samuel and Maria.

The man rose, deliberately leaving his staff fireside—no longer in need of it. He slung his bag around him. Yoseph rose, following suit.

Turning to the couple the man spoke in a gentle, hopeful voice, "It is time for us to make our way back. Having come this far, will you come further? Will you become the newest branch of our family gathered?"

The sun was ascending. A fragrant wind blew in from the west. The sound of waves crashing in a far-off sea called him home.

L.M. BROWNING

Browning grew up in a small fishing village in Connecticut where she began writing at the age of fifteen. As a longtime student of Religion, Nature and Philosophy these themes permeate her work. Raised a Catholic, she studied both the Traditional and Apocrypha doctrine before her spiritual search eventually crossed into the other religions of the world, compelling her to investigate: Judaism, Tibetan Buddhism and the ancient traditions of Shamanism and the earth-based faiths.

Browning is a Pushcart Prize nominated poet. In 2010 she penned a three-title contemplative poetry series: *Oak Wise: Poetry Exploring an Ecological Faith, Ruminations at Twilight: Poetry Exploring the Sacred* and *The Barren Plain: Poetry Exploring the Reality of the Modern Wasteland.*

WWW.LMBROWNING.COM

MARIANNE BROWNING

Marianne Browning has spent her life along the coast of Connecticut. From an early age she felt an inward pull to explore her spirituality. She earned her Bachelor's degree in Psychology, though her true education was had over a long journey of experience and introspection. In the early 1990's, after several years of difficulty, Marianne underwent a spiritual awakening and entered into a time of redefinition and meditation during which she departed the traditional path—questioning all that she had been taught in an effort to find genuine truth. Having no desire to hold a place in the chaotic world of business, Marianne chose to focus her efforts on her home and loved ones. Leaving behind many modern conveniences, she chooses to live a simple life. She is gifted in the old-world skills of: quilting, sewing, crocheting, baking and furniture restoration. Marianne continues to reside in New England where she tends to home and family.

HOMEBOUND
an imprint of HIRAETH PRESS

GOING BACK TO GO FORWARD is the philosophy of Homebound. We recognize the importance of going home to gather from the stores of old wisdom to help nourish our lives in this modern era. We lend voice to those individuals who endeavor to translate the old truths into new context. Our titles introduce insights into mankind's present internal, social and ecological dilemmas.

It is the intention of those at Homebound to revive contemplative storytelling. We publish introspective full-length novels, parables, essay collections, epic verse, short story collections, journals and travel writing. In our fiction titles our intention is to introduce a new mythology that will directly aid mankind in the trials we face at present.

The stories humanity lives by give both context and perspective to our lives. Some older stories, while well-known to the generations, no longer resonate with the heart of the modern man nor do they address the present situation we face individually and as a global village. Homebound chooses titles that balance a reverence for the old wisdom; while at the same time presenting new perspectives by which to live.

CPSIA information can be obtained at www.ICGtesting.com
Printed in the USA
BVOW011231021211

277335BV00002B/37/P